W9-DAW-358

Goodbye, Jimmy Choo

Goodbye, Jimmy Choo

Annie Sanders

ORION

First published in Great Britain in 2004 by Orion,
an imprint of the Orion Publishing Group Ltd.

Copyright © Annie Ashworth and Meg Sanders 2004

The moral right of Annie Ashworth and Meg Sanders to be identified as
the author of this work has been asserted in accordance with
the Copyright, Designs and Patents Act of 1988.

All rights reserved. No part of this publication may be
reproduced, stored in a retrieval system, or transmitted
in any form or by any means, electronic, mechanical,
photocopying, recording, or otherwise, without the prior
permission of both the copyright owner and the above
publisher of this book.

A CIP catalogue record for this book
is available from the British Library.

ISBN 0 75286 135 2 (hardback)

Typeset at The Spartan Press Ltd,
Lymington, Hants

Set in Adobe Garamond

Printed in Great Britain by Clays Ltd, St Ives plc

All the characters in this book are fictitious,
and any resemblance to actual persons living
or dead is purely coincidental.

The Orion Publishing Group Ltd
Orion House
5 Upper Saint Martin's Lane
London, WC2H 9EA

To McVitie's, who
have sustained us
all the way.

Chapter 1

Izzie glanced at the clock, then redoubled her efforts. 'Get in there, you bitch,' she hissed. 'I haven't got time to mess around!'

A glance in the shiny metal lids of the Aga confirmed her worst fears. Quite apart from the fact that the curved surface made her look like Barry Manilow's ugly sister, she was a mess, and there was evidence of the struggle all over the kitchen too. In just over an hour, she'd have to appear in public with every trace carefully cleaned away. No one must ever know the ghastly truth of what had gone on. If anyone found out all her careful work would be ruined. How had she got herself into this god-awful situation? But time was running out. She grabbed a bread knife.

'I'll cut your bloody legs off, I'm warning you! This is your last chance.'

Barbie lay on the kitchen worktop, unmoved by the threats and surrounded by cake crumbs. Once more Izzie jerked her upright and, ignoring the accusing stare of the painted blue eyes, thrust her into the top of the cake. This time she went in up to the waist and stayed upright.

Muttering a fervent prayer of thanks, Izzie started to patch up the damage: cake fragments unceremoniously jammed in to fill the crater in the top, then a light skim of butter cream to stick on the all-forgiving royal icing. Once that was in place, with a few strategically placed icing rosebuds and some jelly sweets, she'd defy anyone not to be impressed by 'Princess Barbie in a Crinoline' – even if the sponge cake was bought and hacked into shape after her pitiful effort sank without trace in the bloody Aga. The first thing she'd do if she ever got any spare money would be to yank out that temperamental monster and replace it with a nice biddable gas oven.

There – finished. Now to do something about her hair – like wash out the icing sugar for a start. Only twenty minutes until Sue 'twin-set' Templeton's awful lunch party. ('What that woman doesn't know about cardies, you could write on the back of an M&S label,' had been Marcus' remark.) She wasn't Izzie's type at all, and the feeling was clearly mutual. Izzie was quite aware she'd only been invited to make sure she delivered the cake on time. The prep-school set, of which Sue was the lynchpin, wouldn't bother with her otherwise, despite the mysterious ex-London allure that still clung to her – just. This was definitely the last time she'd let herself get suckered into doing a cake for some posh kid's birthday. She'd rather be ostracised altogether than go through ordeal by Victoria sponge again.

She stormed upstairs and turned on the shower. Her entirely undeserved reputation for being good at birthday cakes, she realised, was based on those she'd produced for her own children's parties. What no one had tumbled to was that she had simply snaffled her ideas from the displays in the Jane Asher shop in Cale Street, so she'd allowed the fiction to continue – and this was the price! Sue Templeton's ghastly adenoidal brat had demanded a cake for her birthday, and Izzie, against her better judgement, had complied at once. She'd have to keep the whole cake thing well hidden from her old mates in London. What would they think if they knew she was now rubbing shoulders with the Mercedes Mums?

Blimey, she thought as she applied shampoo, an invitation to join the august company of that lot was quite a step up rural Ringford's social ladder, but it had been long enough coming. After two years, she still wasn't sure she'd mastered the steps of the complicated social dance of the provinces. It wasn't that she hated the country. Intellectually speaking (not a thing she did a lot of nowadays), she could see all the advantages. The schools were fine and you didn't have to go private; there were no syringes in the sand pit at the recreation ground; the air was clear (apart from the crop spraying, the slurrying and GM trials down the road). She'd even developed a sneaky affection for the funny little shops in Ringford High Street – learning to live without squid pasta and giving up hope of Jo Malone opening a branch there. On the rare occasions she went back to London now, she realised her friendliness with shop assistants in Upper Street was hopelessly inappropriate, and returned home with a rather pathetic sense of relief. OK, so she'd lost her urban edge, but in all the ways you could calibrate, quality of life here was better, even though it hadn't been her idea to come.

But in the ways you couldn't measure, Izzie knew there was something lacking. Those intrinsic bits of London: the buskers on the South Bank, violet-coloured fondant icing on those mini-cakes from Konditor & Cook, or leisurely Saturday mornings spent reading the *Guardian* from cover to cover while the kids were at tap.

She fumbled for a towel, water trickling over her eyes. No, what she really couldn't bear a moment longer – and somehow, this Barbie thing had brought it all into intolerably sharp focus – was the permanent feeling that there was no one round here she could share even the memory of these delights with, least of all Sue Templeton. Izzie couldn't get this crowd at all, and she was torn between not even wanting to understand them, so sod the lot of them, and longing to feel a part of something. No wonder she was bloody confused.

Now, as she combed her wet hair, she thought back to her hopes when they moved out of London. Downsizing had seemed the sensible thing to do and Marcus was so keen to do it. They'd sold their house in Islington – oh all right, Stoke Newington – and bought this sweet Victorian cottage in Hoxley. They'd been reliably informed by the agent that it was a highly 'desirable' village (meaning it had no council houses), so they'd packed up without a backwards glance. In fact, Marcus had been thrilled to shake the dust of London off his feet, and he'd even lost touch with his old friends.

Izzie had talked it through with all the publishers she worked for as a copy editor, and everyone had agreed that they'd carry on as before. It would be just the same, only she wouldn't be able to pop in to pick work up or deliver – but no problemo. And the Jiffy bags of page proofs, designs for approval and sheets of illustrations to check kept hitting the doormat. She could work in her pyjamas (a long-held ambition), fit it all around the kids, and everything went on as before.

She untangled some clean knickers from the over-stuffed drawer. Frankly the new school had been a bit of a culture shock. Liberal though she was, Izzie was a stickler for correct spelling and grammar – and that extended to tattoos. Instead of the Tobys and Tashas of North London, here most of her children's classmates were Waynes and Kellys whose main entertainment after school was PlayStation2, shooting pigeons with air rifles or, most mystifying of all, Irish dancing.

So why had she agreed when Sue Templeton, non-working wife of the BMW-driving proprietor of a sign-writing firm, with kids at the local prep school, had asked her to make a Princess Barbie cake for snotty Abigail? She buried the question and dried her hair while simultaneously hopping on one leg trying to pull on Gap low-slung combats. Would her black cashmere sweater have shrunk so far that it would leave a strip of unappealingly white back on display when she leant forward to serve herself quiche? There was bound to be quiche.

Within twenty minutes she'd arrived, and parked rakishly between driveways on Millstone Meadow, the newly built estate of executive homes in Long Wellcote that was *chez* Templeton. 'Stepford Drive' Marcus had christened this mock-Georgian abomination, and Izzie had to admit wryly he had got it right again. Hopping over the precisely alternated clumps of blue and white lobelia that passed for imaginative planting, she glanced at the car she had parked behind. A bloody huge Beamer, naturally. But the woman inside it didn't look very Stepford.

She was blonde, of course – it seemed to be some sort of legal requirement if you drove a BMW – but she'd got the shade exactly right: somewhere between Gwyneth and Cate, without veering dangerously towards Jerry (or even worse, Geri!). Puffing grimly out of the window on a hands-free cigarette, this woman was gripping the steering wheel and seemed to be muttering to herself, a ferocious scowl on her face.

Shrugging, Izzie composed her face into the bland smile she thought fit for such an occasion, then, gripping the cake board more firmly, she rang the doorbell.

White 'toaster' sliced bread. Oven chips. Frozen crispy pancakes. Turkey drummers. Maddy's heart sank as she watched the shopping of the woman in front of her passing through the checkout. Did these philistines know nothing about real food? She looked down at her own trolley. It had been a struggle to find them, but she'd managed free-range duck breasts, those scrumptious but obscure little French choccie biccies the children so adored and some balsamic vinegar that looked just like the stuff they'd bought in Tuscany last year. God, she missed that little deli on the corner of Draycott Avenue.

She looked at her watch; twenty minutes before she had to be at Little Goslings to pick up Florence and get to the lunch. If the woman in front didn't get a move on packing her pathetic selection of fast food, she'd be late and Clare Jenkins, the rather obsequious proprietor of the nursery, would give her yet another reproachful look. She had no right to of course, when Maddy had offered so generously to back pay the extortionate fees when Florence had started there three weeks into term.

Her three-year-old's education had already cost them an arm and a leg. With the sudden move up to this godforsaken county, she'd had to forfeit a term's fees to the nursery in London where Florence had been so settled. They'd had to reserve a place there for her almost before conception – it made joining The Hurlingham seem like a picnic. Little Goslings just outside Ringford was, frankly, a comedown, and the fact that she had promised to enrol nine-month-old Pasco very soon was another reason why the staff had no right to come on all superior with her.

The woman at the checkout was now searching through her ghastly, faux-leather handbag to find her purse. Maddy sighed and tapped her fingernails on the handle of her trolley. It was going to be a close-run thing. While she waited, she looked the woman over. She seemed to sum up everything that was so common about everyone in this hayseed community. The woman's white T-shirt – probably a man's and undoubtedly from Matalan – was pulled tight over a huge, insufficiently supported bust, and hung out loose over a vulgarly over-patterned flared skirt, creased at the bum. And her shoes, oh God her shoes. Light beige sandals bearing up heroically under the strain of the fat feet squeezed into them.

Maddy looked down smugly at her own soft-as-toffee, pale blue suede driving shoes which she'd found in a gorgeous little place on Walton Street. She hadn't been able to resist buying another two pairs in different colours. She sighed again. Her monthly hair cut at John Freida was one thing, but would she be able to justify a trip up to town now just to satisfy the imperative of decent footwear or after a few more weeks living here, would she too be drowned in a sea of mediocrity?

Grabbing a last-minute bunch of bright orange gerbera from the flower section, she paid for them and a packet of Marlboro Lights at the cigarette counter as she left (delayed even longer by the bloody losers queuing for the Lottery). The fact that the flowers cost three times as much as they should, being out of season, would almost certainly be lost on her lunch hostess, Sue Templesomething. She manoeuvred the trolley at precarious speed around the car park and stuffed the bags into the back of her car. They'd brought it in the days when they had to negotiate the perils of the traffic on the Fulham Road – the TV screen in the headrests was a godsend for entertaining the children. But now they were in the country, its height from the road gave her a sense of superiority over other cars that felt appropriate.

Turning out of Ringford, she headed on to the more rural roads towards the nursery and Huntingford. She could feel her hands relaxing on the wheel as she looked over the hedges at the fields and the view beyond. Summer was holding on for dear life, and there was a heat haze that hung over the hills in the distance, making each one less distinct than the one before it. A tractor in a far-off field looked like a child's toy and was busy ploughing up the remnants of the summer wheat, she guessed, to prepare for a crop she certainly wouldn't recognise. Her agricultural knowledge was sketchy to say the least, but the whole picture of undulating countryside was, she supposed, a pleasing one, and went some small way to reminding her of the positive reasons for the move here.

Simon's announcement that he had decided to abandon the City and had bought an IT company 'somewhere lovely in the country' had landed on Maddy like a bombshell. OK, so they had ranted and raved about the parking difficulties of SW10, and fantasised occasionally about the delights of a big garden and the sound of bells from a village church, but Maddy had thought that was all just in fun. Simon, however, had rehearsed all the reasons why it was the best thing for the family to get out of town, even before presenting her with a virtual *fait accompli* one evening last May over a glass of chilled white Bourgogne. He'd even had Colette, their French nanny, look after the kids for the weekend, and had driven Maddy around the country lanes, seducing her with a carefully vetted pile of estate agents' details of houses with idyllic pictures and even more poetic descriptions. He'd then seduced her again after dinner at a rather gorgeous hotel he'd booked them into, as if making love in the country was somehow superior to doing it in the city.

Huntingford House had been everything she had lusted after: Queen Anne, brick built, with big sashes and dormer windows peeping out of the roof on the second floor. The type of house you see in the opening pages of *Country Life*. It had all the right bits in all the right places: sweeping drive, old roses in an acre of rambling garden, and a kitchen bigger than the whole downstairs area of their house in Milborne Place. The décor hadn't been quite so gorgeous. The Formica units, fifties central heating system and shag pile carpets *had* to go. But with the help of her old boss, Felicity Cook, and an instinctive good taste acquired by osmosis after years living within spitting distance of the Boltons, she was in the process of replacing avocado bathroom suites with CP Hart, and exchanging William Morris curtains for yards of Zoffany. She was now well on the way to creating the home she wanted it to become. Somewhere that would turn visiting London chums green with envy.

Will's school too had been a persuasive factor. Simon had arrived home gripping a copy of *The Good School Guide* with the page already marked. Eagles had been described as having 'all the elements of an inner London Prep, without the traffic'. That was good enough for Maddy. By an amazing stroke of luck, they had managed to secure a place left by a child whose parents were relocating and, despite another hefty financial penalty for starting late, they were in. Maddy had been heartened by the other parents in the car park. OK, so there was an alarming plethora of gold shoes and appliquéd T-shirts, but there weren't too many common accents and the head, Mrs Turner, a rather tall, anorexic-looking woman in her mid-forties, Viyella suit and high shoes, had assured them that most parents worked 'in fields like IT and medicine'.

Colette was just wiping the remnants of lunch off Pasco's face when Maddy burst into the kitchen with the supermarket bags. 'I'm late for that woman's little "get together",' she gasped, planting a kiss on the baby's head. The petite French nanny had been Maddy's bargaining tool for the move. Either she came too or Maddy wasn't budging. Colette, despite (or perhaps because of) being from deepest France, seemed even more cynical about a move to the back edge of beyond than Maddy. In fact, Colette's rooms at the top of the house had to be first for an overhaul as an added incentive and she was now ensconced in luxury with her wide-screen TV and Malabar curtains, while the rest of the household were having to put up with bare plaster and barer floorboards.

'Oh, Maddy, leave the shopping,' cooed Colette in that drop-dead sexy accent. 'I just change Pasco's nappy and he be ready. Come on, little man.' She called back over her shoulder, 'The builder want to talk to you about the spare room.'

'He'll have to wait.' Maddy quickly packed Ben & Jerry's Phish Food into the big American freezer and plonked pots of coriander and fresh basil on to the windowsill, brushed her hair and applied some lipstick, by which time Pasco re-emerged smelling clean and delicious in his nanny's arms.

'We'll be back after school pick-up,' she said, taking the baby from Colette. 'I can make a pretty good guess what sort of women will be there – I've met them all at the school gate – and it's not looking like a gathering from the social pages of *Tatler*. Pasta for the children's supper? With that lovely plum tomato sauce you do so well – and I've even managed to track down some fresh Parmesan. There is a God!' Is that an expression the French understand? she wondered as she swept out of the drive. God, her command of her mother tongue must be slipping.

By the time she pulled up outside Little Goslings, a substantial Victorian house with every window festooned with a child's jolly drawing, it was ten past one and she was well prepared for the disapproving looks she'd receive from the nursery nurses.

'Florence has had a lovely morning,' gushed Clare Jenkins, the name of the nursery emblazoned on the sweatshirt stretched across her ample bosom, 'haven't you, Florrie?' (To flatly refuse to give her name the correct French pronunciation was one thing, but *Florrie*!) 'We've done a drawing of mummy and your lovely new house. She's had some banana and raisins for a snack,' then she added, almost mouthing the words as if to protect Florence from the knowledge that she had a negligent and tardy mother, 'but I think she's a bit hungry. It's lunchtime, isn't it, Florrie darling?' Oh stuff you, thought Maddy. Wouldn't anyone be if all they'd had since breakfast was a handful of raisins and some banana?

'Thanks, Clare. See you tomorrow. Come on, *Florence*,' she said, emphasising the name and grabbing her rather fractious daughter's hand. 'We're off to meet some nice new friends.'

Twenty past one now and Maddy wasn't quite sure how late you could be for a half-twelve invitation around these parts without appearing completely rude. She lit a cigarette, confident that she wouldn't be allowed to smoke chez Templeton, *that* was the name, and opened the window wide so it wouldn't choke the children. Back home, you could turn up virtually when it suited you. Lunches had been long and fun, with nannies (usually from ex-eastern bloc countries) entertaining various offspring in the garden. She'd then return home around five and escape the tea-time warzone, with the excuse that she had to get ready to meet Simon in town for whatever dinner or party they were attending that night.

She overtook a couple of horseriders at speed, and vaguely returned their enthusiastic gestures. Did she know them? No, somewhere in the back of her mind she knew she wasn't achieving all she should in life. 'If Madeleine puts in half as much effort into her school work as she does into her social life, she will go far,' her headmistress had written on her leaving report from Queensgate. Maddy knew she had been right, and, though she endeavoured to read serious books and always to scour the Weekend section of the *Daily Telegraph*, life was too much fun. She justified her lifestyle by consoling herself that Simon earned quite enough to make her working unnecessary – and what could she do anyway with a couple of A levels, and a few years picking wallpaper for the rich and clueless?

What galled her now, as they drove towards Long Wellcote, was the thought that at least in London she could make sure she went to the right exhibitions and operas, and kept up with the sharp end. The closest thing Ringford had to offer in terms of culture was a framing shop with prints of Provençal lavender fields in the window. She glanced in the rear-view mirror at her beautiful children: Pasco with a dark colouring that suggested his European grandparentage, and Florence with her blonde curls, so like Simon, and her thumb in, gripping her beloved rabbit with her other hand. Suddenly she had an image of the woman she was in danger of becoming: a country mumsy who spent her life going from school playground to bloody coffee morning to bloody toddler group to bloody boring lunches, talking about potty training and school fundraising. It just wasn't her bag.

Hers was more Prada, and the prospect loomed terrifyingly of a life without one, or for that matter, lunch at Harvey Nicks,

Jimmy Choo's or a couple of hours shopping in New Bond Street.

Royally pissed off, she finally found Sue Templeton's house at the other end of the village and pulled up outside, behind a new Peugeot MPV with a 'Don't Kill the Countryside' sticker displayed in the back. The house, a pastiche of Georgian splendour, complete with porticoed porchway, sat on the corner of a road of other unimaginative boxes and, through the new privet hedge, Maddy could make out a garden strewn with garish plastic trikes.

As Maddy jerked on the handbrake and turned off the engine, she could feel herself about to weep with despair. 'Sod the bloody countryside,' she wailed out loud. 'It deserves to die.'

Chapter 2

Izzie could hear Sue Templeton's loud, unrelenting voice long before the door opened. Her big face fell when she saw who it was. 'Oh it's you,' she brayed. 'We were beginning to wonder if you were coming. At last, is that the cake? Abigail will be thrilled.'

Of course it's the bloody cake, you dopey tart, thought Izzie, but smiled artlessly and mouthed invented excuses for her lateness. Sue shepherded her through the oppressively narrow hall.

'Bring it through,' she ordered. 'Fortunately we haven't started eating yet.'

'Oh, you shouldn't have waited for me. Sorry, I should have called to say I'd be late but . . .'

'We weren't waiting for *you*,' Sue retorted, then thinking perhaps it was a bit too rude to speak that way even to Izzie, corrected herself, twinkling revoltingly. 'I mean we're waiting for our guest of honour – Mrs Huntingford House!'

'Mrs who? I don't think I've met her. What an unusual name!'

'No, Isabel,' Sue explained as if to a tiresome child. 'She's the new woman who's moved into Huntingford House. Come up from London, husband did something seriously important in the City, setting up a business locally now – to do with computers I think,' she honked. 'Isn't it always?'

Rolling her eyes to indicate that the details of the business were not the important part – only the size of the bank balance – Sue flapped her hands irritably at the hesitant Izzie and ushered her through. 'Her little boy is at Eagles with ours, and I thought she'd like to get to know us all better. So important to make sure you have plenty of friends when you move to a new place!'

Laudable sentiments, but Izzie suppressed a cynical smile. Sue's hospitality had never been extended quite so freely to her. Izzie could tell by the sense of anticipation in the overheated kitchen that Mrs Huntingford House had been identified as something of a social catch. This should be funny!

As they entered the room, Izzie could hear stifled laughter then a hurried, 'Ssshhhh!' She felt herself tense up even further. There were three women already seated at the table: Linda Meades and Clare Lorrimer were so inseparable that she always thought of them as one, a bit like Ant 'n' Dec or Rosencrantz 'n' Guildenstern. Meades 'n' Lorrimer kind of blurred into a sea of silky camel knits, silky camel hair and too-orange fake tan – all in a flawless eggshell finish. Even the lipgloss was co-ordinated.

Shoe-horned in close to the wall opposite was Fiona Price. Looking frumpy and uncomfortable – her one concession to femininity a pair of gold earrings shaped like stirrups – perspiration beaded her bleached moustache in the airless kitchen, and her arms were clamped across her boobs. Fiona reminded Izzie of an overstuffed armchair, but any idea of cosiness was deceptive. Affectionately known in Izzie's house as 'Frau Schadenfreude', her speciality was spreading the word. She was more effective than Reuters, and, like CNN, seemed to function 24/7. What bothered Izzie the most, though, was the obvious delight she took in other people's misfortune. When a friend's husband had been banned for drink-driving, Fiona had virtually pinned Izzie to the wall outside Boots to impart the sordid details.

True to form, the women all pretended to have forgotten her name, greeting her with vague but perfunctory smiles, so she had to go through the indignity of introducing herself again. From then on they ignored her, talking instead about the sweeping changes 'Mrs HH' had made to the house since she'd arrived. Each had some juicy tit-bit of information to impart, gleaned from the carpenter, the postman, the man at the deli in Ringford, the florist and more, testifying to the lavish lifestyle and effortless chic of their still-absent guest.

Stuck for something to say, Izzie eventually piped up. 'There was a woman in a car just in front of me when I parked. Perhaps that's her and she's forgotten the house number.' Sue went to peer through the lavishly swagged curtains on the front window. 'Yes that is her! I'll go and get her. Isabel, do put that cake down and could you pour a glass of wine . . . ?'

But a ring at the doorbell cut off Sue's string of commands in mid-stream. She fussed with her hair, pulled lint off the inevitable knitwear and, bracing herself, went to answer the door, her accent poshed up as she greeted her guest in rapturous tones. From her vantage point by the kitchen window, Izzie watched bemused as the others preened themselves for the arrival of this new marvel.

The woman who walked through the door, the very one she had seen in the BMW, was clearly a cut above her welcoming committee. Yes indeedy – a different breed altogether. Very urban chic but kind of effortless. This woman was a class act, and it wasn't just the hair; everything about her screamed entitlement, languor, money – such an irresistible blend. Izzie blinked rapidly as she strove to itemise her gorgeously under-stated ensemble. Her accessories were perfect, from Gucci shades pushed up on her head, to the soft glint of Patek

Philippe on her wrist, right down to powder-blue suede driving shoes revealing a hint of slender tanned feet, the beautiful baby on hip and exquisite little girl in tow. Even the slightly petulant expression and hint of a frown line between the carefully shaped brows fitted perfectly.

Izzie prided herself on being able to scent good breeding at a hundred yards – it was a gift that had come in handy through the years – and this was an absolutely prime example. The arrival's bust was slightly larger than hers and she looked a few years younger, but apart from that they were about the same size. Izzie wondered fleetingly whether she could get friendly enough with this vision to find out which charity shop she honoured with her cast-offs.

'Oh sorry, this is Isabel Stock. Isabel, Madeleine Hoare. She's made this lovely cake for Abigail's party this afternoon. Isn't it gorgeous? Every little girl's dream. A perfect fairy princess. And another little Barbie to add to the collection!'

Izzie winced as the newcomer's incredulous glance swept over the pink monstrosity. She had to say something, to dissociate herself both from the ghastly conceit of Barbie in a Victoria sponge and icing crinoline and from the other women there, before she was dismissed along with them. Over here! she felt like shouting. I'm not like them. Honest! I used to live in London too. I'm interesting really.

The Madeleine woman paused, tilted her head and arched an eyebrow, scrutinising the icing.

'Christ! It looks like a stag party for toddlers. Are those jelly tots or silicone implants?'

Izzie was startled, not sure how to react and then from somewhere dug up a witticism. 'Just the job for Abigail's party,' she mused. Madeleine stifled a laugh and at that moment there seemed to be a connection – almost imperceptible, but it was there. She shot her a quick glance then looked more closely at the cake.

'How on earth did you get the wretched doll to stand up? Did you shove her in there with brute force?'

'Pretty much,' replied Izzie. 'It was either that or cut off her legs.'

A shocked murmur ran round the room, but the newcomer's eyes sparkled with mischief. 'Sounds a bit like *Boxing Helena*,' she challenged, now staring straight at Izzie, who came straight back with, 'Not so much *Boxing Helena*, more Nigella meets Hannibal Lector.'

Madeleine's peal of laughter was all the more pleasing because of the uncomprehending stares of the others there. Izzie, who was still clutching the cake despite Sue's orders, had a look of sheer delight on her face as the significance of what was happening began to sink in. Apart from the two of them, the room was in puzzled silence, but in Izzie's head an angel chorus was crooning. For the first time in two years someone, apart from Marcus of course, actually seemed to be on her wavelength.

'It's Maddy by the way,' she said, as if for Izzie's ears only.

'Mine's Izzie, to rhyme with busy.'

Disconcertingly, the rather exquisite little girl holding on to her mother's leg giggled shyly. Maddy whispered conspiratorially: 'I'm sorry, Florence thought you said *Zizi* – which is the French word for a willy . . . !'

Izzie snorted with mirth. 'No way! I never knew that. I'll book my Eurostar seat right away.'

Sue muscled in, puce with anger. 'Well, I think it's a marvellous cake,' she chirped, and whisked Maddy off to the beanfeast going on for the other children in the playroom.

Left undefended in the kitchen, Izzie felt her balloon of happiness slowly deflate as the others looked her up and down. Trying to hang on to that elusive feeling of confidence, she placed the cake firmly on the pristine Corian work surface, then turned round to confront them with a smile bravely pinned to her face.

'Wine, anyone?' she said perkily, and seizing the bottle in its frosty plastic insulated jacket ('icy condoms', as Marcus had dubbed them) sauntered over to the table. She really didn't fancy sitting next to the Frau at the far end, but Linda and Clare had formed an apparently impenetrable barrier on the far side, and the fug of 'Opium' and 'Mitsouku' that surrounded them was enough to repel all boarders, welcome or otherwise. Sitting at the head of the table seemed presumptuous so she sat down on the only other chair, opposite them, and surreptitiously moved it as far from Fiona as she could. Three sets of eyebrows shot up and meaningful looks were exchanged.

'Well, Izzie, you look as tired as I feel,' murmured Clare with phoney solicitude. 'Working hard at the moment? That lovely little house of yours must take some keeping up. Give me modern, any time. So much easier!'

Linda joined in. 'How's that hunky husband of yours – Marcus? I haven't seen him at the gym lately. Not that *he* needs it; he's in such fa-a-antastic shape. I remember him saying while we were in the sauna one time that you had a joint membership. Don't you ever go? So good for the posture – and the skin!'

Posture! Skin! Izzie's shoulders had gradually hunched up round her ears, and she could feel her own face now going blotchy with rage. How dare these ignorant trollops try and get her going! Well today she wasn't going to give them the satisfaction. Summoning up the remnants of her self-control, she strove to remember Marcus' nicknames for them. Linda he referred to as 'the Lizard' – all sunbaked and scaly with swivel-ling eyes and a tongue that kept flickering in and out. Clare was 'Daisy', and there was indeed something cow-like about her huge, over-made-up eyes and wobbly, pushed-up boobs. Yes, that definitely helped. Izzie sat up straight again and smiled broadly.

'Marcus is really great at the moment, thank you. How clever of you to remember *his* name. He often used to mention seeing you both at the gym. But you know Marcus, he always has such funny stories to tell when he's been anywhere, and he makes me just curl up with laughter with the things he tells me. He hasn't had time to go there lately and, you're so right, he really is in wonderful shape. We get plenty of exercise together though! The house – well, what can I say? We're so happy there. We always dreamt of living in a house with character and charm, and we've certainly got that. I suppose people always choose houses to suit the way they are. I'm sure yours suits you down to the ground, Clare.'

The simultaneous intakes of breath round the table told Izzie she'd hit the mark, and she sat back, pleasantly surprised at how easy it had been. She was saved from further interrogation by the return of Sue and Maddy, their hostess still braying and honking her way through her monologue.

When they reached the table, there was an unexpected pause in the running commentary and Izzie looked up to see Sue glowering at her. Oh God! What had she done now? Sue stomped off to get another chair which she shoved in next to Izzie, scraping the leg spitefully down her ankle, then banged another knife and fork down next to hers. Izzie looked in surprise at the cutlery (very scrolly, repro Georgian). How very remiss of Sue to forget to lay a place for Maddy!

Lunchtime chitchat was steered expertly by Sue towards subjects about which Izzie knew nothing – and cared less. Someone's dog had come into season, someone's car went like a bomb, someone else was going to Dubai for half-term. Izzie kept schtum, but was encouraged by Maddy's scant contribution to the conversation. As pudding, a plate of individual sticky strawberry tarts, was produced, Sue looked theatrically at her watch. 'Oh Izzie, look at the time. You'll have to be going, won't you?' she said pointedly, then turned conspiratorially to Maddy. 'She has a bit further to go to collect her children from school than *we* have, you see.'

Bewildered, Izzie put down her fork. 'I will have to leave in a bit, but I'm all right just for a moment.' She laughed uncertainly.

'No, no. I won't have you rushing. It's just not fair on those poor little children of yours if you're late. I won't have it on my conscience! It was such a nice surprise that you decided to stay on for lunch, but we won't keep you any longer. Thanks for the cake. Smashing.'

Now on the other side of the front door, Izzie shook her head in puzzlement. What on earth was going on there? It was only when she was parked near St Boniface's, a good twenty minutes before the children were due to come out, that it all fell into place. With a sickening lurch, Izzie realised she hadn't been invited for lunch at all. She was supposed to drop the cake off and go – or have a glass of wine at the most. Sue had set the extra place only when it was clear she wasn't budging – and the strawberry tarts! Of course, there had only been five.

Quite out of character, Izzie felt tears pricking in her eyes. She leant her head on the steering wheel and howled.

Maddy awoke the following morning full of resolve. She had escaped Sue Templeton's at a time she hoped wasn't indecently early, only to be swamped by a wave of despair, not helped by the misery a couple of glasses of wine at lunchtime can precipitate. Those two hours had confirmed her greatest fear – that this was the way life would be from now on.

As she had pulled into the Eagles' car park, she had vowed that the minute she got home she would hurry along the completion of the spare room and invite friends for every weekend stretching out as far as the eye could see. Turning off the engine, she had sat in the car and glanced back at the children asleep in their car seats, soft little mouths fallen open, oblivious to the world as only sleeping children can be. Sequestered there, warm in the early autumn sunshine, she had decided she would wait until Will's teacher opened the school door to let out the flood of children before she got out to greet him. Just at that moment, she couldn't have borne another second of banal chat and provincial platitudes with the other mothers.

Now, as soon as the radio burst into life at six-thirty, she jumped out of bed and headed for the shower.

'What the hell's got into you?' mumbled Simon, without even opening his eyes. As a rule, Maddy never stirred until she had downed a mugful of Earl Grey and she was sure Colette had dealt with the messy business of Coco Pops, toast and baby mush with Will, Florence and Pasco downstairs.

'I want to get a move on.' She stomped across the floor, wincing as she stepped on a nail proud of the floorboards. When would the goddamn carpets arrive?

'Well, wonders will never cease.' Simon yawned as he swung up on to the side of the bed, crumpled and tousled from sleep. He sat for a moment summoning the energy to stand up. Maddy paused for a second and looked at her husband. With his broad shoulders, and thick unruly fair hair, he was such a good-looking man, she thought, and God I must love him to have sacrificed everything.

She stopped and put her hands on her hips. 'I'm just fed up of waiting on everyone – carpenters, carpetlayers, the decorators – today I'm going to be dynamic and kick some butt.'

'I love it when you get arsey,' he chuckled, pulling her by the arm so she tumbled on top on him on the bed. Her nose filled with the scent of his body. 'You know you're in your element really,' he kissed her nose. 'This place will be beautiful when you've finished – you are so clever,' his mouth moved to her ear, 'and so sexy,' he murmured softly, his breath sending delicious shivers right down to her toes.

'Oh you English boys, you love to be dominated – must be all that boarding-school repression.' She could feel her body responding to him, despite her resolve. 'Shall I play matron?'

'Oh please,' he groaned, 'I could really go for you in one of those uniforms.'

'Right, Hoare Minor.' Maddy playfully rolled him over, as he started to pull at the drawstring on her pyjamas. 'A cold shower for you, my lad, and PE on the lawn – look sharp!' and slapped him on the backside.

'Spoilsport!' he called after her, laughing, as she headed for the bathroom

She was like a woman possessed over the next twenty-four hours. The builder, who went under the implausible name of Crispin, positively reeled under the barrage of Maddy's requests and deadlines. Suddenly the woman who had wafted around, waving her hand vaguely and talking dreamily about bleached-string-coloured walls and obscure door handles made by companies from London he had never heard of, was behaving like a whip-cracking foreman. Maddy wasn't completely green. She knew he'd been hoping to stretch out this job for a while, when she'd accepted his estimates without question. She was prepared to bet that, when he'd smelt the size of the budget involved, he hadn't shied away from adding a nought or two. Now perhaps he'd begin to panic that the holiday he'd no doubt planned on the back of this little earner may not happen at all.

When she wasn't barracking Crispin, Maddy stormed from room to room, with the phone glued to her ear.

'I don't care what the warehouse says,' she shouted imperiously. 'You said three weeks for the carpets and it's been four. I want them by the end of the week or you can forget it.' She jabbed her finger on the disconnect button, confident that she'd see the carpetlayers' van in the drive on Friday. At sixty-five quid a square metre, they weren't going to risk losing this contract.

Sure enough, eight-thirty Friday morning, two surly-looking blokes were carrying rolls of carpet upstairs and the rest of the morning was spent to the accompaniment of banging. Excited at the prospect of being able to step out of the bed the next morning to feel soft wool under her feet, she rang Simon at work.

It took a bit of time to get through, and Maddy was impatient in her excitement. Lillian, Simon's secretary, seemed to be stalling her. 'I'm sorry, Mrs Hoare, he's rather tied up at the moment. Can he call you back?'

For a brief moment Maddy was disconcerted. Simon would usually interrupt anything to speak to her. She hung up and instantly forgot it as Pasco crawled across the hall towards her. She scooped him up into her arms and nuzzled her nose into his soft neck.

'I do think, Mr Pasco Hoare, that we just might be getting somewhere with this blasted house. Now all we need to do is find someone half decent to invite here.'

'Let's celebrate,' she said, when Simon finally called back, sometime after lunch. 'The carpet's gone down. How about supper at that new place in Ledfinch? I'll book, though I can't imagine they'll be that busy. Do these peasants go out for meals?' He agreed but sounded a little distracted. She reckoned he must be dealing with some new client – not entirely confident she knew what exactly Simon would do in a discussion with someone in business. Funny, she mused, grabbing her keys to go off and collect Will from school, you can marry someone, share their bed and have their children, yet you haven't a clue what they do for ten hours a day.

'I thought I might go down to London on Monday and have lunch with Pru,' she ventured after they were seated at their table that evening and had ordered. Simon looked weary and not terribly interested in the menu or the surroundings of The Vinery in Ledfinch. To Maddy it was an amusing, and not completely unsuccessful, stab at mixing country pub with brasserie. Large leather sofas had replaced pub seating, and instead of beer mats the tables were minimalist, with a single flower in a tiny vase and a bowl of olives.

'It would be fun to see her,' she continued, 'and I thought I might go back to the house. The new people have found a couple of things in the attic we'd forgotten. Some old stuff of Mémé's.'

Obviously suspecting that somewhere between these two appointments, Maddy would find the lure of Selfridges irresistible, Simon smiled indulgently. 'Go easy on the autumn collections, will you? Or at least stick to just *one* complete new outfit.'

'Oh darling,' Maddy laughed, 'you can't honestly expect me to find anything half decent in Ringford, can you?'

'Whatever,' he replied and took her hand over the table. 'You are happy here really, aren't you, darling?' It was an odd question. Simon was usually so upbeat, never one for quiet introspection. He was a bull-by-the-horns man, equally capable of doing a hard day's work and then being the life of the party until the wee hours whenever they went out in London, which had often been four or five time a week.

'Once we get the house shipshape I will be.' She tried to sound as jolly as possible in an attempt to shake off her slight feeling of unease. 'How's everything at work?'

'Oh fine, fine,' he replied and leant back, yawning and stretching in his chair. 'Couple of problems to iron out and it'll be fine. These damned American venture capitalists are proving tricky but we'll get there. Jeff Dean is flying in from New York on Monday. I thought I'd go and collect him at Heathrow and try and soften him up before we get to the meeting at the office.'

They chatted on about the children and Maddy's idea for making a cottage out of the ramshackle sheds in the garden, then she finally made him laugh with her description of the Templeton lunch. 'The whole house was a shrine to a DFS furniture showroom. Sue is absolutely ghastly. There was this Izzie woman there who seemed like she might be quite fun. In fact, she's refreshingly different from the appliqué brigade – a bit boho, sort of reminds me of a little elf. Anyway, she arrived with this extraordinary cake for Abigail's birthday. Christ, the poor woman! I thought she was the nanny or something. Sue treated her like dirt.'

Later as they lay in bed, wrapped around each other and satiated in the aftermath of comfortable and familiar lovemaking, Maddy fell asleep to the still unfamiliar silence outside and the strong smell of new carpet.

Simon lay wide awake beside her.

Instead of Selfridges on Monday, Maddy spent an hour or so, after a giggly lunch, absorbing the familiar smell and bustle of Knightsbridge. A couple of hours with Pru Graves was always a tonic. As usual they'd gossiped about old school mates and Pru updated her with tales from the world of PR. Maddy in turn had regaled her with anecdotes from Huntingford, the school playground and the neighbours, playing up their awfulness.

'God, darling,' Pru's heavily made-up eyes had been wide at her tales of hop-festooned kitchens and 'country' pubs with play barns, 'as your townie therapist, I insist you come down twice a month for treatment.'

Later, as Maddy ran her hands over the soft leather trousers on the racks in Joseph, she wasn't convinced twice a month would be enough.

She returned to her car bearing some stiff carrier bags and a satisfied smile. But as she pulled up outside their old house in Milborne Place, her euphoria turned again to panic. It was almost desperation by the time she was greeted with a big hug by the new owners, a Sunday newspaper editor and his petite wife. How Maddy had loved this house, with its beautifully regular façade, its high narrow hallway, floor-to-ceiling windows and French doors to the garden. Simon and she had sat so often there on the terrace reading the papers and drinking coffee on summer Sunday mornings. Letting go of the house had not been a bereavement. It was more like relinquishing a lover, and having to watch them go off and marry someone else. Houses, thought Maddy, are fickle things.

Thankfully, yet somehow painfully, little had changed inside except for the furniture. She cast her eye covetously over the chrome kitchen units she had so carefully chosen, and thought about the dinner parties they'd had. Friends drinking wine and laughing late into the night. Even the grandeur of Huntingford House seemed to diminish. This was her real home. Suddenly she felt tired and resentful. What the hell had she agreed to relinquish here? She had lived in London all her life, except for a year living with her adored grandmother, Mémé, in Paris to prefect her French. Slice her in half and she was city girl through and through.

After tea and conversation about a London she was beginning to know less and less about, she squeezed the box of Mémé's dusty bits and pieces from the attic into the boot of the car, careful not to crush the carrier bags containing her new purchases, and headed out of town and on to the A40 towards Huntingford and what, to Maddy, felt like purdah.

As she opened the front door, the children, fresh from their baths, flew into her arms and the next half-hour was spent opening presents she had bought them. Florence pranced about enchanted by her new pink tulle dress, and Will disappeared with a remote-controlled car he had coveted from the Harrods' toy department. OK so it was a spoil, but Maddy felt that somehow she had to make up for the deprivation she felt sure the move had inflicted on them.

Later and with Simon not yet home, she poured herself a glass of wine, lit a cigarette, went through the post and tried to seek inspiration for supper from the rather pathetic contents of the fridge. Then she noticed the light flashing on the answering machine.

'Maddy, it's Sue. Sue Templeton.' Maddy raised an eyebrow.

'Lovely to see you for lunch last week. We're planning a little get-together for the mums from class, Thursday week. Do hope you can come. I'll call back.' I bet you will, thought Maddy. Beep.

'. . . er Maddy, it's Izzie. You know from the lunch last week. The one with the horrendous cake. I just wondered if you wanted to come over for lunch or something er . . . sometime. I'm sure you're too busy but if you're not . . .' Beep.

'. . . er Maddy, sorry Izzie again. I forgot to leave my number. It's 225571. Speak to you soon.'

Maddy took a slug of wine and smiled slowly. Yes, that just could be fun.

Chapter 3

Izzie crouched down beside the phone and groaned, covering her furiously blushing face with both hands. What a cock-up! And after all the preparation too! She had started psyching herself up to call Maddy Hoare last week. The question was, would Maddy want to get together with her for lunch or a coffee? Izzie, frankly, couldn't care less about being rejected by the Stepfords. She'd have rejected them first if she could have. But if Maddy gave her the cold shoulder, it really would be upsetting. Thank God Marcus hadn't witnessed her lamentable performance. He'd have teased her mercilessly.

Or maybe he wouldn't. He'd appeared quite uninterested when she told him about Maddy. Normally people were his favourite subject. She'd only mentioned her in the course of relating the story of the Templeton débâcle anyway, because she'd thought it would make him laugh. He'd been a bit down about the tedium of his temporary work lately, and the best way to cheer him up was usually to poke fun at herself. He'd always hoot with laughter, tousle her hair, tell her she was a scream. Somehow, having him laugh along with her at the Stepfords made the whole thing seem different, less hurtful. Together they'd made up daft names for Sue and the crew, speculated on their sex lives, marvelled at the blatant malice. But when she told him about Maddy, and their quick-fire conversation, how good it had made her feel, he'd frowned.

'She sounds ghastly, sweetheart! Just the sort of person we left London to avoid. God preserve us from that kind of Euro-trash with their highlights and Vuitton bags, and those horrible shoes with little knobbly things on the back!'

She happened to covet some driving shoes, but she didn't mention Maddy again.

After the fiasco of the Templeton lunch, the rest of Izzie's week had gone pretty much as usual. She'd pottered around at home, trying to help Marcus with a new idea he'd had – taking photographs at weddings and other dos (she was at a loss for a moment to think what these other dos might be). Of course, it was fantastically expensive setting up with all the equipment – the cameras he'd had as a student were hopelessly out of date – and it had made a bit of a dent in their holiday fund, but he'd been so excited about the possibilities it would open up for him. He'd carried her along with his enthusiasm – just like he had when he'd bought that old Triumph bike before they were married, and they'd spent weekends zooming around the countryside, her clinging on to him for dear life.

By Friday, she'd run out of excuses not to call Sue Templeton to thank her for lunch. Fortunately, the answering machine had been on.

With the unexpected arrival of a knitting book to copy-edit super fast, Izzie was head down over the manuscript, and it gave her another excuse to put off the nerve-racking business of calling Maddy. Knitting was really not her thing, and she'd fibbed to the editor that she could take it on. She'd had to get some background info from the library even to begin to make head or tail of the manuscript. God alone knew if she was doing it right, but it was work! So the last few days had passed in a blur of 'knit one, slip one, purl one, pass slip stitch over'.

By Monday she couldn't delay it any longer. If she didn't call now, Maddy wouldn't even remember who she was. So that was how she'd come to leave that pitiful message.

The following day she'd finished the blasted book and sent it off, after carefully checking that each jumper had a front, back and two sleeves – beyond that, she couldn't be too sure. Picking up the children at three-fifteen made a pleasant change from the eye-crossingly dull work. Waiting in the drizzle, she shifted restlessly from foot to foot with her arms crossed and shoulders hunched against the cold breeze that always seemed to race across the playground. She'd come out without a coat again, but at least she'd remembered to bring the kids a snack.

True to form, Charlie was out first, a dishevelled eight-year-old torpedo streaking through the doors as soon as they were opened. He dumped his bags and coat at her feet, took the offered muffin as if it were his due and was sharing it with two friends, but there was still no sign of Jess. Year One were always last. Eventually she came mincing out, socks pulled up neatly and her book bag clutched firmly in one hand, her classmate Susan Summerscales holding grimly on to the other. Izzie groaned.

'Jeth ith by betht fred!' announced the permanently congested Susan. 'She thayth I cad cub for a thleepover thoon.' Her parents couldn't have predicted the lisp and the adenoids, but surely even they should have realised that christening a child Susan Stephanie Summerscales was making oneself a hostage to phonetic fortune.

'Smashing!' Izzie muttered. Feeling her hair starting to frizz uncontrollably in the rain, and offering a tea date as consolation, she urged the children through the throng around the school gate.

'Let's get home so you can see Daddy.'

Charlie looked hopeful. 'D'you think he'll let me take some more pictures with his camera?'

'Well, sweetie, cameras are very expensive. They're not toys, you know. And no more close-ups of my backside, please.'

Marcus had not returned by the time they got home. The answering machine, however, was flashing. Taking a deep breath, Izzie pressed the button.

'Hi, Izzie! Maddy here. Thanks for your call. Sorry I didn't get back to you yesterday – sodding plumber, driving me round the twist. Yeah – I'd love to come for lunch. I'll be a bit tied up later in the week. Tomorrow any good?'

The children came scampering downstairs when they heard the first yell. It took them a moment to get over their astonishment, then, whooping and shrieking, they too joined in the little dance Izzie was doing round and round the kitchen table.

Maddy was pretty relaxed over the next few days. For the first time in ages she was feeling positive – the weather was warm for October and summer still hung in the air. The garden was tumbling with colour and they'd managed to eat the odd lunch outside on the mossy terrace. The house was really beginning to take shape – the kitchen was finished, and she'd even found a passably nice table lamp at the rather old-fashioned furniture shop in Ringford – but best of all, Izzie had proved to be what Maddy had so hoped she would be – fun and intelligent. They couldn't be more different really. Izzie was sort of fluffy, with a mass of wild, dark hair and pale skin, and those amazing blue eyes. She wore combat trousers, tie-dye T-shirts and denim jackets, and very ugly lace-up boots, clothes that Maddy wouldn't have been seen dead in, but somehow the look worked for her. Effortless and eccentric. Maddy couldn't quite imagine they had that much in common, but she just might become a friend. She cautiously let herself believe there was a chink of light in the long dismal tunnel here.

It had started with Izzie's lunch last week. Maddy had had a suspicion that she shouldn't tip up late. It was one thing to keep

La Templeton waiting, but something had warned her that she should not mess with the sensitivities of this rather vulnerable-looking woman with the slightly bobbled black cashmere sweater.

She hadn't really had time to imagine the sort of house Izzie would live in, but she was pretty confident that an executive box it wouldn't be. When she'd called back the night before to give her instructions, Izzie had told her to turn into Hoxley and look out for a 'tatty brick hovel with a far too narrow gateway'. When Maddy had pulled in, scraping the sides of the car down the unclipped hedge, somehow she hadn't been surprised by the toy-strewn front garden and look of general chaos, but she recognised a pretty house when she saw one. An old-fashioned, deep pink rose rambled around the casement windows, and mismatched terracotta tubs by the door overflowed with fading summer bedding.

The overall picture of shabby-chic, inside and out, seemed to fit with the little she knew about Izzie. The woman obviously had style, and had certainly once had money: the bright modern paintings on the walls (painted by Izzie's father, she learnt later), the bookshelves heaving with intellectual stuff, and the odd holiday read crammed in between, the heavy crewelwork curtains, mellow kilim rugs, unusual modern ceramics sitting on nice bits of oak furniture and a baby grand piano. It had all the right ingredients, and blended with ease. But Maddy couldn't help noticing the worn arms of the sofas, and walls, scuffed and crying out for a fresh lick of paint. Things chez Stock obviously weren't as prosperous as they had been.

Lunch in the cluttered, aqua-painted kitchen had been fun, once Izzie had a glass of Chablis inside her and had stopped flapping. She'd obviously faced a culinary crisis at the deli, and the kitchen table heaved under a variety of foods which would have better suited a buffet at a European Union trade delegation: the decanted contents of little plastic deli tubs containing tired-looking feta and olives, oily pasta salads, salami, more olives and sun-dried tomatoes. Maddy freely admitted she was a food snob – it was either genetic or learnt during her stays in Paris – and she had always loathed olives. Her heart had sunk. She was certain this wasn't the sort of thing Izzie usually produced, and it had bothered her a bit that Izzie felt a ham sandwich wouldn't have sufficed. But keen not to offend her hostess, she'd gamely forced down a couple of black olives and a shedload of French bread.

The wine had loosened Izzie's tongue, and she'd told Maddy about her life BC (before children). Izzie's London was clearly very different from the one Maddy had inhabited – where the hell was Stoke Newington anyway? – and Maddy found herself uncharacteristically underplaying Milborne Place and the life they had led. What they were both agreed on, however, was the awfulness of La Templeton's little coterie.

'Blimey!' Izzie had shrieked, as she grappled with making two cups of coffee after lunch. 'That lunch was hard going. I've had more laughs at a wake. I've got to admit they're not exactly my type.' She'd suddenly looked a bit alarmed, as if she'd overstepped the social mark, so Maddy found herself agreeing quickly.

'Mine neither! But at least I'd only met the women a couple of times at school. Why were you honoured with an invite?'

Izzie snorted, as she opened the fridge door for the milk. 'I thought they'd let you know the moment my bum was out of the door – I got the wrong end of the stick and thought I had been invited for lunch, but when I saw the portion-controlled strawberry tarts, the penny dropped. I was only there to deliver the cake – that's why Sue hussled me out. Miss Congeniality she isn't!'

Maddy had kept her face deadpan. 'But she's my new best friend, and I'm hoping Fiona's going to give me the in on the gossip.' She'd watched with glee as Izzie's face fell. 'In fact, I'm having them all back to my place and I was hoping you'd join us,' she'd let a smile creep over her face. 'I've just got to dig out my paper doilies.'

'And don't forget the quilted loo paper, love,' Izzie had giggled. 'The amazing thing is Sue's the style guru to her set – the Martha Stewart for the Stepford Wives.'

'Stepford what?'

'Oh that's one of Marcus' nicknames – he comes up with something for everyone.'

Maddy was intrigued. 'And what's mine?'

Izzie had coloured, so Maddy had quickly changed the subject by asking sheepishly if she could smoke. Izzie had dug out a saucer and hesitantly asked if she could bum one too. 'I haven't for years, but it's just a poke in the eye to that lunch – thank God you didn't light up there. Can you imagine the disgrace!

'So,' Izzie had asked, trying not to cough as she coped with the novelty of the cigarette, 'what brings you out to the frozen shires? Sue mentioned something about your husband setting up a new company.' Maddy had found herself telling Izzie about Simon's dream of being the great IT entrepreneur, and her horror at having to up sticks to the sticks. 'He was pretty canny,' she'd said laughing. 'He put on a charm offensive and whisked me around the area, studiously playing up the good bits and omitting the bad. He's always been good at that.'

'How did you meet him?' Noticing Izzie had stubbed out her cigarette, half smoked, she had realised she couldn't remember the last time anyone had asked her that. Once you have kids people tend to forget you were ever a single entity, and everyone she had met here was more interested in whether she was settling in or fishing for invitations to check out the house. It was fun to recall how she'd been introduced to him through a mutual friend, and how he'd wooed her in the old-fashioned way with tickets to Covent Garden, and dinner at Quaglinos.

'Then he showed his true colours and took me to an England game at Twickenham. Well, I hadn't a clue what was going on, except that it was very noisy and bloody cold. England lost and that was the end of my rugby-watching career, thank God! We did the big white wedding in Richmond, where my mum lives, and then we procreated . . . What about you and Marcus?' She'd hoped she'd got the name right.

Izzie had seemed a bit dismissive somehow. 'Oh nothing so glamorous. I met him at an advertising party. I was working for Greville Dane, you know the children's book publisher, as an editor, and a friend invited me along. Marcus was a copywriter for a big ad agency – Mitchell Baines McCormack – they did all those trendy jeans ads in the eighties with the big American cars. I thought he was a dish – all leather jacket and sparkly eyes, very witty and amusing – and he sort of swept me off my feet. Anyway we moved in together and did the eighties two-mortgage thing. We were far too trendy-lefty to get married or anything like that, but then I discovered I was pregnant with Charlie and, well, I made an honest man of him!'

Izzie had trailed off and had looked down into her coffee, smiling. Maddy, ashamed of her curiosity, had felt compelled to ask, 'So why here then – did the agency move?'

'Oh God no! Far too provincial.' She suddenly looked cautious and Maddy was sorry she had asked. 'No, there was a pretty aggressive takeover, and heads had to roll. In advertising you are only as good as your last campaign, and Marcus had had a lean period, so his head went on the block. It was all pretty hairy, so we decided to sell the house – and made a bit of a killing – and came here.'

'Any sign of a job?' Maddy had winced at how different things were for her, with her big house being overhauled at huge cost by the builder, and here was Izzie clearly struggling. She wasn't sure she'd ever met anyone like this. It was a whole new experience.

'Oh, he's doing some freelance for an agency in Oxford, brochure-writing, that sort of thing, but not quite so glamorous. And I'm still editing stuff here and there.' Izzie had suddenly seemed evasive, and keen to lighten the tone. 'So now you know why I don't quite make the grade with Old Templeton. That and the fact that I don't share her passion for plug-in air fresheners and coffee mornings.'

They had both been gasping with laughter when the door had opened and Marcus Stock had come in. He had seemed surprised to find someone else there, but had kissed his wife and shaken Maddy's hand.

He was a good-looking man, and Maddy could understand the devotion with which Izzie had talked about him and his wonderful advertising career in London. He looked lean and fit, with keen eyes and thick, wavy brown hair down to his collar. But it was also clear that he was a bit drunk.

'Bloody hell it's smoky in here,' he'd drawled. Izzie had jumped up, and fussed around getting another mug for him.

'Instant, darling?' he'd teased, draping an arm over Izzie's shoulders. 'Wouldn't the real thing be a bit more suitable for our guest?' He'd turned to Maddy. 'So how are you enjoying the frozen north?'

'Oh it's grim but I can cope.'

'Can't say we miss London one bit, do we, darling?' He'd smiled warmly down at Izzie. 'Moving here was the best thing that ever happened to us, wasn't it?'

Maddy wasn't entirely sure that Izzie would concur, but she'd made some muttered agreement about how she thought she'd get used to it in time. Over coffee, Marcus had been witty and charming, dominating the conversation with little anecdotes about local life, and on the surface it had been all very jolly. But his arrival had put an end to the easy conversation between her and Izzie, who was now saying very little, and Maddy felt vaguely disappointed. Finishing her coffee, she had looked at her watch, and lied that she had to collect the dry cleaning before she got the children. But she had given Izzie a parting hug with a warmth she really meant.

'Thanks, that was fun – let's meet in town for coffee soon. Have you got a mobile? Here's my number. Let's meet after the school drop-off one morning.'

Over the next couple of days she had been tied up sorting out the electrician and the plumber, who had managed to chip one of the new CP Hart basins. Simon hadn't come home until very late on either night – she'd given up and chucked his dinner in the bin – and he'd seemed distracted and even snappy when she'd tried to share her domestic crises with him.

'God, darling, I don't know,' he'd said rather brusquely, grabbing a beer from the fridge. 'Get the ruddy man to pay for a new basin.' Maddy was confused. Even on the most hectic days in the City, when the markets were teetering on the brink of Armageddon, he'd manage to find something amusing about the day, and come home and regale her with it. He was always positive, taking her in his arms and kissing her hair. 'Who cares what's happening, my darling? It's only money and someone else's at that!'

Maddy had put his mood down to the pressures of running his own business, assured herself it would all be fine as usual, put it out of her head and cracked on with the house. The following Wednesday she had packed off Colette and Pasco to the local toddler group – run by Janet Grant, the vicar's wife, and rather gruesomely called Ragamuffins – and treated herself to a trip to Burford. What pleased Maddy's sensibilities most about this agonisingly bijou Cotswold town was that the shops sold antiques as good as any she would find up Kensington Church Street or on the King's Road, but at less ludicrously inflated prices. Burford was OK. It had kudos. It reassured her that there was civilisation only a few miles away.

She had felt a bit sick with guilt as she'd looked in the rear-view mirror at the two rather delicious garden urns in the back of the car. She'd paid for them with the credit card as quick as she could to somehow lessen the pain – even her unfailingly generous husband would flinch if she came clean about how much they had been – but she'd felt pretty sure that if she positioned them somewhere fairly discreet in the garden, he wouldn't notice them for a while.

Feeling elated the previous morning, she'd called Izzie first thing before heading off to school, and they'd met for coffee in town. Now as she drove to collect Will from school – thankfully it was Friday and she had a couple of days' break from the tedious trip – she thought about the morning they had spent together. Had she handled it right? Over coffee at Costa's – well, you could smoke in there – Izzie had bemoaned her paltry wardrobe and Maddy had persuaded her to come shopping. Acutely aware that Izzie's budget was probably pretty tight, Maddy had employed all her tact, and her unswerving eye for a pseudo-designer bargain, and was rather chuffed that she'd managed to find just the thing in Libra on the High Street.

Libra exuded the superior atmosphere of a provincial boutique that is very generously bringing designer fashion to the masses, but its pristine chatelaine, who had a face like a prison warder in make-up, was smart enough to clock Maddy straight away. Izzie hung back – Maddy suspected that she had never set foot in the place before – but Maddy brushed aside the woman's obsequious overtures, put on her best 'sod you' face and headed straight for the sale racks, where, in among appliquéd T-shirts and casual 'slacks' for the golf club, she had dug out a pair of gorgeous wide-legged woollen trousers and a powder-blue angora jumper. Izzie had taken some persuading to take off her jeans and T-shirt but, despite the rather dubious Italian 'designer' label, the clothes had fitted her beautifully. When she'd looked self-consciously in the mirror, her twinkly blue eyes had lit up.

'Honestly, Maddy, you are a genius. If I didn't know better, I'd think it was Armani!'

Maddy had resisted the urge to investigate the real Armani on the new season rails, and the two of them had left the shop, Izzie gripping her new purchases with the excitement of a child, and had given Maddy a big hug of thanks.

Maddy smiled to herself now. Yes, it had been fun. Will chatted all the way home about his day. He seemed to have made a friend called Sam who he wanted to invite home to play, and despite Will's alarming caveat that Sam be allowed to bring his Power Ranger suit with him and that he couldn't eat dairy, Maddy felt happy enough with the world to promise that she would ring Sam's mother on Monday and put a date in the diary.

It wasn't until much later, after she had unloaded him and the weekend shopping from the car and gone to her bag to get out a fag, that she saw she had a voicemail message on her mobile. It was Simon's secretary.

'Mrs Hoare, it's Lillian. Mr Hoare has asked me to let you know that he will be late leaving tonight, as he has to put in a call to the States. Er . . . I wonder if you could call me back if you get a chance. I'm off a bit early, so if you get this before four could you possibly ring?' Maddy looked at the clock. It was four-thirty. Damn she'd missed her. And he'd be late again. She'd been asleep when he got home last night, and left, with a brief kiss on her hair, first thing this morning.

Colette had asked for the weekend off to see friends in London and Maddy had concurred – she didn't ask often and the poor girl needed her fix of urban life too – so she promptly forgot about Lillian's unusual call as she ran headlong into the maelstrom of the children's baths, story-reading and bed. With Florence and Pasco tucked up, she poured herself a glass of wine and curled up with Will on the sofa: he engrossed in a *Star Wars* video and she casting a casual eye over the paper. She only ever read the headlines, page three (just as saucy in the broadsheets in their own rather Tory way), and the features section.

As she closed the paper, bored by an interview with an ageing rock star about his battle with depression, a small heading on the business pages caught her eye. 'Americans pull out of IT deal.' There were only a few lines: '*Regus, the leading US venture capitalist, has had cold feet about backing a major software development initiative with Workflow Systems. Insiders say the Oxford-based company, which was to be floated on the AIM, is unlikely to survive the blow.*'

Will felt his mother's body stiffen beside him. 'What's the matter, Mum?' Maddy smiled reassuringly, but her stomach lurched with nausea and panic. 'Just some rubbish in the paper. Come on, little man, off to bed.'

Once she'd tucked him in and checked for monsters behind the curtains, she came downstairs and dialled Simon's office number. Lillian's voice came on: 'This is Workflow Systems. The office is now closed, and will be open again at eight-thirty on Monday morning. Thank you for calling.'

Strange, she thought. Simon usually picked up any evening calls if he was there. She punched in his mobile number. It rang and rang and then clicked through to the voicemail she remembered him recording in the kitchen. She could even hear Will and Florence shrieking in the background.

'Hi, this is Simon. I can't take your call at the moment, but if you leave your number I'll get back to you as soon as I can.'

'Darling, it's me.' She didn't really know what to say. 'Will you be back soon? Can you call if you won't? Love you.'

By eleven she was getting fussed that he hadn't called back, and though she tried to get gripped by some Bruce Willis film in which he saved the world – again – she kept flicking channels, and getting up to pour herself another drink or light another cigarette. At 11.15 she heard his tyres on the gravel drive and, flooded with relief, rushed to the front door. She pulled it open. Oh Christ, oh Christ, it was a police car. Had he been done for drunk-driving and they'd brought him home? Did they do that sort of thing?

A policeman and a policewoman got out with almost painful slowness and, as she watched with fascination as they put on their hats, she vaguely registered that Simon wasn't getting out of the back.

'Good evening. Are you Mrs Madeleine Hoare?' Perhaps he was down at the police station and needed bailing out. Would they take a cheque? 'Do you mind if we come in?'

Maddy ushered them into the sitting room, switched off Bruce Willis and tidied up the papers strewn on the sofa.

'It's about your husband, Mrs Hoare.' The policeman paused and glanced at his colleague. 'I'm afraid he has had a accident, driving on the B42 hundred earlier this evening.' Why did they always refer to bloody road numbers? Maddy thought, irritated. 'He was taken to the John Radcliffe Hospital, but I'm very sorry to tell you that he died in the ambulance.'

Maddy smiled. 'No, that can't be right. He's been calling America. He's at the office. He's coming home.'

'Can I make you a cup of tea?' the policewoman asked. Maddy noticed she had very poor skin, and her hair was in a bun, rather like a ballet dancer's.

'No, I don't drink tea this late, it keeps me awake.' She was aware she was babbling. Her arms had gone cold, and she wanted to throw up.

'Mrs Hoare,' said the policeman patiently, 'is there someone we could call to be with you?'

Chapter 4

Izzie passed the rest of the week in a cloud of happiness. The lunch had gone really well, and she thought Maddy had been impressed with the unusual food she'd offered.

Even better, Marcus hadn't drawn his usual caricature of Maddy. After she had left, Izzie had braced herself for some kind of comment, but Marcus had been refreshingly quiet. No, quite unexpectedly, he had come down with a cold, and the poor love had spent the next few days in bed, while Izzie clucked around him and tried to keep the kids from disturbing him.

Maddy had been as good as her word, and the shopping spree had been a tantalising nibble at how the other half live. Any more of this and she'd have blonde streaks and regular tennis coaching like a proper prep-school mummy! With a whole new outfit to her name, Izzie felt a million dollars and not even Marcus' gloomy snuffling could put a dent in her happiness.

Unable to contain her excitement, she'd worn the new jumper the very next day (she'd hidden the trousers just for a bit, and couldn't bring herself to part with the lovely stiff, shiny paper carrier bags and tissue they'd come in), and was filling the car with diesel, when a good-looking, slightly older bloke in a Lexus had stared at her intently. Worried that she had a smut on her nose, she'd looked down, away, up in the air – anywhere but at him. Then on the way out from paying, he was there at the door as if waiting for her. Opening it with elaborate care, he'd smiled and said roguishly, so only she could hear, 'I only know of one person with bluer eyes than you – and that's me!'

She'd darted away blushing, and drove off hurriedly, crunching her gears. She had glanced in the rear-view mirror to see him watching her. 'Bloody hell, I've been chatted up! Me! Married with kids. How amazing!' She'd roared with laughter, and had pulled into a lay-by. Maddy would love this! Still giggling incredulously, she had left a message on her mobile, telling her the whole story.

At home, she composed herself and set about skimming the chicken soup she'd put on earlier for Marcus. He hadn't fancied anything else to eat for a couple of days, though he'd raided the kids' treat box while she'd been out, leaving nothing for her to put into their school bags for break but a couple of Amaretti biscuits.

She thought she heard a rustle of papers as she went upstairs, but when she popped her head round the door, he appeared to be asleep. She turned to creep out, but was arrested in her flight by his rasping voice. 'Darling? Z'at you? Come and sit with me for a while. It's so boring when you're out.'

She perched next to him on the bed, stroking his forehead with the tips of her fingers, and made the stupid mistake of asking him how he felt. For a moment he was stoical about his symptoms. But only for a moment.

'. . . and my throat feels a bit worse than yesterday, so I think I might need some of those lozenges that make it feel numb, you know, the ones in the little tube, and I got this awful pain under my ear when I blew my nose earlier. Oh, could you empty the bin for me . . . ? It's full of paper tissues. The ones you got were a bit rough, and now my nose is red, so I used some of that Clarins stuff you put on when your face goes blotchy. It feels a bit better now. Any chance of a cup of tea, lovey? Children all right, by the way?'

Once she'd related her morning's doings, carefully omitting any reference to the man at the garage, she went to make him some tea, checked that the soup was just simmering. By the time she went upstairs with it, and a couple of hot cross buns, toasted and buttered for a treat, Marcus was sitting up in bed and had resumed reading the paper. He stared at her as she came in.

'New jumper? I haven't seen that before, have I? It makes you sort of fluffy. Bit of a new look for you, isn't it?'

'What do you mean?' she challenged, bristling slightly. 'Fluffy-cute like a rabbit? Or fluffy-ditsy like Meg Ryan?'

'More fluffy dog hair like Fiona Price!'

'Right you!' Looking back later on what she did next, Izzie did see it was clumsy but she was provoked. She'd picked up the pillow without thinking and had meant to boff him on the head with it. How was she to know he was just taking a sip of tea? It had taken half an hour to clean up the resulting debris and she doubted she'd ever get the stain out of Marcus' fleece dressing gown. There was nothing hoarse or croaky about his yell as the hot tea splashed across his chest and trickled down into his lap. 'At least,' she ventured once it was all sorted, 'it's cleared up your throat.'

She made up for her clumsy impulse by being extra nice to Marcus for the rest of the day. She cut a chunk of baguette lengthways into sticks and buttered each one, just the way he liked; she brought the good radio upstairs so he could listen to *The Archers*; she even cut his toenails for him – well beyond the call of duty. Her mobile made a funny little bleeping noise, just when Pam Archer was about to harangue Tony (again), and she dashed downstairs to get it. Peering at the screen, she could see it was a text – her first ever – and she fumbled to open it.

'of course he was hitting on u! u look fab in that jumper. c u l8r'

Izzie spent some time decoding the message, then some more time working out how to send one back. She was quite pleased with the result, which she thought came over as modern and dynamic:

wanna meet 4 coffee nxt wk.

She sat down at the kitchen table with a satisfied smile on her face. New jumper, text messaging, new best mate (jumping the gun a bit there, maybe), new blue eyes. She stretched her legs out and leant back, her hands clasped behind her head. Things were looking good!

By the following week, Izzie's elation had evaporated. She checked and rechecked her mobile, but there was no reply from Maddy. She really couldn't do any more without being unbearably pushy. She suppressed the uncharitable thought that Marcus may have taken a call from Maddy and simply forgotten to tell her, but to be on the safe side, she had dialled 1471 every time she had been out.

Pissed off with herself for even caring, and with nothing better to do, she went into efficiency mode for the next few days, clearing out cupboards, defrosting the freezer, and tidying away old toys. Digging out the stepladder, she heaved herself and a box laden with Duplo up into the loft with difficulty. There was a funny, fruity scent in the cold air. She sniffed. Where was that coming from? Shuffling boxes and old tea chests around, she soon found out. A lusty growth of mushroomy things was blossoming under the eaves and had spread on to some old velvet curtains folded against the rafters. This could not be good!

As he closed the trapdoor the following day, Frank, the lovely builder from down the road, shook his head and sucked the air through his teeth. 'This isn't good, Izzie. What you've got here is a big case of dry rot – and that won't wait for no one.' He promised a quote by Monday, and she spent the weekend nauseous with worry, not even daring to tell Marcus. How much would it be? She tried to imagine the worst. Could it be as much as a thousand?

'It's going to be five grand, Izzie love, even if you do the minimum. Proper job, you're looking at seven.' Frank's kindly voice down the phone at eight-thirty on Monday morning couldn't soften the blow. 'It's not something you want to leave. I'm pretty busy, but I could fit you in before the end of the month.'

When she finally broke the news to Marcus, he was even more clueless than she was about how to raise the money. The only solution that presented itself was the building society. That was one humiliating meeting! Five minutes in, it was crystal clear that they could no more extend their mortgage than win an Oscar.

Standing in the sitting room a couple of days later, idly wondering if she were too old to go on the game, her glance fell on the piano. A fine old boudoir Bechstein, it had been part of her life and had stood like an old friend in her parents' sitting room. She'd learnt to play on it, sitting on her mother's knee until she was tall enough to reach the pedals. Now the children were doing the same – only last night Charlie had been sitting with her practising his scales, his face screwed up with concentration, his tongue poking out as his little hands fumbled for the notes. It felt like a body blow, but it was the only solution.

'This veneer's rather stained,' said the prissy little man from the piano warehouse, a few days later. He shook his head patronisingly, and she felt like setting fire to his horrible patterned acrylic sweater. 'People just don't know how to treat pianos. I suppose you've been using it as a side table. It's a crime to treat a piano as fine as this like a piece of furniture – it's a work of art.'

'Thank you for reminding me,' she hissed through her teeth. His attitude changed, however, when he sat down to play it and a Schubert Impromptu flooded the room. 'Oh – you've had it tuned – it has a very fine tone.' He hit a wrong note and trailed off. Fed up with his censorious manner, she leant over and, picking up where he had stopped, she completed the piece in the upper register. With sudden respect, he suggested a price that would comfortably cover Frank's quote, but she couldn't meet his eye as she arranged for him to collect it. She made damned sure it would be tomorrow when she knew she wouldn't have to be there to witness it.

Marcus was sympathetic that evening, when she told him tearfully what she'd done, at the huge sacrifice she had made. But he couldn't hide his relief that the problem was solved. She brushed off his clumsy suggestion that they could replace it with an upright, and took herself off to bed, drained with misery – what would her mother say when she plucked up the courage to tell her?

But the next day, Marcus finally made the jibe she'd been waiting for since Maddy had come to lunch. He caught her in the doorway, coat on, making her escape before the piano men arrived, and checking her mobile once again. He shook his head knowingly. 'Your new mate turning out to be a bit of a disappointment, is she?'

'No, of course not. It's just that I was expecting a call.'

'From Maddy, I presume.'

'No. Well, yes. I was just checking—'

'Izzie, my little darling. I warned you about her type, didn't I?' He put an avuncular arm round her shoulders. 'She was filling in time. She was probably at a loose end that day. Don't take it to heart, sweetie. You're worth ten of her. People like that can be very cruel and insensitive . . .'

Tears had started to prick in Izzie's eyes, until his last sentence. She turned to him, stony-faced. 'Thanks for your advice, Marcus, but I'm sure Maddy will get back to me when she's free.'

He looked uncertain for a moment, and was about to say

47

more, but Izzie turned on her heel. 'They'll be here any minute. I'm going to pick up the children,' she called over her shoulder. 'They've got swimming this afternoon, so we won't be back until later.'

And silently mouthing, Drop dead, Marcus, she swept out of the house.

Too early to pick up the children, she went to bury the accumulated misery of the past week at the supermarket. Mooching round the store, trying to resist the biscuit aisle and looking to see what was reduced, she failed completely to notice Sue Templeton standing dead in front of her. She nearly knocked her over with the trolley – in her current mood, she would have been quite happy to do so – and her scowl seemed to take the old cow by surprise.

'Oh Izzie, fancy meeting you here. You look different somehow. Have you lost some weight?'

Izzie stared at her startled. It was so unlike Sue to say anything that could be construed as a compliment, she knew it must have been spontaneous – and genuine.

'No, I don't think so – we don't have any scales, but my clothes don't feel any different. How are you?'

'It must be that sweater then. Been at the sales, have we?' That was more like it. Sue was back in her stride now, but Izzie's 'bugger you' mood prevailed.

'No. Popped into Libra with Maddy the other day. We both bought loads!'

Watching Sue's mouth drop open was worth the fib, but when her expression turned to one of solicitude, crossed with avid curiosity, it was Izzie's turn to be wrong-footed.

'What an awful business! Have you heard any more details?'

'I . . . er, no, no more details.'

'Those poor little children. My heart bleeds for them. How's she coping? No one's seen hide nor hair of her.'

'Coping? Oh . . . as you'd expect. Up and down, really.'

The awful lurching in Izzie's stomach was getting worse. Her mind raced to put together the hints of Sue's cliché-ridden drone. If she hadn't started this stupid charade, trying to impress Sue with her intimate knowledge of Maddy's life, she'd have found out by now. She framed her question with care.

'So when did you hear about it?'

'The very next morning. Gary had heard something on the traffic news. Of course you'll know. It took them ages to clear the road, and the car was a write-off. The fire brigade got him out, but he didn't even make it to the hospital. Terrible mess apparently, but isn't it lucky no one else was involved?'

Suppressing a sob, Izzie stumbled away from Sue, muttering something about fetching the kids. She paid for the groceries in a daze, shoved the bags in the car and left the trolley spinning in the car park as she gunned the engine and drove to school. On the way, she groped for her phone, found the number, and left a message when no one answered.

'Maddy, it's me. I'm on my way.'

Her face looked set and horribly white in the rear-view mirror, so she pinched her cheeks and tried to relax her shoulders before she went into the playground. Never had the children been picked up so quickly or efficiently. They seemed to sense her urgency.

'I've got to pop out for a bit this afternoon, darlings, so I thought you could miss swimming for once.'

In the back, the children silently exchanged a high-five. Mummy never relented on the swimming, no matter how they tried. At home, Izzie unloaded kids, bags and shopping at top speed before calling up to Marcus. 'Can you put the shopping away and feed the kids? I've got to go over to Maddy's straight away. Not sure when I'll be back.'

He was downstairs like a shot. 'What on earth? But I've been stuck here all afternoon. And now you want to race off to see

49

that woman. She leaves you hanging on for days, and you go haring off there at the drop of a hat—'

'Stop now, Marcus. Just stop it.' She put her hand on his chest. 'Her husband, he's . . . her husband is dead. He was killed in a car crash. I have to go. She's not answering calls. I have to make sure . . .'

Marcus fell back, his face pale, nodding in mute agreement.

'Yes, go. I'll do the kids, don't worry 'bout that. See what you can do. If there's anything we can . . . I'm sure there won't be, but – take your mobile and call me if . . .'

She squeezed his arm, touched by his unquestioning support. 'Thanks, darling. Love you lots.' And, jumping into the car, she set off for Huntingford House, trying not to think what she would find when she got there.

She located the house without much difficulty. It was easily the largest in the village, and she felt a little ashamed at a brief stab of envy. Maddy had all this, but no Simon to share it with now. What a tragedy! Guiltily remembering her uncharitable feelings towards Marcus only a few hours earlier, she breathed a silent prayer of thanks that her husband was safe and sound at home with their children. He had been wonderful, stepping into the breach like that. She really must be more patient with him. Resolving to lead a better life in every way, Izzie took a deep breath and marched up to the door.

She couldn't hear if the bell had rung through the heavy oak panelling, so she applied herself to the chunky brass ring, banging it hard again and again. She was just deciding whether to peep in through the windows when a faint clunking and rattling reached her ears. After what seemed like ages, the door slowly opened and her mouth dropped open. For a split second she thought it was Maddy. But although the resemblance was startling, the differences were more intriguing. The woman at the door regarded her coolly, her grooming immaculate, her clothes classic but severe, her make-up understated, but her jewellery . . . well, the only expression for it was 'bling bling'! It had to be Maddy's mother.

'Can I help you? Is there something you want?'

Her accent was almost faultless, but the too-careful enunciation betrayed her French origins. This was Seizième meets Sloane Square.

'I'm here to see Maddy. I'm a friend – Izzie. I live near by.'

The woman's face relaxed, the eyebrows returned to their normal patrician arch, and she extended her hand. 'Oh a friend, at last! I'm Giselle, Maddy's mother. Every day I've been telling her – "Call someone. Get on with your life! See your friends." When her father died, I didn't spend my time crying. Within a week I was at the beautician again, and the hairdresser. A woman owes it to herself to look her best. If you look right, you feel right. Come and see for yourself. She bites her nails, her hair's a mess! She's chain-smoking. So bad for the complexion . . .'

Izzie followed her and the running commentary. The message was clear. Never mind the loss of your husband, just look at those open pores! Glancing around, it was obvious to Izzie that Giselle's attention to sartorial detail did not extend to helping around the house. Stacks of papers were piled up against the walls, a school bag was disgorging its contents over the floor. Stacks of unironed laundry wilted on the stairs like dispirited passengers delayed in the departure lounge on their way to their final destination. But the little woman, with her fabulous legs, danced on in front of her, seemingly oblivious to the chaos, chattering away and gesticulating vividly.

Through the kitchen door she plunged – Izzie vaguely registered a symphony of blonde wood and chrome – still talking, talking, talking, with Izzie in her wake. How Maddy coped with this was beyond her – and now, of all times.

Maddy. She was sitting at the far end of the kitchen table, quite still, a cigarette burning down in her hand, staring through the windows. She looked bloody awful: hair un-washed, stained sweatshirt, not a scrap of make-up. But worst of all was the blank, blank look in her eyes. Slowly she turned to face Izzie, her face strangely serene, her voice a quiet mono-tone. Giselle threw her hands up in despair and departed, still talking.

'Oh hello, Izzie. Lovely to see you. Can I get you something? Cup of tea, perhaps?'

Izzie swallowed hard. This was scary. Not what she'd expected at all. Histrionics she could have coped with. Out-pourings of grief, no problem. She had big hugs and supportive talk ready and waiting. But this calm detachment, unruffled and undemonstrative, was disconcerting. Obviously, she'd have to take her cue from Maddy, and the mother wasn't going to be any use at all. She rolled up her sleeves.

'No tea thanks. Can I get one for you? Have you eaten?'

Izzie moved around the kitchen, emptying half-finished cups, stacking the dishwasher (which she found with some difficulty behind a blonde wood façade), clearing plates of congealed food, talking as she did so in a low, calm voice, the way she used to do when the children were babies. Maddy turned her face to follow her, but seemed barely to see her. No eye contact. Izzie couldn't imagine the landscape of pain she was gazing at so fixedly. All she knew was that she had to be there, to provide some kind of a link, to help Maddy back to reality.

After some time, Maddy looked up, puzzled. 'Where did *Maman* go? I can't bear having her here. She's got no idea at all. She just goes on and on all the time. Make her leave, can you?'

Izzie blanched. 'Are you sure, Maddy? I mean, I would have thought you'd want someone close to you at a time like this. Is she helping with the children? Isn't she getting your shopping in and stuff like that?'

Maddy shook her head irritably. 'Does she look like she'd help with the children? She's got no bloody idea at all. She lets Pasco play with her jewellery, then freaks out because he puts one of her earrings through the floorboards. She tells Will he's the man of the house and has to look after me. She even gave Florence her Chanel lippy to try out, then told her off for blunting the end.'

She broke off, her face crumpling and soundless tears running down her cheeks. The tissue she'd been twisting in her hands was useless – she'd shredded it into tiny pieces, dropping them on top of a pile already in front of her on the table. Izzie darted forward with a packet of soft tissues from her bag and thrust a bundle into Maddy's limp hands.

A soft cough behind her made Izzie jump. A small, dark-haired young woman had come into the kitchen and looked expectantly at her. 'Excuse me, Madame. You are her friend?'

'Er, yes. Yes, I suppose I am. You must be Colette. How are the children? Where are they?'

Colette beckoned her out through the door, and Izzie followed, mystified.

'I feed them upstairs. I make like a little *pique-nique* every night and they think it's a game.' She shrugged sadly. 'I don't know what else to do!'

'I'm sure that's just right, Colette. Is there anything I can do to help. Have they finished eating?'

Colette looked a little uneasy. 'Oh, Madame. Maddy, she don't go to the shops since the *enterrement*. There is nothing in the fridge now. I don't know what to give them tomorrow.'

Izzie nodded firmly. 'Right. I see. Let's go and make a list then.'

The fridge was just as Colette had described, and the freezer was little better. Together they worked out what would be needed for the next few days and Izzie got ready to return to the supermarket. From upstairs floated a warbling soprano singing Puccini. 'What on earth . . . ?'

'Maddy's mother. It's all she do. She come downstairs, she tell Maddy to pull herself together, then she goes upstairs and has a bath. I hope she go soon.'

Back in the kitchen, Maddy was now standing by the window, staring at the sunset. She jumped violently when Izzie touched her arm.

'I'm going to get some groceries. I won't be long. Do you want to come? Can I get you some ciggies?'

'Yes. Yes – the children need some bits . . . I don't know. Just some . . .' Giselle rustled into the room.

'It's all right, Maddy, I've done a list with Colette. Twenty fags OK or shall I get two packs?' Izzie ignored Giselle's scowl. In a satin peignoir with her hair wrapped in a turban, she pursued Izzie to the front door, haranguing her on the harm smoking would do to Maddy's complexion.

'Madame,' Izzie said firmly as she stepped through the door, 'I reckon her complexion is the least of her worries at the moment.'

Yikes. Another fifty quid gone. Even choosing the generic brands, the shopping still came to more than Izzie could afford. She'd have to sort out the money with Maddy later. Back at the house, everything was much the same. Only now, the hall was full of luggage. Giselle's voice floated from the kitchen. 'See if you can get those floorboards up. Those earrings were very expensive. I'll get your friend to take me to the station. Your stepfather will pick me up at Marylebone. I'll call you tomorrow. Now, for goodness sake, wash your hair. I'm sure darling Simon wouldn't want you to let yourself go.' A sound very like glass shattering was followed by a shriek.

By the time Izzie had got back from the station, and had cleared up the broken jar and sticky marmalade, Colette had put the groceries away. Maddy still hadn't moved but the pile of shredded tissue had increased. Izzie made fresh tea, pressed a cup into Maddy's hands and sat down next to her.

The silence drew out. At last Izzie could bear it no longer. 'I'm so sorry, Maddy. You must be feeling terrible. I'm sure it'll ease with time.' God – that sounded trite.

Maddy turned to her, seeming to see her for the first time that evening. 'Come on, Izzie, you know that's crap.'

Izzie looked down into her mug, mortified by her crassness.

'I'm sorry. I didn't know what to say.' There was a long, long pause.

Finally Maddy spoke. 'I've lost everything.'

'I know nothing could ever replace him but, Maddy, you've still got your children and this lovely home.'

Maddy laughed mirthlessly. 'No, Izzie. You don't get it. Everything.' There was a long pause as she lit one cigarette from the butt of another. 'I spoke to the lawyers today. The house is OK, he put that in my name, but what am I supposed to run it on? He's left me with nothing. Absolutely nothing. There's no mortgage so not even any life insurance.' She paused again, gazing down at the tissues in her hand. 'There's worse. It looks like he put our savings into the business – the money we had made on our house in London after we'd paid for this.' Izzie vaguely calculated how much Huntingford House must have cost – Maddy was talking about figures Izzie could only dream of. "Everything will be OK," he always used to say. OK?' Maddy looked up into Izzie's eyes. 'Nothing for me, nothing to pay the bills . . .' Her voice cracked. 'Nothing for the children.'

Maddy opened the fridge and surveyed the contents, surprised to see it was almost full with cheeses, packets of sausages and fresh pasta and something that looked like lasagne, in a serving dish she didn't recognise. Where had all that come from?

She wasn't hungry but, before she'd left today, Izzie had reminded her to eat. Maddy closed the fridge and opened the biscuit cupboard. That too seemed to have sprouted packets of KitKats and crisps. She took out a digestive from an open packet, nibbled it but, losing interest, dropped the rest in the bin. She lit another cigarette and noticed that she only had three left. Damn. She'd have to stop at the garage on the way to school.

Leaning against the sink as she smoked, she looked out of the window at the garden. Autumn seemed to have arrived without her noticing, and the leaves from the trees were strewn all over the lawn. Some she saw were still green, ripped too soon from the branches by some gale before they had had time to turn colour and die. Like Simon.

She glanced at the clock, and then had to look again realising she hadn't registered what it said at all. She'd have to leave to collect Florence in a moment. On the sideboard, next to a bundle of papers and unread school notices, she saw Simon's mobile, returned with his 'effects' by the police. Out of some masochistic urge she picked it up and tried to listen again to her last message to·him, but the save option had expired. She felt a wave of despair.

Hearing a crash from the sitting room, followed by a wail from Pasco, she rushed in to find him sitting on the floor surrounded by the debris of a vase he had pulled off the side table. It had been a wedding present. Suddenly she was overcome by a wave of anger mixed with guilt at having left him unattended.

'You stupid boy,' she screamed. 'Look what you've done! That was precious!' Pasco wailed even louder, his face bright red with grief and tears pouring down his face. Maddy felt suddenly mortified. She picked him up and clutched him to her. 'Oh God, darling, I'm so sorry. It wasn't your fault. I'm sorry. I'm sorry.' She sat down with him and cuddled him close, his snotty nose rubbed over the front of her cardigan and his tears now mixed with hers as they trickled down her face. Her chest ached with the effort of crying, and she felt like throwing up.

'What are we going to do, little man? What the hell are we going to do?'

She rocked him gently in her arms and sobbed with him. He was tired and fractious, she knew. He hadn't slept at all on the drive to Burford, the urns in the back of the car. How long had it been since she'd brought them home with such guilty glee, and had inveigled Crispin into helping her get them out of the car and hide them behind the outbuildings? Two weeks, maybe three? The man at the shop had been crestfallen when she'd called to ask if she could return them, but had made damned sure he bought them back from her for less than she had paid. She'd had to get them to him today. The car was going tomorrow and she'd never get them in the back of a Fiesta.

She lay back on the sofa as Pasco quietened in her arms, his sobs now slowing to vague hiccups, and looked over at the shards of smashed vase on the floor. Simon had thought the vase too ornately French and vulgar, but she'd loved it. It reminded her of Mémé's apartment – so stylish, so dark, every surface packed with fascinating trinkets that, as a child, Maddy had loved to run her fingers over.

Simon had never really fitted in on the few times they'd been to stay there. It had vaguely irritated her, but she'd teased him for being so British and reminded him that it was her French genes that made her so good in bed. Was it disloyal to admit now that anything about him had annoyed her? No. Not now. Not now she was mad as hell with him.

She had no recollection of the week leading up to the funeral, only that her mother had lent her a hat to wear at the church – 'so becoming, darling'. Simon's brother, Rory, had identified his body – she simply couldn't have – and she supposed he must have dealt with the funeral arrangements too. Will had been there at the service, quiet and brave and so grown up, and she had focused all her attention on him so she hadn't had to catch anyone's eye. What had the vicar said in the eulogy? She couldn't recall. Nor could she remember any of the people who had attended and kissed her and squeezed her arm afterwards, muttering platitudes about how 'sincerely sorry' they were.

She knew Izzie had been around the house – had she overlapped with her mother? – and it must have been she who had stocked the fridge and piled up all the letters of sympathy on to the hall table. Maddy hadn't opened many – they all said the same thing – what a lovely man he was and how if there is anything they could do to help she must call – but the phone had been predictably silent. How embarrassed people are about death.

She had vaguely registered how brilliant Izzie had been with the children since Colette had gone. That conversation had been painful. She knew she couldn't justify the cost of keeping her on – Maddy's meetings with the bank had made that plain – but she hadn't had the courage to face the truth. It was Colette herself who had finally forced the issue, and her leaving had been an emotional one. The children, in their grief, had clung to her and made her promise to come back. Maddy knew she would, but it couldn't be to work here. Her mother had been appalled. 'Darling, she is a gem. What *are* you thinking of?' But Maddy's pride, and some sense of self-preservation she couldn't quite rationalise, had stopped her yelling, 'Because I can't bloody afford her any more. I can't afford anything.'

She gently strapped the now sleeping Pasco into his car seat and set off for Little Goslings and Florence. How much longer she would stay there Maddy couldn't say, but it wouldn't be much past Christmas. The interview at Eagles had really been about the effect Simon's death might have on Will, and Mrs Turner had sat primly with her long rather masculine hands folded in her lap, nodding reassuringly and smiling with gentle sympathy.

'Of course, Mrs Hoare, I will make sure his form teacher keeps an eye on him. What a tragic situation for you all.'

She had been so lovely that Maddy had had to look away and try frantically not to cry. And it made it so much harder when she had to tackle the subject of the fees.

'Mrs Hoare, I can assure you the school and the governors have had this situation before, and we know it takes time to sort out probate on your husband's estate. We want the very best for Will as we know you do, so let's talk about this at the beginning of next term when you are clearer about what your financial situation will be.'

As she drove now towards Little Goslings, for the last time in her comfortable shiny car, Maddy's throat hurt with the pain of holding back her grief and her head ached with self-pity, and the headmistress's understanding and lack of it. You've got no idea, she thought. There is no money now and there won't be then.

She thought too about the impromptu visit from Lillian to the house some days after the funeral with personal stuff from Simon's office. She was a funny little woman, hard to put an age to – forty-five maybe fifty? She'd stood in the kitchen refusing to sit down, nervous and unsure, brave with her purple coat and vibrant orange hair. Unemployed.

'Mrs Hoare, I'm sorry you didn't get my call until it was too late,' she'd said. 'I wanted to warn you that Mr Hoare's behaviour wasn't right that afternoon. He'd been on the phone all morning, looking so desperate, then he went out at lunchtime . . . I think he did drink quite a lot . . .' She'd left the rest unsaid, given Maddy a clumsy embrace and left in her bright green little car.

Maddy gripped the wheel, slowly beginning to let the anger she had buried for so long boil to the surface. 'How the fuck could you leave me like this, you bastard, you deceitful, lying bastard?' she said out loud. 'Did you think so little of me that you couldn't let me in on your worries? I hate you. I fucking hate you.'

Chapter 5

Izzie had slipped into a routine during the past couple of weeks. She'd kiss Marcus goodbye in the morning, drop Charlie and Jess at school, go to the shops if there was anything she or Maddy needed, pick up a paper, then drive over to Maddy's. She wasn't sure how much Maddy registered her presence – that spaced-out calm of the first day was still pretty much in place, although it was occasionally punctuated with periods of stormy tears and furious resentment. But whenever Maddy had cursed Simon for leaving her in the lurch, calling him names that chilled Izzie to the bone, she would later be assailed with the bitterest guilt and grief. Once or twice Izzie had found her lying on her bed, curled in a foetal position sobbing so hard that her whole body shook uncontrollably.

Izzie did what she could. The practical things were the easiest: loading and unloading washing, stocking the fridge, helping Will with his homework, or playing with Pasco after Colette had to leave. Even answering Florence's heartbreaking questions. This she could take in her stride.

It was how to be with Maddy that was worrying her. If they'd known each other for longer before this dreadful tragedy, she would have had a reference point. Up and down, calm and crazy, resigned and resentful – Izzie wasn't sure which was the real Maddy. It was like trying to piece together a jigsaw without having seen the picture on the lid. She hadn't even known Simon. All she had to go on were the photographs Maddy had shown her with such fervour. They revealed a big, confident man who was smiling in every one, from the glamorous wedding pictures, to the snaps of him buried in the sand with Will standing triumphantly beside him with a spade.

So she could give no feedback when Maddy spoke about him, speculating endlessly on what had gone wrong, on the signs she shouldn't have missed, forensically combing through her memories of their last weeks together, reproaching herself for not being the wife he could have shared his problems with.

Izzie could only listen. She knew enough about bereavement to realise that Maddy didn't want platitudes. The best gift she could give her was the space to feel what she was feeling, and to take her as she was, day by day, hour by hour. Some instinct made Izzie believe that Maddy had an inner strength that she was only just testing, and that it would see her through, in the long run. Some days, however, that belief was stretched to the limits.

It was a Wednesday when things came to a head. She had walked straight into the house, as usual, and tucked a couple of shepherd's pies, made the night before, into the freezer. Maddy's car – the Fiesta now – was parked at its customary rakish angle in the drive, but of Maddy there was no sign. Florence was at nursery, Pasco was grizzling, bored in his playpen in the kitchen, and the remains of his porridge was congealing on the high chair. Worried now, Izzie picked him up quickly and clutched him to her. Feeling the dampness from his nappy, she started rushing from room to room – no sign. Her heart was pounding in her chest when, from an upstairs window, she spotted a trail of footsteps on the dewy lawn. Almost crying herself, she followed the dark ribbon on the grass into the orchard, and there Maddy stood, barefoot and still in her pyjamas, her hair wild and uncombed, looking up at the sky through the branches of the trees.

Mustering all the control she could, Izzie spoke quietly. 'Maddy, come in now, you'll get cold. I'll put some coffee on for us both. Who took the children in today?'

Maddy turned, looking slightly irritated at having her reverie interrupted. 'I did, of course.'

'In your pyjamas?'

'I wore my dressing gown,' she replied defensively. 'And it wasn't cold.'

'Come in now,' Izzie reiterated more firmly. 'It's time to get dressed. And we've got work to do today. I'm going to put Pasco into his cot for a bit while we get you dressed.' Izzie cuddled him as they went upstairs together and changed his sodden nappy before settling him safely into the cot, surrounded by a ludicrous number of toys. He'll be fine, thought Izzie, while I sort out his mother.

'Right, Maddy.' She steered her across the landing. 'No more pyjama mooching.'

Maddy allowed herself to be undressed, and shoved under the warm jets of the power shower she had chosen with such care less than six weeks before. Izzie's hand shot round the glass door to pass her shampoo, conditioner, shower gel in rapid succession, and Maddy performed her usual routine bit by bit, waiting for the next command, then meekly responding.

Izzie, for her part, was struck by how similar it all was to getting Charlie to wash. 'Rinse the shampoo out thoroughly, now. Have you done your feet? Don't forget in between your toes. Is this the stuff you like?'

As Maddy let the water rinse off the shampoo, Izzie perched on the side of the bath and watched her for a moment as the water cascaded over her drooping head and down over her slim body, until the glass steamed up and obscured her view. She seemed almost childlike, passive and unresisting in her raw vulnerability. Izzie had to look away.

She scanned the room, so perfectly put together with its honey-coloured walls and white and chrome fittings. Every tap, every plug, even the toothbrush mug yelled *quality*. No Buzz Lightyear bubble bath or foam alphabet letters here to ruin the effect. Beautifully lit glass shelves either side of the basins groaned under stylishly packaged jars of creams and lotions. Unbearably, one still held Simon's shaving gear, silver shaving bowl and badger-hair brush, silver-backed hairbrushes and discreet bottles of Penhaligon aftershave with rounded glass stoppers. His toothbrush stood forlorn and dry in a glass.

Unable to witness the desolation in the midst of this luxury any longer, Izzie reached into the shower to turn off the water, and hand Maddy a towel. Dried and moisturised, she sat quietly on the bed and Izzie noticed, as she brushed the tangles out of her hair, the dark roots that would once have vexed Maddy beyond endurance. Izzie opened the wardrobe – where to start? It was almost anal in its neatness. Like her mother, Maddy was clearly fascinated by clothes. T-shirts were piled by colour; socks and tights rolled and placed in honeycomb drawer organisers; cashmere knitwear arranged by sleeve length and by tone from palest pink to deepest turquoise, like a paint palette.

'Is this the capsule wardrobe, hey Maddy? More like a space shuttle!' Izzie laughed lightly in an attempt to lift the mood. 'My cupboard's just a lucky dip. What do you feel like wearing then?' Maddy shrugged and tugged distractedly at the tie on her towelling bathrobe. Eventually, Izzie laid out on the bed a pair of pale blue capri pants, a white long-sleeved T-shirt and a cashmere V-neck in a deep sea-green. On the smooth beech shelves, she found bras and knickers, carefully matched, and enough of them to last a month. Each one in shell pink or palest blue and more lacy and delicate than the last.

Suddenly Izzie felt overwhelmed by the intimacy of it all –

she'd had to intrude too far. She went to check on Pasco, who was chewing his donkey's ear.

She stroked his soft little head. 'Fancy your mother taking Will and Florence to school in her pyjamas. Just you wait – it's the start of a trend. They'll all be at it soon – ditching their new pastel loafers and going barefoot! I'd pay good money to see that.' Pasco gave her a gummy smile and bounced up and down on his bottom.

A puzzled exclamation had her racing back to Maddy, who was frowning in perplexity. 'These trousers can't be mine. They're far too big.' She was right. They were hanging off her. And now that Izzie really looked, she could see that the bra was loose, and her ribs visible under the lightly tanned flesh. Maddy must have lost a stone at least.

Maddy let her head tilt right back, laughing slowly. 'I'd have given anything to have lost this kind of weight six months ago. Look at me! I've found it! The weight-loss programme that works. Roll up, ladies, it's the bereavement and bankruptcy diet!'

Izzy had to head this off. 'Come on,' she said briskly. 'You're not going to tell me that someone who loves accessories as much as you can't find a belt! There – that's a bit better. Now you're the best-dressed scarecrow in the whole county. Right, come on. I've got big plans for us. Bring Pasco downstairs. He's in for a real treat!'

Intrigued now, in spite of herself, Maddy obediently trotted downstairs, nuzzling Pasco's soft neck. 'What is it? What are we going to do? Are we going out?'

'Nope. Something far more innovative than that! We're going to clean the kitchen. Now. Take me to your Mr Muscle. We're going to get Marigolded up.'

Maddy looked around the kitchen as if for the first time. 'You've got a point. One foot sticking to the floor, I can tolerate. But not both.'

Izzie was throwing open cupboard after cupboard. 'OK. I give in. Where's the hoover?'

'I've no idea. Somewhere in the utility room, maybe?' She peered inside and shook her head in wonder. 'Look at all this stuff. I may not have any money, but it looks like I'll never want for Toilet Duck!'

Brandishing brooms and dusters, they got stuck into the kitchen. First Maddy mopped the floor, then Izzie wiped down all the surfaces and covered the floor with crumbs again. Then Maddy carefully cleaned windows with the floor cloth, leaving them dirtier than before. Izzie struggled to empty the Dyson cylinder into the bin, but in banging it, created a mushroom cloud of dust. Pasco meanwhile was busily emptying pasta shapes and posting them into Izzie's handbag. With a shriek of horrified laughter, Maddy scooped him up and spun round with him in her arms. Now they were all laughing as they looked around at the carnage. Every surface, as well as they themselves, was coated with fine grey dust.

'Well, you've got to admit it,' said Maddy at last, wiping tears of laughter from her grimy face, 'we've made a big difference. It was pretty dirty when we started. Now it's a complete shit heap.'

And they all started laughing again, Pasco delightedly sticking his grubby fingers into his mother's mouth.

After a damage-limitation exercise that involved a cursory hoovering up – nothing they could mess up too much – Izzie went to tidy up the papers in the hall while Maddy took everything out of the fridge and wiped the shelves.

'I've only dropped one jar and I've found a yoghurt that expired in September,' yelled Maddy from the kitchen. 'Not bad, eh? Think I dare risk making a cup of coffee?'

'Live dangerously, girl,' replied Izzie, and tidied away some coats from a heap by the front door. Under them, she found a large wooden wine crate and, deciding it wasn't her place to look inside, took it with her into the kitchen.

'I found this under some rubble. Is it something of yours?'

Maddy stared blankly for a moment then seemed to remember. 'Wow! I'd forgotten about that. It comes from my grandmother's apartment. Let's have a look.'

Izzie set the box on a chair and lifted Pasco out of his mother's arms. Carefully Maddy placed the wine crate on to the table, treating it like some kind of exhibit at Sotheby's. Izzie watched as she flexed her fingers, like a pianist about to perform a concerto, and ran her hands over the smooth mellow wood. 'What have we here?'

With one hand, Izzie quickly piled up the detritus that covered the table, so Maddy could spread out her finds, and took off the kettle. This was important, an event that merited a plate of biscuits too. For the first time in weeks, Maddy seemed to be taking an interest in something, a vague flush of colour tinged her cheeks, and Izzie didn't want to destroy the fragile moment.

Maddy couldn't be sure, but the box must have arrived in a packing case with the furniture sent over from Paris when Mémé had died three years ago. She'd obviously taken one look at the dusty, yellowing newspaper on top and condemned it to the loft with Simon's old school trunk and the oddments she could find no place for in their house in London. Maddy had only been able to make a flying visit for her funeral – Florence had been very tiny – but Giselle had stayed behind in Paris with her sister, Claudette, who lived in Antibes (though was careful to stay out of the sun), and the two of them had gone through the ghastly process of clearing their mother's bits and pieces.

Maddy had started half-heartedly to do the same with Simon's, but she had stopped after lifting out an armful of his clothes from the wardrobe and burying her nose in them to take in the smell of his body. It was too soon and too final. Only yesterday Will had come plodding out of the cloakroom like Christopher Robin wearing Simon's wellies which came up to his thighs, but Maddy had snapped at him and told him to put them back straight away. Then, seeing his face begin to crumple in confusion, had relented.

As she now lifted off the paper from the top of the box – a front page from *Le Figaro* – it revealed a piece of Chantilly lace, folded and stiffened from being there so long.

'Oh that's beautiful.' Izzie took the delicate filigree from Maddy hands and unfolded it carefully, keeping it out of Pasco's reach. 'This is the sort of thing you pay a fortune for in those *brocantes* places – I remember we went to one on a Sunday once when we were on holiday in Provence, oh aeons ago . . .' Maddy could sense that, by her jabbering, Izzie was trying to encourage her to keep going through the box, and suddenly she loved her for her enthusiasm and interest.

'It's funny really – Mémé wasn't big on lace. She was incredibly elegant, in a fifties sort of way. Always dressed to the nines in case someone called unexpectedly – you can see where my mother got it from. She was all Chanel and pearls, and she smelt divine.' Maddy paused but Izzie stayed silent and waited. 'When I was little I used to fiddle the whole time with the things on her dressing table, trying on her rings and her necklaces. I'd prance about in her dressing gown and high shoes, smother myself in Guerlain until I stank. She was such a lady – surprising really cos she wasn't born to it.' Maddy stopped and put her hand back into the box.

'Really?' Izzie prompted. 'I sort of imagined she was French aristocracy.'

'Oh no no no,' Maddy smiled, lifting out a pile of curled and faded papers. 'Real peasant stock from further south.' She narrowed her eyes, thinking. 'She went to Paris in the thirties to look for a job in a couturier – she was always mad about fashion. I think she was one of those girls who modelled the collection for the smart ladies who come for a private fashion show. All very *Vogue*.'

Maddy started browsing the curling papers in her hand, the dust getting on to her fingers. They looked like old photographs. 'Anyway, she met *Grandpère* when he came to the couturier with his mother to buy her some clothes – now he *was* top drawer. Really posh Parisian banking family – and it was a *coup de foudre, la grande passion* – apparently he came back and waited until she knocked off work that evening – Mémé used to tell me all this with glee, really playing up how smitten he was – the French are so fucking pleased with themselves – anyway the family was horrified and all that, but she charmed the pants off them . . . Oh look, here's a picture.'

She handed Izzie a black-and-white photo of Mémé in a coat with a thick fur collar, her hair neat and bobbed, on the arm of a devastatingly handsome man whose chest was puffed out with pride. Izzie giggled. 'They look so young but so sophisticated.'

'Here's Mémé in about nineteen eighty – must have been in Nice or somewhere.' The photo, in colour this time, showed an old woman in a wicker chair on some kind of terrace, and you could tell from the light it was taken beside the sea. She was wearing a large straw hat, and a sort of greenish kaftan.

Izzie gasped. 'God, she's the image of you! Your mum was right, better get off the fags if you want to look like that at fifty-odd.'

'Oh don't you bloody start,' laughed Maddy. 'And anyway she smoked like a chimney with a long cigarette holder!' Suddenly she shrieked with laughter. 'Look at this – oh my God! – this is one of me in my teens – must have been about fifteen – when we went to stay with Aunt Claudette in Antibes.' A group of teenagers, nubile bodies in swimsuits, were all leaning against each other, laughing, and holding up glasses of wine as if in a toast. Izzie took the picture from Maddy. 'Your figure was great even then, you cow. You all look so bronzed and carefree.'

'And rich,' added Maddy wistfully. They *had* been spoilt. Villas, maids. It had been idyllic.

'Well, I didn't want to say it. But money obviously didn't do anything for your taste in haircuts. Look at you all! I had a boyfriend once with hair like this guy here – horribly early eighties and New Romantic. Didn't that much hair gel cause an oil slick in the Med? Who is he?'

Maddy looked up from the other pictures, hearing the end of Izzie's question. 'Oh that's Philippe, my oldest cousin – he's a surgeon. That's Adele, his younger sister – she eloped with the boy next door. She teaches English. They've just adopted a little girl from Senegal.' She hoped she wasn't boring Izzie.

Izzie peered closer. 'And who's this skinny one? He's cute too, in a callow kind of way.'

Maddy looked again at the photo. 'Oh that's Jean Luc, another cousin. He's my aunt's son and he runs a farm in the Cévennes now. Isn't he lovely? He's one of my favourite people. Thank goodness he's shaved off that moustache though. He was doing the moody student thing, writing poetry, playing the guitar. I was madly in love with him in those days, but then so was half of Nice.'

She looked down again. 'Look at this – here's my mum and my dad.' The picture must have been taken soon after he and Giselle were married – they were both wearing sailing clothes and were holding on to each other as only newly-weds do; the wind had caught their hair and they were both laughing at the camera. For once her mother looked carefree and dishevelled. Maddy's eyes filled up with tears, but they didn't feel like the tears she'd shed over the last few weeks. Not angry and desperate, just sad. The sort of tears that come when your memory's been stirred and you realise how much you miss the time when life was perfect and uncomplicated.

Izzie looked closely at it. 'I can see why she fell for him, but somehow I imagined someone dapper and distinctly continental . . .' She paused. 'Well, I don't really know your mother but . . . no offence.'

Maddy sniffed and laughed. 'None taken. Dad was very English. Almost aristocratic really, public school and all that. Can't imagine how they were ever compatible. The rest of the pictures are of long-lost cousins.' Maddy made a pile on the table, and then delved into the box for more. 'Good grief, I remember this.' She pulled out an old clockwork toy, a monkey on a bicycle, and gently placed it on the table. As she turned the key, the monkey's legs began to move up and down and its head clicked from side to side. Pasco clapped his hands with glee.

'Don't touch, sweetheart,' said Izzie. 'They're quite valuable, you know. You ought to hang on to it for the children when they are older.'

'I don't think it will quite compete with a PlayStation2 for entertainment value, do you?' snorted Maddy.

'It's so sad when old things just disappear out of your life.' Suddenly Izzie sounded deeply sad and, fleetingly, Maddy wondered why. 'Jess thinks my Sasha doll is an antique.'

'God, I had one of those. I adored it! Used to brush her hair for hours.' Maddy delved into her box of delights again and gently pulled out something wrapped in white tissue paper. She looked at Izzie with hammed-up anticipation. 'Oooh treasure!'

'This could be it,' laughed Izzie, wide-eyed. 'The Fabergé egg that your grandmother stashed away for you to discover and sell when you fell on hard times.'

Tantalisingly slowly, Maddy unwrapped the tissue. They both guffawed as Maddy revealed a hideous terracotta vase with little curly handles and black, decorative squiggles up the side. 'Oh tragedy – it's one of my mother's few lapses in taste – ghastly. Chuck it quick!'

As Izzie lobbed the vase into the bin, Maddy had a final

delve. 'Nope that's all, no hidden family jewels or tiaras.' She lifted up the box and then put it down again and felt into the bottom. 'Hang on, it's too heavy to be empty. There must be something else under this paper.'

Pulling out another brittle, yellowed sheet from *Le Figaro*, Maddy revealed a thick leather-bound ledger, about the size of an A4 notebook, bulging with papers slipped between the pages. The cover was mottled brown and held closed with two pieces of ribbon shiny with age.

'What on earth is this?' said Maddy, as she carefully undid the knot and opened the cover. The spine creaked with age, and on the first page was handwritten in faded brown ink and in that distinctive loopy writing all French people seem to have, '*Le journal de Luce Ménestrel 1847*'.

'That's a family name – I wonder who she was.' Maddy turned over the next page and, as Izzie looked over her shoulder, they both fell silent feeling they had found something significant and grave.

The writing inside was minute and would have been hard to decipher in English, virtually impossible in old French. As Maddy continued to turn the pages, dried and faded flowers fell from between them, revealing the shadow they had left on the paper. The loose sheets that had been tucked inside seemed to be torn from other bigger bits of paper and had the odd word or numbers scrawled on them.

'How good's your French, Maddy?' whispered Izzie, as if in reverence. 'I can't understand a word of this, but then I only managed a C at O level.'

'I'm not quite sure. I can recognise the odd word . . . I think this says *onagre*, that's evening primrose I think, *cire d'abeille* – that's beeswax. Oh there it is again . . . and *sauge,* which is sage. Hang on . . . *pétale* . . .'

'Well, even I know what that is,' laughed Izzie.

Maddy read on only vaguely listening, lost in the effort of

working out the fine script. '*Lavande, la rose, jacobée, digitale*, that must be foxglove . . .' Maddy struggled with the next word. 'God knows what this means, *centpertuis . . .*'

'It seems to be a kind of gardening journal. Perhaps Luce was some early Vita Sackville West,' Izzie wondered, 'or the Charlie Dimmock of her day.'

'Maybe – do you think she used to wield a spade without her stays on? No, this seems to have lots of measurements next to the words, like *ajouter deux tasses de lavande* . . . add two cups full of lavender. It's almost like a cookery book but with plants and herbs.' Maddy absent-mindedly picked at the biscuits that Izzie had laid out on a plate on the table, and started to nibble one. Just at that moment Pasco, who'd dropped off, started awake in Izzie's arms and both women jumped in surprise.

'Christ, Izzie, look at the time, it's five to three. We've got to get to school.' She hastily put the book back in the box, along with the other bits, and started to gather up their coffee cups from the table.

'I'll have a look at it later and dig out my dictionary.' Suddenly, overcome with good feelings, she put down the cups, turned to Izzie and gave her a huge hug. 'I've loved today. You have been wonderful, I can't thank you enough for putting up with me and all the shit that's been going on. You are the best thing around here.' She had really meant it, but she could see Izzie look away almost with embarrassment yet with pleasure on her face. For a moment they were both a bit ill at ease, then Izzie grabbed her bag and slung it over her shoulder.

'I'll speak to you tomorrow,' she said, adding, in her best Jean Brodie voice, 'and make sure you have something to eat, young lady.'

Maddy drove to collect Florence at break-neck speed – or as fast as a five-year-old Fiesta would let her – but by the time she reached Will's school, she was clearly late and he was the only child left in the classroom. He looked disconsolate and very small sitting at the table in his little grey cap and school coat.

'Mrs Hoare,' said his form teacher quietly as Maddy entered the classroom, with Florence and Pasco, 'can I have a quick word? We've had a rather bad day, I'm afraid,' she continued quietly. 'William has been quite disruptive in lessons. Of course, I understand what he has been through and I have been really very lenient with him.' Maddy could feel the hurt well up inside her, and a primeval desire to protect her poor little son. 'But he's been so *rude*,' continued the teacher. 'To me and Mrs Lovett, the classroom assistant, kicking and punching. He even poked Sam with a pencil, and they are usually such good friends. William is such a lovely boy,' you don't have to tell me that, thought Maddy, suddenly desperate with loathing for this woman, 'but we can't tolerate that sort of behaviour when it affects others in the class.'

Maddy gathered up her children, muttering something about talking to Will later, and left as fast as she could. She felt devastated and mortified. What had she been thinking of? She had been so enveloped in her own grief over the last few weeks, she had failed to see the effect it was having on the children. She'd assumed that so long as there had been someone there with them, so long as they had been fed and bathed, they'd be all right. How stupid and selfish she had been. Of course Will was hurting. He'd lost his father, and all she had done was withdraw inside herself. Something about today, the clearing up and the delving through the box and into the past had made her wake up. She had to preserve herself and her sanity for the children, if not for herself.

For the first time in ages – if not ever – she let them help her make the supper. Florence put the sausages on the baking tray and Will broke the eggs for the pancake batter for pudding. Pasco completely emptied a cupboard of Tupperware all over the kitchen floor and for once she let him. Maddy dug out the unopened Mary Berry Aga cookbook someone had given her as an 'essential for moving to the country', and she created an enormous mess making Scotch pancakes. The children smeared them and each other with butter and jam, and ate them warm at the table. Leaving the debris, Maddy whisked them up for a bath, and they splashed and giggled as much with delight at the bubbles as at the fact that their mother was giggling with them.

They each picked a story, and they cuddled up on her bed to read them. When was the last time she had done this? She gently lifted the two sleepy little ones, and tucked them into their beds, turned on their night lights and kissed their fragrant skin.

'Mum, can I stay in your bed tonight?' Will asked when she came back into her bedroom, lit softly by the bedside light.

'You're a big boy – don't you want to stay in your own bed?' She climbed in next to him and he snuggled up to her.

'But you must be lonely without Daddy.' His thumb went into his mouth.

'Yes, darling, I am lonely without Daddy. And you are too, aren't you?'

'Is he happy where he's gone? Will there be anyone else to play cricket with, now he's not here?'

Maddy couldn't bear it. Her face ached with the effort of not crying, but what the hell? What was the shame in showing her son that she missed Simon too. She let the tears fall.

'I hope he's happy. I know he didn't want to go there because he wanted to stay with us, but I'm sure it's a very nice place. Like a beautiful garden where the sun always shines.' She almost began to believe it herself. 'And I'll play cricket with you.'

He traced her tears with his fingers. 'But you're hopeless. Daddy says you throw like a girl.'

'But I am a girl! Perhaps you could teach me? Then I could be as good as you.'

They cuddled a while longer until she felt Will's body relax and his breathing become slow and regular. It was tempting just to fall asleep next to him, fully dressed, but she knew she'd feel foul in the morning, so she put on her pyjamas, and feeling suddenly cold and tired, pulled out one of Simon's fleeces from his wardrobe. It was her favourite – thick and soft – they had bought it for skiing in Colorado in the short gap before she was pregnant again with Florence.

Wrapping it around her, she pottered downstairs to tidy up and get a drink of water. There on the table was the wine box, and she idly pulled out the pictures to look at again. How fast time passes. It seemed such a short time ago that she had been twenty and lazy and convinced that everything would come to her without her having to try. There was a photo here of her and Simon, with Will on her knee aged about six months. She looked blooming and Simon so big and proud and capable. She hadn't want to show it to Izzie. Not quite yet.

She looked again at the other things, and then pulled out the journal, turning the pages once more and squinting at Luce's script. She went to the sitting room and climbing up to the shelves, pulled down her dictionary, went to put on the kettle and made herself a mug of tea.

Chapter 6

'Right. I'll be back as soon as I can, but I've got to pick up a few bits first. Frank said they'd definitely be here this morning, and the skip's being delivered before ten. If Frank gets here first, you can let him sort the skip out. But if you can just hang on until I get back, I'll take over.'

Marcus grunted. This was bad timing. He had arranged to take a portfolio of his photos to show an old college friend who had set up a gallery in Oxford, and was itching to be off, even though the meeting wasn't until lunchtime.

Even to Izzie's untrained eye, his photos looked impressive, if slightly contrived. He'd assiduously sought out bridges with the odd bit of graffiti and places where the canal looked slightly rancid, but if he'd turned the camera even a little, there would have been barges, swans, healthy-looking children on expensive bikes. After days tramping through fields in his new photographer's jacket, he'd also come up with a series of images of telegraph poles, tractor ruts, corrugated iron and shadows. He was taking it all terribly seriously, had been reading up on Cartier-Bresson, and kept talking about 'decisive moments', but making their part of the world look as if it were suffering from any vestige of social deprivation or blight would have taken a skill well beyond Marcus'.

He'd spent ages the night before swapping the prints around, to get them in a pleasing order 'for the full narrative force to be felt'. Although he'd kept asking her opinion and demanding that she come and look, he'd seemed too preoccupied to listen to any comment she ventured. In the end, she stuck to what she knew she was good at, and made him cups of tea. From what he said, a lot could hang on this meeting.

Giving him a goodbye hug, Izzie stowed the children in the back, their school bags in the boot, and breathed a sigh of relief as they set off. She'd got her mobile with her, and switched it on so Marcus could let her know as soon as Frank got there. Seconds later, it bleeped at her – that was quick! But it wasn't Marcus, it was a voicemail. The children safely kissed good-bye, she called the answer phone. 'You have one new message, received today, at 5.32 a.m. To hear your message, press one.'

Oh God! It was Maddy. Please don't let anything be wrong. The voice was crackly, hard to hear but the tone was urgent. 'Izzie, can you get round here quick? I need to see you as soon as possible.'

There was only one thing for it. She'd have to get Marcus to wait while she went over. His voice when he answered her call was a little terse. 'You on your way? Great! I can't afford to be late for this, you know!'

'Darling, I have to go over to Maddy's. There must be something wrong. She left me a message really early, and I've only just got it. Could you bear to hang on just a bit?'

'Oh for God's sake,' he snapped. 'Not again! You're over at her house all the time. I'll tell you this, you'd better bloody hope there's something wrong with her, because if there isn't I'll personally go over there and wring her sodding neck! OK, if you must, but hurry up.'

She winced at the sound of him slamming down the phone, and stood dithering by her car. What to do for the best? She knew today was important to Marcus, but he didn't really have to leave quite so early. He was right, of course. She had been neglecting him, and being with Maddy wasn't quite such an act of charity on her part as she had led him to believe. But now it seemed that Maddy was in crisis again. Izzie dialled her number, but it rang and rang. There was really no choice.

She let herself in the house, and called out, hoping she wouldn't find a scene like yesterday's. The sound of muttering and crashing around led her to the kitchen, and she opened the door to a fug of cigarette smoke. Sitting at the table, Maddy was once again barefoot in her pyjamas, but with a huge fleece zipped up halfway to reveal her lacy vest. Oh God! Had she really delivered the kids to school like that?

'Hi! Thought you were never coming! Take a look at this. It's fantastic.'

Gradually, Izzie felt the coil of fear in her stomach unwind. Maddy was OK. In fact, she was more than OK. Her eyes were shining and, although she looked pale and knackered, she radiated an energy that was deeply contagious. Before her on the table, still liberally strewn with Coco Pops and crumbs, was an array of sharpened pencils, a stack of paper covered with notes, numbers, lists and lots of question marks – and the *Journal de Luce Ménestrel*.

'Want a coffee? There's some left in the pot. I've been working on this all night. Started about eight and just couldn't tear myself away. Where have you been? I called you ages ago – way before the kids woke up – Oh!' Realisation dawned. 'Were you worried? I'm sorry, I didn't think. It was just so exciting, I couldn't wait to tell you.'

'Well, yes. I did think there must be something up. I was afraid I'd find you with your head in the Aga or something. I'm just so relieved it's something good at last.'

'Oh Izzie, I'm sorry. I promised myself yesterday I wouldn't be so self-absorbed, and now I've gone and done it again. I've been a lousy mother these last few weeks, and now I'm turning into a lousy friend too. You've been so patient. Please don't give up on me now. Look, you sit down there, have a look at what I've done, and I'll bring you a drink.' And she shot up to get a mug.

Izzie shook her head and laughed. Maddy was like a grey-hound on speed – all twitchy and wild-eyed. She must have been hitting that cafetière all night! Turning over the notes Maddy had made on the back of Simon's company letterhead, Izzie began to see why she was so excited. Recipes for an ointment to strengthen the nails, an infusion to make the hair grow, a table about what to pick at which phases of the moon – it was fascinating stuff. Maddy had rendered it into English without losing the archaic style. The result was charming – really atmospheric, and the character of the woman who had written it so long ago sang out from the pages.

She looked from the translation to the original, admiring the detailed little sketches Luce had done, and an idea began to germinate in her mind. By the time Maddy returned with the coffee (too strong to drink), Izzie was as excited as she was, pacing the room, her face alight.

'You know what this kind of reminds me of? That *Country Diary of an Edwardian Lady* thing that was so popular. Do you remember? There was spin-off stationery, cosmetics, tea cosies – probably even condoms! It was huge, and it all started with something like this. Someone found an old book and published a replica. Maybe you could do that. I could even help you do a book proposal, help you find an agent.'

'Whoa, slow down there, Red Rum! This is now, not then. No one's interested in this kind of thing any more. That went out with smocks and lacy petticoats.'

'Don't dismiss it, Maddy. It might be a goer. See if you can translate the rest of it. But for goodness sake, do it on the word processor – it'll be much faster.'

Maddy looked sheepish. 'Not the way I type, it won't. And

there's another flaw in your master plan. Luce goes on and on about a particular plant, *centpertuis*, about how it's got healing powers. It's in loads of the recipes, but I can't find it in the dictionary. It's probably extinct – eradicated by the rapacious farmers grubbing up all the hedgerows – unless of course they can get an EU subsidy for keeping them!'

'You could find that out. Try the Internet. Or phone that cousin of yours. He'd know, wouldn't he?'

'Actually, that's a good idea. I must call him. Haven't spoken to him since the funeral, and then I didn't talk to him much either. Mick Jagger could have turned up and I wouldn't have even noticed.'

Izzie's phone rang. Marcus was shouting so loudly, Izzie was sure Maddy would be able to hear every word. She quickly moved across the room. 'Get your arse back here now! I've got a ruddy great skip blocking the drive so you'll have to give me your car. I want to leave for Oxford in half an hour.'

He rang off without giving her a chance to speak. She looked awkwardly at Maddy. 'Do you mind awfully? I have to get back.'

'Of course I don't mind. No, you get back home. I've got plenty to be getting on with. I might come by and see you later. What are you having done?'

'Oh, nothing nice, I'm afraid. I found dry rot in the loft. They're going to replace most of the roof timbers, so of course the slates have to come off.'

'Ooh – that sounds pricey. Bad luck. Well, I'll definitely come by. My chance to cheer you up for a change!'

Izzie had an idea. 'Hey – maybe we should cook up some of those recipes in the book. See if they work. Shall we give it a try? If you're going to get it published, we'll have to check out that they're do-able! Just think. You could become a publishing magnate. Your money worries are over!' And laughing, they walked out to the car together.

At home, Marcus was seething. 'The morons just left the skip there. Have they no brains at all? How am I supposed to move my car?'

'But, Marcus, didn't you think to ask them to put it further along?'

'Don't you start! Don't you bloody start! I was inside, sorting out my contact sheets. By the time I'd finished, they'd already buggered off.'

'Will you be back in time for me to fetch the kids?'

'How should I know? Probably not. You'll have to phone them and get them to move it. If you'd been here, it wouldn't have happened in the first place.'

Izzie bristled. 'Now hold on! The whole reason for one of us being here was to make sure something like this didn't happen. Don't blame this on me! If it wasn't for me, we wouldn't be able to have this done at all!'

'Yes, I know, I know. Can we leave this for later? I'm going to be late as it is.' And he grabbed the keys, gave her a brief kiss, shoved her seat back and drove off, spitting gravel from the back wheels.

'Drive carefully,' she said quietly to the vanishing car.

Maddy always felt excited when she dialled Jean Luc's number. It thrilled her to think that she had punched in some numbers here in her kitchen, and the phone was ringing in his big mas hundreds of miles away in the Cévennes. It was lunchtime so with a bit of luck he'd have come in for a quick bite to eat and she'd catch him.

Beep. Damn she'd forgotten they were an hour ahead. He was out and she had so wanted to talk to him. She left a message. '*Salut, Jean Luc. C'est Maddy à l'appareil. Tu peut me rappeler aussitôt que possible? Je t'embrasse. A tantôt.*'

Disappointed, she put down the phone. She'd felt fired up by Izzie's idea of a sort of *Country Diary* and had wanted to get her teeth into the project. He'd call back, she was sure, so she pulled up her sleeves and started to tackle the washing-up. Will had gone into school far happier the last couple of mornings – they'd even done some pictures together with sticky paper and shells for Show and Tell – and she felt quite smug that she was finally getting a handle on being a proper mother.

I bet Sue Templeton never lets her kids loose with the Pritt stick, she thought, as she wiped the kitchen table and stacked the dishwasher. She imagined the scenario in that perfect kitchen. 'Abigail dear, that's enough paint. No, not on Mummy's curtains. *Abigaaaiiil, don't touch a thing . . .*'

It was time for Pasco's sleep, so she tucked him in, set the mobile above his cot swinging and was coming down stairs with a pile of washing when the post plopped on to the mat. There were a couple of flyers for carpet cleaning services, a standard circular from her bank offering her a £30,000 loan 'just a phone call away, Mrs Hoare' – oh wouldn't *that* be marvellous – and a letter addressed to her. It was Crispin's bill for the building work so far.

Maddy had to make herself a cup of coffee and light a cigarette before she dared open it. Then all she could bring herself to do was peep inside without even pulling out the invoice. Two thousand, eight hundred and seventy-four pounds. Plus VAT. Including one thousand, two hundred pounds from the last unpaid invoice. Thank you for your valued custom.

Oh bloody hell. She'd had no idea that it would be this much. She felt vaguely nauseous. What was this about the last one being unpaid? Anything that looked vaguely like a demand for money – Visa bills, the phone bill, Peter Jones, Harvey Nichols, school fees – had always gone on to a pile for Simon to deal with. What was going on?

She couldn't remember the last time she had written a cheque. In fact, she'd never done bills, full stop. Any kind of financial transaction had been dealt with by the family solicitors after her father's death, by Peter, her stepfather, or by Simon. And a mortgage? What the hell was that? Adverts on the television for variable rates and APRs had always gone right over her head. They were for the great unwashed.

Not for her. Her father's hefty legacy had been more than enough, helped by a small but regular salary from the interior designer she'd worked for in Chelsea Harbour.

She suddenly felt rather ashamed of herself. Everything had always been so easy, and it wasn't just the money. After school, which, to be frank, had been more like a social event from start to finish, she'd fallen on her feet working with Felicity Cook. A well-known interiors whizz, Felicity was flavour of the month at the time and anyone who was anyone had their house flounced and frilled by her. So tasteful, so agonisingly eighties, so expensive.

It had been an era of money and loads of it. Even the Yuppies could buy taste by the yard and Felicity had no qualms about talking them into doing so. These Emilys and Fionas hadn't even glanced at the bill and had simply paid, thrilled by their new colour schemes which so cleverly brought together the roses and peonies of Colefax & Fowler's glazed chintz with ginghams, ribbons and bows.

But Crispin's bill was frighteningly itemised: stud walls, plastering, carpentry, paint. How expensive it had been to create the understated, sublime décor that now filled Huntingford House. She looked around her and felt almost sick as she did a mental calculation of the contents of the kitchen alone.

The phone rang suddenly beside her. 'Madeleine sweetheart.' It was Jean Luc with his deep, earthy voice, and she could almost hear his teasing smile.

'Brilliant to hear you. How are the vines?'

'Asleep. And what about you? I so wanted to call, but I didn't think you would want to hear from anybody. I barely saw you at the funeral, you looked wonderful, of course, but I don't think you were there with us at all, were you?' How refreshing and how typical of him to cut to the chase. 'How are you coping?'

For once she didn't mind letting on. 'Bloody awful frankly. And I've just had a bill from our builder that would make your hair curl.'

'*Comment*?' Jean Luc's English was good, but obviously not that good. 'Oh make the man wait,' he said once she'd explained. 'So, little Madeleine, what's so urgent? Have you finally seen sense and decided to leave that horrrrrible country you live in?'

'I wish,' she replied, and for a fleeting moment wondered if it might be worth selling everything and buggering off to France where the children could roam vineyards and get brown as berries. 'I'd have to come by horse and cart though, we're that short of money.'

Jean Luc snorted with disbelief. 'You? Now that I would like to see!'

'Oh get lost. Now *écoute bien*. I've something a bit odd to ask you. What's *centpertuis*?'

'Have you gone mad, woman? Why on earth do you want to know that?'

'It's just something I read somewhere and I think it's a garden plant, but I can't find it in my dictionary.'

'Garden plant!' Jean Luc laughed deeply. 'Madeleine, it is the nightmare of my life. It's a *mauvaise herbe* – how do you say it? – a weeeed. It grows everywhere and I have to spend a fortune having it dug up – it's the only thing which makes me wish I wasn't organic.'

Maddy roared with laughter. She'd envisaged a sweet-smelling plant with a delicate flavour that might be the secret ingredient in some Provençal recipe.

'I think it is fairly unique to France, a bit like your couch grass – but it stinks. God, the smell is *incroyable*!'

'Can you send me some?'

'*Send* you some? Don't tell me – you want to add it to one of your disgusting English dishes?'

'Oh yes,' she joked back. 'It goes so well with steak and kidney pie. No, I've found a book in Mémé's things and it's rather intriguing. Lots of recipes, but not for food I don't think. It says Luce Ménestrel on the front – does her name mean anything to you?'

'*Mais oui*. She was Mémé's great, great grandmother. Quite a girl from what I know. Listen, darling, I have to go. Someone has arrived at the door – the chicken man I think – I'll do a bit of digging around and let you know what I find about her, and I'll get you some weeeed. How many lorry loads would you like? I can't say I'm not worried about you – *centpertuis, merde*! – speak soon.'

They said their goodbyes, and when Maddy put down the phone she felt excited. A weed! He'd promised he'd send her some, so scribbling down on a piece of paper some of the other – more common – herbs from Luce's notebook, she decided to ignore Crispin's bill and go on a shopping spree. OK, so it wasn't Selfridges, but spending money, now that was something she was good at.

When she finally found the farm shop down a track outside Ringford, it was not quite what she'd expected. She'd looked it up in the Yellow Pages and imagined something like the one at Chatsworth, crammed with goodies and with serving assistants in crisp white aprons and hats. This one was more like a shed, with chickens strutting about outside – much to Pasco's glee – and a small selection of sad-looking plants. A blackboard encouraged you to 'order your turkeys now for Christmas'. Maddy had forgotten about all that. How different it was going to be this year. No Simon. No obscenely bulging stockings for the children. Will and Florence would have to experience a steep learning curve about how the other half of Santa's round lives.

Inside the shop it was freezing, and a young, rather over-weight girl stood behind the counter in fingerless gloves, a fleece and a grubby apron. Cardboard boxes filled with filthy carrots and potatoes were piled up on the floor, and a man was using them to fill the shelves next to cabbages and thick, juicy leeks. A fridge displayed tubs of clotted cream, locally cured bacon, pâtés which had gone a bit crisp at the edges and, rather in-congruously, a few jars of rolled eels.

Maddy was looking around hopefully at the rather un-prepossessing selection and was putting things in her basket, when the door opened behind her and someone came in, bringing with them a blast of icy air which lowered the temperature even more.

'Well hello, Maddy.' Maddy felt herself flinch at Linda Meades' voice. She'd managed to avoid her since that awful Templeton lunch. 'I didn't expect to see you in here. Didn't see your car outside.'

'No. You wouldn't have.' I'm not going to give her the pleasure, she thought. 'I've got a new one, a sweet little Fiesta. Just the thing for nipping around the lanes. My old bus was just so unwieldy I found. Now, with this one, I can slip into the tightest parking spaces.'

Linda smiled rather uncertainly. Not knowing quite what to say, she looked down into Maddy's basket, which was full now with every bunch of parsley, thyme and sage that the shop possessed.

'Gosh, that's an interesting selection of things. Making soup?'

'Oh no,' said Maddy, looking too at the basket as if she couldn't imagine how the herbs had got in there in the first place. She thought fast. 'Stuffing . . . Yes, stuffing. We've got a huge houseful this Christmas, and the turkey will be a whopper, so I thought I'd get ahead and do the stuffing for the freezer.'

'Right,' said Linda slowly. 'I cheat I'm afraid. I find the stuff from M&S is just as good. Less bother you know. But how *are* you?' She put on her caring voice. 'How's *things*?'

Things? What things? Things like I've just lost my husband who's left me with no money; things like having to sell my car and doubtless having to take my son out of your precious prep school. Suddenly she felt livid. Maddy had been the woman to know when it looked like her life was perfect and these sort of women could all boost their social standing by being associated with her. But then there had been that rather embarrassing and messy death of her husband, and where had they been then?

'*Things* are fine thank you, Linda. Just fine. Now if you don't mind I'd better go and pay and . . . get stuffed!'

Pasco couldn't quite understand why his mother was laughing so much once they were in the car. But he joined in anyway.

The following morning bought a bank statement, and the final demand from BT. Her account showed she had the sum from the sale of her car, which wasn't much considering she hadn't done a part exchange, and the remainder of her monthly slug from Simon which must have gone into her account the day before he died. Time to tackle this, Maddy Hoare, she thought and, lighting a cigarette to bolster her, started to dig through Simon's desk. For an ex-banker he was very disorganised. Notes were shoved in files with no sense of order. She began to make piles on the floor – things for the bin, unopened bank statements, circulars and letters about the conveyancing of the house.

Pushed into one corner was a pile of ski brochures, balancing precariously on top of a pile of envelopes and more papers. She pulled it in front of her and started to sort through, opening each envelope as she went, and with each one feeling more and more sick. The water rates, insurance for her car, Crispin's last bill, unopened; the invoice from the kitchen fitters, including the kitchen units. God, had they been that much? The bathroom suite, including glass shelving, and the carpenter's bill for the bespoke bath surround and cupboards; her Visa bill including her last foray up the Fulham Road; all unopened. It took over an hour to find everything she was looking for, and to sort through everything she hadn't been.

Stunned, she walked back into the kitchen and, like an automaton, sat down with her diary and wrote in the dates when the insurance, utility bills, council tax were due to be paid. Apart from the phone and school fees for January, which she could just about cover if she was very careful over Christmas, none of these was due before March. But then there was Crispin's bill, the carpenter, the bathroom, the kitchen. And then they had to eat.

Slowly and hesitantly she started to write down the figures due on the back of an envelope, and twice she checked the final figure. She let the pen fall on to the paper. It couldn't be right, could it? How the hell had this happened? Simon must have simply picked up the bills from the hall table and stuffed them away, in denial. She looked around the room, at the exquisite turned detailing on the blonde wood, the huge dresser she'd had made specially to fit the big wall by the door, the American fridge she'd lusted after. She'd talked him into buying all of it, justifying the expense with well-thought-out and oh-so-rational arguments about how it was 'pointless to spoil such a beautiful ship for a ha'penth of tar', and Simon had merely concurred. But then he always had – whether it was the darling mirror she just had to put over the fireplace in Milborne Place, or the sweet little hotel on St Kitts which would be so romantic for a couple of weeks, just the two of them.

She ran her hands over her face. Had she really milked him dry? Not perhaps in the old days, when he was earning a shed-load and getting bonuses that would make you raise your eyebrows in disbelief. But recently? Her face burnt at the thought that he had simply gone along with her whims to keep her happy about the move. Meanwhile things had been going badly wrong at work.

She'd heard Crispin's van crunch into the drive earlier and, like a coward, she went back to the study with a bin liner for the rubbish pile she had accrued and avoided him until he was up the ladder replacing some guttering. Finally, she made him a cup of coffee and went outside.

'Good morning,' she called up to him. He looked down the ladder at her and started to come down.

'Thanks, that's just what I needed. It's bitterly cold out here.' He swallowed a mouthful. 'That guttering is not too good you know. I think we're going to have to fix it all the way round.' He took another gulp, and waited for the usual 'whatever you need to do' from her.

Maddy looked at him. It would make a paltry dent in her debts, but he seemed a nice enough chap. She thought she'd try her luck.

'Crispin, since my husband died, I've had a rethink, and I'd like to stop and think a bit more about the project . . .'

His face fell. 'Oh, well. I've ordered those new sashes you wanted for the top windows. They're pretty rotten you know. And I can't store them, cos I haven't got a yard at the moment. The previous place I rented has gone up for sale for development.'

Maddy couldn't remember having agreed to any replacement windows – perhaps he'd asked her when she was so low she hadn't even known her own name. She realised now just how much had gone on around her as she had sat in her cocoon of grief. If she didn't stop him, Lord knows what the next bill would come to.

'No, Crispin. I haven't been exactly honest. You see I'm going to have to tighten my belt a bit on finances. Actually you are going to have to stop.' She felt tears well up and she turned away from him. 'I don't think I can even meet your last bill, I'm afraid,' she finally choked out. 'In fact, I know I can't.'

Too polite to gasp in disbelief that a woman surrounded by

such affluence could possibly be strapped for cash, he stood in silence. They both gazed around the garden, shrouded in the dankness of the November day, like a couple of vague acquaintances who had met unexpectedly. Maddy couldn't think where to go from here. Izzie would know. What was the deal when you couldn't pay a bill? Would he sue her?

The misery of the dewy grass, wet pathways and lifeless, dormant plants seemed to match her mood. Then through the bare trees she saw the garden sheds where so recently she had hidden the urns with him. Would it work?

'Crispin, you said you hadn't got a yard.'

'Yes, that's right.' He looked puzzled.

'How's this for a deal?' For a moment she prayed she might be on to something. 'You use my sheds as your yard – they're secure and there's a separate driveway which goes out to the lane at the back – and set off the rent against what I owe you?' She looked at him encouragingly.

'Well, it'll take a while. I only paid two hundred quid a month at the old place.'

'Hopefully soon I'll be able to pay you back properly,' she was treading water frantically now, 'but do you think it would work? Does it sound fair?'

There was a long silence.

'OK, it might be professional suicide as far as my cashflow is concerned, and you are going to have to pay me what you can whenever you can too.'

'You are top of my long list of creditors,' she lied, and spontaneously she kissed him on the cheek. 'Crispin, you are a darling.'

Chapter 7

Izzie rubbed her eyes. When were they holding the awards for the 'Most Boring Website Ever'? This government agency was a sure-fire winner. Mind-numbing though it was, it was reasonably well paid, and there was about two weeks' worth of it. With Frank still crashing around in the loft and shaking his head sadly whenever she asked him how it was going, she was not in a position to be picky.

The whole Marcus thing had calmed down since the day of the great Oxford expedition. He'd apologised for getting shirty, and seemed quite up about the meeting. He was trying too – kept asking her about her work, had massaged her shoulders one night, they'd even made love, and he'd actually made lunch one day – cheese on toast, but still. He'd seemed resigned to the time she was spending over at Maddy's too, provided she sorted the kids out herself. Definitely a change for the better!

When she arrived at Huntingford House, forensic evidence in the kitchen – half-drunk cups of coffee and overflowing ashtrays – revealed Maddy had had a working lunch. But she was nowhere to be seen, although from the fresh pile of notes, she had clearly been busy translating the journal.

Izzie made fresh tea, buttered a few scones and took some out to the sheds for Crispin, whose reassuring, bear-like presence and quiet comings and goings had lifted the mood of the whole place. A smell of sawdust filled the air, and Izzie found him contentedly sweeping up shavings and making small repairs to the sheds he would be using. He was a bit of an enigma, old Crispin. Obviously well bred and educated, he seemed as comfortable with her and Maddy as he was with his hairy-arsed colleagues. She had noted with amusement that he answered his mobile as 'Chris' – much more suitable. Crispin was the name for a bishop or a diplomat, not a jobbing builder.

'Thanks, Izzie. That's smashing! She was around earlier, and her car's still here, but I haven't seen her. She was out roaming the fields earlier with Pasco. Came back with a big basket of Rowan berries.' He shook his head, laughing quietly to himself, and went back to his work.

Her shoes too light to go trudging, Izzie went back into the house to wait. She was just correcting Maddy's spelling in her notes – erratic to say the least – when she heard the scrunch of a car on gravel. A moment later the doorbell rang out. Probably someone looking for Crispin. Yep, through the glass panels she could definitely see it was a man, and a pretty big one too. She opened the door with a cheery, 'Hello! If you want the sheds, they're further on up the drive. Can't miss 'em.'

But the man who turned round at the sound of her voice was definitely not a contractor. You don't get a tan like that in Ringford in November. Instead, Izzie found herself staring up at a bronzed face, slightly puzzled, clearly amused, somewhat familiar. She knew her mouth had dropped open, but she didn't seem able to close it.

He looked at her intently and, with lean brown hands, he pushed his floppy hair back off his forehead, and shook his head slowly. With a soft French accent like honey dripping on hot toast, he responded, '*Non*. Not the sheds. I'm looking for Madeleine, my *cousine*. Is she here? You are a friend?'

So this was the cousin from the photo. 'Oh yeah! Maddy's

told me about you – I'm sorry, I've forgotten your name . . . er . . .'

'Jean Luc.' He smiled, his eyes crinkling warmly at the corners and shook her hand. 'Is Maddy here?'

'Yes – I mean, no. She's around, just out in the garden somewhere. She'll be back in a minute. Come in and have some tea.'

'In the garden? That doesn't sound like her! I've got some things for her – I'll bring them in.'

She watched with unashamed pleasure as he strolled over to the mud-splashed Range Rover, and stretched luxuriously. He was really quite an attractive man – they sure knew how to breed them in that family. By no means eye candy, he had a kind of battered charm, a bit like an old suitcase. Izzie led the way into the kitchen, and he followed, carrying a couple of wine boxes.

'Are you staying long?' she asked, filling the kettle at the tap.

'Ah hah! Your famous English hospitality.' He laughed richly as he put the crates on the table. 'Well, there is nothing much happening on my farm, so I crept away, but I cannot stay too long here. I have horses, and they miss me when I am away. But I have to check my little *cousine* is all right.'

He took in the kitchen. 'She has done a lot since I was here last.' Then he swung round and looked straight at Izzie. 'How is she now?'

She answered carefully, trying to make her response as sincere as the question had been. 'It's been hard for her. There's so much for her to take on board. I mean her life has changed totally. I'll admit, I've been worried at times and I didn't know what to do to help her. But just in the last week, I think she's starting to feel – not exactly feel better – but it's as if her compass is pointing ahead again, as if she knows the way she has to go now, even if she's not sure how to set about it.'

Jean Luc frowned and nodded slowly. 'Yes, I can feel what

you mean. It's a strong image. You must be a good friend to her if you can see all this. But I don't remember seeing you at the funeral.'

Making the tea, she thought hard before she replied. 'It seems strange now I put it into words, but I haven't known her long. I never even met Simon. We met up a couple of times, but when I heard about the accident, I came right over and – well, I've been here almost every day since.'

He shrugged his square shoulders, easing them inside his thick leather jacket. 'Sometimes it happens like that. She is very lucky to have you.'

'She certainly is!' Maddy's voice came from the door. 'Hello, stranger – what the hell brings you here?'

He spun round, and Maddy flew into her cousin's arms, squashing Pasco between them. He picked them both up, squeezing them tight, streams of delighted French bursting from them simultaneously. Izzie smiled to herself and got on with making the tea, discreetly clearing the table before they sat down.

She shyly produced some scones she'd made at home. Jean Luc exclaimed in delight. 'Most of your food is *sheet*, but proper tea I love.' Then he went out to the hall, returning moments later with boxes full of food he had brought with him. 'When you come to England, you have to bring your own food.' He laughingly deflected their jeers. 'Oh yes! Really.'

Like a magician, he produced pots of jam sealed with wax, honey, pâtés in glass jars, cheeses, big tomatoes, a couple of frisée lettuces, some cured ham, several bottles of local wine, olive oil and a home-made looking bottle of vinegar . . . on and on it went. The women clapped and gasped in delight, reached into the boxes, giggling as he pretended to slap their hands away.

'Last, but not least. Please don't open this, my little Pandoras!' He produced a tightly sealed plastic bin bag, and announced dramatically. 'Madeleine, you have made me a smuggler! Here is a bag of the smelly weed, just for you. The disgusting, the unspeakable *centpertuis*. I can't begin to guess – I don't even want to guess – what you are going to do with it. But I had to come here to check if you really are crazy!'

'And now? What do you think?'

'Now,' he replied, putting his arm round Maddy's shoulders in an affectionate squeeze. 'Now I am quite reassured. You are completely crazy, but you have a crazy friend too. *Ca-y-est! C'est bien!* You are quite fine, giggling like schoolgirls!'

Izzie jumped to her feet. 'The kids! I'm going to be late. You too, Maddy! Lovely to meet you, Jean Luc.' And she dashed from the room.

Marcus was busy that evening, too busy to ask her what she had been up to, and she had to admit she was relieved. She was a bad liar and didn't entirely trust herself to be off-hand in her description of Maddy's cousin. Marcus had always been the jealous type and he was bad enough when she started drooling over Jeremy Paxman during *Newsnight*. He never left her unchaperoned during *University Challenge*. Boss-eyed from a further tango with the government quango, she gave up at ten-thirty and surrendered herself to the pleasures of *Sex and the City*. For the first time she found herself analysing the characters' flirting techniques – it was so contrived and she knew she'd never be able to imitate them even if she wanted to. There was no doubt Jean Luc was a bit of a flirt, and today had been fun. She'd revelled in the attention. 'Oh for God's sake, Isabel,' she berated herself as she turned off the TV. 'He's French. They do flirting at baccalaureate.'

The next day, Izzie returned to Maddy's house straight after the school drop-off. They'd arranged by phone the night before that this would be the day of the great cook up. She only hoped it would go better than the thyme and parsley hair conditioner Maddy had already attempted. She'd had to throw the pan out, and the backs of Izzie's ears were still bright green.

Maddy was in the kitchen, weighing out the *centpertuis* for the base tincture that seemed to appear in most of Luce's recipes. Izzie looked around for Jean Luc, and hovered near the cooker. 'So,' she ventured at last, 'did you eat all that cheese last night?'

'No way!' retorted Maddy. 'Can you imagine the nightmares you'd get from that lot? Jean Luc made some yummy soup. I thought we'd have the leftovers for lunch. He should be back by then.'

'Oh – right. Well then, let's get on with this. Have you got an apron I could use?'

Maddy looked her up and down, and bit her lip to suppress a smile. 'Yes. You'd better cover that jumper up. Wouldn't want to get any green smelly goo on it, would we? You're looking particularly scrumptious today. Your hair looks nice like that.'

Izzie pretended to concentrate on the recipe. 'I just blow-dried it differently for a change, you know.'

'Yes, I know,' Maddy replied cheerfully. 'I absolutely know! Now, are you ready for me to open this bag? Jean Luc says it smells worse than his socks – and having gone camping with him, I can tell you that's pretty appalling! With just him rattling round in that huge old farmhouse, I don't suppose he bothers much. Ready? Pheeeew! He wasn't exaggerating. Here – add the water. It might smell better once it's boiled down.'

Two hours later, the *centpertuis* had been reduced to a small quantity of goo but smelt far worse. Even with all the windows open, the stench was appalling. The two women stared into the pot in disgust at the evil, bubbling mess.

'God, this is vile!' laughed Maddy.

Izzie glanced at the translated notes from Luce's book. 'Oh Lord! We've got to simmer it for another half-hour. Luce is very specific about her timings, isn't she? I'll set the timer so we don't forget.'

'Fat chance of forgetting something this smelly! For God's

sake, pass me the pan lid. I'll stick it in the bottom oven. The stench is making me gag. Oh sod it! I've burnt my wrist on the door. This had better be worth it.'

'Quick! Run your arm under the cold tap,' said Izzie as Maddy pulled off her oven glove and inspected the red weal rapidly forming on the inside of her forearm. 'That looks nasty. Hang on – doesn't Luce say this goo is supposed to be good for burns? Have a go!'

Izzie wiped a dollop of cooled purée from the wooden spoon they'd stirred it with and gently dabbed it on to the burn.

'Do you think it's all right to use it neat?' asked Maddy doubtfully, peering down at her arm.

'It's just a plant. Can't do any harm, can it?'

Maddy grimaced. 'They said that about hemlock. Actually it feels quite soothing.'

They heard the front door bang, and a deep voice call out, '*Oh non! Cet 'est pas possible!* The smell is just awful!'

This time, Jean Luc embraced Izzie too – three kisses – then held her at arm's length, his hands cupping her shoulders and looking her up and down appreciatively. 'You look like a summer sky, Izzie. That blue – just perfect for you.'

He turned away to unpack the groceries from supermarket bags. 'I was nearly chased from the store,' he complained. 'How do you buy cheese in England if you don't open it up and smell it? And what is so terrible about squeezing melons? Does that make me a pervert? This is a crazy country. You should see the market in St Jean du Gard. You would love it. So full of colour, fragrance. You must come over again soon, Maddy – both of you, why not?'

Maddy took off her apron. 'Tempting idea, but right now I'm hot and sweaty after all that boiling – I'm going to have a shower. We'll have lunch in about half an hour, OK? Jean, why don't you open a bottle of that Coteaux du Languedoc? I bet Izzie's never tried it before!' And she left the room.

Silence fell. Izzie pretended to read Maddy's notes, now splattered with drops of green sludge. She was acutely aware of Jean Luc moving quietly round the kitchen, but didn't dare turn round. She heard him getting down plates from the rack and mixing up a dressing for the salad. The silence was agonising. What was it about this man? Why couldn't she just behave normally? The sound of the cork squeaking, then popping slightly as it left the bottle was followed by a clink of glasses and a mouth-watering 'gloop-gloop'.

Jean Luc cleared his throat. 'Er, Izzie . . . you want some?'

He held out a glass of the black-red wine and smiled slowly. Izzie sat down at the other side of the table, and took a slug, nearly choking on the earthy, full-bodied flavour.

He smiled ruefully. 'Yes – wines from the south can be a bit too bold.' He sat back with his wine, content in the silence.

Izzie could stand it no longer. 'Gosh, isn't it quiet now?'

'Yes, isn't it? Wherever Maddy is there seems to be lots of noise and laughter. It's always been that way – when we were children, she was always was the wicked one. She used to drive Giselle crazy, mind you, that's not far to go. Have you met Giselle?'

Thank God. He'd got the conversational ball rolling, and she could relax. 'Oh yeah. Once met never forgotten. Within five minutes of meeting her she had me driving her to the station!'

He laughed. 'That sounds just like her. She's an institution. *Notre Gigi nationale.*'

'Gigi! That doesn't sound like her at all.'

'I know – it's why I always call her that.'

'Maddy must be much more like her father.'

'I think so yes, except for the addiction for clothes. I don't really remember him, but I do remember playing football with him on the beach. He used to organise us all into games. He had such energy.'

'Jean Luc, how did he die? What with Simon, I haven't dared ask.'

'Oh it was so stupid. He died during a routine operation – for a knee injury from rugby, I think, when he was young or something unimportant like that, but it went wrong. Giselle fell apart, though she's reinvented her history now, and that was when they came to spend long summers with us in Antibes.'

'I've seen the pictures,' said Izzie, remembering the fresh young faces of the teenagers in Maddy's box.

'At first I was very angry about it – I was adolescent and bad-tempered. I hated her because everyone felt sorry for her, and I was expected to keep an eye on her. But after a while I began to look forward to them coming. Then Peter – have you met him? – anyway he arrived on the scene and he's such a good man. He simply took on Giselle and Maddy with all their sadness.'

Izzie shuddered. 'God, imagine having that happen twice in your life.'

'That's why it's so amazing that wherever Maddy is, she manages to make it fun. But come on, Izzie, I don't know much about you – except that you've been a very good friend to her.'

'Oh well not much to tell. All very boring really.'

'I doubt that very much. Do you have children?'

'Yes, two. Charlie is eight and Jess is six. They're a great team but they take turns to drive me crazy. What about you?'

'Me? No. No children.' Izzie was desperate to ask more, but couldn't catch his eye as he fiddled with a loose button on his cuff. 'But we were talking about you, Izzie, so stop trying to change the subject. You don't look like a country girl – have you always lived here?'

Under his gentle questions, she found herself telling him about the move to Ringford, and even about the trouble she was having settling in with the natives. But for all the details she gave him, to which he listened with quiet intensity, she found she was deliberately avoiding the subject of Marcus. She couldn't quite work out why, or maybe she didn't want to. And stranger still, Jean Luc didn't seem curious about the missing link. But within no time, she was telling a man she had only just met about feelings she had barely ever voiced even to her own husband.

'But don't you realise,' he smiled, 'that these dreadful women you talk about feel entirely threatened by you. You are intelligent. They are cretins. You have charm. They are vulgar.' Izzie could feel herself flush. Get a grip, woman! 'And you have ten times more verve than they could ever hope to have.' Suddenly the kitchen timer burst into life. Phew! Saved by the beep. She leapt to her feet and grabbed a tea towel. 'Time for lunch!' She carefully lifted out the dark green Le Creuset, and placed it on top of the Aga.

'Well, that's the end of that pan,' laughed Jean Luc. 'She won't want to use it again now.'

'I'd better give it a stir and make sure it's not sticking.' She went as if to take off the lid, and he came to stand beside her.

'For God's sake, don't take that lid off,' shrieked Maddy as she reappeared, her hair wet and tousled from the shower. Jean Luc moved away quickly. 'The neighbours will be asking awkward questions about the state of my septic tank!'

'Oh ladies! It's no worse than your usual English cuisine!' he muttered into his wine glass, then ducked to avoid the tea towel Izzie had lobbed at him.

The three of them chatted and laughed over lunch, Jean Luc embarrassing Maddy with stories about their youth and her ghastly first boyfriends, egged on by Izzie.

'Oh he was rough,' Jean Luc shook his head in disbelief. 'Not a nice boy at all. Giselle went crazy. Motorbike and those tattoos on his arms 'ere and 'ere.'

'Speaking of arms,' Izzie suddenly remembered the burn, 'how's yours now, Maddy?' she asked, pulling back Maddy's sleeve.

'Oh that. I'd forgotten all about it.' They both peered closely at her barely marked skin and their eyes met in amazement. 'Well, look at that! Seems the old bird was right about this stuff after all.'

It took days to get the smell out of the house. Maddy had opened all the windows in the kitchen until the children and the poinsettia on the windowsill had started to complain of frostbite.

It had been an anticlimax when Jean Luc left and, with only a few weeks of term remaining, the looming horror of Christmas was beginning to worry her seriously. Without Simon it all seemed so pointless and it took everything she had just to drag herself out of bed in the morning. And then there was the cost! Florence, whose unspoken grief had manifested itself in the need again for a nappy at night, had her heart set on some ghastly plastic pony she'd seen advertised on ITV. Will's wish list was a second-mortgage number. Gameboy Advance, CD-ROMs, Action Man, go-kart. She knew they were out of the question this year, but out of a passionate desire to make up for all they had lost, Maddy wondered whether he'd settle for a home-made version – perhaps Crispin could knock something up in the sheds?

Stephen Chester from Chester Goodwin, the big auctioneers in Oxford, had been so obsequious when he'd toured the house that it was all she could do not to punch him. Good public school etiquette, which oozed from every pore of his tweed-clad body, forbade him from making any enquiries as to why Madam wished to raise the cash. He had simply gushed suitably about the house, and then became intimidatingly businesslike when it came to the sticky subject of valuation. He peered closely at the massive gilt mirror – the one she'd bought for the overmantel in London, and which now took pride of place in the hall – and tapped his cheek with his pen, then jotted down a brief description on his pad. He tried, and almost succeeded, to cover up his excitement at the walnut tallboy in the spare room, and ran his hand lovingly over the long oak dining-room table and large carver chairs.

Maddy had followed him round, trying to act nonchalant, as he peered, considered and wrote down notes. 'It's only furniture,' she kept reminding herself. It can always be replaced, but as she spread out the contents of her jewellery box on to the kitchen table, she almost lost control.

Watching his chubby hands picking up and putting down her rings, necklaces and earrings, she felt as if she had been violated. 'Some interesting pieces here, Mrs Hoare,' he said oleaginously, 'though of course a successful sale entirely depends on how interested the collectors are.' He looked closely then carefully discarded several pieces, and she felt a mixture of relief and outrage that they weren't good enough for consideration. 'This is especially pretty.' He had picked up an oval diamond brooch that Mémé had given her for her eighteenth birthday and was holding it very close to his eye. 'Yes, very interesting. There is a growing market for this style of art deco jewellery. I think this could easily sell,' and he made another note on his pad.

The letter with his list of suggested reserve prices had arrived a couple of days later, and for another two days she had picked it up and peered at it, then put it down in disgust. The final figure, if she put all the pieces he had suggested into auction, would just about cover the outstanding invoices for the work already done on the house, except Crispin's bill, but only if she included Mémé's brooch with the lots. Trying to sound as cool and detached as she could, she rang to confirm her agreement.

She put down the phone and surveyed the kitchen. The sale might raise enough but it wouldn't come close to leaving them enough to live on. It was no good. She'd have to get a job.

Izzie was incredulous. 'A temping agency? Maddy, when was

the last time you even went into an office? They have computers these days you know, all the typewriters are condemned to museums. What are you going to offer them?'

'Well, people must still drink tea.'

'Yeah right.'

'But can I ask you a big favour? I'm going to try that agency in Ringford – WorkWorld or something – could you possibly have Pasco for a couple of hours tomorrow morning? He'd love to play at your house and you know how much he loves you.'

'OK, you don't have to lay it on. I've got to finish this bloody quango stuff, but he can always sort out my CDs while I'm doing it. How is he at ironing?'

'You're a doll. I'll bring him over about nine-thirty.'

Maddy was serious. She felt happier leaving Pasco with Izzie than anyone else. She knew he'd be happy, safe and looked after, so next morning, putting on her black Jean Muir 'funeral' suit – she assumed that was the sort of thing efficient secretaries wore – and using a belt to hold up the now much-too-big trousers, she dropped the children at school and set off for Izzie's.

The narrow driveway was taken up with a skip, now full to the brim with sick-looking timbers. The house was swathed in scaffolding, and two men were crawling over the roof. The damage was clearly worse than Izzie had let on, and Maddy wondered just how much it must be costing them to put right. Izzie just seemed to muddle along without complaint, but this must have put a hell of a dent in their budget. Marcus got to the door first, and she tried to smile warmly.

'You look smart,' he opened with, rather coolly. 'Swanning off to lunch somewhere posh?'

Not a very good start. She really couldn't put her finger on it, but on the few times she had met him now, his charm seemed rather phoney, and when Izzie wasn't around, he was verging on hostile. Had she done something to offend him? 'Izzie very sweetly said she'd look after Pasco, while I go into town for a meeting.' That sounded important and professional. 'He's terribly good and I won't be long.'

His reply was cut short by Izzie bolting down the stairs. 'Hi, little mate,' she said, as Pasco put his arms out to her. 'Are you coming to play with me this morning? Fancy a biscuit? Let's go and find you one.' She looked at Maddy, as Marcus went back into the kitchen, and said quietly, 'Remember, they are called word processors, and you are familiar with Windows XP.'

'Is that a new type of Jag?'

'Ha ha. Just say it, and if they've something for you, I'll give you a crash course on my computer.'

'Crash it will be,' laughed Maddy. She gave Pasco and Izzie a hug and promised she'd be back as quickly as possible.

No, thought Maddy as she tried to find a parking space, Marcus really is touchy. Whenever he was around, Izzie seemed to lose her spark, glancing at him nervously as if not quite trusting him to behave. She certainly hadn't been like that with Jean Luc. The old rogue had brought out the best in her like he did with everyone. His charm was hard to resist. For a silly moment she fantasised about Izzie and him getting it together. Jean Luc deserved some happiness. But she couldn't imagine it really. Besides, there was no way on earth Jean Luc would move over here. Not for anyone would he tolerate British supermarket shopping. Daft idea.

'So,' repeated the rather brisk woman at WorkWorld, 'you haven't been employed since 1994.' She pursed her lips. That plum-coloured top is so wrong for her, thought Maddy, and that hair! It looks like it was cut at the garden centre.

'I take it you are familiar with Microsoft Office and Power Point?'

'You just plug the machine in at the wall, don't you?' The woman looked sceptical. 'I'm very efficient, and I'm a quick learner . . .' Maddy finished weakly. Nothing she seemed to have said so far had impressed, and she could feel this interview was running away without her.

The woman half-heartedly scrolled down the computer screen in front of her. 'Well, Mrs Hoare, I'm not sure we have anything to match your . . . skills just at the moment, but we will keep you on our books and I'll been in touch if anything comes up. I take it you can start work at a moment's notice?'

Maddy thought about Pasco at home all day, Florence at Little Goslings and the school pick-up at three-thirty. 'Oh yes, not a problem.'

'Lovely. Well, thank you for coming to see us, and I'll be in touch.'

Don't hold your breath, thought Maddy as she got back to the car. Pulling out of Ringford, her mood hit rock bottom. What the hell was she going to do? Who was she kidding that she could earn money? The only thing she could do was spend it. Stuck behind a tractor, the journey back to Izzie's was a slow one. She'd left London so she could get out of traffic and third gear, but things didn't seem to be any better here. If only she could turn back the clock, to before that day in May when Simon had said he wanted to move out. Had she followed her gut instinct and said no, he'd still be alive, they'd still have their lovely house and she wouldn't be acting out this humiliating charade in her little black suit.

As she turned into Hoxley, she spotted a home-painted sign by a gate advertising local honey with a bright orange bee painted with childish ineptitude. An idea popped into Maddy's head and she pulled in. Half an hour later, her small enquiry about buying wax had led to a lecture on honey production and a full-scale tour of Mr Norman Jacks' hives – luckily the bees were asleep because she hadn't fancied putting on one of those beekeeper's hoods. In her smart suit, she'd have looked like something from a Vivian Westwood collection. She'd also found out about a Christmas Fayre – an annual event at

Ledfinch Manor, a huge pile Maddy had remembered passing a couple of times, and quite the highlight of the local Christmas calendar according to Mr Jacks, who muttered something about 'load of nonsense'.

Izzie handled the delicious slabs of wax with awe. 'Brilliant – let's see if you can get a stall at this jamboree and sell some of Luce's recipes, but let's hope the wax improves the smell, or when people open the jars, they'll run a mile.'

'One thing that struck me while I was looking at Mr Jacks' little production line – are there restrictions on producing something people are going to put on their skin? We don't want the great and good of the county spending Christmas in hospital with second-degree burns.'

'To the Internet, my girl,' directed Izzie, leading her through the cottage. 'The source of all information that's useful, and plenty that isn't.'

'Can we look at some naughty sites too?' giggled Maddy conspiratorially.

'Type in "skin" on a search engine, and God knows what we'll find. Jess was looking up about ponies the other day, typed in "riding" and . . . well . . . you wouldn't have believed what came up.'

Izzie led her through the sitting room.

'Hey, something's missing,' said Maddy, pausing to look around the room. 'Where's the piano?'

'It's on the roof.'

Maddy looked at her for a moment not quite understanding. Then the penny dropped. 'God, you didn't have to sell it, did you?' Maddy was incredulous. 'Not that beautiful thing?'

'Darling, I had no choice. It was that or going on the game, and I didn't think Marcus would make much of a pimp.' Izzie tried to laugh, but Maddy could see the depth of her distress. Her own furniture hadn't meant anything like as much – but with the loss of the brooch, she could relate to the terrible sacrifice Izzie had made. Maddy hadn't realised money was that tight for her and Marcus too.

Izzie briskly led her through to the study, as if she couldn't bear to look at the empty space left by the piano, and somehow they found her desk in among piles of newspapers, old magazines, books which had overflowed from shelves and were piled precariously on the floor, and large sheets of book page proofs.

'God, Izzie, how the hell do you work in this state?'

'A tidy desk is the sign of a sick mind. Now what do you need to know? Trading standards I suppose.' As she went online and started typing in key words, it suddenly struck Maddy that Izzie kept saying 'you' whenever they talked about Luce's recipes.

Maddy squeezed on to the chair beside Izzie. 'Hey, Mrs Stock. You're not leaving me to do this project on my own, are you?'

'Well, she was your relation, wasn't she? And the stuff is coming from your cousin, it's really—'

'Wait right there a moment,' said Maddy, putting her hands on Izzie's to stop her typing any more. 'I'm not doing this hare-brained project without you. If you aren't going to do it with me, then we can forget it right now.'

Izzie looked uncertainly into Maddy's eyes, then a broad smile spread across her face. 'I'm with you, girlfriend. Give me five!'

Everything moved incredibly slowly for the next few weeks. Izzie's stoicism over losing the piano made Maddy determined to be brave as she watched the walnut tallboy, dining table and carver chairs, a commode, an oil painting (that she'd never actually liked) and her beloved gilt mirror being wrapped in blankets and placed carefully in the back of the van. Rather pathetically she wrapped the brooch in bubble wrap and the driver put it carefully in his pocket. 'Should get a bit for this lot, love,' he said, slamming the back of the van shut. 'But you won't miss it in a place this size I expect.' Maddy could have kicked him.

Frantically seeking displacement activity, she phoned Gail Thwaite-Mickleton, the Fayre organiser, and managed to sweet-talk her into giving them a stall – someone had apparently had to drop out – and gave her some flannel about the quality of their product and how it would fit in with the woman's high standards. 'This isn't some two-bit event, my dear,' Gail T-M had brayed. 'We only want products of the very best quality.'

The only problem was they really had no product yet to sell – high quality or not. Izzie's investigations had revealed the rigorous regulations that went with cosmetic production, and Maddy had used her best sultry tones with a nice-sounding man at the trading standards office in Oxford to help her find laboratories that tested cosmetic products for them. It helped that Luce's recipes were about as natural as they come. To make life simpler, they had settled for now on producing just Luce's '*baume panacé*' – healing balm – which contained nothing but *centpertuis*, beeswax, olive oil and lavender, something Izzie had finally sourced from a rather twee dried flower emporium in Cheltenham. It was worth the inflated price – the fragrance sweetened the awful smell, though only slightly – but Izzie was incensed at the amount she had been charged for it. 'This is daylight robbery – in summer my garden's awash with it!' All of the other recipes they had tried so far had been a disaster. The healing balm might smell awful, but at least it didn't look like half-rotted lawn clippings.

Now all they could do was wait until they got the results. Meanwhile they had the packaging to think about. Maddy didn't imagine for one minute that the type of women who came to these fayres would settle for creams in the selection of old marmalade and jam jars Izzie had found in the cupboard under her sink.

'No, they'll never fall for that,' said Maddy, as they both looked despondently at a washed-out jar of Bonne Maman apricot jam sat in the middle of Maddy's kitchen table. They were feeling panicky. Only days to go until the Fayre: a large pan full of green healing balm which closely resembled pig swill; no jars and no accreditation to sell it anyway.

'Have you any old jars of Clarins we could use?' suggested Izzie hopefully.

'Good God, woman. Clarins? I wish. I'm reduced to lard these days.'

Izzie suddenly sat up. 'I've got it. What about those sweet little kilner jars that Jean Luc brought with the pâté in?'

Maddy smacked the table in excitement. 'You're a genius. They're in the cupboard over there.'

There were only five of them, but they looked unusual and rustic enough that they just might do. They scraped out the contents, spreading some of it on crackers and eating as much as they could – this was good stuff and a tragedy to waste – until they both felt thoroughly sick. The rest went into the apricot jam jar, which Izzie put in her bag for Marcus' supper.

Once the jars were clean and the old labels soaked off in hot water, they looked even better. Now all they needed were labels. Maddy dug out a roll of white stickers she used to mark the children's snack boxes and they both sat at the table again.

'Now what?' said Maddy. 'I can't do anything, my drawing is retarded.'

Izzie picked up one of the children's crayons from the table, and started to doodle on a piece of paper. 'Well, first we need a name. Is there a sort of ancient French name we could use? Tante Luce or something.'

'Sounds a bit like an apple pie brand you'd find in the freezer compartment at Tesco's. It needs to be countrified. "Old Slurry"?'

'Oh that'll get them excited! Eve Lom had better look out!' laughed Izzie. 'Get serious, Maddy. You're the frog.'

'OK. *Pays, paysanne*? Country something. Luce's recipes are almost like spells, aren't they?'

'What? Like country magic?' said Izzie, half-wittedly.

'No more like magical country.'

'Like Narnia or the Wizard of Oz.'

'Yeah right. I'll be Dorothy. Oh the hours I spent watching that film. I can date my shoe obsession back to those ruby slippers. You can be Toto. You've got the hair for it. Right,' Maddy scribbled some words on the paper in front of her. '*Magique, sortilege, secret* . . . er . . . *enchantement du pays*?'

'Too clumsy.'

'Enchanté. I know, what about *Paysage Enchanté*. It means sort of magical country . . . ?'

Izzie started to write out the letters, copying the thin, florid, distinctively Gallic script from Luce's notebook. Beneath she doodled and half sketched out a long, veined leaf of *centpertuis*. It looked very plain and uninspiring on its own. Then, flicking through Luce's book on the table, she picked out a dried stalk of lavender, straw coloured now but still perfect in shape, and sketched it on the paper.

'That's wonderful,' said Maddy, coming to look over her shoulder. 'You're good at this, aren't you? Must have got it from your dad. Can we put the two plants together?'

Izzie thought for a moment, with her head to one side, then sketched out another leaf more boldly this time, and entwined it with the lavender motif. Rattling through the pot of children's crayons on the table, she pulled out a deep purple and soft grey green, and coloured in the design. They both looked at the finished effect. It was simple, almost contemporary, yet captured the earthy element of the recipes.

'God, I haven't done any drawing for ages – I'm so rusty, but it's a start. I'll work on that over the next few days.'

'Brilliant. If we do another label on the back with the ingredients and all the bunkum we have to include, in the same script, it'll look really professional.'

The next morning Maddy was back on the phone to Jean Luc. He was resolved. 'Now I know you are both mad. You want four dozen empty pâté jars? What are you going to put in them – don't tell me you are going to pass off that smelly weed for tapenade?'

'We've just got this idea,' said Maddy. 'We're going to mix up one of Grandmère Luce's recipes and see if we can sell it. Call me desperate, but, Jean Luc, you know I've got to make some money somehow. Things are even tighter now.'

'It's not such a crazy idea.' Maddy was surprised that for once he seemed to be taking her seriously. 'I've done a little asking around the family, and her village, St Estèphe. She was something of a legend. A sort of white witch.' Maddy could feel a tingle of excitement. 'Apparently she had a little business going where she would cook up recipes for ointments and creams, and the villagers would pay her with cheese and vegetables. A kind of barter system. People came for miles for her magical potions – she even had orders from highly placed people in Paris, or so she used to claim.'

Maddy scribbled frantically on the back of an envelope as he talked. 'What became of her?'

'Well, she must have had children, or we wouldn't be here.' He laughed. 'I think she was a kind of earth mother – a hippy before her time. I can imagine children and chickens running in and out of the kitchen around her feet as she stirred her secret potions.'

'This is great stuff! Oh, can I beg another favour?' she asked apologetically. 'When you send over the jars, could you possibly chuck in another bag of *centpertuis*?'

'I'll have to triple wrap it, or you'll kill a few sniffer dogs at customs! Take care, *ma petite*, and say 'ello to Izzie for me.'

Maddy laughed knowingly, blew him kisses down the phone, and as soon as he hung up, dialled Izzie's number.

Soaking in the bath that night, enjoying the last drops from a bottle of Clarins Bain aux Plantes 'Relax' – there wouldn't be any more where that came from – she wondered where they were going to go with this Luce thing after the Christmas Fayre. Even if they sold the whole batch, they'd hardly be able to afford a turkey each. It had been fun getting all the ingredients – a nice distraction from grim reality – and the combined effect of the fresh, delicate green in the jars, with Izzie's naïve but pretty labels, was irresistible. It made you want to open the jars and plunge your fingers into the cream. This was too good an idea to drop.

Padding down the landing in her dressing gown, she scooped up Will's discarded socks, and the little jingley rabbit Pru Graves had given Pasco when he was born. She stared at it. Pru! With her PR contacts, she'd know whether there was any point developing the idea somehow. Maybe selling it at the farmers' market or the health food shop. Didn't she represent some niche make-up brand that was always been mentioned in magazines like *Elle*? This would be small beer for Pru, but she knew her stuff.

Two cups of tea and an ashtray full of cigarette stubs later, Maddy had scribbled down everything she knew about Luce and the ingredients, with a grovelling covering letter. Tomorrow she would stick a few jars in a Jiffy bag and send it off to Pru. Nothing ventured nothing gained!

Chapter 8

Talk about cutting it fine! Izzie was delirious from tiredness, having spent the three previous nights working until long after midnight on the hand-lettered labels for the jars (which hadn't actually arrived yet) that would contain the healing balm (which they hadn't made yet because they were waiting for more *centpertuis*), and they hadn't even had the first batch certified by the testing labs as safe for sale. The Fayre was tomorrow!

This event wasn't anything as ordinary as a 'fair' of course. Ooh, no! That came nowhere near encapsulating the weight of pretension, the frenzied preparation, the desperate anticipation that accompanied this yearly shindig. Raising money for charity was, of course, a laudable endeavour, but it was very much the supporting feature here, not the main event. The real reason for the Fayre was to see, to be seen, and to be seen to be looking fabulous, doing marvellously!

They were under no illusion as to how they had managed to secure a stall so late in the day. Invitations, hotly sought after, had been issued way back in June. Their admission resulted solely from the misfortune of one Rosalind Franks, whose famous Liberty Print tissue-box covers graced the spare rooms of right-thinking people throughout the Cotswolds.

Rosalind's nasty dose of amoebic dysentery had apparently been the talk of Ringford and just showed what could happen if you went somewhere Third World on your travels. Opinion was divided hotly between her having opened her mouth in the shower and her having succumbed to a drink with ice. Whatever the cause, Rosalind had apparently been poorly since her return, and hadn't stitched a single tray cloth, pincushion or carrier-bag tidy for months. Maddy and Izzie were clearly a poor substitute for the stall Rosalind has held for years, but it was either them or a great big gap.

The two of them had spun like dervishes preparing pots of the balm to deliver to various labs for testing. Different labs seemed to test for different things – fungal spores, allergens – and they all seemed to be at different ends of the country. Maddy had been all for going ahead without the accreditation, but Izzie had slapped her wrist.

'Which one of us is going to stump up the five-thousand-pound fine then, clever clogs?'

'We could always choose the prison option,' Maddy had replied. 'Maybe *they* could find me a job? Look what it did for Jeffrey Archer . . .'

They were both quietly confident they'd get the accreditation – most of the ingredients were time-honoured components, and known to be safe. The notable exception was their secret, never-before-tested magic formula, the boiled, strained *centpertuis*. They now discovered, from an old botany book at Ringford library, that the evocative English name for it was 'lop-ear'. Eradicated in the Middle Ages from Britain, it was apparently still a big problem in parts of France, particularly round vines. Jean Luc could vouch for that.

Once she returned from the school run, Izzie made herself a huge mug of leaded coffee, did all the stretching and yawning she needed to stop her voice sounding too sleepy, and dialled the now-familiar number. 'Mr MacNamee, please.'

The answering voice was Yorkshire, with a side order of world-weary cynicism. 'Mrs Stock, I presume?'

Izzie summoned up all the charm she could muster. Whether this long-range flirting on her part was having the least effect, she couldn't guess, but she had to give it her best shot! 'Good morning to you, Mr MacNamee. How clever of you to guess it was me! And how are you today?'

'Not so very clever, Mrs Stock. After all, you have phoned me three times a day, every day for the past three weeks.'

'Oh dear! Has it been that often? I do hope I haven't made a nuisance of myself, it's just that—'

'Yes, I know, Mrs Stock, you've explained more than adequately several times. The Fayre is on tomorrow and, yes, you did explain the significance of the spelling, and you did explain about your unfortunate friend and her personal problems, and you did tell me all about the dry rot and the piano.'

'Oh, I have been wittering on, haven't I? I hope I haven't been boring.'

'No, I'd say that's the last thing you've been, Mrs Stock. I can safely say that no other client has ever, ever been so entertaining – or so persistent. So it's with mixed feelings, Mrs Stock, that I have to tell you that the results are all in.'

Oh God no! What was this?

'Mixed feelings, Mrs Stock, because I've enjoyed our little chats, and I'm frankly sad to put an end to them, but I'm pleased to tell you, though I shouldn't really, not over the phone, that all the test results are in, and your product has been given the all-clear. The ingredients you have used seem to act as a natural preservative, so you won't need to put in any additives. I'm sending out your accreditation today, and I hope you'll receive it tomorrow morning. Before you ask, I'll make sure it goes out first class. I'll even write urgent on the envelope. Is that all right? Happy now?'

'Oh yes, Mr MacNamee. I certainly am. I could hug you!'

Embarrassed coughing came from the phone, followed by a gruff, 'Well, that won't be necessary, but thank you for the sentiment. I shall follow your progress with interest. If you're as determined about marketing your product as you have been about seeing it through testing, I expect you'll be taking over the world in a month or two!'

Jubilant even in her exhaustion, Izzie reached for the phone to tell Maddy the good news, but it rang as she reached for it. It must have been telepathy.

'It's here! It's come! A crate of dinky little pots and a load of *centpertuis.* Jean's had it vacuum-packed so it's stayed fresh and there's loads of it. He put in a note – says we owe him big time because he had to go and ask some of his neighbours to give him some. They agreed, provided he dug it up for them. He says his back's killing him, and everyone around thinks he's taken leave of his senses!'

'Well, wait till you hear my news! Darling Mr MacNamee has just told me that the balm has been certified. Thunderbirds are go! Just think, Maddy. We're in business. Literally in business!'

'Well, that calls for a celebratory coffee. My place or yours?'

'Oh God – no more coffee. I think I've given myself permanent kidney damage, the amount I've drunk in the last few days. How 'bout a soothing camomile tea?'

'Nah,' drawled Maddy. 'That's for wimps. And don't forget, we've got to boil up another batch today. Can you come over here later, and we'll get cracking?'

Izzie finally kissed Maddy goodbye at 2 a.m. and drove home cautiously through the clear, frosty night. Her tiredness had evaporated and she felt wired and excited. It would have been great to be able to tell Marcus how hard they'd worked potting and labelling all the balm, but she knew he'd be fast asleep by now. She'd imposed on him enough recently, expecting him to act the househusband on top of his own work – she had come back only briefly to put the children to bed and then disappeared back to Maddy's – so she doubted there would be bunting out to welcome her home now. She'd have to make it up to him.

He was fairly taciturn the next morning when she enthused about the night's antics, while she juggled making packed lunches for the children, press-ganging Jess into practising her recorder – Charlie was now obliged to use a neighbour's upright for his piano practice – and bustling them out of the door to the car and school. Not sure when the Fayre would finish, she'd called in some favours and billeted out the children to a friend's for tea. Asking Marcus to step into the breach alone yet again might be, she knew, a step too far.

Gathering all their spare change in a sandwich box for the float, they set off for Ledfinch Manor and following the neatly stencilled sign, parked round the back of the William and Mary pile. The area was jam-packed with Range Rovers and Mercedes, punctuated by the odd scruffy little estate – trade no doubt.

Women were everywhere. Any men present looked uncomfortable and edgy, impatient to get away once they had unloaded the piles of stock, and back to a world they understood. No, this was strictly a female event. And they came in such variety! From statuesque county types, complete with padded waistcoats, pie-crust collars and velvet hair bands, to the pinched, briskly efficient professionals, aprons jingling with change, enjoying a quick ciggie outside and sniggering at those unfortunate enough to have stepped in the huge desiccated cow pats that the free-range Highland cattle had left behind.

Inside, the place was awash with oestrogen (much of it, Izzie suspected, HRT) and the noise level was incredible. Well-bred voices, strident yet languid, cut through the throng. 'Serenaaa! Ovah heah, dahling! Put the découpage frames theah. Thet's it, dahling. Looks smeshing!'

Izzie and Maddy had a corner pitch in the draughty hallway. Quite a good one, actually, fairly near the entrance door, and they set out their wares. Maddy had found some Provençal fabric – not quite geographically correct – gay in blue, yellow and white, and they swagged it over upturned boxes to create different levels on the splintery trestle table they'd bagged. With some photographs of the Cévennes, including a rather arty one Maddy had taken a couple of years ago of Jean Luc silhouetted against the rising sun, and a wildly exaggerated history of Luce and her struggles which Izzie had bashed out in a moment of inspiration on her PC, it looked very fetching. After some debate, they'd decided to risk £4.99 a pot. But would anyone buy?

Before the doors opened for business, they took it in turns to tour the stands and check out the competition, and returned moderately heartened.

'I've never seen so much useless tat assembled under one roof. You could live several lifetimes without needing any of it,' said Maddy.

'*Au contraire, ma chère*,' contradicted Izzie. 'I see now that my life has been incomplete without knitted socks with multi-coloured individual toes.'

Maddy was rooting for those little painted wooden plaques that hang on the front door, informing visitors of your where-abouts. 'Honestly, if I was a burglar, I'd be laughing. It's an invitation to walk in and nick stuff! "I'm in the garden", "I'm walking the dog". I know – let's do a more cutting-edge range, "I've been sectioned under the Mental Health Act", "I'm rogering the window cleaner". Those'd sell nicely!'

Then the punters swarmed in, most brandishing lovely wicker baskets with elasticated Liberty print linings (bought from Rosalind the previous year). There appeared to Izzie to be two distinct sub-species of the same breed. The alpha females sported stretch capri pants, cashmere polo necks and sheepskin gilets, glasses perched on top of their highlighted heads. The less genetically favoured were in comfy loafers, shapeless cords and regulation green quilted jackets with corduroy collars. All came armed with lists of people to buy for – lumpish teenage nephews, aged uncles and strings of difficult godchildren. They were like a plague of uppercrust locusts. And buy they did.

They snapped up floral wellies, overpriced colourful resin keyrings, and stuff to stop their ponds from getting clogged with duckweed. They cooed over hessian utility belts and bags for storing their garden tools, joke golf books, novelty aprons, chef's hats for their husbands' barbecue efforts, and embroidered cushions bearing witticisms like 'Etonians do it against the Wall'.

Lord, how they bought! Money was changing hands like a bear market at the metal exchange, lubricated still further by glasses of mulled wine, spicy and sweet, on sale by the door. The noise level steadily rose, faces became redder and shinier and shrill laughter broke out above the hubbub. The organisers looked quietly delighted.

Maddy and Izzie began to enjoy themselves. Their stall was attracting quite a bit of attention, and their pile of little pots steadily decreased. From their first rather apologetic efforts, they gradually improved their sales technique until, by three-thirty, they had the smoothest patter and no stock left. Absolutely none. The ladies with their sensible, wind-chapped, horsey faces had gone for the healing balm with zeal. Eyeing Maddy's golden glowing complexion and Izzie's delicate pallor, they probably thought they were buying into their secret.

'If only they knew,' whispered Izzie, out of the corner of her mouth. 'The only reason I don't look about eighty is a fanatical avoidance of the lacrosse field all through school!'

By the end of the afternoon, and once they had given the agreed percentage to the organisers, they were left with a tidy pile of fivers. Maddy stuck to her insistence that they share everything, so they split it and for that Izzie, cleaned out by the dry rot payments, was profoundly grateful.

Maddy looked tired. 'Well, I'd call that an unqualified success,' she said as they stowed the empty boxes into the car. 'Do you think we charged enough? If we'd had another twenty pots, I reckon we could have sold them too.'

Izzie nodded emphatic agreement as she swung the car over the rutted paddock back towards the drive. 'I think we were definitely getting into our stride by the end. It seems a shame to end it like this. Do you think we should make more and keep going?'

'I don't see why not, if we can get a regular supply of *centpertuis* and some more little pots. Do you think Jean Luc would be game?'

Izzie blushed under Maddy's close scrutiny. 'Well, how would I know? He's your cousin, after all. Why don't you ask him?'

Maddy whistled with exaggerated insouciance. 'I thought you could ask him, next time you two *speak on the phone*.'

Izzie swerved. 'How did you know about that?'

'Well, my love, remember when you left your mobile at my house last week?' Izzie's face burnt. Oh God! Maddy turned the screw. 'I couldn't work out where the buzzing was coming from to start with. We had a *lovely* chat when I finally found your phone under a pile of ironing. He was as surprised to hear me answer as . . . well, as you look now! Funny you didn't give him your home number . . .'

Izzie slapped at her leg. 'Oh shut up.' She felt like a teenager being given the third degree. 'Anyway, he gave me his number because he wanted me to let him know how you are. He always asks for a full report – what you've been eating, what you've been doing. He's very concerned about you!'

'Yeah right.'

Izzie drove on in silence for a while, frowning slightly, then burst out laughing. 'Maddy, you are incorrigible!'

'Oh and I meant to tell you. Some publisher rang too. Said they had something in the pipeline for you after Christmas. I said I'd see if you could fit it in, but that you'd had to put your rate up.'

Izzie was horrified. Maddy had put the final nail in the coffin of her sickly career.

Maddy paused theatrically. 'They said that would be fine, and they were very grateful you could find time for them.'

The last couple of weeks before the Christmas holidays flew by, as they always do. Izzie got on with all the usual stuff: cards, decorations, provisions, mince pies and Christmas pud to make, plus the nativity costumes to create – well, tea towels and dressing gowns, sandals, snake belts and walking sticks, but still! This year, however, she had to do it all on a tighter budget than ever.

For a change they were going to spend Christmas with Marcus' parents, Ray and Gwen, for the first time since the children had been born. Visits were supposed to be on a strictly fair rotation, alternating with Izzie's parents. But there had been a sort of hiccup when Marcus' brother, Adrian, had gone to live in Melbourne and they'd got out of synch. This had caused all sorts of tensions and cross-currents of bad feeling that Izzie only vaguely understood – Marcus' family were always squabbling. But she was very aware that after such a long gap, this Christmas had a significance beyond that of peace on earth and goodwill to all men. She was dreading it.

Marcus and his parents had always been a sore topic in their marriage. The bottom line was that they were both acutely aware that she came from a very different background. Her dad was an artist, her mum a secondary school teacher. They'd never had much money, but she and her brother had sailed through grammar school. Home life had been rich in intellectual conversation, music, European travel, books, artistic friends always swapping ideas over glasses of cheap plonk at the kitchen table.

Right from Marcus' first visit to their house in Norwich, he'd tried very hard – perhaps a little too hard – to fit in with the lefty, liberal-thinking bohemianism, but her parents had been gracious and tolerant as always.

Marcus' upbringing had been much tougher. Staunch Thatcherites, and life-long *Express* readers, his parents had been one of the first to buy their council house and were proud of the improvements they'd made to it. Not bad for a factory foreman and a dinner lady. But their proudest achievement was Marcus, and on every visit they asked him avidly about a life they could not even conceive of. Yet he always brushed off their well-meant enquiries.

Izzie reacted by trying desperately to make up for Marcus' reticence. She found herself blowing his trumpet for him, despite his glares. It was so difficult to strike the right balance. Whatever she did, she seemed to get it wrong. If she got matey with Gwen, having a giggle with her over peeling the sprouts, for instance, she was worried Marcus would think she was being patronising. If she was quiet, she feared he would think she was a snob. She wouldn't dare go down the allotment again with Ray after last time, although she'd really enjoyed lifting the carrots for lunch with him and seeing how tenderly he nurtured the hyacinths he was forcing for the house. Marcus had been uncomfortable about that, as if he was sure his dad would say something crass. It was insulting to Ray and even more so to Izzie.

Taking the kids to stay at Ray and Gwen's little semi did add an extra layer of stress, but they were so delighted by their grandchildren, and the feeling was mutual. Izzie allowed her strict rules on sweets between meals to go by the by – a policy she regretted at bedtime when she had to peel them off the walls, their blood sugar level was so high.

Maddy had been understanding about the delicate diplomacy that in-law visits required and the impending sojourn. Maddy's own in-laws sounded a pretty tricky bunch, but she had such a different set of problems now that Izzie didn't like to go on too much. It seemed so petty. Funnily enough, the thing she was dreading about Christmas was not seeing Maddy. It would probably only work out as a week apart, at the most, but the intense effort leading up to the Christmas Fayre had been such fun, and now Izzie couldn't help feeling that Christmas itself would be a let-down. She hugged Maddy and the kids goodbye after they met to exchange tiny token presents – no money for big ones – but Izzie couldn't resist the shocking pink feather duster she'd found in Ringford Market. She had a sneaky feeling that the cassette of French songs Maddy had recorded for her had a hidden agenda.

The second week of January and Maddy was profoundly relieved that the whole nightmare of Christmas and New Year was over. She had always hated this time of year – what on earth was there to celebrate when it was early January, more foul weather was inevitable and it was weeks until spring? But this year had been infinitely worse than any before it.

They would usually have spent Christmas in Hertfordshire with Simon's family, which included his two married brothers, their enthusiastic wives and hordes of cousins. They were a hearty lot who did the festivities in good English fashion, with lots of booze, a huge lunch (with Simon's father, Alan, getting more touchy-feely and red in the face under his party hat as the day went on), then wellies on and a 'bit of fresh air' down the fields with the dogs. This was more like a route march organised by Simon's formidable mother, Cynthia, and Maddy was expert after years of practice at thinking up excuses to avoid it.

Cynthia had been quite a looker in her youth, but hardened to the world after raising three sons, she had the complexion of a woman who had stood on innumerable touchlines watching rugby. Her very existence revolved around the men in her life, and she had no time for fools or those who didn't 'muck in'. Sensible, forthright, she was the kind of woman who had a voice that could strip paint, who based her politics on the leader column of the *Daily Mail*, who played golf with an impressive handicap and who dressed from the catalogues advertised in the back of the Sunday supplements.

On Maddy, Cynthia had never quite been able to get a handle. She thought she had her taped as a well-bred gal who would be just the right sort of wife for her beloved youngest son. But when Cynthia had met the Chanel-clad Giselle during the lead-up to the wedding, and had to suffer her very continental approach to nuptials, she had to readdress her assumptions and had thereafter treated Maddy with a certain amount of caution.

Maddy was determined not to follow the Christmas tradition – the gap left by Simon would have been a yawning one – so she had virtually invited herself and the children to stay with Giselle and Peter, in their handsome Georgian house at Richmond. Panic stricken by the thought of the place being wrecked, Giselle had practically cleared out the toy department at Peter Jones so Will, Florence and Pasco would have no reason to touch anything during their stay other than their new toys. For all her inability to cope with anyone under twenty-five, Giselle was a lioness when it came to guarding the perfection of her house, and sticky fingers on her silk curtains was something up with which she would not put.

Needless to say, on Christmas morning Pasco had been more interested in the wrapping paper than the contents, and even that had been short lived. One broken lamp and a pot of handsoap rubbed into the bathroom carpet later, and Maddy was relieved when they packed up the car with the horde of presents on Boxing Day. Just before she pulled away, Peter, a rather diffident bear of a man, had leant into the car window as if to say a final goodbye and had pressed a cheque into her hands. It was made out for five hundred pounds.

Gobsmacked, Maddy had opened her mouth as if to say, What on earth . . . ? Peter had simply put his hand on her shoulder and said, 'Think of it as an extra Christmas present,' and had turned to walk away.

'What are you doing at New Year? Want to join us?' Izzie had asked very thoughtfully on 27 December. But for once Maddy was economical with the truth. 'Oh, I've a couple from London coming to stay. We'll stay in and have a piss-up I expect.'

In fact, she had curled up with a cup of hot chocolate in front of the TV, watched as much as she could stomach of hearty hogmanay celebrations from Edinburgh Castle, and had been in bed with her book by nine-thirty. The whole experience had been made more painful by the fact that Will kept reminding her how much fun Daddy had made Christmas, and that Pasco had decided to start walking on New Year's Day. Simon had recorded Will's and Florence's first steps devotedly on the camcorder, but even when Maddy eventually found the ruddy thing, she couldn't get it to work.

The next morning they awoke to a freezing house. No heating. No hot water. It took her ages to work out that they must have run out of oil. Frankly it hadn't even crossed her mind that oil ran out, and 'with the backlog of Christmas', as the woman at the oil supplier call centre had been at pains to point out, it would be a few days before they could fill up the tank. Cold, frustrated, angry at herself for letting it happen (in the knowledge that Simon wouldn't have let such a situation occur), she felt desolate and lost. And when the tanker did finally arrive, she could only afford for them to half fill the tank.

The same day the children went back to school and nursery, and she took down the pathetic decorations. Packing them up into boxes haphazardly and fighting back tears, she put them away as fast as possible in a cupboard on the top floor and collected up the Christmas cards. There had been a flood of them this year, each one had a little note of support. The only one that hadn't was from Pru. 'What on earth was that little parcel you sent me?' she had scrawled hastily on her corporate offering, which rather incongruously showed a picture of a posh spa on the front (one of her clients no doubt). 'I'll be in touch in the new year – loads of kisses Px.'

Now, sitting down at the kitchen table during Pasco's rest, she scribbled a note to Giselle to thank her for Christmas and the wonderful presents. They had given her a pale grey cashmere roll-neck, which was beautiful but seemed inappropriate when cash was so short, and a Nigella Lawson cookbook that was even more so when her budget ran to chicken nuggets and beans. Something stopped her, however, from mentioning Peter's cheque. She had a feeling Giselle had known nothing about it, and that perhaps Peter knew more about her predicament than he was letting on.

The sale at the auction house had gone moderately well, the only big disappointment being the gilt mirror which only just made its reserve. She'd banked the cheque then written out copious other ones and tucked them into envelopes with the rather aggressive reminders which had arrived from the kitchen fitters et al. She had earmarked most of Peter's money for Florence and Little Goslings. She had taken the decision to reduce Florence's hours to three days a week, and Clare Jenkins had swallowed her feeble excuse that she felt Florence would benefit from spending time at home. 'Oh yes, Mrs Hoare, bonding is so important at this age.' Eagles had been brilliant, the governors having written her a very supportive stay-of-execution letter about 'never wanting to interrupt a child's education if at all possible'. But the cash wasn't going to last long, the phone was predictably quiet on the WorkWorld front, and the year loomed ahead of her dismally cash free.

She had the key in the door on the way back from school

later in the afternoon when she heard the phone ring. Stumbling into the hall she grabbed it.

'Will,' she shouted, putting her hand over the receiver, 'just leave your sister alone, and no, you can't watch *The Weakest Link*. Hello?'

'A sea of domestic calm and serenity I gather,' said an amused voice at the other end. 'Darling, is this a good moment?'

'No, Pru, your timing is crap, but how are you? Have good festives?'

'Oh usual thing. Gruesome day with Graham's family, then back to DINKY heaven as quick as was politely possible. Now listen, I won't keep you cos I'm sure you have supper to rustle up. About this gunge you sent me. From what I could make out from your scrawl, it all sounds rather intriguing. There just might be something in it – well, it certainly isn't the fragrance – but I like the story. I've got a plan. I need to talk to you and your friend a bit more about it. I don't suppose you can get down here to civilisation, can you?'

Maddy took in the chaos of school bags, caps and coats all over the hall floor and the screaming coming from the upstairs bedrooms. It wasn't just the logistics of childcare if she went down to London – though God knew she ached to go – it was the cost too. Could she really justify the petrol for a meeting that may come to nothing? She was pretty damned sure Izzie couldn't.

She'd obviously hesitated too long. 'OK, I get the message,' laughed Pru. 'At huge personal cost to my delicate sensitivities, the mountain shall come to Mohammed. Can you meet me at whatever provincial little station is nearest to you?'

Maddy put down the phone with a fluttering of anticipation in her stomach. It was time to come clean to Izzie about what she'd done.

Pru looked totally out of place as she stepped off the train at Ringford two days later. Immaculate in a navy suit, perfectly tailored camel coat, deep burgundy velvet scarf, and armed with Louis Vuitton, she looked around her with momentary panic until she spotted Maddy waiting at the other end of the platform.

'Daarling.' She flung her arms around her in a fragrant embrace, and stood back to look at her old friend. 'You look . . . well, bloody awful frankly. And what have, or rather haven't, you done to your hair? Don't they do highlights up here in the sticks, or are you rediscovering your French roots?'

'Very funny! Come on, Izzie is waiting for us at the house – she's looking after your godson for me – and she's dying to meet you. How's London? I want to know *everything*.'

Pru nearly shrieked with disgust when she saw the little red Fiesta parked in the car park, and gingerly shoe-horned herself and her briefcase into it as if she might dirty her coat on something vile left on the seat. On the short journey home, it started to rain and she peered out through the windscreen wipers like the first westerner to enter East Berlin.

'Oh how quaint, a village Post Office. Do people really use them? And all these signs for the Countryside March. Don't tell me they're planning another one. Bloody pain that day was for nipping into Knightsbridge – the inconvenience!' Maddy smiled as she listened. It was heaven to have someone who felt the same way.

Pru spent the rest of the journey as if she had a bad smell under her nose, and when they pulled into the drive and Maddy stopped the car, Pru stepped out in her high heels on to the now muddy driveway as if it were liquid cow pat.

'Christ – how do you put up with it?'

'Oh fortitude and copious amounts of gin,' laughed Maddy. 'Come and meet Izzie.'

Once she was ensconced in the house – 'Oh darling, I knew it would be a haven of exquisite taste in a sea of mediocrity' – and had given Pasco some cars which were entirely unsuitable and clearly stated on the packaging 'not for children under 36 months', Pru settled down at the kitchen table with a glass of wine. Her warm response to Izzie, who had been thrilled by Maddy's initiative but was struck dumb with awe on meeting this pillar of public relations, reminded Maddy why Pru was such a good mate.

'Now, girls, about this smelly gunk you so kindly shared with me. It smells like a council tip, but I think the story is rather beguiling. What I want you to do is run it all by me again, show me this Luce woman's scribblings and then I suggest we cobble together a bit of a press release.'

Maddy was puzzled. 'You mean, you're interested? We just wanted your advice on farmers' markets and the like.'

'Would I have come all this way for some two-bit farm-shop operation, darling? Let's think global! I have a feeling that this product might just appeal to those jaded luvvies in the beauty departments of magazines and papers who are full of New Year flu and scrabbling around for something to interest their rich and pampered readers.'

By the time Maddy put her on the return train to London three hours later, Pru had filled about twenty sides of A4 paper, had thumbed through Luce's journal and had tucked the last of the samples they had left into her Vuitton handbag. 'God! This is a bit of a quantum leap!' Maddy said to Izzie when she got back from the station and they'd given themselves a congratulatory hug. 'But if anyone can stir up interest, Pru can. She's formidable to say the least and there's not a journalist worth knowing whose number isn't in her little black book.'

The flu Pru had mentioned was now rife all over the country, and everyone Maddy met over the next few days had already had it, had it now or was brewing it. Will came home from school shivering a week after Pru's visit, and Maddy put him into bed with some Calpol and a hot drink. The next day

Florence was showing signs of it too, so Maddy battened down the hatches over the weekend.

'God, I want to die,' sniffed Izzie down the phone when Maddy called her on Saturday. 'I've just got back from drama club with Charlie and Jess and, even though I'm wearing three jumpers and my old skiing thermals, I can't seem to get warm.'

'What on earth were you doing out? You should be in bed. Where's Marcus?'

'Oh I think he's photographing some event of the Mayor's. He won't be back until later.' Feeling helpless that she couldn't lend a hand, Maddy made Izzie promise to stick on an epically long video for the children, and get herself into bed with a hottie.

Fortified by orange juice and cigarettes (she was convinced she got less colds than non-smokers), Maddy managed to stave off the lurgy, despite the children's best attempts to sneeze all over her. But on Monday morning Will was still not well enough to go into school. No sooner had she put the phone down at 8.15 from telling the secretary that she was keeping him at home, than it rang again.

'Mrs Hoare, it's Mara Fields here from WorkWorld. It's very short notice I know but we've had an urgent request from the doctor's surgery on Cherry Tree Walk in Ringford. They are down to one receptionist, what with the flu epidemic, and need someone to step in right away.'

'You mean now?'

'If you can. You did say you could work at short notice.' Me and my big mouth. 'It's quite unusual for us to supply temps to a surgery, but in the circumstances they had no option but to call us, and most of our regulars have been struck down with the bug too.'

Trying to sound efficient, and covering up her panic about what on earth she was going to do with the children, she wrote down the details and promised she'd be there as fast as was humanly possible. She then phoned Izzie who still sounded like death warmed up. 'Oh Maddy, I'm so sorry, I still feel lousy, Jess is off and Marcus is coming down with it too. You can bring them all over here if you like . . .'

'No way – that's the last thing you need. I'll cope – somehow!'

Frantically looking for inspiration, and Florence's *My Little Pony* comic she was whining she needed, Maddy's eye fell on the parish magazine. Could she fall on the mercy of the good vicar's wife in her hour of need?

Janet Grant bustled in ten minutes later in her duffel coat, sensible boots and bobble hat from under which poked out a thatch of wiry greying hair. 'Don't panic, Maddy. I'm sure I can manage – you must be Florence,' she said to the sulky-looking little girl who was hiding behind her mother. 'You'll tell me where everything is, won't you? I've even brought some Play-Doh from the playgroup box – we can do that, can't we?'

Maddy heard a wail of tears as she slammed the front door and ran to the car. She scraped away as much of the ice from the windscreen as she could with the edge of a cassette tape box, and by the time she climbed back into the car, the crying had died down. 'God bless Janet Grant,' she muttered. 'I promise I'll go to church more often.'

The surgery was pandemonium when she finally got there at nine. Unanswered phones were shrilling, the waiting room was full to bursting with pale, coughing patients, most of whom, it seemed to Maddy's untrained eye, would have been better off in bed with a glass of Beecham's Powders. A lone receptionist was trying to juggle the queue waiting at the desk demanding appointments with a GP. She almost hugged Maddy when she told her she had come from WorkWorld. 'I'm Margaret, practice manager. Just chuck your coat there and answer the phone, can you? Tell them that we are completely full up today, if they have the flu to stay warm and drink lots of fluids, and if they are bleeding to go to A & E.'

Over the next two hours Maddy must have answered about fifty calls. By eleven, surgery was running seriously late, the computer had crashed twice and Maddy had inadvertently booked a vasectomy patient into the well-woman clinic. She had never had much patience with ill people, and when she told a particularly persistent caller to 'stop making such a fuss, it's only flu' she got a very old-fashioned look from Margaret.

By eleven-thirty she was gasping for a cup of coffee and a fag. 'Any chance I can see Dr Fellows today?' said a friendly voice across the desk.

Maddy was just about to brush her off, when the speaker, a rather smartly dressed, elderly women in her sixties, suddenly said, 'Didn't I see you at the Christmas Fayre at Ledfinch Manor?'

Maddy smiled. 'Yes, that was me. Did you buy much?'

'Oh lots. Do all my Christmas shopping there. Bought some of your cream actually – terrible whiff, but it's good stuff, isn't it? I'm a mad keen gardener – in the local club, you know, dahlias my speciality – but since using your cream my hands have never been so soft. My friend Sylvia put some on her corns and they just went! Fantastic!' She leant forward con-spiratorially. 'I'm here about my piles. Do you think it would work on them too?' and they both roared with laughter.

'Oh I'm so pleased – not about the piles I mean. You could always give it a try. Do tell your friends about it, won't you?'

'I already have, my dear. They want to know where I got it. Do you sell it locally?'

'We're hoping too. I'll let you know, Mrs . . . ?'

'Bates. Lally Bates. I think I live near you. You're at Huntingford House, aren't you? Thought so. It's looking marvellous. Terrible state it was in and you've done wonders. Look, put me in with Dr Fellows when you can, and why don't you come to a WI market with your pots? They'll go down a storm.'

Maddy had made her an appointment, and had waved her goodbye, when Margaret came over. 'Mrs Hoare,' she said with a face like thunder, 'it is one thing to waste precious time chatting with patients when we are so busy, but quite another to recommend ointments without a doctor's approval, especially for something as personal as – ' her voice dropped to a whisper, '*haemorrhoids*. I'd appreciate it if you would just do the job.'

Maddy kept her head down for the rest of the day, and finally left at six-thirty when the last patient had coughed and snuffled his way out of the surgery door. She had a feeling she wouldn't be asked to help out tomorrow, but she'd done nine hours, so the pay would be better than a poke in the eye.

Janet had clearly done sterling work. The children were bathed and in pyjamas when Maddy let herself in the front door, the house smelt of baked biscuits, the kitchen was pristine and the table was strewn with pictures they had drawn or painted, and interesting collages using dried pasta and string.

'Janet, I really don't know how to thank you. You have been a brick.'

'Oh Maddy, think nothing of it,' she replied as she shrugged on her duffel coat. 'I'm delighted I've been able to help, especially when I know you've had such a tough time. Bereavement is so difficult and debilitating. If you would like to join one of our Wives Fellowship meetings we'd love to have you. Just coffee and a chat. Lots of fun. Anyway must go – but Nick and I are there to help whenever we can.'

Tired and emotional after her long day, tears welled up in Maddy's eyes and she planted a kiss on Janet's cheek. With a surprised look on her face, Janet disappeared into the night.

She tucked the children into bed, administered Calpol and Olbas oil, changed out of her clothes into her pyjamas and went down to make herself a piece of toast. As she waited for it to pop up, she turned on the answering machine which flashed three messages. They were all from Pru. She listened, rewound and listened again, then she picked up the phone and dialled Izzie's number.

'It's me.'

'Hiya. I was just going to call you,' mumbled Izzie, her voice still thick with cold. 'How did you get on?'

'Don't ask. I think I've been fired. But listen. We've got a problem.'

Her heart pounding with panic and disbelief, Maddy recounted what Pru had said in each increasingly excited message. She heard Izzie squeal.

Chapter 9

First thing next morning, Izzie reported for duty. The combination of shock, panic and excitement at Maddy's news seemed to have blasted away the lingering symptoms of her flu and she was positively hopping from foot to foot as she let herself into the house.

'Flood of enquiries? Is that really what she said? What are we going to do?' she demanded. 'Two hundred pots! We can't possibly come up with that much balm in three days. We haven't got any pots for a start, no *centpertuis*, no lavender, no wax. The only thing we have got is Jean Luc's olive oil!'

Maddy shook her head helplessly. 'I've been up all night thinking it through. It'll certainly take more than just the two of us this time. We'll have to get help. And I haven't managed to get hold of Jean Luc yet, though I've been trying his number all night. He's going to be gobsmacked when we tell him how much more *centpertuis* we need!'

Izzie looked momentarily disconcerted. 'Isn't he answering his phone? Didn't he go home last night?'

Maddy eyed her cautiously. 'No, I don't think he did. He's left the answer phone on, and he's not picking up his mobile.'

Trying to look nonchalant, Izzie set to work loading the dishwasher and making coffee, while Maddy ran through the possibilities she'd come up with for helpers over the next few days. 'I know Crispin's at a loose end at the moment. I feel terrible about it. He'd pretty much banked on working for us for the next six months, and he's only got bits and pieces of other work lined up. Thanks.'

She took the coffee Izzie offered and patted the seat next to her. 'Look, I've started to make a list. I haven't asked anyone yet – I wanted to check it out with you first. What do you think?'

Izzie peered at the piece of paper. 'Janet Grant, yes and she'd be brilliant with the kids, wouldn't she? Who's Lillian? I don't think I've met her. I could ask Marcus, too. I'm sure he'd help us out.'

'Mmm,' replied Maddie quickly. 'I wouldn't want to get in the way of his photography, and you might need him to pick the kids up if we're really pushed. But we could keep him in reserve. Lillian was Simon's secretary at Workflow Systems. She's a bit shy, but terrifically efficient.'

'But Maddy, we can't pay them. We're going to be stretched enough as it is to pay for the ingredients and the packaging and everything. Are we just going to ask them to do it as a favour? You could offer Crispin your body, but I don't think Janet or Lillian would be too keen!'

'Oh I don't know. Janet wears comfortable shoes, and she practically has a moustache.' Maddy smiled wickedly. 'No, I've thought about that already. It's only going to be for a couple of days. We'll have to offer them payment in kind – a kind of barter thing. For a start, we'll feed them – that goes a long way with Crispin, I can tell you. He could eat toast for England! I thought I could offer Lillian some of my clothes – well, you should see the stuff she wears – and I've got too many jumpers, you said so yourself. Not sure about Janet – maybe she'd be satisfied if I offered my soul – but she did ask if she could take foliage from the garden for the church flowers. I may have to offer her a whole tree for this, but I reckon it'd be worth it!'

'What about me? What can I offer?'

Maddy waggled her eyebrows suggestively. 'I've thought about that too. You can offer Jean Luc some irresistible incentive to get us some more of that sodding *centpertuis*. I warn you, he drives a hard bargain!'

Izzie fidgeted, looking down. 'If he's been out all night, he might not be very interested in anything I have to offer. You'd better play the cousin card. I think that would—'

The phone interrupted her, and Maddy answered. 'Jean Luc! At last. Where have you been? Izzie and I were worried!'

Izzie flapped her hands and mouthed a silent 'Noooo!' at Maddy, who turned away laughing and lapsed in French. '*C'est pas vrai? Toute la nuit? Cinq? Tu doit-être crevé. Ah oui, on s'inquietait, Izzie et moi. Izzie surtôut.*' She paused and laughed knowingly. '*Demande lui toi-même! Je te la passe.*'

And she passed the phone to Izzie. What the hell had that been all about? She took the phone cautiously and found herself speaking rather stiffly. 'Hello? Jean Luc?' Even to herself she sounded embarrassingly English. 'Yes, we were wanting to ask you for some more *centpertuis*, please.'

'Izzie? It's really you?' His voice sounded warm and smiley, and in spite of herself, Izzie felt her stomach clench. Get a grip, girl. 'Wonderful to hear your voice. I feel better already, but I'm sooo tired.'

'Well, um, we need quite a bit this time. About four times as much, actually.'

'Oh non! My poor back! It is only just recovering now. I am sooo out of condition, I think. But for you two, I will do it.'

'The thing is,' she gabbled on primly, 'we need it very fast this time. We have to have the stuff made up in three days, and more of those little pots. Two hundred actually.'

'*Non! Tu plaisantes!* You are joking! Oh, Izzie, I can't bring it over this time. I'm all tied up here. You know how it is – no one else will do but me. But I'll make the phone calls – there's a wholesaler in Grasse. I'll make some time to dig up more *centpertuis* this morning before I go back to bed.'

Izzie's back was growing more and more rigid as the conversation went on. 'Yes, well, we'd be very grateful,' she concluded frostily. 'If you could let us know where we can source the pots, we won't have to trouble you again. I'm sure you must be exhausted after last night.'

'Oh yes! But it was so exciting. Every time is like magic. I'll send you both photos.'

'Jean Luc, I'm really not sure I—'

'They are so adorable. I have two of them here. One white, one black.' He paused theatrically. 'I've got five altogether now.' He started to laugh, and suddenly she got the feeling she was the butt of some joke she didn't quite understand. 'And more on the way. The sweetest little *lambs* you ever saw.'

'Oh! Lambs. Of course, lambs. It's lambing time!' She laughed, relief pouring into her. 'Jean Luc, it's so great to hear your voice . . . Yes, I wish I was too . . . of course I would . . . I can't wait . . . Yes, of course . . . Me too . . . Now off to bed with you, young man! You've got to be in good shape for digging up the *centpertuis* for us!'

God! I must get a grip, she chided herself. I'm a married woman.

A few hours later, the troops had been rallied. Of course, Lillian had had no trouble finding temping work in Oxford, but by a stroke of fortune was free for the day and agreed readily to drive over to Maddy's at lunchtime. Izzie sat back in admiration as she listened to Maddy laying on the charm to persuade her. She'd missed her vocation this woman: she'd have got a first-class honours in schmooze.

Crispin had been run to ground and it only took the word 'lunch' for him to drop everything. Janet had bustled over after taking the local primary school children for hymn practice, and had arrived in a cloud of patchouli and dog hair. One of Izzie's super-deluxe shepherd's pies had been liberated from the freezer and was soon steaming seductively on the table in front of them. As Izzie dished up, Maddy addressed her battalion, explaining the situation, offering terms and trying her darndest to be persuasive.

'So the thing is, we absolutely have to get the balm to Pru's office in London by Wednesday afternoon at the latest. That way, she can get the samples out to journalists on Thursday ready for editorials in weekend editions of the paper. And I'm afraid that means it's going to be all hands to the pump as soon as we get the ingredients and the pots – probably tomorrow morning – Jean Luc is organising that.'

There was a nail-biting silence.

Janet was the first to wade in with gushing enthusiasm. 'Even if it means working all night, I'll sign on the dotted line straight away. I think this could be rather fun! And you don't need to worry about a whole tree – but if I could make free with my secateurs among your shrubbery, I'd be very grateful. I've got my eye on that Camelia williamsii. Can't wait to get going on that lovely glossy bush of yours!'

Crispin, Izzie and Maddy all suddenly studied their plates with ferocious concentration.

'I don't know anything about cooking or stirring or anything,' said Crispin, through a mouthful, and trying to wipe the smile off his face, 'but I can help with loading up and you can use my van for delivering the stuff.'

Two down one to go. Everyone turned to look at Lillian. She was hesitant. 'I've got to be in the office during the day tomorrow, but if I come over as soon as I've finished, I'll gladly help, er Maddy! And . . . well, I've always admired your chic, so if you're quite certain about those jumpers . . .'

Maddy and Izzie exchanged triumphant glances as their odd assortment of guests tucked in with relish. A rather fine Chateau Léoville-Barton from Simon's cellar added to the party atmosphere, and discussions turned to practicalities. Soon Lillian was showing her form.

'We, er, we do have a terrific amount to do. Is there anything we could be getting on with before the pots and the ingredients get here?'

Izzie groaned. 'Well there is, but I'm afraid no one can do it but me! I'll have to do four hundred hand-lettered labels, two hundred for the front, two hundred for the back, so I'd better get cracking!'

'Hold on a minute, Izzie,' Lillian interrupted, flushing slightly at her boldness. 'I could help with that. If you can give me one of each type of label, I could scan them at work tomorrow and print out as many as you need. I'm sure no one would notice.'

'Lillian, you're a genius!' shrieked Maddy. 'But will you have time?'

Lillian shrugged modestly. 'Oh Maddy, I get my work done so much faster than all the other team assistants there, I've got bags of time on my hands.'

'Lillian, I could kiss you. I'll double your jumper allocation for that!' Izzie quickly found Lillian the labels she been using to copy from, and she left shortly afterwards, beaming in her new mint-green pashmina.

Back in the kitchen, Janet gathered up her bags. 'What are the other ingredients you need, apart from the stuff your cousin is sending?'

'Not much really,' explained Maddy. 'That's the beauty of it. It's actually quite a simple recipe. Just beeswax, *centpertuis*, olive oil, which we've got, and lavender. That'll be the problem.'

'Lavender? Is that all? Good heavens, I've got a good friend, met her at the peace camp at Greenham actually.'

Maddy and Izzie exchanged incredulous glances.

'She runs a holistic health centre in Wales, and they make

some of their own remedies and oils. They've got fields of lavender there and I know they dry it. Shall I give her a call?'

'You lifesaver! If you could, that would be great. We could go and collect as much as she could spare us – today, if you could arrange it.'

'Well maybe that's something I could do,' chipped in Crispin. 'If you could fix me up some sandwiches for the journey.'

'I'll pack you a proper Famous Five picnic,' Izzie promised. 'Hard-boiled eggs, as much fruit cake as you can eat, ham sarnies and . . .' they all joined in, 'lashings of ginger beer!' And laughing as they left, Crispin and Janet, an unlikely alliance, planned his route to Wales for the lavender mercy dash.

Later that afternoon, Izzie went to pick up all four children so they could have supper at Maddy's. The car park at Eagles was just as appalling as she had feared – and worse. She felt horribly conspicuous, but couldn't resist a triumphant little smile at Linda, Fiona and Clare, clearly put out when Will bolted out of the classroom and threw himself into her arms.

Back at the house, while the children were busy watching cartoons and spreading muffin crumbs all over the sofa, Maddy told her that Jean Luc had called again. He had found a supplier for the pots, negotiated the best deal he could, gone out to dig up a load of *centpertuis* and arranged for an overnight courier to pick up everything they needed that evening.

'The man's a saint,' Maddy exclaimed. 'It should all be here in the morning. And he's offered to pay for this load.'

'God! That's going to cost a fortune.'

Maddy put a restraining hand on her arm. 'Oh you needn't worry about him. Jean Luc's loaded. He may play the simple farmer, but he made a stash as an art dealer in his thirties. He just dabbles now. The farm's what he really loves. But being Jean Luc, he's even managed to make a success of that!'

Izzie's eyes sparkled. 'God! Could he be any more perfect?'

'Well, there is a dark side. I suppose I should be the one to break it to you – he's got a secret collection of Jean Michel Jarre albums.'

'That's hard to forgive. But honestly, we've got to get him to invoice us, just to keep things businesslike.'

'He's promised to, although I had to threaten him.'

Next morning, with an early courier drop-off, they were ready for business. Crispin had spent the night at the holistic health centre, but was due back with a van-load of lavender within the hour. Lillian had phoned to say she would bring the labels by about seven that evening, and Janet had turned up carrying pots, double-boilers, sieves, jelly bags, funnels and ladles – amassed during a lifetime of jam-making – and clanked her way into the kitchen.

'Right, *mon capitaine*, what's first?' she looked around, rubbing her hands together. 'Let's clear some space. Let the dog see the rabbit, eh?'

Within an hour the first batch of *centpertuis* was bubbling foully, and the whole house stank. Janet, who seemed oddly immune to the stench, had been commissioned to prevent it sticking to the pan, and was poking at it with a wooden spoon. Maddy had scoured the countryside, following up leads from Mr Jacks, and had probably now bought far too much beeswax. Izzie alternated melting the wax and mixing it with the oil with cuddling Pasco. She hadn't yet broken the news to Marcus that she'd be out all night. He had been a bit iffy about the amount of work she was putting in for no financial gain – he called it a jobby, half job half hobby – and she couldn't in all honesty blame him. She was beginning to wonder herself if it was all jam tomorrow. She'd deal with Marcus later, but he got there first. She put down the spoon and delved into her handbag for her trilling phone.

'Hi. Where are you?'

'Er, at Maddy's,' she said hesitantly.

'Surprise, surprise! Look, I've got to go to Oxford. Piers has called me about the pictures. I won't be back till late, so don't bother cooking for me.'

'Oh Marcus, I was hoping you could look after the kids tonight. We've got a rush on with the balm. It's rather exciting really—'

'Sorry, can't really help this time. Got to go, darling. Bye.'

Maddy looked at her as she put the phone back in her pocket. 'Are you stuffed for tonight then?'

'It's my fault really, I hadn't arranged it properly with him and—'

'We'll do a sleepover then. Go and get their sleeping bags when you pick them up and they can all stay here. Will's been asking for ages if Charlie could stay. Go on – problem solved!'

Janet bustled over. 'All the children here together? What fun! Perhaps we could do a little treasure hunt in the garden. Bagsy Pasco on my team!'

By seven o'clock, the children were all fed and bathed. They'd flatly refused to eat in the kitchen, wrinkling up their noses at the smell, and Janet had set up a picnic area in the hall, complete with tent made out of the clothes horse, picnic rug and thermoses of Ribena. They were in seventh heaven. Good thing too, because the kitchen resembled a Chinese laundry, running with condensation and with jelly bags and pillowcases full of boiled *centpertuis* hanging from upturned stools, dripping slowly into Pyrex bowls. Earlier Crispin had dumped orange boxes of lavender sprigs on to the utility-room floor, and had had to be revived from the trauma of having to sleep on a futon and eat lentils at the holistic health centre, with a full English breakfast and copious cups of PG Tips.

'It was horrible,' he'd whispered to Izzie out of Janet's earshot. 'All those hairy legs, and they kept telling me I had too much yang energy just cos I asked if they had Sky.'

Once fortified, he was persuaded to cut up the lavender to

add to the melted beeswax and looked wonderfully incongruous stirring the jam pan for hour after hour with a wooden spoon and wearing Maddy's Cucina Direct denim apron.

'Right,' said Maddy, rubbing her hands. 'It's gone seven. Janet's doing her *Jackanory* bit upstairs, I think I've just heard Lillian pull up outside, so Crispin take that apron off – and we'll all have something to eat, then it's all systems go.'

Once more they raided the freezer and realising that the Aga and every saucepan in the house had been commandeered, had to resort to jemmying off chunks of frozen chilli to defrost and cook in the microwave. Confident that this was something he *could* do, Crispin stepped forward with his – carefully washed – chisel and soon they were all sitting down, oblivious to the chaos and dipping hunks of French bread into steaming bowls.

Replete, and with a glass of (more) good wine cradled in her hands, Izzie sat back in her chair and looked at this motley bunch around Maddy's kitchen table. What funny turns life takes, she thought. It took a moment for her to recognise what she was feeling. Her children were safe and content asleep upstairs, she was working hard on something that interested her, chattering and laughing with new friends who seemed to value her, and Marcus was finding his feet at last. With a jolt, she realised she felt happy.

Seven hours later, all she felt was knackered. Two in the morning and the production line was slowing at last, but it had been relentless all night. Janet and Maddy had been carefully measuring and blending the cooled lavender-scented oil and beeswax mixture with the strained *centpertuis* at the kitchen table. As each vatful was ready, Crispin would lug it over to Izzie, who had been voted the one with the steadiest hands for filling the pots with the least mess.

'Why me?' she'd whined.

'Darling,' Maddy had explained, 'I've seen what you can achieve with a Barbie and a sponge cake.'

The filled pots went on down the line to Lillian, who had wiped each one down using Maddy's best damask dinner napkins, having already got through a drawerful of tea towels, then snapped each one shut and carefully stuck on the labels. She carried out this task with extraordinary concentration, and, during a moment's rest, Izzie had watched with fascination as she peeled each one delicately from the backing sheet with her orange painted nails and placed it perfectly straight on each little pot.

Crispin had kept up a running total and at two-fifteen the cry went up: 'That's it. Two hundred on the pallets. Any chance of a cuppa?'

There was a ragged cheer, and everyone downed tools. They all looked utterly creased. Izzie put the kettle on again and dug out the teapot. Janet pushed back her wiry hair with exhaustion, inadvertently smearing green goo everywhere. Lillian arched her back and yawned, then went to burrow in her bag.

'I think this calls for a celebration,' she said coyly and, with triumph, plucked out a confectioner's box wrapped in ribbon. 'Doughnuts! I picked them up on the way here.' She undid the wrapper like a child. 'Wasn't sure what you'd all like, so I got a selection. Cinnamon and apple, toffee, custard and jam of course.'

'Cor, I could murder a doughnut,' said Maddy, slumping exhausted into a chair and lighting a cigarette. 'Lillian, you are a marvel. Help yourself to another pashmina!'

The next couple of weeks of deathly silence were agony. It seemed like a century ago that they had worked through the night, then borrowed Crispin's van and bombed – or rather rattled – down the M40 that miserably chilly afternoon to London, to deliver their hard-earned treasure.

Brazenly, they had planted themselves on a double yellow line and Izzie had sat nervously in the car to fend off traffic wardens, while Maddy, who had to charm the languid young girl on the reception desk into helping her, had lugged the pots up two flights of stairs to Pru's Covent Garden office. Luckily Pru had been out, because it was unlikely she would have been able to tolerate the sight of her friend in baggy joggers and a singularly unflattering jumper of Simon's. What would the vision of a client in her doorway who looked more like a bag lady have done for her business image?

Pru had called the following morning and had been suitably rude about having a reception area clogged up with palletfuls of little jars of healing balm, but since then there had been nothing. Izzie had made tentative enquires at the health food shop, but they could scarcely contain their indifference. Maddy bit her nails, smoked virtually continuously and tried to occupy herself with projects to take her mind off the wait. A call from some old London friends, trying to persuade her to join them for a week in Klosters at Easter hadn't helped. It had been such fun last year and she ached to go, but it would have made a large hole in a grand or two she simply didn't have. It was a door to a part of her life she'd have to shut firmly now. Christ, meeting the grocery bills was challenge enough. She tried to sound as upbeat and positive as she could, made some plausible excuse about not being able to leave Pasco, and tried even harder not to slam down the phone.

Every day had been punctuated with calls either from Izzie or to her, in which they tried to reassure each other that something would happen soon, *surely*? Izzie was busy with the editing job Maddy had sorted for her before Christmas – or at least she tried to take the credit for having done so – and making up time with Marcus. WorkWorld had come up with a couple of days here and there for Maddy, covering for sick staff, or those who could afford a week away in February. But each job was more dispiriting than the last – especially as she was clearly no longer trusted to deal with the public – and the evening she came home from a day spent answering the phone at a software company, during which she had managed to cut off their most important client, she drank a whole bottle of wine on her own.

Feeling like hell the next morning, and with Pasco irritable from an ear infection, she decided it was time to bite the bullet and start clearing out some of Simon's stuff. Grabbing a roll of bin liners, she resolved to fill them with his clothes to take to the charity shop in Ringford. If she did it fast enough, she reasoned, she wouldn't have to look and the memories would stay at bay.

Planting Pasco in a pool of unexpected winter sunshine on her bed with a pile of toys and fabric books, she pulled open the cupboards and set to. In went T-shirts and ties, hundreds of suits, jeans and jumpers. She ripped down belts, his bow tie and cummerbund, his dinner jacket (which had cost the earth), and his morning suit (which had cost even more). She pushed it all into the bag so fast she almost ripped the plastic.

'I'm doing fine, I'm doing fine,' she muttered like a mantra, as she filled each bag frantically, desperately trying not to think about the times he'd worn them, or to imagine someone else wearing them now. What would she do if she bumped into a man in Ringford High Street, and he was sporting one of Simon's Hermès ties or Gieves & Hawkes suits? She pulled out fleeces – hastily shoving her favourite into her own cupboard and slamming the door – polo necks for skiing, handmade shirts from business trips to Hong Kong in candy colours. Stuff, stuff, stuff. Eventually four bags bursting to the gills sat on the landing.

Pasco still seemed happy perched on the bed, thumb in mouth banging shapes with a toy hammer. The shelves were almost empty now, so she started another bag for things to throw away, things too old and worn even for the charity shop. Shoes. In went suede brogues for weekends, and leather

Oxfords for work before dressing down became *de rigueur*. Trainers, sailing shoes and walking boots, shaped to his large and wide feet. She tried not to notice the worn leather soles and still tied laces – oh how irritating it had been when he'd pulled off his shoes without undoing them! Be cross with him, she told herself. There was the old Harlequins T-shirt, and a rugby shirt from the days when he'd played for a local club on Saturday afternoons.

At the back of the shelf she found his old yellow corduroy trousers he'd loved so much but she'd persuaded him were too young fogey. She grabbed armfuls of socks, handkerchiefs, tatty T-shirts and swimming trunks. A lifetime of events. Empty clothes that now meant nothing. Meaningless and futile. And then there was the pile of his boxer shorts.

She went to grab them too, but for a fatal moment she hesitated. Then she touched them gently, running her hands over the neat pile. All brightly coloured. Flowery or striped, tartan and spotted. He'd been very particular about his boxer shorts and it had been a bit of a joke between them. Every time they had gone away he would buy a pair, as a sort of ritual. There were ones from Saks Fifth Avenue, Paris, Barcelona. It was like a world tour in pants. God, how gorgeous his body had been in them. He'd been so big and strong, muscular with fair hair on his chest and arms.

For weeks she'd buried the thought of sex, and had gone to bed each night in nightclothes as asexual as she could lay her hands on. Now her mind flooded with the memory of his warm body and about how well he knew how to turn her on. How sometimes it had been gentle and familiar, and at other times frantic and erotic. When was the last time they had made love? Had she properly shown him how much she had loved him?

Her sob came out almost like a retch, and she ran into the bathroom and heaved over the loo, again and again. She felt weak and shivery, but still she retched. The phone shrilled next to the bed. Rinsing out her mouth, tears pouring down her face, she hurried to pick it up before Pasco could reach it.

'Maddy, it's me—'

'Oh God, Izzie.' By now her sobs were almost uncontrollable, and her legs buckled under her as she slid down the side of the bed. 'I miss him. I just miss him.'

It seemed to Maddy, when Izzie had finally left, after rushing over to administer tea, tissues and tenderness, that she would not have howled so uncontrollably to anyone else. She wasn't sure she'd ever laid herself so open, made herself so vulnerable. Thinking back now it was almost embarrassing the things she had told Izzie in her hysteria. She'd railed about his annoying habits – how he never emptied the bins, took his pants off with his trousers, always mislaid important documents – and had been almost graphic about their sex life. Had she really told her about that time in Vienna? But Izzie had simply sat next to her, gently rubbing her back, and had listened without saying a word.

No, had it been anyone else on the phone earlier she would have sniffed, swallowed her grief and been brave. But somehow Izzie had made her open the floodgates and, in a debilitatingly exhausting way, she felt some kind of relief that she had cried so violently. She had rid herself of a huge burden by admitting, at last, that she was lonely, that she missed his voice and his laughter, someone to share the responsibility.

Maddy looked at her face in the mirror now and tried halfheartedly to reduce the puffiness around her eyes before she faced Little Goslings and the school playground – why did her eyebrows always go red when she cried? That night she was so exhausted, she slept more deeply than she had for ages and wasn't even wakened by Florence crawling into her bed. She just woke to her warm body curled next to hers.

'You're not doing the rest of the clearing yourself,' Izzie had ordered bossily as she left. 'I'm coming over next time.' And true to her word, she arrived on the doorstep at about nine-thirty the next morning with a bag of fresh croissants, bullied Maddy into eating them with some of Jean Luc's preserves from his box of goodies, and then they rolled up their sleeves and attacked the cloakroom. With uncharacteristic efficiency, Izzie produced a couple of boxes, and began pulling open drawers, tugging out woolly hats and mis-matching gloves.

'Your anal attitude to your wardrobe obviously doesn't extend to the cloakroom, Mrs Hoare. This is a mess.'

Her head ached with exhaustion from yesterday's out-pouring. Could she do this? 'Oh, the outdoor stuff was strictly Simon's domain. He thought this room would be like the gun room of some country squire, with a place for fishing rods, Purdey's and a brace of pheasant hanging from the ceiling.'

'What on earth is this?' squeaked Izzie, as she took down a spanking new Barbour from the peg. 'You really were going to take this country business seriously, weren't you? This is so crisp and shiny as to be almost obscene. Is it yours?'

'Right, as if you'd see me dead in something like that!' Maddy laughed finally, extracting a cricket bat from Pasco's over-enthusiastic ministrations. 'He was so proud of that – we bought it in one of those ghastly huntin' shootin' fishin' shops on Jermyn Street as a sort of celebration of our move.' She smiled ironically, remembering how he'd bought a tweed flat cap too, and had posed in front of the shop mirror. 'I made him take me to N Peal afterwards, so I could get a big cardy to shore me up against the howling country air.'

Izzie continued to hold up the offending coat in mock horror. 'He could at least have run it over a couple of times in the car to give it that beaten-up look . . .' She stopped suddenly. 'Oh Maddy, I'm so sorry, that was . . . that was really tasteless. I'm . . . honestly . . .'

The look on Izzie's face was nothing short of pole-axed. She couldn't take her eyes from Maddy's. But Maddy simply dropped the pile she was sorting and went over to take Izzie in her arms. 'It doesn't matter – I hadn't even thought you were being tactless. I have no more energy to cry anyway.' Then from nowhere she felt a bubble of laughter shoot up to the surface. 'It's quite funny really,' she snorted. 'I've got this sort of image of someone like Sue Templeton driving frantically backwards and forwards over a coat . . .' she could barely speak now, 'like . . . like Kathy Bates in that awful movie . . .'

Her tears, wonderful tears of mirth, poured down her face. Izzie started to smile uncertainly.

'*Misery*?'

'No, I'm fine really,' replied Maddy, stamping her feet and trying to control her hysterics. She could feel Izzie's shoulders shaking with laughter too, as she caught the mood.

'No, you cretin,' Izzie howled now. 'That's the name of the movie . . . Stephen King . . . with James . . . Caan . . .'

'Aaah,' was all Maddy could reply, and collapsed on to the floor rocking with laughter. Pasco waddled over to her and threw himself into her arms, and for a few moments she thought she'd be sick again, this time from the effort of laughing.

From the kitchen, they could vaguely hear the sound of ringing. 'Isn't that your mobile?' Izzie was pressing her cheeks as if in pain.

Maddy pulled herself and Pasco to their feet. 'It'll be my mother. She always calls the mobile,' she sniffed and wiped her eyes. 'She lives in some misguided hope that I'm always "out and about keeping busy".' By the time she got to the kitchen the ringing had stopped and there was a voice message. She pressed the button to listen and Izzie held her ear close to the phone too, to hear what Giselle had to say.

'Daarling, it's *Maman*. Good to see you are too busy to answer the phone, but I've just been reading the *Telegraph*. What on earth is all this about you and your friend making some cream of Luce's? Couldn't believe my eyes – it must be you. Have you taken leave of your senses?'

The message finished, and Maddy looked at Izzie in disbelief. Without saying any more, she ran to grab her purse. 'Hold the fort for a moment. I'll just see if the village shop has still got a copy,' and without looking behind her, ran out and slammed the front door.

The speed with which she dived into the shop and grabbed one of the last remaining copies of the *Daily Telegraph* must, she thought, have confirmed the villagers' growing suspicions that she had lost the plot completely since Simon had died. Maddy virtually threw the money at Miriam behind the counter, gasped a breathy 'thanks' and legged it out again.

She laid the paper on the table and smoothed it out with her hand. 'Where will it be?'

'Well, I only read the *Guardian*, of course,' smiled Izzie, superciliously, 'but it's hardly likely to be under world events or obituaries, is it? Try health and beauty.'

Maddy flicked over the pages, virtually tearing the thin paper in her haste. There, on the left-hand page, next to a big article about diet drinks, were two columns of text, with a small picture of one of their, *their*, little jars with Izzie's drawing plain to see, under the headline: 'Pots of Gold'.

Maddy ran her finger along the lines of text and read the words aloud:

Well it had to be French, didn't it? Only those clever continentals could create a beauty treatment that would be the elixir of life. But luckily for us British women, it was rediscovered by a couple of country housewives . . .

'Housewives?' Izzie gasped in disdain. 'How dare they?' Maddy read on:

These two Cotswold earth mothers, Madeleine Hoare and Isabel Stock, stumbled by accident on the notebook of a nineteenth-century relative of Madeleine's from the Cévennes region, and they have recreated at their scrubbed pine kitchen table . . .

'It's bloody limed oak,' shrieked Maddy incredulous. 'Pleeese!'

. . . a healing balm which they allege is the cure-all, treat-all cream that should be the only one to grace our bathroom shelf. The ingredients couldn't be more '*naturel*', including an obscure little plant exclusive to the vine-growing regions of France. The jar is delightful, the cream a mesmerising shade of green, and though the smell might put you off, it's no pain no gain when it comes to the pursuit of perfect skin. When I tried some on my winter pallor, I have to confess an overnight improvement. Could this discovery have us chucking out the cleansers, toners and moisturisers we so cherish? I could be convinced.

Paysage Enchanté '*Baume Panacé*' (healing balm) costs £24.99 (plus £3 p&p) for a 100ml jar and is available by mail order from Huntingford House, Huntingford GL53 0XX (01547 324867)

They both stood in stunned silence for a moment. Then read and re-read the article.

' "I could be convinced",' whispered Izzie in awe. 'Do you know what this means? Only the bloody beauty editor of the paper thinks we're on to something. This kind of editorial most cosmetic houses would kill for.'

Maddy felt panic grip her. 'She's put in my phone number, Izzie. Pru's gone and put the phone number on the ruddy press release. You know what's going to happen – we're going to be inundated with calls from wrinkled and careworn readers. And look at the price she's put – that's five times what we were charging at the Fayre. We don't take credit cards, we haven't even got much stock left. What the hell are we going to do? What's the readership of this paper?'

'Oh I don't know – million and a half?' Suddenly the phone started to ring.

It wasn't until after she got back to school and had fielded a further ten calls on the answering machine, that it stopped ringing long enough for her to get hold of Pru. She finally tracked her down in a taxi, and had to shout to make herself heard above the noise of traffic in the background.

'What the hell have you done? The phone has been non-stop all day – it's gone crazy.'

'Well that's gratitude! Actually, darling, I had no idea the papers would pick up the press release so quickly. Listen, I'll call you back this evening and we'll sort out how you can cope, but in the meantime take names and address and ask them to send a cheque payable to you. You have thirty days to fulfil a mail-order request anyway, so don't panic.'

That evening, Izzie came over after the children at both houses had been put to bed and they sat down at the table with notepads and pencils, laughing at their efficiency.

'Right, let the meeting commence,' said Maddy pompously. 'What's on the agenda?'

'Well, Madam Chairman, we have had a squillion calls from people wanting pots of gunk when we have practically no stock and no raw materials to make any more.'

'Thank you. Item two: panic! Izzie, this is dire. We're going to have to get organised. Don't we need to set up a company or something, so the cheques can be paid into that? And it would help if we could take credit cards. And what about the stock?'

'I feel sick,' said Izzie, refilling their wine glasses. 'I've always been terrible at this kind of thing – I deliver my accounts to the accountant in a shoebox. Let's face it, neither of us is renowned for our financial expertise, are we?'

'If in doubt, make a list.'

Over the next half an hour they wrote down everything they needed: bank manager, credit card facility, pots and *centpertuis*, lavender, more oil, Jiffy bags, labels and a new phone number. Valium, Maddy added as an afterthought.

She leant back in her chair. 'You know who we need?'

'Lillian.'

'Got it in one. I'll call her tomorrow, meanwhile let's phone Pru again and see what she has to say.'

Pru was remarkably uncontrite about the predicament she'd put them in. 'Frankly, darling, I'm amazed, but I think the product has just hit a nerve. Perhaps we're all fed up with the horrors of the twenty-first century – global warming, cloning, collagen injections, botox, nano-technology. With what you are offering, it's cheap at the price. I was going to put it at forty-five pounds at one point but I knew you'd blow a gasket. Now, you are both brilliant women, so get yourselves sorted and get as much help as you can. You need to decide if you want to take this seriously.' Maddy could hear her inhale on her cigarette. 'Oh, by the way, I had a call from the *Daily Mail*.' Maddy gasped. 'Nothing to worry about but they want to come up and do an interview with you both. Can I tell them Friday? But listen, girls – you're going to have to think about your image here. If we're going the "back to nature" route you're going to have to hide your Dualit toaster and forget about wearing anything Christian Lacroix. Think Mrs Beeton meets . . . I don't know, Greenpeace!'

Chapter 10

When the *Daily Mail* journalist and the world-weary photographer finally left, Izzie and Maddy slumped against the closed front door, wrung out and gasping for a glass of wine and a fag.

'Oh God!' Maddy groaned. 'I'm never going to live this down!'

The phone rang again. It had been non-stop all morning. 'Look, you get that,' Izzie heaved herself up. 'I'll get the essentials. Where's the corkscrew?'

'*Paysage Enchanté*?' Maddy purred in her professional voice. 'Yes, certainly. No, I'm sorry, we don't take credit card orders. Yes, certainly.'

She gesticulated wildly at Izzie, miming her need for a pen to take down the details. Izzie hurled a crumpled envelope and an eyeliner pencil, scavenged from the depths of her crumb-strewn handbag, and Maddy wrote down a name and the size of the order, then hung up, rolling her eyes. 'We've got to get a more efficient system going,' she sighed, adding the envelope to a pile of other scraps of paper. 'This is pitiful!'

Izzie laughed ruefully as Maddy handed back her eyeliner, now blunted beyond use. 'I reckon we've bottomed out. We couldn't get any more inefficient.'

'Don't you believe it! I've got an order here somewhere written in wax crayon on one of Pasco's nappies! Clean, of course,' she added, seeing Izzie's horrified expression as she poured out two generous glasses. 'But I was upstairs at the time, and I didn't have a notepad handy.'

Izzie looked around at Maddy's once beautiful kitchen. She'd have given a kidney to have one like it, or at least the way it had been before they trashed it for the interview. 'Do you think we got the subliminal message right for them?'

Maddy groaned theatrically. 'Well it must be right, cos it's got everything in it now I hate.'

'Yeah, yeah! I know, but it won't take long to restore to its former beauty, and if it works and the orders keep on coming in like this, we could be solvent again by, er . . . actually, I have no idea at all! And we can go back to being "cashmere Maddy" and—'

'Oxfam Izzie?' supplied Maddy helpfully, ducking the tea towel. 'OK, sorry. All right, even I can put up with it for one afternoon. You realise we're going to need help with the money side.'

'God! Is there anything we *can* do?'

'Well, we know how to make the balm – and we are pretty talented at stage design. This house looks like a set for the West End.'

Izzie gazed around at their efforts. 'Yeah, *Les Miserables*!' A delve through the cupboards earlier that morning had revealed a rich seam of props: a large pestle and mortar, a mezzo-luna chopper and board, some large earthenware bowls – all unused.

Izzie had busied herself, steaming labels off bottles of Carluccio's olive oil infused with herbs and put them out on display. A load of Robert Welch cast-iron ware was dusted off and arranged artlessly on the counters – what the hell was Maddy doing with a recipe book stand anyway? – copper-based saucepans, salt-pigs, wooden spoons. A lot of it Maddy seemed to have forgotten she ever had. Some items looked like wedding presents that had never even been opened – it was like the stock room at Divertimenti. By the end of the morning, virtually everything Maddy did use in her forays into the kitchen had been replaced by things she had never used.

The hallway had proved less of a challenge. By the judicious use of dried flower swags, bought at great cost – both in terms of money and personal credibility – from a boot-faced woman in Ringford, who took great exception to their giggling, they had camouflaged the ultra-modern light fittings. By stacking up wellies and walking boots, and the unused croquet set along the wall, they had created a reasonably homespun rustic effect.

'I can tell we've got it right,' Izzie had laughed, 'by the fact that you look like you've got a nasty smell under your nose when you stand back and look at it!'

Maddy had moaned, in mock distress, 'My house, my beautiful house! It looks like a commune. All stripped-pine, scatter cushions, macramé knickers and knit-your-own yoghurt.'

Preparing the house had been a picnic compared to transforming their own image. 'You were right, you do look like a pig without your eye make-up!' Izzie had gasped as they stood back and gazed at themselves in the bathroom mirror.

The final look they'd achieved was somewhere between Doris Day and Looby-Loo – all scrubbed rosy cheeks and neutral lippy, and thanks in no small part to Izzie's hoard of old maternity clothes.

Their enthusiasm was clearly not contagious, and the journalist and the photographer had looked afraid that they might catch something, accepting the offer of murky camomile tea without enthusiasm. The questions had been predictable, and within minutes Maddy and Izzie were working like a double act, expounding (and expanding) the virtues of Grandmère Luce as if they had known her personally.

'Yes, she was an inspiring lady, all right,' Maddy had heard herself gushing. 'In some ways, I'd like to think I could bring some of her amazing spirit into my life today, and perhaps to share it with other women. Finding her book was like a link going right back through the years!'

Izzie had winced at the mawkish claptrap, and tried very hard not to catch Maddy's eye. For some reason they had both adopted a gracious, oh-so-sincere manner not unlike that of Mrs Thatcher in her more mellow moments. It was very hard to drop, once you'd started.

The only tricky moment was when the hack had tried to steer Maddy into talking about Simon. Izzie could see Maddy's eyes narrowing – she'd murder Pru – and jumped in quickly. 'Our children are everything to us. We feel it's vital to create an atmosphere in our homes that will give them a solid basis in today's hurried world.'

Maddy had calmed down now. 'And the healing balm really works!' she chimed in. 'That's the thing to remember. By tapping into Luce's wisdom and knowledge, we're bringing women something they've lost over the years – and something they'll recognise as being of value as soon as they see it.'

Izzie now took a large glug of wine. 'Well, thank heavens that's over. Never again!'

The morning's post had brought another deluge of orders. After they'd snatched some lunch, Maddy set too again making up the recipe and Izzie, in a burst of efficiency, went through the pile of scribbled phone orders and prioritised them in date order. She'd finished punching out the figures on Will's Fisher Price calculator, and the final figure made her gasp.

'Are you sure these toy calculators work?' She turned to Maddy. 'Cos if they do, we've got about six hundred pots to make up this week.'

Maddy turned from the pan she was stirring on the Aga, 'Well, this lot is only going to do about a hundred, and that's it. We're out of ingredients. We need more of everything.'

'Right then. Where's the phone. I'm going to make some calls.'

Two hours later, she'd contacted every beekeeper in the county she could find in the phone book, but the lavender was proving a problem. She put the phone down despondently, and turned to Maddy who was with Crispin, making him a cup of coffee and a hot cross bun. 'Everybody is saying the same thing. If we buy it dried, even from the wholesaler, it's going to cost the earth. And that will slash our profit margin.'

'Why don't you ask those hairy women in Wales to sell you some of their essential oil?' he asked, spraying crumbs over the table. 'They do all the extracting and everything in the summer, when the lavender is fresh, and the oil keeps almost indefinitely. It's biothermodynamic, or something. They kept banging on about it when they were giving me the massa . . .'

He trailed off sheepishly. But not soon enough. Maddy was on his case in a flash. 'Crispin, were you about to say massage, by any chance?'

'Well, yeah. I had a bit of a headache, after the drive and everything, you know. So one of them did my aura, and then another did my meridians. I didn't ask them, or anything. And it's not like I enjoyed it . . .'

Izzie laughed, shaking her head incredulously, 'You really got your feet under the table there, didn't you? I reckon this biodynamic thing could make a great story. Maddy, have you got Pru's number to hand? If we can get hold of this lavender oil, we should tell her all about it.'

'Just as long as we don't have any more journalists here, I'll tell her anything you like!'

Over the next two days, Izzie had visited about half a dozen of the beekeepers. Although most of them had a standing arrangement with a company in a local town that supplied the cosmetics industry, they were more than happy to sell their excess to Izzie and Maddy, particularly as they offered to collect it by car.

It was Maddy's job to lure Lillian away from her lucrative temping work in Oxford. It wasn't as easy as they had hoped and she'd had to dangle the offer of lunch as a last resort. She then put in a call to Jean Luc. Izzie listened as she gabbled down the phone at him in French, too fast for her to keep up with what she was saying, though she heard her name being mentioned a couple of times.

'Right,' Maddy said when she had finished and referred to the notes she had made. 'He says he's found a bulk supplier of organic olive oil in Provence, but it don't come cheap. I'll call them later, and he's promised me a consignment of *centpertuis* by Tuesday. He's over here anyway on some other business.' Izzie worked hard to quash her glee at the news. Maddy laughed. 'He's incredulous that he's actually encouraging this stuff to grow.' She mimicked his accent: ' "I can't believe what you've got me to do, Maaaddee. A weed I struggle with for years – suddenly I'm giving it the best soil!" '

Driving home later that morning, Izzie had time to think for the first time after all the frantic activity of the last few days. Reordering the materials they needed would make a heavy dent in the mail-order money they had already deposited into Maddy's bank account. It was all getting very confusing. Just how much money did they have exactly? All the cheques were for £27.99, which didn't seem that much, but they must have banked four hundred already. She did a mental calculation.

'Fuck me sideways!' Maddy shouted incredulously when Izzie phoned her on the mobile. 'Over eleven grand? Are you sure? We're in the money, babe! If we ever manage to wash the smell of this stuff out of our hair, we should go out and treat ourselves – oh and the kids, natch!'

Half an hour later, with Pasco asleep in the buggy, they sauntered into the bank and Maddy withdrew four hundred pounds, then handed Izzie a wad of notes. 'Here you are. All of Ringford at your feet. Where do we start?'

They stood outside the bank, gazing around hopefully. 'This is scary – normally I can spend money for England, but looking round, I can scarcely contain my indifference!'

At a loss to find a single thing for themselves, they spent the next half-hour in displacement activity, and indulged the kids at Woolies. 'How come it doesn't count if you spend money on your children?' asked Izzie, from behind an armful of Action Man and Animal Hospital boxes.

Maddy pulled down a huge pack of Stars Wars Lego. 'Same as when there's no calories in their leftovers at tea.'

Armed with huge bagfuls hooked over the handles of the buggy, they made their way back to the car. 'God!' Izzie stopped in her tracks. 'I've forgotten Marcus.' Leaving Maddy with the car keys, she dashed back to the chemist and, in her haste, she grabbed the simple option – a gift pack of Clarins for Men, on special offer with a rather dinky little black toilet bag. He'd like that!

When she unloaded the spoils at home after school, the kids were delirious, and within minutes the boxes were ripped open and she was unwinding those maddening plastic-coated wires that were wrapped around Action Man's unfeasibly meaty thighs. Marcus, when he got in, was soon caught up in the atmosphere. Whisking Izzie into a frenetic and totally inept tango round the kitchen, with the children whooping enthusiastically, he seemed genuinely pleased at her excitement, and kissed her with unexpected ardour. Later she caught him poring over his new skin care, reading the instructions with the greatest attention. Maybe this was going to be the answer to everything!

Next morning, after very little sleep, Izzie was at Maddy's bright and early to make up for bunking off the day before, unable to wipe the grin off her face. Maddy looked a little puffy eyed, and Izzie suspected that bringing home treats for the kids had reminded her of far happier times. She rubbed her friend on the shoulder. 'OK?' she asked quietly.

'Yeah – fine. Really. I had a bit of a bawl last night after the kids were asleep. I wanted to get something for Simon. Silly really . . .'

The phone rang. Damn, they hadn't switched the answer phone on! But Maddy looked pleased. 'Pru! Did you speak to those *Mail* people? What did they say?'

She listened quietly as Pru spoke, frowning slightly, then glanced up at Izzie, strapping on a clean apron in readiness for the day's boiling and stirring. 'Yes, of course. If you really think we need to. I mean, things are going fine here. We're more or less managing to keep up . . . Well, of course. Will next week do? Oh all right then . . . Yes, we'll come as soon as we can!'

'Now, as I understand it from what you've both said,' concluded Pru, looking down at the sheets of paper in front of her, 'you want to keep a low profile and just tick along as you are.' She leant back in her office chair and put her pen to her lips ponderingly.

Maddy looked at her and was nervous. This wasn't a Pru she was used to. This was Professional Pru, and she didn't like the look of her at all. Suddenly she realised that things had changed dramatically. Izzie and she had become a brand, a client, a brief.

'I think,' Pru said finally, leaning forward over the desk and twiddling her pen with both hands, 'that you are wrong.'

Izzie glanced at Maddy alarmed, but Maddy could only look quizzical.

'I believe,' she went on slowly, 'that the press have focused in on this earth mother message. The cream itself works wonders, that we can't deny, and the fact that it does is what will keep it selling. But it's a tough market out there, and you are not the first to put together a natural cosmetic product. Let's face it, the country is awash with natural products.' Maddy and Izzie sat like children listening to her, both with a sense of foreboding about what she was about to say. 'But there's another side to the story of *Paysage Enchanté,* and that's you two and Old Granny Luce.'

Izzie and Maddy looked at each other again. 'Go on,' said Maddy hesitantly.

'The *Daily Mail* reporter rang me back twice after interviewing you both, wanting to know more details and to check facts about Luce's journal. And it got me thinking that our best hope of success – real success – is to major on you both and the earth mother element.' She took in their bemused faces, before carrying on. 'You are both mothers living in the countryside. Maddy is coping on her own – big sympathy vote—'

'Now hang on a minute,' Maddy interrupted, suddenly feeling very uncomfortable indeed, 'you're not exploiting—'

Pru held her hand up to stop her. 'Not exploiting, no. I just think we can get some mileage out of you both as women who run your own families, and have good traditional values. If we put the right spin on it, we can turn you into the Luces of the twenty-first century, with your farmhouse kitchen, chickens and hordes of children all with blooming health and rosy cheeks.'

Maddy wasn't sure whether she liked the idea of Rhode Island reds running amok around her Mark Wilkinson units.

Izzie had, at last, seemed to find her voice. 'Well, didn't we talk to the *Daily Mail* about that already? Won't that do the trick without . . . without . . . ?'

'Izzie, I don't really think it's enough.' Pru sounded quite gentle with her and Maddy wasn't sure whether this was out of sensitivity to Izzie's natural shyness, or, and she was ashamed for feeling so cynical, a deliberate ploy to make sure Izzie went along with what she had to say.

'I had a request this morning from *Country Lifestyle.* They want to do a profile of you both with lots of luscious vegetable garden shots, children playing in the orchard, dew on the grass, you know the sort of thing. And they want to do it soon to get it in the May issue. In fact,' she paused and referred to a sheet in front of her, 'they are dropping a feature to put you in.' She looked up. 'In PR terms, girls, that's dynamite. But you are both going to have to play up the back-to-nature card. You know, dress down a bit, bake lots of cakes . . .'

Izzie glanced at Maddy and they both smiled. 'Izzie's your woman for that!' she laughed, lighting a cigarette.

'—Izzie, those low-slung combats are too *now*, you're going to have to wear skirts, be feminine, a bit vulnerable but basically strong and capable. Maddy, those highlights are going to have to go, and, this is the hard bit, so are the fags.'

Maddy blew out a plume of smoke. 'Oh for goodness sake, Pru!'

'Exactly, *goodness* is what it's all about. You have got to be wholesome, good, pure.' She warmed to her theme. 'When Anita Roddick started the Body Shop, she lived and ate the environmental be-kind-to-animals message and that was half the secret of her success. When this *Country Lifestyle* journalist comes up – I've said Tuesday, if that's OK – you two are going to have to be as handmade and wholesome as the healing balm. Those women who slap it on every night have to believe that it will magically make them finer people. That, thanks to you, they will be better mothers and wives, they'll be superb cooks of organic wholesome foods to send their angelic children off and out happy and fulfilled. They will have crisp, fresh linen dancing on the line, a permanent smile on their face, a basket full of flowers over their arm.'

'All right, all right we get the message,' laughed Maddy, stubbing her cigarette out in the ashtray. 'Save your prose for the press release. OK, let us know when this woman wants to come, but this had better be a one-off.'

Pru looked serious. 'I don't think it will be. I have to say that the press response to this product is unprecedented in my experience. You are getting little mentions all over the place, and where the papers lead others will follow.'

'Can I smoke in here?' Maddy leant forward fifteen minutes later to address the cab driver through the glass.

'Sure, love. Just don't stub the butt out on the seat.'

'Maaaaddy,' said Izzie, reproachfully. 'You heard what the guru said.'

'Oh sod it. No one's going to see.'

The cab pulled away from the kerb and joined the queue of traffic. 'Now where did you young ladies say you wanted to go – Marylebone, was it? You know, you two look a bit familiar. Have I seen you on the telly? Or was it . . . ? I know, it was in the paper, wasn't it?'

'Nooo,' said Izzie loudly, her face creasing into a huge smile as she looked at Maddy. 'Think you must have muddled us up with someone else.'

'I've had an idea,' said Maddy suddenly, and she leant forward again to talk to the cab driver through the glass. 'Can you take us to Sloane Street instead?' She sat back in her seat. 'Let's not go home straight away – Pasco's with Janet and we've plenty of time before we need to get back. Let's go and have some fun. We've still got most of that money we took out – and the rest is in my account – so lunch is on you via me! Here begins the missing link in your education. You haven't lived until you've experienced the delights of the GTC café.'

Maddy dragged her through the door, and made a beeline for the café at the back. Izzie looked around her at the exquisite bags, furniture, silk throws and chinoiserie as if she had entered a different world. 'My mum used to despise this place. Said it was the playground of the ladies who lunch, but I think secretly she desperately wanted to come here.'

'Oh, it's still full of ladies who lunch. You'll see.'

They were early enough to secure a table quickly and, like a child on a treat, Izzie gazed around at the faces of the women seated around them, all with Peter Jones bags tucked by their feet. She leant forward to Maddy conspiratorially.

'How come they all look so bloody healthy?'

'Courcheval, darling, or perhaps Mauritius. Where else?'

'It's all so . . . entitled,' marvelled Izzie, 'in a sort of under-stated way. I bet you had your wedding list here.'

'Only part of it, darling. Peter Jones for the essentials, of course, and Les Galeries Lafayette in Paris for the French rellies!'

It took some persuading to get Izzie to have the two-course lunch ('look at the price!'), but after a bowl of soup, mountains of sun-dried tomato bread, a dainty little salad, and a glass of wine each, they both felt more relaxed, and listened in intently to the conversations going on around them.

'So how are the Northops?' brayed the sleek, tanned brunette beside them.

'Oh, busy as ever,' replied her friend, trying to get a piece of recalcitrant rocket salad into her mouth without smearing the dressing down her chin and her cream polo neck. 'Camilla's going to Cheltenham I hear.'

'Was she at Tarquin's party? Victoria said Ben was so drunk he threw up all over the Crucial Trading seagrass carpet in the hall. Alco-pops I suppose. God, they're only thirteen!'

'In our day it was straight vodka,' whispered Izzie. 'Or Lambrusco cos you didn't need a corkscrew!'

'Maddy? It is Maddy, isn't it?' She felt a hand on her shoulder, and turned to see Daisy Smythe-Mayhew, prize-winning school bitch and wife of one of Simon's old work mates. They air-kissed each other on each cheek. Mwah. Mwah. 'I hardly recognised you, you look so much . . . darker. How's everything in the shires?'

'Oh, muddling along thanks, Daisy. This is my friend, Izzie, who's from the shires too actually. We've just come up to town for a shufti.'

Daisy briefly looked Izzie over and dismissed her. 'And how are you coping?' She lowered her voice. 'So sorry to hear about

Simon and everything. Charles said things had been going so well for him.' No he didn't, thought Maddy, stiffening, I bet he hadn't got a kind word to say, the pompous old bastard.

'It's been difficult, but the children keep me sane. We've just set up a little business venture, Izzie and I.'

'Always a good idea to have a bit of pin money. Listen, I've got to dash, couple of things to do before I collect the sprogs, but do come and see us, won't you? We'd love to hear your news.'

They air-kissed again, said their farewells, and they watched as Daisy left the café like a ship in full sail, bearing GTC and Trotters carrier bags fore and aft.

'Cor! Small world, hey?' said Izzie.

'No. As Giselle would say, "thin upper crust".'

'I've never seen you in action like that before,' Izzie was wide-eyed with admiration. 'Do you really want to go and see them?'

'No, I bloody don't,' Maddy hissed through her teeth. 'Nor does she want to see me. She's not just a cow, she's as thick as shit and the only person stupider is her husband! Simon loathed him. Now come on, my girl,' she tucked some cash in under the bill and picked up her bag, 'lesson two in how the other half live, and this time it's strictly for us.'

An hour later, and they were waiting for a Circle Line train at Sloane Square station, Izzie gripping on to her stiff White Company carrier, into which she had stuffed the new pillow-cases in their Peter Jones plastic bag, too shame-faced to display the temporary deviation from her usual left-wing tendencies.

'You shouldn't have taken me into Jo Malone,' she said, as though it had been all Maddy's fault she'd parted with thirty-odd quid for some body cream. 'That was deliberately cruel.'

'Think of it as research and put it on expenses,' laughed Maddy. 'We have to see what we are up against. Did you notice how all the staff in these shops wear black suits with white T-shirts? It's sort of gear *de rigueur*. I think, old girl, it should be our mission to make sprigged cotton the new black.'

'How many mail-order requests will there be when we get home, do you suppose?' Izzie said later when they finally found a seat and the train pulled out of Marylebone. 'If yesterday's post was anything to go by, we're going to be inundated.'

'Have we bitten off more than we can chew?' Maddy gazed out of the window and into the back gardens of the houses beside the railway line. She felt light-headed after the wine at lunchtime, and despondent as she always did when she had to leave London behind. Kilburn, Dollis Hill. Neasden. How weird to think that the people who lived here, with their busy individual lives, might actually have read about them in a paper too, written out a cheque and put it in an envelope to send to *her* house. OK, maybe not Neasden.

'Without a doubt,' replied Izzie, leaning back in her seat and sighing. 'But in a way it's fun. It's actually the most fun I've had in ages.'

'Yes, but if we're not careful it's going to run away with us,' Maddy leant forward in her seat. 'We've never done this kind of thing before and we need to get ourselves sorted out. We're going to need people to help to get the pots out,' she counted the list on her fingers. 'Money to pay them, money to buy the raw materials, premises. And the children? Who's going to look after them when we're busy? I don't think Pasco is quite up to sticking on labels yet.'

'When you put it like that, it's a bit scary, isn't it? I really think we ought to try and nab Lillian full-time. She's fun, she's efficient, and she hasn't – yet – got a permanent job. Do you think she'd come and help?'

'It's definitely worth a try. At least she knows how it all works. But we need to think about the business side of it.' She glanced out of the window again. 'We need someone who could advise us – not a bank manager type. They're too terrifying and we wouldn't know which words to use.'

'Oh I don't know. I'm quite good at "can I extend my overdraft?" '

'Do you know, Izzie,' Maddy looked down at her hands sheepishly, 'until now, I've never, ever been short of money in my life.' She plucked up the courage to look up and check Izzie's reaction. She was smiling in disbelief. 'Until Simon died and left us with nothing, I had never been in a situation where I couldn't really buy whatever I wanted. Not yachts and diamonds, but if I set my heart on something, I pretty much got it. The best furniture, designer fabrics, nice clothes.'

'I'd noticed!'

Maddy smiled. She wasn't sure Izzie believed her, but she couldn't bring herself to admit how much she'd had to sell. 'But there's probably only so many jumpers and scarves Lillian will accept, and I'm not sure Tods and clam diggers are quite Crispin's scene. His diggers are more JCB . . . no, I don't like not having cash in the bank. I'm a spoilt brat really and this situation is just not me. I want to sort this whole business thing out so I never have a scare like that again. I want to know that we're handling the money right and that we make what we should.'

'OK, let's get some help. Who do we know? My parents are even vaguer about bills than I am and Marcus is "a creative" so we can forget him.'

They both looked idly at the fields and farms that now flew by past the window. It struck Maddy that Izzie never really discussed the balance of her marriage, and she wasn't sure, despite how much she had revealed about herself, just what she knew about Izzie. Her response to Jean Luc had not been quite what you would expect from a married woman. The mere mention of his name made her behave like a teenager. I might think Marcus is a jerk, she thought, but if Izzie thinks he's so great, there must be something about him to admire.

'Er, tell me,' she faltered, 'what has Marcus said about all this press response. Is he excited?'

'Well . . .' There was a millisecond's hesitation. 'Less than I'd hoped. I try not to talk about it too much what with him not working. It doesn't seem fair that everything's going right for me at the moment, especially when he's trying so hard. Men can be so proud. I consider anything I earn as being *our* money, but I think, deep down, he feels he ought to be the provider. Perhaps the extra pressure of having to step in to take care of the children has been difficult for him too, what with his photography project and all that.' Good old Izzie, loyal to the last. Maddy let the subject drop.

'How the hell are we going to fake this country thing?' said Izzie after a while. 'My wardrobe is old business clothes, half of them still have shoulder pads, and the rest is jeans.'

'Don't think I'm much better.' Maddy yawned. 'I don't think Prada would really work, do you?'

They both lapsed into silence again, and Maddy could feel her eyelids drooping.

'I've got it,' Izzie sat bolt upright and kicked Maddy's foot as she did so. Maddy started awake. 'Janet.' Izzie's eyes sparkled. 'Janet is the country icon – she's to the country what Anna Wintour is to urban chic. Do you suppose she'd let us raid her wardrobe!'

Maddy snorted. 'On yer bike, love. You're not getting me into bloody Alpaca sweaters and thong sandals. I'm not that desperate!'

'The whole prospect does sound pretty dire,' Izzie conceded, and slumped back in her seat. 'I was too late for the hippy era. We're going to need a make-over to get the image right.'

'And if Pru gets her way, we'll be making the Summer of Love look like the miners' strike.'

Izzie's prediction had been right. There was a massive pile of mail-order requests waiting for Maddy when she got home at three-thirty. Janet, once again, had done her angel of mercy bit taking care of Pasco while they'd been in London. She was obviously out now collecting Will and Florence. Maddy smiled at the vision of her standing in the playground, among the appliquéd army.

She picked up the pile, there must have been a couple of hundred of them, and carried them into the study to join the others which were piled up on the desk and all over the floor. There were envelopes in all shapes and sizes, some typed, some handwritten in big scrawly writing, others in tiny anal script – all wanting one thing, a piece of a miracle. Again the enormity of responsibility washed over her. The Easter holidays were looming and what on earth was she going to do with the children when there were all these orders to get out?

By the time the aforementioned rushed in, Maddy had gulped down two mugs of tea, smoked several cigarettes, first checking that the Wholesome Police didn't have their binoculars trained on her window, and was feeling more human. She made a fresh cup for Janet and persuaded her to have a biscuit and sit down at the table while she started making supper.

'How did it go in the Smoke?' Janet enquired, dunking her ginger biscuit in her tea.

Maddy laughed wryly. 'Yes, smoke. That came up among other things,' and as she put a pan on to boil for pasta and chopped up bacon for carbonara, she told Janet all about Pru's marketing plan. 'It's just not us, Janet,' she said. 'I'm about as much earth mother as Joan Crawford.' She put down the knife and took a deep breath. Oh what the hell.

'Janet, you're the right sort of person for this image. You're such a good person and I'm just flighty – and obsessed with designer labels.'

'Oh no, Maddy, you're so elegant. Everybody in the village thinks so.'

'Well, that's sweet of you to say so. But Izzie and I just wondered whether, just for this *Country Lifestyle* interview, you would let us borrow some of your . . . er . . . lovely clothes,' she finished lamely.

'What a thrill!' gushed Janet. God, this woman was game for anything. 'I've got a barn dance on Saturday to organise and Sunday, well, that's a work day for us God botherers as you know, but can you both come over on Monday and we'll see what we can dig out. I'm not sure anything I have will be right, and of course it'll all be far too big for you both, but with a couple of belts and a following wind . . .'

Right, thought Maddy the following morning, Thursday. One problem sorted and just the small issue of honouring hundreds of mail-order requests and a company to establish. After another long day at Izzie's, straining more *centpertuis* into the giant vats Izzie had tracked down at a catering wholesaler, she collected Will from a superheroes party at Ringford Community Centre and limped home aching with stiffness and exhaustion. The evening was a trying one. Will was too fractious to do his school reading, and Florence flatly refused to put on her nightie, opting instead to go to bed in her pink ballet tutu. Too weary to care about either issue, she gave in and by the time she had finally settled them down enough to sleep, it was well past eight o'clock.

She was drinking a glass of wine and pulling off bits of meat from a cold chicken in the fridge – too exhausted to bother cooking herself supper – when the phone rang.

'Maddy darling, it's Peter.'

'Oh hi,' said Maddy through a mouthful. 'This is an unexpected pleasure – I didn't know *Maman* let you near the phone!'

He laughed his deep, aristocratic laugh. 'She's gone to a charity fashion show with Josephine in town, so I have a lovely evening of peace and the crossword. Now listen – just a thought but I'm playing in a seniors' golf match over the weekend, and I'm driving down tomorrow. Can I drop in on my way and steal a cup of coffee from you?'

'Oh I'd love that. I might be up to my ears in beeswax, but so long as you don't mind that. What time shall I expect you?'

Peter's big Mercedes pulled in to the drive on the dot of eleven, as he had predicted. He really was an enigma, thought Maddy, as she watched him get out of the car in his yellow Pringle V-neck and golfing trousers. He was one of those constants in her life. A man of few words, solid, laconic, distant. At first she'd resented him for not being her real father, but he had simply taken her teenage moodiness, and later the arrogance of her twenties on the chin. Then suddenly he would surprise her. Her wedding, for example, which had been out of this world, the cheque pressed into her hand at Christmas, and then this, a visit out of the blue. She suddenly felt intrigued.

He gave her an awkward hug and pressed a huge bunch of yellow parrot tulips into her hands on the doorstep and, inviting him into the kitchen, she bustled about exclaiming how lovely they were and finding a suitable vase.

'There's a very odd smell in this house,' he said, bending his tall frame into a kitchen chair and taking Pasco on to his knee.

'Oh that's our secret ingredient! Not very appealing, is it? But the addition of a bit of lavender takes the edge off things.'

'How's it going? I keep seeing bits and pieces about you everywhere, and Giselle has even taken to tearing bits out when she sees them and sticking them in a file.'

'It's OK,' said Maddy hesitantly, putting a mug of coffee in front of him but out of Pasco's reach. 'The response has been really quite amazing and Pru – you remember Pru Graves, the one who made a pass at Simon's brother at our wedding?'

'Did she ever find the rest of her clothes at the end of the party?'

'Boy, she was drunk, wasn't she? Well, she's quite the businesswoman now, runs her own PR empire and is giving us her advice. She says that the response has been unprecedented and that we need to get ourselves sorted.' Maddy sat down opposite him with her coffee cradled in her hands. She was desperate for a fag, but had only allowed herself one so far this morning. 'Honestly, Peter, you should see the response we've had. Come and look at this.' She extracted Pasco from his arms, before he smeared jammy dodger into Peter's pristine sweater, and led the way through to the study, throwing open the door dramatically.

Peter laughed deeply at the envelopes piled haphazardly everywhere. 'It looks like Santa's grotto in early December.' Pasco started whinging, desperate to wriggle out of her arms.

By the time she came downstairs after putting Pasco down for a nap, Peter was sitting at the table again and had commandeered a piece of scrap paper from the sideboard.

'This is what you need to do. You need an accountant.' He scribbled down the name Geoff Haynes on the paper. 'Talk to this guy. I used to have dealings with him in the City, and he lives out this way now.' He put the number next to the name. 'Next you want to open a business account, with a trading name. Geoff will tell you that you need to set up a limited company. He'll also advise you on VAT, mail order and so on. Next you need premises. There must be industrial units around Ringford. Call a commercial estate agent. Don't Suggs & Travis have a branch here?' As he made each suggestion, he wrote it down.

The list seemed to go on and on. Lawyers, professional indemnity, health and safety, staffing. By the second cup of coffee, Maddy had given up and lit another fag.

'Oh I wish Simon was here. He'd have explained it all to me. He was so dynamic about this sort of thing.'

Peter looked at her, aware that he was bamboozling her with details. Suddenly he put his hand on hers. 'The irony is, my darling, that if Simon were here none of this would have happened. And for the first time in ages there is an excitement in your eye – in fact, it might almost be the first time I've ever seen it.' Maddy smiled a little uncertainly. This was rather too honest.

'You've been a lucky girl all your life. And for once you are doing something because you have to. Your husband was a wonderful man in many ways, but he was an idealist.' Maddy frowned. 'Workflow Systems would never have been the hit he wanted, but still he went and sunk all his savings and everything you made on the house in London into it.'

'How do you know?' Maddy finally got out.

'Once a City man always a City man. I watched his progress with interest, though of course I wouldn't have dreamt of wading in with advice. He was . . .' Peter struggled for a moment to find the most apt word, 'impetuous, and I'm afraid to say it was a trait which never did much for his career.'

'Oh Peter, do I really want to hear this?'

'No, maybe not. But I want you to realise that, in a way, he has given you a fantastic opportunity. The chance really to use that pretty sharp brain of yours, because I may be your old fool of a stepfather, but I have watched you grow up. I love you very much, and I know you better than you think.'

Half an hour later, he heaved himself out of the chair and said his goodbyes. 'Darling, just call me if you want any help.' He hugged her really warmly this time. 'I'll do anything I can. It keeps the old brain ticking over, and keeps me out of your mother's way.'

She watched him from the front door, as he got back into the car. What a surprise he was.

'Oh, by the way,' she shouted as he wound down the window to wave, 'where is your golf match? Do you have much further to go now?'

He smiled, called, 'Hertfordshire,' and pulled out of the gate.

Chapter 11

Priorities, priorities! Izzie and Maddy were redefining theirs by the minute. With the threat of another interview hanging over them, everything else faded into insignificance.

'I had no idea we were going to be subjected to this kind of scrutiny,' Maddy complained, swigging strong coffee like it was going out of style. 'These people will be wanting to go through my knicker drawer next. And as for giving up smoking! It's the bloody limit! What other pleasures do I have in life?'

'Well, speaking as someone who *has* gone through your knicker drawer, I can see that would fill a whole issue of *Country Lifestyle*. Thanks goodness it's only us they're interested in – we won't take more than a double-page spread.'

It was Monday and they were due at Janet Grant's house to find suitable outfits for the photo shoot. They decided to walk – a concession to clean living – and the crisp air nipped colour into their cheeks and, less attractively, noses as they strode along. The whole journey took ages because Pasco insisted on jumping in every ice-covered puddle in his tiny red wellies.

The drive leading up to the handsome rectory was overhung with branches that threatened to whip them in the face if they strayed too close to the relatively mud-free verges. They hopped along, avoiding the pot-holes as best they could and passed by a large and elegant bay window, bedecked with stickers – CND, Amnesty, Greenpeace, Musicians' Union – and little stained-glass panels depicting cats, lighthouses, irises. The effect was like looking through a kaleidoscope. Inside they could make out a large table with several lumpy shapes spread around it. One of the lumps detached itself, and waved – Janet.

'Come round to this door,' came a disembodied voice. 'The front one sticks – we never use it,' then Janet's cheery, shiny face appeared round the corner of the house. 'Come in, come in! Lovely to see you both. I've been looking out some bits and bobs.'

In the gloomy house, the clutter and dust failed to disguise the beautiful proportions of the arched hallway, and despite jackets hung on every doorknob and over the tops of open doors, the beauty of the panelled wood was undisturbed. A broad curving staircase with slender balusters was so encumbered with piles of books, clothes, papers and crockery that only a narrow path remained up the middle of the worn runner.

Janet led the way into the kitchen – the room with the bay window and a strong smell of boiling marmalade. Here, added to the disorder, were two teenagers, a pseudo-goth girl and a droopy, skateboard-type boy, with loose-fitting sweatshirt and enormously wide jeans. He reminded Izzie of a dripping candle. They eyed the visitors with silent hostility.

'Tamasin and Oscar,' trilled Janet. 'My younger two. Cosmo and Jamilla are away at uni.'

Tamasin made a quick inventory of their clothes from the corner of her eye, Izzie noticed. Oscar blushed furiously and pulled a woolly hat down further down. 'Tammy and I had such fun this morning, sorting through my old things . . .'

'All your things are old,' hissed Tamasin, glaring at her mother's plump rear as she bent over to pick up a laundry basket from the flagged floor.

'Well at least I'm conserving the world's resources, sweetheart. I know how important that is to you! So here you are. Take your pick.'

'Mother, you can't seriously be proposing to lend your hideous clothes to . . .'

Izzie decided to take action and reached out to shake Tamasin's unwilling hand before she realised what was happening. 'I'm Izzie and this is Maddy. Lovely to meet you – and you, Oscar. Yes, your mother has kindly agreed to let us borrow some of her clothes for a magazine shoot we're doing later on this week. They are perfect for the image we're trying to project. I guess you can regard it as dressing up – rather like you're doing with your goth look. Now, in '78 on the King's Road it was all about . . .'

An astonishing transformation took place. Tamasin sat bolt upright, her black-lipsticked mouth open like a child's and her eyes suddenly bright. 'You were *there*? Like actually *there*?'

Izzie decided to camp it up a bit. 'Oh yes, naturally – we all were. Malcolm, Johnny, Jordan, Vivienne. You just bumped into people all the time. I remember one time with Jimmy Pursey in this changing room at Flip in Covent Garden. Well, I won't go into that now . . .'

Oscar looked puzzled, but more animated. 'Jordan?' he croaked. 'The one with the—'

'No, you cretin,' snapped Tamasin. 'For God's sake – we're talking about important political gestures here. An empowered youth movement. Not some slapper with implants.' She turned back to Izzie. 'Go on!'

Izzie knew she'd caught her fish, and began to reel it in. 'Some other time, maybe. It's so kind of you to help us again, Janet.' She smiled at the older woman. 'This is the second time you've baled us out – and I've got a feeling it won't be the last.'

'Nonsense,' laughed Janet, looking unusually bashful. 'It's lovely to be able to help, and to get a chance at playing with these adorable little children of yours.' Pasco was already clamped to Janet's sturdy leg, and was starting to investigate the basket. 'Now, sweetie, what do you think would suit Mummy in here?'

Item after item, one scarcely different from another, was dragged out of the basket. All dung-coloured and shapeless, they could have passed for floor cloths but Janet held them up like treasures, 'Oh these dungarees!' She didn't notice her daughter theatrically sticking her fingers down her throat. 'They're marvellous with this little cambric blouse. I've looked out some shoes too.'

She gestured to an amazing array of what looked like leather Cornish pasties.

'Cor! Have you contacted the Birkenstock museum? They'd pay a fortune for a collection like this!' Maddy goggled at the display that now decked the kitchen table and most of the floor. 'I think we've struck gold.'

Half an hour later, Maddy and Izzie packed their choice into recycled plastic bags. With real emotion, Maddy and Izzie hugged Janet goodbye, aware of the calculating, puzzled gaze of Tamasin, who was clearly incredulous that anyone could be more interested in her mother than in her. They were just struggling down the drive with the bags when Oscar loomed up beside them. 'I'll help you – if you like. I can carry them for you. You shouldn't . . . Well, I'll do it – if you want.'

Maddy shot him a killer smile and he flushed violently. 'Thanks, Oscar! You're a darling.'

On the way back to Maddy's house, he gradually opened up. He played in a band, he wanted to take up surfing, he read science fiction, he was hoping to find some work during the holidays and at weekends (Izzie made a mental note of that fact, just in case) – every teenage cliché falling into place with a resounding thud. But underneath the veneer of apathy, he was as kind, thoughtful and solid as they would have expected a son of Janet's to be. He mumbled a goodbye to them at the door, suddenly embarrassed again, and shambled off home. Inside, and at Maddy's insistence, they carefully laundered the clothes on a delicates wash, with loads of fabric conditioner, then put them to dry over the Aga.

'We may have to dress like peasants,' complained Maddy, spraying the damp garments with the best part of her new bottle of Jo Malone Lino nel Vento, 'but we don't have to smell like them!'

The next day and with Maddy lunching with Lillian, Izzie's project was to prepare for the *Country Lifestyle* interview. She took a long cool look at the house and garden. Pru had been right in her debriefing after the *Daily Mail* feature hit the news-stands. They really hadn't been convincing enough.

She tried to imagine what Pru would say . . . 'Think peasant – but sexy. More organic, darling. I want to smell the authenticity!' OK then – this called for some capital investment.

The out-of-town supermarket in Ringford prided itself on its out-of-season fruit and veg – 'queer gear' they called it. Into her basket went everything that looked luscious and wholesome and she returned to Huntingford House in triumph!

An hour later the kitchen and hallway were bestrewn with galvanised buckets of eggs, bowls of earthy mushrooms, pots of growing herbs (plucked from the plastic and cellophane wrappers and plunged into clay pots of compost). Janet's quilts and woolly wraps replaced Maddy's suede jackets and pink Boden mac, and Izzie had carefully rubbed soil into the gleaming limestone floor.

'It looks like shit!' exclaimed Maddy delightedly as she arrived back. 'You're a genius! Let's have a cup of coffee and then we'll tackle the garden together once we've picked up the kids. Have we got anything to feed them?'

'Yeah – I did Tesco. Sausages, pizza, alphabet potatoes, pasta and peas. Everyone's taste catered for.' Izzie put the kettle on. 'How did it go with Lillian?'

'She's a funny old stick,' sighed Maddy, pulling off her shoes and wiggling her toes. 'She's so prim and proper – Simon used to reckon she needed a good rogering – but d'you know I think we may have underestimated her. It took two dry sherries to get her to loosen her stays a bit – and by the end she was quite pink in the face and giggly. Thanks.' She took a gulp from the mug Izzie put in front of her. 'She earns a packet it turns out, and there's no way we could match what she's getting, but I think she liked it here. She kept talking about that night with the team and the doughnuts, and I have to say I shamelessly played on it.' Maddy smiled smugly. 'She starts on Tuesday.'

'Result!' Izzie punched the air. 'This calls for a biscuit.'

'No it doesn't,' said Maddy, reaching for her bag. 'This calls for a fag.'

Ten minutes later Maddy set off to collect all the children, after Izzie had run through the drill at St Boniface's, and left Pasco helping Izzie prepare supper. With everything cooking away in the Aga, they wandered out into the almost untouched garden. Among the dormant shrubs, daffodils were starting to peep their heads, and purple crocuses and snowdrops nestled around the bases of the trees. Box plants and tatty lavender lined the brick pathways. Someone long ago had obviously designed it with care, but now the remnants of last summer's perennials still cluttered the borders and slimy leaves clogged the bases of the hedges. 'Just you wait and see, Mr Pasco,' she said, nuzzling his ear. 'It may not look much now, but by tomorrow, it will even impress Alan Titchmarsh.'

The children piled out of Maddy's car a short time later and ran screaming with excitement up the stairs, leaving a heap of school debris in their wake. 'Supper won't be long,' Izzie called after them.

'Well,' said Maddy, dropping her keys on the sideboard. 'St Uglyface's was an education. I can't remember the last time I saw shell suits, and so many of them in one place. I must alert

Vogue that they are staging a comeback. And what about that woman who looked like Jimmy Saville? Frankly some of them gave me an apocalyptic vision of what can happen when cousins marry.'

Izzie chuckled. 'You snob! Better steer clear of Jean Luc then.'

'I'm sure I heard someone call a child Lacey-Marie. What's that about?'

'I thought you were impressed by double-barrelled names? We've got plenty of them at St B's too you know . . . the trouble is, it's their first names.'

Fed and replete, the children went out into the garden to burn off some energy, pursued by their mothers. 'Right, I've got a plan,' said Izzie. 'The magazine is bound to want to photograph your gracious garden, so here's what we do . . .'

By the next morning, which dawned bright and sunny, they had perfected their spiel. One thing Pru had stressed was that they weren't to be New Age in the orthodox sense – not Glastonbury and free love. They were to be in the vanguard of a New New Age, so New, in fact, that it was Old. Well, it had made sense when Pru had said it . . . This wasn't the quasi-Eastern stuff people had been kicking around since the turn of the millennium – the yoga, the chakras, the yin/yang bullshit. This was to be a return to pagan European spirituality, with female wisdom in harmony with nature and in tune with the seasons. That was why Izzie knew the garden had to be just right. She'd seen photos of the veg gardens at Villandry in the Sunday papers and that, in a kind of tatty version, was what she had wanted to achieve.

They were lying in wait for the journalists this time, seasoned campaigners that they now were, like actors awaiting their cue. Izzie was in the back garden, with a cotton scarf tied round her head and a hoe in one hand. Maddy had rolls, bought from the deli that morning, warming in the Aga ready to pop into a huge basket lined with dock leaves. As the Alfa crunched its way up

the drive, Izzie threw herself into concentrated hoeing – realising belatedly that she didn't actually know what this entailed.
But she swung the metal bit at the bottom to and fro a bit,
trying not to damage any of their arrangement. Once she was
reasonably sure she'd been clocked, she turned round and gave
the newcomers a seraphic smile and a wave of welcome.

'Oh, I'm sorry. I must have lost track of time. When I'm out
here, I just forget everything else. It's so peaceful! Let me
introduce myself. I'm Isabel Stock. You must be Araminta,
and Giles, is it? Lovely to meet you. Shall we go into the house?
I think Madeleine is still baking for the day.'

These two are a bit posh, Izzie reflected worriedly. Araminta
was unhealthily thin, very fair, very county, although she looked
like the sort who'd be allergic to horses. Giles was the beefy
type, resplendent in thick cords, a waistcoat (he would have
pronounced it 'wesskit') and the sort of horrible tweed jacket
that country blokes wear shooting. He was lugging an alumi-
nium box of cameras and seemed to do most of the talking.

'Smashing part of the world this. Used to have a bit of a bolt
hole over Rousham way. Jolly cold in winter, though. Could
never get the bloody fire going. Took a girlfriend down there
one time – she had to skip with my dressing gown cord in the
morning to get warm. Funny thing – never really saw her after
that.' Funny thing, thought Izzie. Is missing the subject out of a
sentence part of the curriculum in public school?

They went through the story again, with far more aplomb
this time and took it in turns to bustle about like headless
chickens, engaging in pointless domestic tasks – wiping mushrooms, pretending to churn butter (they'd tipped a few spoon-
fuls of marge in the bottom of the tub and produced it with
pride after a couple of turns of the crank), prodding at the
centpertuis, and slowly melting the beeswax. Pasco pottered
around the floor, looking a bit girlie in one of Janet's treasured
baby smocks. They were both hoping he wouldn't hitch it up to

reveal his disposable nappy. By the time they provided lunch – goat's cheese quiches and a gnarly salad, distressed to make it look home made – they'd already posed for at least two rolls of film. It seemed to be going rather well.

As they made their way out into the garden, Izzie could hear herself waffling on about the products. 'We believe strongly in natural remedies – organic, of course – and we use them on ourselves and the children – and the animals.' What the hell had made her say that?

'Oh you keep livestock too?'

'Um – yes. Of course. Not much, you now, just some chickens and a goat or two.'

'Oh, maybe we could do some pictures with them later. That would be terrific.'

'Ooh no,' said Izzie hurriedly. 'The . . . the billy goat is very aggressive – doesn't like men. He'd butt Giles soon as look at him!'

'So would I,' breathed Araminta fervently. 'But he's got a fiancée.'

It didn't take long to set up the first shots in the garden. Against the background of apple trees, Izzie and Maddy posed decoratively, making sure that their petticoats showed below their dirndl skirts.

In the vegetable patch, the serried ranks of broccoli were wilting a little, even though Izzie had watered the florets when she'd stuck them into the ground. The leeks were standing up well, though, as were the carrots, bought at huge expense with leaves still attached and thrust into the soil in neat rows. There was a sticky moment when Maddy caught one of the red cabbages with the heel of her clog, and it rolled out of alignment with the others. Fortunately, Araminta and Giles were engaged in a rather heated private conversation of their own, and didn't notice Maddy busily trying to nudge it back in place.

The couple broke off and continued with the shoot in a slightly embarrassed way. They'd got a lovely scene set up, with Maddy holding a basket over one arm, while Izzie sat on a wooden bench, struggling to pod peas. What was it with mange-touts?

When Crispin arrived back with the children, he'd entered into the spirit of it all – if anything a little too enthusiastically. All collarless shirt and moleskin trousers (tied with string below the knee, presumably to keep his ferrets where he wanted them). He introduced himself as the gardener, and Izzie let him wax lyrical about the soil, and the composting operation he claimed to have set up.

The children's costumes were not quite so successful. Izzie and Maddy had laid out four outfits in Florence and Will's bedrooms, and left instructions that they were to put them on as soon as they got back from school. Just like dressing up – what fun! The girls had complied reasonably well and looked ducky in their little pinafore dresses, but Florence appeared in her Barbie clippy-clop shoes and Jess was waving a magic wand. The boys had got halfway there – Will had donned the cord breeches but had on his *Toy Story* check shirt and cowboy holster. Charlie had put on all the gear but had also found some hair gel and a pair of sunglasses – Men in Taupe. The children were all ravenous, as ever, and a mutiny was steadily brewing over the lack of Jaffa Cakes, normally a permanent fixture on the kitchen table. Wholemeal shortbread just didn't fit the bill. They were pressed into staying still for the last few shots with whispered promises of as many Jaffa Cakes as they could eat, and Araminta and Giles pulled out of the drive at last.

Over supper – peanut butter sandwiches and a mountain of biscuits by way of compensation – Izzie voiced something that was worrying them both: the looming spectre of the Easter hols.

'Well, I hate to say it, but once again state wins over private! We only get two weeks at St Boniface's and they can do the play scheme for the first week. My parents, God bless 'em, have offered to have them for the second, so I'm going to be able to work pretty much as normal.'

'Yeah, yeah! I know – pay more, get less. But can Charlie spell bugger? You see, we get a better class of swear words at Eagles. I'm just going to have to muddle through with the kids here. I mean, it works all right with Pasco, so it can't be all that much worse, can it?'

Izzie shrugged eloquently and passed along the Jaffa Cakes. 'We'll soon see, won't we?'

Geoff Haynes, the 'accountant' Peter had suggested, was definitely more of a Geoffrey. Geoff was far too common for a man of Haynes' imposing presence. Nor was he the stringy, greasy stereotype Maddy had always imagined accountants to be. And it wasn't just his height – though he was a towering six foot two at least. He had the dark grey suit, perfect midnight blue shirt and cufflinks (always a sign of class) of a man who would cut a much more appropriate dash in a board room in Canary Wharf than on Ringford High Street.

He looked too young to be completely retired – he couldn't have been more than fifty – but when Maddy had called him over the weekend, he had been evasive about the type of companies he had worked with in London, just referring to the bit of consultancy he did 'here and there'. She'd come across types like him before though, through work events with Simon, and gut instinct told her that he had been involved in some fairly blue-chip stuff. He was certainly more FTSE than face balm, and anyway Peter wouldn't have put her in touch with a wide boy, would he?

In fact, Maddy suspected that Peter had already squeezed in a phone call to Geoff since his visit on Friday, and when Izzie and she met him the following week at Locations, a rather chi-chi joint in Ringford (or, correction, the only chi-chi joint in

Ringford), he seemed a bit more briefed and ready for their sales pitch than perhaps he ought. Maddy just made a mental note to thank Peter when she got home.

Pen at the ready, she had knuckled down to listen to what he had to say. After a couple of hours and a couple of bottles of very drinkable Bordeaux, she had pages and pages of information about what the two of them needed to do to get the business kosher.

'I think, ladies,' he concluded as he stirred his coffee and flashed a fabulous set of teeth, 'that you have a very interesting idea here, and if it would help I would be delighted to act as your "consultant", if you will. Leave the tiresome details to me. You just need to concentrate on getting your product out, but we can arrange regular meetings, perhaps twice a month while things are getting under way and then take it from there.'

'But Geoff . . . rey,' drawled Izzie, her face flushed from the effect of the wine, and pretty punch drunk by the force of his dynamism, 'you can't be doing this out of a favour to Maddy's stepfather. How much do we pay you for your services?'

'Let's just see, shall we?' he replied. 'I'll very much take a back seat, and we'll see how things pan out. Perhaps when you float the company, I can become a shareholder.' They all laughed heartily at this – imagine Maddy and Izzie on the stock market with their little pots of gunge.

Out on the street, he kissed them both on the cheek in a very gentlemanly fashion and they all made a date to meet again the following week.

'He's a bit of a dish,' giggled Izzie, taking Maddy's arm as they walked off down the street. 'That distinguished grey hair and those twinkly eyes. I could rather go for him.'

'You are a woman of eclectic tastes, Mrs Stock. I thought you went for the bronzed agricultural type.'

'Oh give over,' laughed Izzie and punched her, rather too enthusiastically, on the arm.

The following morning they met at nine-thirty outside the bank and, with Pasco holding hands alongside, they made a beeline for the business manager. The whole ordeal was pretty painless, no thanks to Pasco's attempts to dismantle the point of sale boards, and within minutes they had opened a healthy business account with the funds to date transferred from Maddy's account. Izzie rubbed her hands with glee. 'Once that fat chequebook arrives, it's pay day!'

By the next day, Lillian was ensconced in Maddy's study. She had arrived like a gust of wind in a curious pale green mohair coat which, with her orange hair and one of Maddy's cream pashminas, made her look not unlike the Irish flag. Within minutes she had unloaded a PC from the back of her car ('I filched it from Workflow Systems before the liquidators moved in,' she explained sheepishly), had handed an astonished Maddy a list of stationery she would need, and was beginning to put names and addresses on to a database.

'Well, Hurricane Lillian is here,' whispered Maddy to Izzie when she arrived later on in the morning. 'I offered her a cup of coffee a few minutes ago, but she says she doesn't have a break till eleven.'

'At least someone knows what they are doing around here.' Izzie took off her coat and hung it over the back of the kitchen chair. 'I had a call from that business banker yesterday afternoon. She said she didn't want to say anything in front of you at the branch yesterday, but Marcus and my banking record is so poor they are a bit dubious about allowing me to open another account.' She slumped into the chair, almost in tears. 'They say I need a reference. Who the hell will vouch for me?'

Maddy stopped midway through filling the coffee mugs. 'I don't believe it. They can't do that!'

'Oh Maddy darling. You are so wonderfully naïve. Of course they can. I don't think Marcus and I have been in credit since he was made redundant. Once the mortgage payments and all that go out each month, the bank has to fund everything. I almost wrote to them last year to thank them for our Christmas presents. She was very apologetic but certainly got her point over.'

'Well, I'm phoning Peter.' And before Izzie could stop her, she lit a cigarette – her first of the day, boy was she doing well – picked up the phone and was dialling.

Rather disconcertingly Peter confirmed everything Izzie had said. 'They are powerful institutions, these banks. Listen, darling, leave it with me and I'll make a few calls. Would Izzie mind giving me her banking details, and I'll see what I can do?'

'Now sod them and listen,' said Maddy, putting down the phone. 'We've got work to do. Here's Lillian's list – and we need a ton more Jiffy bags. I'll get on with straining the next batch. Can you get down to that wholesaler outside Ringford and get the stuff from this list? Oh Izzie, get . . .'

'. . . a receipt!' laughed Izzie and slammed the door behind her.

Will and Florence both broke up for the Easter holidays the following Friday lunchtime. Bloody private schools, thought Maddy again, as she collected Will, plus his bin liner full of Easter cards and fluffy chicken pictures which she'd have to leave lying around the house for a time until it was safe to bin them.

'Maaaddy,' came a shriek from across the car park as she stuffed pump bags and the children into the car. Sue Templeton, the other disadvantage of private schools, loomed into view, with Josh and Abigail-the-angelic by her side. 'I haven't really seen you for simply ages. You seem to fly in and fly out these days. And who on earth was that chap who collected them last week in the corduroys tied up with string? Keep hearing about you everywhere. Hardly recognised you and Izzie in your . . . unusual outfits. Quite the country image you appeared in the *Mail*.'

She looked Maddy up and down. Her baseball cap to hide her filthy hair, baggy jeans and fleece, thrown on in haste after a morning (and most of the night before) spent slaving over hot wax and lavender oil, was a far cry from her normal sartorial elegance and it wasn't lost on Sue. She seemed nonplussed.

'I'm itching to try some of your cream stuff,' she said, unconscious of the irony. 'It sounds intriguing. Linda says she put some on Alasdair's eczema and it's made the world of difference.'

'Well,' replied Maddy, fervently encouraging the children into the car and fastening their seat belts, 'you can't beat nature and natural products.'

'Mum,' yelled Will from the back seat, 'can we go to McDonald's?'

'No, darling,' said Maddy through her teeth. 'I've made some lovely fresh soup at home.'

'But we always go at the end of ter—'

'Come on, everyone,' she added hastily, slamming the car door. 'Got to get back. Lovely to see you, Sue. I'll be in touch.' And she was out of the car park like Damon Hill on speed.

Despite the hours they had put in during the last few days of term, and the help offered by Crispin and the ever-wonderful Janet, they were way behind with orders and still requests were pouring in. The biggest problem was space. Izzie's house was really not big enough to accommodate the mixing operation, though it would have been ideal without her children there, and now that Maddy's children were under their feet demanding biscuits and juice every few minutes, Maddy's kitchen was beginning to resemble a Victorian sweatshop.

Breaking point came one sunny morning a few days later, while Izzie and Maddy were up in Maddy's bedroom checking labels for printing quality. The floor was strewn with sheets over which they were poring, when there was a knock at the window. Maddy looked up.

'The gutter,' Crispin shouted and gesticulated through the glass. 'It's finally come down. I'll just go off to the merchant's and get another. It's going to rain tomorrow and you'll need it.' Maddy gave him the thumbs-up and as he disappeared down the ladder went back to her checking. Several labels were faded where the ink had started to run out and she was marking these with a red pen, when she heard another knock. She looked up. There, face pressed to the glass, was Florence.

'Mummy, look! I'm up the ladder.'

'Oh Christ, Izzzzie.' They both jumped up like greyhounds out of the trap. 'Get downstairs to the bottom quick. I'll try and get her through the window.'

'Now, Florence darling, just hold on to the top of the ladder – tight.' She tried to ease up the sash, but it had stuck and as she tried to force it, she could see Florence's initial delight at her adventure turning into sheer terror.

'Mummy, it's wobbling.' Her bottom lip was wobbling even more.

'It's OK, darling. Mummy's here,' she shouted, 'and Izzie will be right behind you any minute.' She took off her shoe and tried to nudge the top of the frame, chipping off the paint as she did so.

'Mummy, I'm scaaaared.' Florence was wailing now.

'Don't panic. We'll have you down in no time, and then we'll all have ice cream.' What the hell use is Ben & Jerry's at a time like this, she thought desperately as she abandoned the shoe and bashed the frame with the heel of her hand.

'It's all right, sweetheart, I'm here.' Maddy could hear Izzie's gently reassuring voice, and saw her head appearing behind Florence on the ladder. 'Now just do as I say, and it'll be fine.' She watched as, carefully and slowly, Izzie helped Florence take each rung, one at a time, until they were out of sight.

Legging it downstairs, she shrieked, 'Lillian, here quick! We've got a problem.' Lillian came rushing out as Maddy intercepted Izzie at the front door and took the howling Florence in her arms. 'It's over. You're safe now.' She turned to them both. 'That's it. This is crazy,' she barked in her terror and relief. 'We can't do this here any more. Lillian, can you put together a list of commercial estate agents and phone them up? We need premises and we need them now.'

Looking at house details had been one thing. Industrial units was something else altogether. The agents Lillian contacted all talked in square metreage, and both Izzie and Maddy were as clueless as each other about what 300sq m looked like, despite the pile of details spread across the kitchen table. Nor were they exactly sure just how much they needed.

As usual Lillian came to their rescue. 'Well, Maddy, if it's any help, Workflow Systems was about two hundred and fifty, and you know how much that was because you visited us once.'

'I can hardly remember, and it was just when you moved in so you couldn't see the floor for PC boxes and desks.' Maddy sighed. How proud Simon had been when he showed her round. 'My little baby' he'd called it, and she'd tried very hard to feign interest. 'It was only once, wasn't it, Lillian? Do you think I should have visited more often?'

Lillian hesitated a fraction too long. 'I don't think so, Maddy. It wasn't always a very happy ship. Pretty stressful actually.' And she changed the subject by picking out a rather dark photograph of a brick barn in a village just outside Ringford which looked unusual. 'This one's pretty cheap – they are offering them at reduced introductory rates to get people in as it's just been converted. Shall I tell them you'll go and have a look?'

The young agent from Griggs, Staples & Davis, in his light brown suit, button-down shirt, cheap tie and narrow shoes, didn't seem to be quite sure how to deal with the two women who rolled up outside Blackcote Farm Business Park the following afternoon. He was even less sure about the five children who poured out of the two cars and ran as though possessed through the barn doors, screaming and shouting in the echoey space. It was a child's heaven. A giant nothingness, just vast concrete floor and bare walls, around which Charlie and Will pretended to be planes, and Jess skipped, with Florence stuck like glue in admiration not far behind. A wooden staircase led up to a mezzanine floor above, with a balustrade overlooking the space below, so, Maddy presumed, the management could check up that the workforce were hard at it.

They looked around in wonder. 'It's a bit grown up,' said Izzie uncertainly. 'Are we really going to be making enough of the stuff to need all this?'

'If the orders waiting to be done already are anything to go by, we certainly are.'

The agent seemed keen to hustle them out as quickly as possible, and once they had confirmed the rental, arranged to come to the house for them to sign for the barn the next day – he wasn't going to risk a similar invasion of the office. When they finally got back to Huntingford House, and dug out pizza from Maddy's freezer, Lillian was ready to go home for the night.

'Have you got time for a cup of tea before you go?' Maddy asked, taking the wrappers off the margheritas.

'I really ought to get going. It's salsa night tonight and I'll need to change.'

'Lillian, you dark horse,' Izzie laughed incredulously. 'I didn't know you were a dancer!'

'Oh it's just a bit of fun with some girlfriends, really,' she blushed, a mistake with her hair colour. 'We used to do line-dancing, but I got fed up with the men there slapping my bottom and yelling yee-ha!' She giggled. 'Anyway the phone has been red hot. Pru called to say one of the women's weeklies is keen to do something on you as soon as you can. I said you'd call her tomorrow. Sue Templeton wants to fix a date for Josh –

is it? – to come and play because they are off to Twois Valleys or somewhere over Easter. Now there's a forceful woman, and Pru called again and said could you ring her about something else first thing. Oh and Peter called. What a lovely voice that man has – he was very enigmatic, but just said to tell Izzie "it's all fine".'

Just how fine didn't become clear until Maddy had time later in the evening to call him back. 'I've been a little underhand I'm afraid,' Peter explained. That would take some believing. 'I didn't pry but the bank wanted confirmation that your business was going to be solvent enough that it wouldn't put any strain on Izzie's personal account, so . . .' He paused. 'I have made a deposit into your business account as a sign of goodwill.' He heard Maddy's intake of breath. 'Now before you say anything, darling, it's just a small sum to show confidence in your venture, and you can pay me back. From what Giselle has told me from her cuttings, that won't take long.'

'Peter, I don't know what to say.'

'Well don't say anything. Now we have both been thinking. What about the children? How are you going to cope over the holidays?'

'I don't know frankly.' She explained about the unit, and the need to get into serious production as soon as possible. 'We could always employ them packing pots, I suppose, but I think Health and Safety might not approve.'

'Now you're a bit more liquid financially, why don't you look into a nanny again? Your previous one is probably tied up, but you are going to need someone – and, Maddy, take care of yourself. We both worry about you.' Maddy could feel the tears well up and she sniffed inelegantly. 'You know,' he added gently, 'Simon would be proud as hell of you.'

She said her goodbyes as fast as she could before she collapsed completely, and poured a glass of wine from the open bottle in the fridge to ease the pain. Everything that had happened over the last couple of months had been so fast, so exhilarating, so exciting, and she realised how much she ached to share it with Simon. It would have been fun to chat about it to him over dinner, ask his advice, laugh with him about the press interviews, the meeting at the bank and the estate agent. Who else would want to know? Who'd be interested enough to listen? She realised how tired she was, and sitting down at the table she laid her head in her arms. Almost every night recently she had woken to find either Will or Florence (usually wet) in her bed. It was comforting to feel their warm sleeping bodies next to hers, but she hadn't had a full night's sleep for as long as she could remember, and there was no one to take over in the morning, no one to ask first thing, 'Please make me a cup of tea. I can't move.'

Everything, she realised, from making sure there were clean pants to paying the phone bill was down to her. If she didn't see to it, it wouldn't happen. Peter was right, she had to get help. She looked at the clock. Nine-fifteen, not too late to call. She pulled out her leather organiser, turned the pages and found Colette's forwarding address and phone number. Her finger hovered over the digits. Was it a viable proposition?

'Maddeee!' Colette sounded reassuringly thrilled to hear from her. 'How is everything and those gorgeous children? Listen. I saw something about you in the paper.' Her voice dropped to a whisper, 'This beetch I work for has the *Mail* rag lying around. What are you doing? You looked wonderful but so theen.'

Maddy couldn't keep the weariness from her voice. 'Izzie and I had this mad idea and it's rather run away with us. I have a study full of requests for pots of this gunk we've come up with, and we're in danger of screwing the whole thing up because we can't get the orders out.'

'What about the children? How will you cope with them?'
'Exactly.'

There was a temporary silence at the end of the phone. Maddy took a sip of wine and a long drag of her cigarette.

'Well,' Colette said finally, giving the word several syllables, 'I would need to give a few days' notice, of course.'

Maddy smiled to herself, and felt her heart lift. 'Oh Colette, would you? I don't even know about money. But it's coming in, because I have a roomful of cheques next door . . . but your bedroom is just the same, just needs a bit of a dust and Florence has made a little camp up there with a table and a tablecloth – it was the vicar's wife who gave her the idea – but it's all still the same. There's no cleaner now but I'm a dab hand with the duster, you'll be amazed, and Pasco's walking, and Will's lost three teeth, and—'

'Maddy, *arrête!*' Colette laughed, exasperated. 'I'll come up as soon as I can, and you can tell me all about it then.'

The following morning, over an orgy of toast and Pop Tarts (which she'd always thought would make a great name for a girl band), Maddy played her ace and told the children about Colette's imminent return. Will and Florence squealed with delight at the prospect of having their beloved nanny back, though Maddy was fairly certain anyone would have sufficed so long as it wasn't their frequently absent and otherwise distracted mother. They piled on to her knee with glee, and in celebration she let them have a Fruit Winder. Now she knew she had really lost her grip on parenthood.

As they wandered off to watch CBBC, she finally located the ringing phone under the breakfast debris.

'Good morning, Mrs Cosmetics Magnate,' Pru said warmly when she answered. 'I hope you're not playing mumsy today cos I bear good tidings. Lillian may have told you that *Country Life* want to talk to you both and I'm in discussions with *OK!* who want to do a little piece on their beauty page. Can I tell them next week sometime?'

'Er, sure.' Maddy absent-mindedly nibbled a piece of leftover toast. 'So long as they don't mind picking their way through cooking vats, children's toys and dirty washing.'

'Oh, I think that image will be ideal, so long as the toys are all wooden or wind-up. But there's more. Wait for this. I've had an intriguing phone call from Elements.' For a minute Maddy was too shocked to take it in. That achingly trendy health and beauty emporium – there was no other word for it – had been one of her favourite London stomping grounds. She would spend hours in the Knightsbridge branch ogling the glass shelves, with row upon row of deliciously packaged goodies from all over the world but all equally *now* brands. Bath oils, creams and lotions you wanted to sniff, feel, almost lick. What could they want with *Paysage Enchanté*?

'They are going softly softly, of course, but want to know if you would be interested in supplying them. I played it terribly cool, you'd have been so impressed.' She was silent. 'Say something, Maddy. Other clients of mine would kill for shelf space there, and you two go and get an approach!'

'How many branches have they got?' Maddy finally managed to squeak out weakly.

'Six. Three in London, Edinburgh, Dublin and Leeds. Shall we set up a meeting?'

'You have to be joking,' squealed Izzie, when she arrived half an hour later. 'Not "so trendy, the carrier bags are a collectors' item" Elements?'

'The very same,' giggled Maddy in delight and they practically danced around the kitchen in their excitement. 'We, us, the pair, *les deux* are only going to be stocked by the sexiest shop on planet Earth.' She pulled down two aprons from the back of the door. 'Come on, girl, we've got work to do.'

Chapter 12

And work they did! Easter wasn't until the end of April. The nights were light and the days wonderfully warm – just as well, because the Blackcote Farm barn was unheated, and there was always a slight feel and smell of damp. No wonder the agent had discounted the rent!

Izzie and Maddy would arrive by seven, and the others by eight, bundled up in layers of jumpers, fleeces, Nepalese hats with earflaps only to cast them off bit by bit into amorphous coloured bundles around the walls as the sun rose higher outside. By lunchtime, they would all go and sit on the staddle stones ranged along the back wall, looking out over the swollen stream and the farmland beyond as they munched their lunch.

One of their staunchest workers proved to be Oscar Grant, who had shuffled up to Izzie one afternoon in Ringford. Looming over her in his school uniform, he'd looked vaguely menacing and at first she didn't recognise him. His friends' slightly timid jeers obviously unnerved him and he shifted from foot to foot, his bent head swaying like a mild-mannered dinosaur searching for tasty greens. 'Lo, Izzie,' he'd mumbled. 'All right?'

'Hi! Oscar!' Izzie was relieved, and went slightly over the top. 'Great to see you. How's, er, things? Been skateboarding lately?'

She wished she hadn't asked, but at least it gave him a chance to overcome his embarrassment. He waxed lyrical about Ollies and goofyfooters, and, no idea what he was talking about, she nodded enthusiastically. 'Right! Gosh – really? That sounds er . . .'

'. . . so anyway, I'm saving up for new wheels, and they're pretty expensive, so I was wondering if you might have any work going during the Easter holidays – not full-time, cos I've got to do some revision too but—'

'Oscar, that would be tremendous. We've been worrying about getting all the orders ready, so any time you could give us would be welcome. Why don't you call me?' She rummaged in her bag for a Post-It note and pencil, then wrote down both her own and Maddy's numbers.

'You've pulled, Oz!' came a muffled catcall from the bus stop, but Oscar didn't blush this time. He glanced over at the tumbling pack of teenage boys with quiet superiority. 'Wrong. Got meself a holiday job.'

The assorted groans and sullen muttering of 'Jammy bastard!' were encouraging. Oscar was still hovering. 'Erm, could I tell Tam that you might have some work for her too?' He glanced uncertainly at Izzie.

'Would she want to? I got the impression she thought the whole thing was too trivial for words.'

'Oh no. Tamz is dead keen only she . . . she doesn't like to ask. She's been cutting out all the stuff in the papers about you and Mrs . . . Maddy. And she's stopped dying her hair.' He trailed off. 'She'd kill me if she knew I'd told you that . . .'

'Don't worry, Oz,' she glanced at him mischievously. 'It'll be our secret!'

So along with themselves, Oscar and Tamasin, Lillian half on admin and half on labelling, Crispin half on deliveries and pickups and half on pot filling, they were managing to keep up with the orders. They were even set up for the summer term, when three mums from St Boniface's would be starting. Now that had been an interesting conversation. Izzie, skulking in the playground at pick-up time, had been surprised as they had approached her. She knew them by sight, of course, but had never had more than a nodding acquaintance with them.

'You're Charlie's mum, en't you?' said the one in the middle, with hair cut into a mullet and the most visible piercings.

'Yeees.' Were they going to complain about that awful rhyme Charlie had been chanting – that one that started: My friend Billy . . . ?

There was a pause. The one on Izzie's left with the growing-out perm tied into a tight pony tail chipped in. 'My Jade's on the same table as your Jess.'

The third of these three graces was short and fat. 'I got Sam'n'Adam in wi' Charlie. We was wonderin' if you and that friend of yours needed any work doin' – casual like. You got that place out on Blackcote, en't yer?'

Now how did they know that? The answer was not long coming. 'My sister's ex-boyfriend's mate was doin' the plumbin' and he saw you goin' there. So we knew you was goin' big, with that face cream stuff. We've been workin' down the plant nursery, potting up and loading the orders, only they said we had to work durin' the 'olidays. Seeing as you've got kids an' all, we was thinkin' you'd understand 'bout that. We could start soon as they go back.'

Izzie recovered her composure. Things were desperate and this could be ideal, but how would Maddy react? She'd have to run it past her. 'Why don't you come over and see us at the barn, tomorrow maybe, when the kids are at school and we'll try to work something out?'

So the Easter holidays were far easier than Izzie and Maddy had dared to hope. With Colette back, Maddy's kids and therefore Maddy were well and happy. She'd even got to grips with the computer, sending e-mails with the best of them, and she'd overcome her reservations about employing the school mums, Angie, Donna and Karen (perhaps it was the association of those last two names that swung it).

It was sad, as term resumed, to say goodbye to Oscar and Tamasin. Tamasin, despite Izzie's fears, had proved herself invaluable within an hour of starting work. She had caught on so quickly to what was needed that, by the end of her time with them, she'd often completed tasks even before Maddy or Izzie had thought about asking her to do them. Her new natural look suited her much better than the Goth too, although she'd cut her hair ludicrously short herself, to avoid the two-tone effect as she grew the dye out. 'We'll carry on at weekends though, won't we, Oz? And at half-term too, if you want us.'

With the three graces, Karen, Angie and Donna, taking over, the atmosphere changed radically and Izzie heard some jokes that shocked even her, but productivity increased. The new workers' disrespectful attitude to the product also endeared them. 'Load o' bloody crap, all this though, ennit? Soap and water my mum always used, an' 'er skin were smashing. And best part of thirty quid? They want their 'eads lookin' at.' This was the judgement of the triumvirate, endlessly mulled over, along with a fairly limited range of other topics including sex, kids, the lottery and a bloke called Shane. But in spite of their feelings on the product, the three were clearly used to hard work and, grimly cheerful, they operated as a well-oiled if rather noisy unit, with Radio One playing loudly all day.

Having regular staff also allowed Izzie and Maddy to get on with strategic planning. Maddy had already been working on one of Luce's other recipes. A moisturiser, called *Crème Rosée du Soir*. 'It's evening dew cream,' she translated. 'I think it sounds rather romantic. It's got the weed extract and rose petals infused in oil – we'd have to get some stonking rose essential oil and, maybe, almond oil and wax – if we haven't made all the bees in the country homeless that is!'

Lunchtimes were also rather different. Without the tabbouleh, pan bagna or chilli bean wraps, sent in by Janet, and shared generally – once Tamasin had got over her embarrassment at her mother's pebble-dashed offerings – they had now relapsed into sarnies, crisps, loads of diet cola purchased from the lunchtime van and Tunnock's caramel wafers by the score.

But Pru had been livid. Immaculately groomed as always on one of her rare visits north, and in stark contrast to the gear she'd insisted they should wear, she had counted off the list of dos and don'ts on her French-manicured fingers. 'No ciggies, no booze apart from French wine, French mineral water, no takeaways, no ready meals, no sliced bread, no processed food, no supermarket for preference. I was wondering about going veggie, but I think if we stick to . . . oh I don't know . . . Guinea fowl, capons and mutton you can go on eating meat.'

'What, no sausages?' Izzie squeaked, imagining the mutiny she'd be faced with at home.

'*Saucisson de Toulouse*, of course – but nothing less recherché. Unless you can find a little place that does home-made organic, of course.'

The list went on and on. Fluoride-free toothpaste, hemp towels, strictly nothing in black, no Lycra and emphatically no eyebrow plucking or waxing . . . 'What?' Maddy and Izzie had rejected that one simultaneously.

'Pru, you can't,' Maddy was outraged. 'You remember what my eyebrows were like at school. It's just not sensible.'

Izzie was aghast. 'You haven't seen my legs without attention. I have this pelt – it keeps me warm in winter – but it has to come off, or I'll stifle in the heat once summer comes.'

Maddy gazed at Izzie with new respect. 'You mean you go all winter without waxing your legs? How revolting! Go on – show us.'

Izzie managed to hold her patchwork skirt down round her ankles, despite Maddy's tugging. 'But what about our families?

You can't expect the kids to change their lifestyle to fit in with our new image. And as for Marcus . . .'

Pru steepled her fingertips together and leant towards them. 'Girls, if I've got this right – and believe me, I'm never wrong – it's not just going to be your families doing all this. It's going to be a good forty per cent of ABC1s in the 25–39 bracket, with spin-off going much, much further. In fact, if one's kids *aren't* eating mulberry bread with wild mushroom pâté, they're going to be complaining that everyone laughs at them in school.'

She also briefed them on what to expect from Elements. 'They are big hitters, I warn you, and they have an extremely well-defined image so they'll have put in lots of work on this presentation.'

Izzie rubbed her hands together. 'I was thinking, we want to make a really professional impression, so do you think we should scrap all the cambric and go for really natty little suits?'

Pru was indignant. 'Have you been listening to *anything* I've been saying? You *are* the brand. You have to carry this through with conviction or it won't work. Natty suits is what they wear – you and Maddy stick to the plan.'

It was harder explaining Pru's policy document and the need to stay 'on message' to Marcus. He shook his head in exasperation. 'Look, I understand that you're working very hard and long hours and everything, and it's great to have some money coming in . . . although I think you ought to have a better fix on just how much you're making . . . but you just haven't considered my feelings in all this. Does it really matter what I do? You're the main story here.'

'I'm not really enjoying all of this either. There are days I could murder a packet of prawn cocktail crisps.' Izzie crossed her fingers under the table. 'But surely it's not too much to ask? You can drink lager at home, if you like. Just don't do it in the pub.' She moved closer, put her arms round his unyielding body. 'We need to be a bit careful that we maintain an image.

We can't afford to be caught out. And think of what we stand to gain. I need you on board, Marcus.'

He stood stiffly, frowning and distant. 'Do you? I wonder sometimes.'

Between the meeting with Pru and the planned meeting with Elements, the May issue of *Country Lifestyle* magazine came out. Izzie arrived at the barn with her copy, hot off the press – well, off the shelves of the Ringford newsagent anyway. She and Maddy had agreed not to peep until they were together – it felt a bit like opening A level results.

'Ready?' They eyed each other anxiously, then, opening the magazine boldly, they both gasped. The photographs were nothing less than amazing, with a dramatic quality that had nothing to do with the weather on the day of the shoot.

'How did he manage to make those clothes look sexy?' Maddy examined the pictures more closely. 'You look like Cathy waiting for Heathcliff. I can't imagine what lens he must have used to give you a cleavage like that – telephoto perhaps?'

'Well, look at you – you're positively Demelza-ish in that one. And what are you doing to that carrot?'

Maddy had flipped to the next page. 'Look at the kids! Who says the camera never lies? They were being little sods that day but he's made them look angelic – all rosy cheeks and pearly teeth.'

The copy was even better, gushing on about 'the idyllic environment' and 'a secure homestead which manages to keep the excesses of the twenty-first century at bay'. 'Both women work hard,' it effused, 'to provide for their families on their own terms; in a context where glass ceilings and boardroom wrangles are irrelevant.'

Izzie clutched her head. 'Oh no. What's Marcus going to say when he reads that?'

Marcus didn't say anything. In fact, he barely glanced at the feature when she showed it to him enthusiastically. As predicted, the coverage resulted in another prodigious surge in sales. There was now a kind of momentum building up, with articles appearing quite regularly and little mentions here and there. One R&B diva claimed that she had been using nothing but *Paysage Enchanté* for years, and had been a fan long before anyone else had caught on. Maddy and Izzie both chuckled at this one.

Buoyed up by this excitement, they marched confidently a few weeks later into the achingly trendy Spitalfields' offices of Elements, although they felt decidedly out of their element in their swirling skirts and frilled shirts. 'Just as well we didn't go for the natty suit option,' Izzie hissed as they swept upwards in the steel and glass lift. 'They seem to be cloning those types here. We might have got lost and never found each other again.'

'God, they're scary. I've never seen so many people like this before in one place. If they're creatives, why do they all dress the same?'

'Relax.' Izzie held up a reassuring hand. 'These are my people. Remember, I used to live in North London.'

Waiting to greet them in the conference room – yin-yang balanced no doubt, for the most positive energy – were a range of identikit designer types. Black suits, white T-shirts, clunky shoes and neo-brutalist haircuts – and those were just the women! The only splashes of colour came from the hair – dyed an alarming range of very non-natural colours. Finbar, a postmodern Irishman who seemed to be their leader, got them off to a flying start.

'We're very excited to be working with *Paysage Enchanté*.' Izzie tried to avoid Maddy's eye. It did sound funny in a Belfast accent. 'We feel that the brand truly enhances our current range-set introducing an excitement-facing urban-rural dialecticism that we think will upscale selling outcomes of both identities in a kind of counterbalancing way.' What? 'By co-mingling, as opposed to intermingling, PE with our other more future-here brands, we think we'll create an increment-alised dynamic, producing an almost,' he did air quotes and both women shuddered visibly, 'ironic tension between the old and the new – with the deliverable of course being . . .' he smiled around at his colleagues who were all nodding in agree-ment '. . . exponentialised client take-up across the board!'

Maddy looked around in confusion. Izzie was frowning. 'Hold it right there, Finbar. Can we just "unpack" that?' Izzie air-quoted and Maddy turned her splutter of laughter into a coughing fit. 'If I'm interpreting correctly your vision of our brand identity, you see it as validating your current image in a Rousseau-esque rural juxtaposition that springs entirely from the contemporary – in other words, externally.'

The clones were gripped.

'I couldn't agree less,' Izzie went on. 'PE's integrity is entirely auto-referential.' They were eating out of her hand now. Some of them were even taking notes. 'We propose a dedicated PE zone in each of your outlets, spatially contiguous with, yet distinct from, your base range area. A kind of syncretic con-catenation with all the imagery that implies. I'm thinking green, grey-green with cobalt *éclats*. Sepia, concealed lighting to create a wash and tonally matched to Provence at two-thirty on an afternoon in early June.'

Finbar's mouth was hanging open and he nodded fast. 'I'm with you! I'm totally there. I can smell the *garrigue*.'

'I knew you'd get it, Finbar.' Izzie smiled at him warmly and they went on to finalise details, with figures, she realised in horror, that would mean more than doubling their output. If only she could double the number of hours in a day. When she mentioned the proposed new rose moisturiser, Finbar almost wet his knickers with excitement, and wittered on about 'creat-ing a synergistic lifestyle experience'.

'I can smell something, but it ain't *garrigue*,' muttered

Maddy as they passed round pantone swatches for the point of sale. 'I didn't know you spoke fluent bullshit.'

On the way out, the drones and clones were deferring to Izzie as though she were the queen ant and she took the adulation in her stride. She was particularly pleased with herself for having requested about three hundred pounds' worth of their existing cosmetic ranges, to help her with the concept, naturally. Finbar hugged them both like old friends.

'It's wonderful to work with clients who have such a clear vision. Ciao, ciao!' he gushed as he closed the taxi door, then waved until they were out of sight.

'Phew – I'm glad I was able to put a stop to that.' Izzie sighed with relief. 'What a bloody nerve – they wanted to put our stuff next to their existing products as a sort of contrast, old and new. But I reckon our stuff is so different in every way, and is giving out such a different message about lifestyle that it has to stand alone.'

'You were fab, girl. Did you make all that up on the hoof or had you been thinking about it before?'

'I suppose I was thinking how the pots could be presented. They would have looked terrible on those glass shelves with the shiny pots – all country mouse and town mouse. But when that awful Finbar started I just saw red. He probably assumed we'd be country bumpkins. What a patronising gobshite!'

Maddy started to chuckle. 'Well you must admit, Madame Cholet, we do look a bit like yokels.'

Izzie looked down at her unshaven legs and pin-tucked blouse, and giggled. 'Yeah, but sexy as hell!'

Really irritated now by the time André, Ringford's most sought-after hairdresser, was taking, Maddy made it plain she was ready to go, paid the bill (£35 – compared to London charges, a snip at the price!), and left as smartly as she could.

She'd promised to meet Jean Luc in town when she was

done. He'd arrived late last night, had been in bed before she'd got back from Blackcote Farm at about one in the morning, and he'd still been asleep when she'd left for her nine o'clock hair appointment.

'I'm shorn,' she said when he picked up his mobile after several rings. 'Where are you?'

Five minutes later she tracked him down in Costa's. The Saturday papers were spread all over the table, except for a small space opposite him where he had placed her steaming cupful, and his head was bent over them intently. He had always loved the weekend broadsheets; it was about the only compliment he ever gave the British. She crept up behind him before he could see her and whispered 'Boo!' in his ear. Starting with shock, he twirled round and gabbled in rapid French. '*Merde*, don't do that to me. My heart's already racing from the amount of coffee I've . . . Good God, Maddy, you look fantastic.' He stood up and enveloped her in his arms. He smelt wonderful, and felt so warm and strong, and for a few moment she let him hold her as he buried his nose in her hair, not unaware of the interested looks they were receiving from the other people in the café.

'You smell of coconuts.'

'Must be André's secret shampoo. What do you think of the cut?' She sat down in the chair opposite and twisted her head around exaggeratedly like a hairspray model.

'You look like you did when we were fifteen – all that fake blonde gone at last.' His eyes were sparkling, and Maddy went quite pink under his scrutiny. 'I like you better this way.'

'Well,' she took a gulp of the strong, hot coffee, 'not bad for the provinces. Did you have a good sleep? I hope Colette was hospitable and you didn't flirt too outrageously with her.'

'She's a lovely girl but a bit young even for me! You must have got in late.' He offered her a cigarette.

'I'd kill for one, but I'm down to two a day and even those I have to have surreptitiously upstairs in my bathroom. I can't afford to have anyone see me with a fag in my mouth. This coffee is subversive enough.' She fiddled with the handle of her cup. 'I have to say it's bloody hard and most of the time I feel like I could kill someone. I'm going to be the first psychopathic hippy ever.'

He put his hand over hers. 'You sound pretty fed up with it all, *ma chere*.'

'No.' The warmth of his hand felt good. She'd missed the feeling of a man touching her even if it was just Jean Luc. 'Just tired and generally crabby and nicotine deprived. Izzie says if she'd known how horrible I was in real life, she'd never have bothered with me!'

'How is she?' he said on cue.

She filled him in on Izzie's bravura performance at Elements. 'She just rose to the occasion, and by the end we were dictating what we wanted from them.'

'I can't imagine that of her.' He stubbed out his cigarette and knocked back the last drops of his coffee. 'She is usually so gentle and sweet. What's that great expression?' he said in English. 'Wouldn't say boo to a goose.'

'She seems to be getting stronger all the time, but I only hope she's using some of her new-found confidence on that husband of hers. He's not really handling her success very well, and I could give him a kick up the arse. She needs the love of a good man.' She looked right at Jean Luc, a smile in her eyes.

'How could any man resist that?' he laughed.

'Now I've got a job for you to do.' She too finished her coffee and picked up her bag. 'We've got a meeting with some designers from Oxford on Monday and, darling, I haven't got a thing to wear!' Jean Luc snorted. 'I know. I know. But it's all the wrong stuff. The new Me has to be in sprigged cotton and *au naturel*. I want you to be my consultant. If you tell me I look nice in something, I'll know it's the last thing I should buy.'

Confused, Jean Luc followed her out of the café, and they

spent the next hour browsing the poor selection of Ringford clothes shops for the poorest selection of clothes. By shop three he was getting the hang of it. 'This is it,' he yelped with glee, selecting from the rail a drop-waisted dress with a tiny pattern of roses and blue nondescript flowers, which, when she put it on and paraded around the shop, looked hardly less shapeless on her than it had on the hanger.

'You look like a sack of potatoes,' he said, in French so as not to offend the shop assistant. 'Perfect!'

The rest of the day was fun, much of it spent with the children, something Jean Luc, for a childless man, had an aptitude for. His grasp of cricket was pitiful, but he gamely had a go for Will's sake and the two of them bowled and batted for what seemed like hours on the lawn, until Jean Luc had to plead exhaustion and retire.

'I won, Mummy,' Will crowed, rushing into the sitting room where she was sewing with Florence, his face glowing with fresh air and pleasure. 'He's not as good as Daddy, but I showed him what to do.'

'Wait till I take you on at pétanque, my boy,' said Jean Luc, collapsing on to the sofa beside Maddy. 'I need a drink. What on earth are you doing?'

'Making a blanket for Florence's Barbie horse, of course. Shouldn't every self-respecting horse have one? Listen, I've had an idea. Why don't we see if Izzie, Marcus and the children are free for lunch tomorrow? She'd love to see you.'

'Yeah cool, Mum, can we?' pleaded Will, and before Jean Luc could protest – well, he was bound to be a bit unsure about meeting Marcus – she was in the kitchen dialling the number.

The children played up horribly at bedtime, not helped by Jean Luc getting Will thoroughly over-excited. Maddy left them to it, settled Pasco into his cot, read Florence a story and plaited the tail of her Barbie horse, then went to have a bath, taking care not to muck up her new hair. But by the time she had slipped on her pyjama bottoms, a T-shirt and Simon's old fleece, Jean Luc was already on his second glass of wine and was cooking steaks at the Aga.

'That was quick. How did you manage to settle him?'

'I taught him how to count to fifty in French, then said I'd give him five pounds if he could say it backwards by breakfast.'

'No sleep there then!'

He gave her outfit the once-over. 'Very chic, darling. If it wasn't for the hair, I'd say you were in grave danger of losing your grip completely.' He handed her a glass of wine, and kissed her on the top of the head. 'You smell clean though. Now sit down. Supper is nearly ready. This cooking machine of yours is about as useful as a huge radiator. It simply doesn't get hot enough to fry these steaks.'

But of course they were tender and delicious. Maddy simply sat there, waited on hand and foot, and ate like a pig. 'That was perfect,' she said, mouth still full and wiping the juices off her plate with some bread. 'God, I love being cooked for. Most evenings I eat the children's leftover sausages, or something you can stick in the microwave.' Jean Luc winced.

They finished their pudding, and talked shop. Maddy told him about the new product line they were going to develop, and between them they tried to work out the volumes of *centpertuis* they would need.

'You know it would be much cheaper if I could get the weed distilled at home. I think I could help you.'

'Oh Jean Luc, that would be brilliant. Then we don't have to cope with huge volumes of greenery. The barn is beginning to look like a giant compost heap. Could it come in sealed containers?'

'I'll look into it.' Maddy sat back in her chair, picking raspberry pips out of her teeth, and they fell into a companionable silence.

Jean Luc took away the plates again, wiped the table and refilled her glass. 'Thank you for that.' She sighed contentedly. 'Simon always used to cook me supper at weekends. He made a mean Spanish omelette, and could do wicked things with a bag of pasta and a tin of tomatoes.'

Suddenly she felt a wave of sadness. 'I think I miss his company most. He was always such fun to be around. You remember how he used to hold the floor at a party, telling everyone indiscreet anecdotes. Giselle loved it, the way he would tease her about her flower arranging class and her shopping trips – she used to blush like a schoolgirl, which on the face of it is quite remarkable. And that time when we all met up for the match at the Parc des Princes, and he insisted we all wore red roses – you two almost came to blows! – didn't France win anyway?' On she nattered, and Jean Luc simply sat there drinking his wine and listening.

'Peter seems convinced that Workflow Systems wouldn't have worked out.' Jean Luc raised an eyebrow. 'He said Simon was too unrealistic. It hurt so much when he told me, but I suppose he was right – Simon was always so positive about everything – and the more I think about those last few weeks the more I realise he tried to protect me from the inevitable.'

'That could have been pride.'

'Maybe, but I think he just didn't want me to know how bad the situation was.' She paused, hardly bearing to say what she had thought but never dared to voice. It was something that had flitted into her head at her most desperate moments, but she had pushed it firmly into the background. 'You don't . . . you don't think he took his own life, do you?'

Jean Luc leant forward and put his hand over hers. 'God, no, Maddy. No man would do that and leave a beautiful wife and three gorgeous children. Nothing, no problem, is insurmountable.' He rubbed his hands gently over hers. They felt rough and solid. 'He may have been unrealistic, but he wasn't stupid.'

His words made her feel slightly consoled, but she wasn't sure she would ever get the notion out of her head. She just wanted to have Simon sitting here, to be able to ask him what had happened.

'Come on, my girl. It's time you went to bed.' He put the mugs in the dishwasher, and started to turn off the lights.

'For the last few months, both you and Izzie have been so wonderful looking after me,' she said, getting up from her chair. 'I feel a bit like a small child at times.'

He came over and stood in front of her for a moment, then leant down and kissed her gently on the cheek. 'No, darling. You are certainly not a child.'

Izzie looked glorious when they all piled out of the car the following lunchtime. She was wearing pink linen cropped trousers and her top was flowery and feminine, but clung to her in all the right places. She's got quite a figure, when she's not wearing combats or saggy skirts, Maddy thought. The colours suited her dark hair and pale skin, and she was positively glowing.

The look on Marcus' face was cautious as he came round from the other side of the car with a bottle of wine gripped tightly in his hand. It suddenly struck Maddy that he'd never been to the house before, and the whole package of the children greeting each other and rushing upstairs with excitement, her playing the grand hostess, Jean Luc embracing Izzie warmly and Izzie as familiar here as in her own home, must have been quite intimidating for him. She prepared to give him the benefit of any doubt.

'Hi, Marcus, lovely to see you, and glad you could come at such short notice.' She leant forward to give him a kiss on the cheek but the response was cool and distant. He shook Jean Luc's hand, and muttered a greeting. What a curious little vignette it was. Marcus shaking the hand of the man who clearly fancies his wife.

She bustled about finishing laying the table, while Jean Luc opened a bottle of wine and Izzie, unconsciously, put on an apron and started stirring the gravy bubbling away on the Aga. They were like a slick *ménage à trois*. Jean Luc handed Marcus a glass of deep red wine. 'I'd rather have a beer if you don't mind.' The atmosphere suddenly went cold.

'I'll have the wine,' said Izzie quickly taking the glass. 'I think there's some beer in the utility room.'

Without speaking, Jean Luc went to find some, and Izzie shot a brief glance in Maddy's direction. 'I thought we'd be eating in the dining room?' She asked finally to fill the silence.

'The table's covered in papers,' Maddy replied quickly, fishing out the gravy boat from the bottom oven and omitting to add that there wasn't actually a table as such, or chairs. 'And besides, Pasco would do his best to massacre it, so I thought it would be cosier in the kitchen.'

'Quite a place you have here, Maddy.'

'Glad you like it.' She wasn't sure Marcus was being entirely complimentary. 'It's not finished yet but once we have some more money coming in—'

'Yes, soon you'll both be the Rothschilds of Ringford. We won't be worthy. We're barely that now.' Fifteen love to Marcus. Why was he being so obnoxious? Couldn't he make the effort even for Izzie's sake?

Thankfully the constant chatter of the children over lunch dispelled the atmosphere, and Jean Luc started them all off in a general knowledge quiz, which involved questions like 'Who has more clothes, Barbie or Mum?' or 'Who designed the pyramid at the Louvre?'

The children giggled at him. 'All right, clever clogs,' said Will. 'What's the name of the captain of the English cricket team?'

Marcus let Jean Luc struggle for a moment, then dryly replied with the correct answer. Thirty-love, thought Maddy, not sure that he wasn't playing singles to Jean Luc and her doubles.

'Who cares?' countered Jean Luc, looking at Will teasingly. 'The English are terrible at cricket.'

By the time they had finished their rhubarb crumble – 'home cooked,' Maddy was keen to point out to Izzie, 'I'm not entirely hopeless' – the score was about deuce, until Marcus was dragged away by Charlie who wanted to show him the great tree he could climb in the orchard. When he had left, pursued by the rest of the children, the three of them sat in an uncomfortable silence. Maddy took one of Jean Luc's proffered cigarettes, and Izzie got up to put the kettle on.

'I'm sorry,' she said, her back to them. 'He's being vile, and it's not really like him.'

Before Maddy could answer, Jean Luc stood up and put his arm around her. 'Izzie darling, it's OK. He must find it a bit strange—'

'Pasco's fallen on the path . . .' Marcus burst in, a crying Pasco in his arms, and stopped as he saw the scene at the Aga. Jean Luc hastily dropped his arm from around Izzie's shoulders, and Maddy went to take her son from Marcus.

'Do you want some coffee too, darling?' said Izzie quickly.

'Only if you are not too busy,' he said. Looking at her hard, he turned on his heel and left the room.

By the time he came back the three of them were on safe ground, discussing the more efficient pot supplier Jean Luc had traced in Reims, and the fact that it was cheaper to have the *centpertuis* strained in France, and Izzie was outlining enthusiastically her vision for the point of sale signs for Elements. Marcus collected his coffee, now tepid, from the Aga and sat down at the end of the table furthest away from them.

'Marcus, darling, you are better at this sort of thing than me. He does this all the time,' she said to Jean Luc. 'He's brilliant on design ideas. Do you think greens and greys on the backing boards will be too dour?'

'Don't ask me.' He poured himself the last of the wine from

the bottle and took a chocolate from the box Izzie had brought. 'It sounds as if you have it all under control already.'

Izzie wouldn't let it drop. She got up from the table and went round to sit beside him. 'Oh please, darling, you've got such a great eye.' She put her hand on his unresponsive one. 'Don't you remember that brilliant campaign you devised for that Swedish paint company? Maddy, you must remember it – with the room reflected like a forest in a lake – it won loads of awards—'

Marcus pulled his hand sharply away, leaving hers limp on the tabletop, and stood up. 'Look at the time. It's getting late – I've got important things to do for tomorrow,' and walked out of the room to rouse the children. Game set and match to Marcus, thought Maddy.

Jean Luc had to leave shortly after too. Maddy felt curiously disappointed as he put his bag down in the hall, and went to say goodbye to the children. It was like that awful Sunday-night feeling you get before you go back to school. He put the bag in his car, then gave her a huge, bear-like hug. 'You're doing great, Maddy my darling. I'll call you when I get back, and we'll arrange shipping once you have a clearer idea of quantity.' He started to get into the car, but paused. 'You know I'm really quite enjoying being your French co-ordinator. It's a long time since I worked for someone else. Why don't you come over at half-term – all of you – and you can meet the suppliers and charm them with your smile?'

'That's a great idea. The kids will love it. I don't know how long it is since Izzie has been away either.'

'Yes . . . yes, Izzie. I think she needs you now as much as you needed her. Call me.' And blowing her a kiss, he drove off.

Monday morning and Maddy didn't feel any better. Leaving Colette with Pasco and a huge list of things that needed doing, including a new pair of shoes for a boy who was shaping up to be built like his father, she dropped the other two at Little

218

Goslings and Eagles as quickly as possible and was at the unit by quarter to nine. Izzie had only beaten her by five minutes.

'The heat's on this morning,' she said without preamble. 'Elements have e-mailed to say they want first delivery by Wednesday and we are already two hundred pots behind schedule.'

'Good morning to you too.'

'Sorry – good morning, and thanks so much for yesterday. Marcus was a prat and I told him so, not something he was thrilled to hear, and it was just lovely to see Jean Luc again. Has he gone?'

'Yeah, he left shortly after you. But fear not, love-sick maiden,' she added, as they went up the stairs to the office, 'he's invited us to go on a suppliers' trip over half-term.' Izzie's face lit up, and she kept bringing the subject up as they worked like maniacs alongside the team.

It was the only highlight of a long and tedious morning. The electric kept tripping out, and waiting for the electrician wasted precious time. By twelve they were up and running again, and by half past two had 600 perfect little pots sat in boxes on a pallet, with the Elements delivery addresses stamped on them, waiting to be collected at three. Five minutes to and the forklift was ready to roll. Maddy and Izzie watched with excitement as the distribution lorry backed into the large doors, and the forklift slid the forks under the boxes and picked up the pallet. Perhaps he hit the wrong lever. Perhaps he lost concentration. Perhaps he was put off by the little group watching him in anticipation. But as if in slow motion, in sickeningly slow and terrible motion, 600 perfect little pots packed in their boxes slipped off the pallet and went crashing on to the concrete floor.

Maddy's immediate thought was not that their first order for one of the most chic shops in the country had just bitten the dust. It was that she was due to pick the children up in half an hour and that Josh Templeton was coming back for tea. Ignoring the need to phone Elements and explain the delay, she immediately rang Colette to get her to dive into the car and get to school. 'Disaster has happened here, I'll be back as soon as I can,' she rattled down the phone. At about the same time, Izzie came off her mobile to Marcus, who'd agreed to collect Charlie and Jess. 'Bloody working mothers,' she muttered under her breath. It then took nearly an hour to work out which jars were salvageable, to wipe them down and repack them into new boxes. Three hundred passed muster, but Izzie had to peel the labels off another hundred and fix on new ones. The rest of their hard work was chucked unceremoniously into the wheelie bin.

'It's the quality really,' said Maddy in her most assertive voice down the phone to the Elements head office shortly afterwards. 'We really weren't happy with the shipment of lavender oil this time, and the beeswax had a couple of tiny flaws which worried us. Being such an exclusive product, we are very, *very*, particular about the quality of the ingredients we use. We'll send you a proportion of the consignment, if you can bear with us on the rest . . .' She listened to the cool response of the woman at the other end of the phone. 'Forty-eight hours?' She looked at Izzie across the desk, panic-stricken. 'Yes, I'm sure that will be fine. We'll have the delivery with you by Friday at the very latest.'

'Oh bloody, bloody hell,' moaned Izzie when she put down the phone. 'Panic stations. We won't have enough for the other orders now. We've just about enough *centpertuis*,' she was dialling as she spoke. 'You call Crispin and see if he can do a mercy dash to the commune in Wales, and I'll . . . oh hello, it's Isabel Stock from *Paysage Enchanté*. Yes. Me again. Now I need your help . . .'

It was nearly six before Maddy finally got home, to find Colette coping brilliantly and the children seated around the table having supper, though Will and Josh were busy discussing the meaning of the word vagina.

'It's an island in the Mediterranean,' said Maddy without

missing a beat and dropping her bag on the side. She took the cup of tea Colette held out to her. 'Oh just what I need. It's been a bit of a day. I can't wait to put my feet up.'

'Yoo hoo! Anyone home?' Sue Templeton. This wasn't what she needed. She put down her tea before she had even managed to put it to her lips, and went into the hall. 'What a lovely place, Maddy,' Sue gushed, trying to peer into the rooms. 'Mind if I have a peep?'

'No, Sue, go right ahead.' Maddy followed Sue into the sitting room.

'What lovely curtains!' Sue stood in admiration. 'I do think terracottas are so restful, don't you? That's why I put them in our lounge. Do tell me where you found such super things. Blacks and creams. What an unusual idea, but then you have such a great room to work with. Are the others all like this?'

'Most of them, yes. Would you like a cup of tea? I'm just having one.'

'Oh there's me nattering on and being nosy, but I do love snooping in other people's houses. They give one such good ideas.' Maddy urged her into the kitchen. 'Oh isn't this super! So modern and contemporary. Is it Magnet? I keep telling Gary we need to do ours again.'

'Mum, we've only just had a new kitchen,' said Josh, astonished.

'Oh sweetie, that was years ago.' She ran her hands over the wooden worksurfaces. 'This would look super in our house.'

'Now, you lot,' said Maddy briskly, 'when you've finished your ice cream – Will, that's enough chocolate sauce – you can have five minutes' play. I'm sure Sue has to get home, and, Will, you have reading to do.' With the children bundled off, she refreshed the pot of tea, and invited Sue to sit down. Sue did so seamlessly without drawing breath. 'I love your new look, Maddy. So peasanty and earthy. Quite a change from the sort of things we used to see you in.'

Maddy was too weary to even try and make conversation, which was fortunate as Sue was making more than enough for both of them. 'So have you got your holidays planned? We're off to Provence this summer. I do so love France, all that effortless style. Gary likes to do the vineyards, to stock up our little wine cellar, so we tend to take a villa and go native. I think next year we might do Portugal again – Gary loves the golf – and the seafood is so good, don't you find? Of course I can't complain. We have just had a super skiing holiday. The chalet was simply marvellous and Arabella, our chalet girl, made the most delish suppers.'

'Maddy?' Crispin called from the back door. She heard him kicking off his boots, and he appeared, grubby and dishevelled. 'What time did you tell that hippy lot I'd be . . . ?' He walked into the kitchen and stopped short. 'Sorry, I didn't know you had company. Hello.' He glanced briefly at Sue, and then he looked again. 'It's . . . Sue, Sue Pilbeam, isn't it? Haven't seen you for years.'

Maddy was pretty confused by the speed at which Sue left her half-drunk tea, picked up her bag, dragged Josh away from his game of dreadnought power fighters on the landing, and, pleading a 'huge list of things to do', was out of the drive like a frightened rabbit. Maddy came back into the kitchen, where Crispin was still standing in his stockinged feet.

'Well, bugger me!' he said, awe-struck. 'If that wasn't Pokey Pilbeam. She's poshed up a bit but still got that magnificent chest.'

'Pokey Pilbeam?'

'That's what we called her at school. She was a right goer was old Sue Pilbeam. Think I had a snog with her once at a school disco, but that wasn't all she was offering as I recall. Hence the Pokey bit. Hardly recognised the old slapper . . .'

It took Maddy at least ten minutes to stop laughing long enough to phone Izzie with this enlightening news.

Chapter 13

Izzie gleefully passed on the hot news to Marcus as soon as he got back from the pub before supper, but he barely smiled. She'd been hoping it would thaw the atmosphere that had been building up between them enough for her to broach the tricky topic of their planned trip to the Cévennes. He ate without looking up from the paper, and she wasn't even sure he was listening to what she was hesitantly explaining.

'So there's no option really.' Izzie looked down at her plate, twisting the pasta round and round the fork without ever raising it to her lips. 'We'll have to get the *centpertuis* boiled down and filtered in France. It's costing far too much to have it shipped over here in its raw state.'

Still no response. 'We were thinking we could go over once the school holidays begin – spend a few days there setting up the operation. We've got access to premises and there are staff lined up.'

At last he closed the paper and folded his arms, looking up stonily. 'All lined up. That's handy. How did you manage that then?'

Izzie concentrated very hard on organising the carrot sticks in her side salad into neat rows. 'Maddy more or less took care of it. She's got contacts over there and she made a few calls.' Damn, why did she sound so apologetic?

'Right – simple as that then? And what about the kids? I hope you're not simply assuming I'll drop everything and look after them again?'

It was time for her trump card and she smiled triumphantly. 'No, actually. Maddy and I thought we might take them all with us. It could be fun for them.'

'Very neat.' Marcus looked away and exhaled loudly, his voice dripping with sarcasm. 'So you won't need me at all this time. What am I supposed to do while you're off in France, then?'

'Do what you want, for goodness sake. You're always complaining that you don't have any time to yourself.'

'Suppose what I want is to have you and the kids here with me. What then?'

'Marcus, make up your mind.' Izzie's patience had worn through. 'You've made it perfectly clear you resent looking after the kids so much of the time, but when I offer to take them off your hands, you get all sulky. I'm trying to be helpful here.'

'Oh you are, are you? Silly me! I though you were just trying to squeeze me out. Again.'

'Look, I'm offering a few free days on a plate. What's the problem?' Izzie stood up abruptly and emptied her uneaten food into the bin, then crashed her plate into the dishwasher.

'I don't know, you tell me! You've got all the answers, haven't you?' Marcus stalked over to the fridge and pulled out another can of lager, staring at her challengingly.

'The way you're talking, anyone would think I was dumping on you. I'm not going on holiday, for goodness sake. I'll be working, making *Paysage Enchanté* more efficient.'

'Oh *working*!' He turned away, sauntered back over to the table and sat down again, with his legs stretched out in front of him. 'Well *that* makes it all right then. If you're working, then you can put everything and everyone to the back of the queue and it's all right, in fact it's fantastic because you're a big fucking success, aren't you? Everyone I meet tells me how lucky I am, how proud I must be, how hard you work. I know how fucking hard you work, because you're never here. You're never here, you never talk to me, you never tell me what you're doing – until you've already done it—'

'Now hang on.' Izzie stood in front of him, hands on her hips. 'That's not fair. I'm not just doing this for me, you know. Do you think I like working all hours making this stuff, having to watch my every move for fear that some cruddy journalist will spot me putting on mascara or something?'

'I assume you do like it.' He shrugged. 'I mean, you've got a choice in the matter. If it's so awful, just stop. Go on – give it all up now.'

'Oh don't be ridiculous. You know it's not as simple as that. I have responsibilities, obligations—'

'And what about your responsibilities to me?' Izzie could feel her heart sink. There was no deflecting the row now. 'Don't turn away from me,' he went on. 'Sit down. We're going to have this out. Basically you just take it for granted that I'll fit in with whatever you dump on me.'

Izzie forced herself to sit, but clenched her fists together on the table. 'That is so not true! All the time you were working, I put my work, my whole life on the back burner, just so I'd be there for you. I kept the kids out of your way when you were tired. I always put your career and what was best for you first, even when—'

'Here we go. I was waiting for this.' He shook his head and rolled his eyes. 'Even when what? When I lost my job, you mean? Do you think I wanted to move to this godforsaken hole . . . ?'

Izzie gasped. 'But I thought you loved it here? It was your idea!'

'What other option was there? It's all worked out fine for you, hasn't it? You've got your own little business, your little mate, your little bank balance.'

'But it's not my money, Marcus. It's ours. For you and me and the kids.'

'Can't you see how excluded I feel from all this?' He thumped the table. 'My life is going down the tubes and your solution is to pop over to France with the kids. Great timing, Izzie. Top marks!'

'But the whole idea is that we'll make enough money eventually for me not to have to work so hard. That way we can all be together. It's what I want. Really! Marcus, you're welcome to come, if you want to,' she lied. 'It's just a question of getting another plane ticket. Look,' she reached for the phone, 'I'll call right now. I'll book you in—'

Marcus slammed his hand down on the table again. 'You're not listening to me. I'm telling you I feel rejected. What do I have to do to get your attention? Send you a fucking e-mail? You're not really interested in how I feel. Just managing me like you do the kids. Well, I'm not a kid, and you can't brush me off!'

Izzie stood up, too angry now to keep a guard on her tongue. 'If you're not a child, then stop bloody acting like one. Take responsibility for yourself for a change. If you've got a problem, do what I do – sort it out yourself. I've got enough crap to deal with, and I don't want yours.'

He sighed theatrically. 'Yeah, you have such a lot to complain about – don't you? Well, where would you have been without me these last months, eh? I've done everything for you, picked up the kids, fed them, even gone shopping for you. And this is the gratitude you show me!'

Izzie felt an icy calm close round her heart, and she stood up looking at him with distaste. 'Yes, of course. You have been helpful, you've done lots of things for the children. But the one thing only you could have done – give me your complete support, belief and love – well, that's the thing you haven't been able to do.'

Marcus seemed to be having trouble focusing. 'Well, from now on you can pay someone to do it all for you, because I'm out of here, and we'll see how you manage.'

And he walked from the house, leaving the door wide open behind him.

Izzie collapsed into her chair. She felt sick, and her lower back was throbbing with tension. Was that it? Was that the end of it? She felt so confused, she couldn't work out how they'd got to that cold hateful place. She felt a surge of remorse. She went through the motions of clearing up, then went upstairs to bed, where she curled up in a foetal position, her teeth chattering. She thought, he doesn't have his jacket. He'll be cold. Then she fell asleep.

The next morning, he hadn't reappeared. She tried calling his mobile phone, but didn't leave a message. The children didn't seem unduly surprised that Marcus wasn't there, and she quickly made up some story about him having to work early. Charlie complained, 'He was going to help me make an assault course for my Action Man tonight. Will he be here when I get back from school?'

Izzie swallowed hard. She had no idea what to say to him. 'I hope so, darling. But let's see later on. Maybe I can help you if he's busy.'

Izzie and Maddy were due to have another meeting with Elements that afternoon, but since Maddy had gone to visit Peter and Giselle, they had arranged to meet outside the head office. A single phone call was enough to ensure that the kids were taken care of, and she explained carefully before dropping them at school just who would be picking them up, and for how long.

Maddy was already waiting on the pavement by the time

Izzie hopped out of the taxi, looking slightly shifty in a puff-sleeved blouse with drawstring neck. Izzie plastered a smile on her face. 'Moll Flanders, I presume?'

Maddy groaned and rolled her eyes. 'Don't! I've had Giselle going on and on about my clothes since first thing this morning.' She gave her a kiss. 'You all right? You look a bit peaky.'

Izzie couldn't face this now. 'Oh – fine, more or less. I didn't sleep very well. Come on. We'd better go in. Can't keep Billy Bullshit waiting.'

An hour later they emerged on to the pavement as if they'd been punched. 'Could you please pinch me?' muttered Izzie, dazedly. 'I'm not sure that wasn't a dream.'

Every element of Elements had undergone some sort of metamorphosis. Gone were the plasma computer screens, the glass-topped desks, the primary-coloured chairs. Gone was the monochrome tailoring, the gravity-defying hair, the NASA-inspired décor. When the gleaming lift doors hissed open to reveal Finbar, it was not as they had known him. Could he be wearing corduroy? Yes, top to toe – brown corduroy. Positively Hugh Grant in his floppiness, and smiling with a gentle warmth.

As the whole encounter unfolded, it became increasingly clear that Elements hadn't taken on *Paysage Enchanté*. *Paysage Enchanté* had taken over Elements, body and soul. The entire company had suffered a sea-change into something rich and very strange. The walls had been made to look like rustic plaster, and swags of carefully distressed damask hung at the plate-glass windows. In place of the coffee machine, there was now an evil-smelling earthenware teapot. Even the staff were dirndled and Birkenstocked.

A lot may have changed at Elements, but the language remained the same, though even Finbar couldn't cloud the message this time. Sales were fantastic. They were crying out for the new range. The shop within a shop idea was working perfectly – and the 'future-here brands' were apparently being somewhat bypassed in the stampede to reach the *Paysage Enchanté* that now lay at the heart of each store, as Finbar had poetically put it, like a pearl within an oyster.

So Maddy did pinch her hard, then hugged her and Izzie tried to match her enthusiasm, as they staggered (again laden down with samples) homewards.

Pleading a headache, she pretended to fall asleep on the train, and tried to imagine life without Marcus. Would he stay in touch? Would he disappear out of their lives? Or would things just carry on as before, and they'd agree to forget about the whole stupid row?

By the time they got into the car at Ringford, she felt she owed Maddy an explanation.

'Oh. I'm sorry. Are you OK?'

'I don't know and I don't know where he is.' Tears spilt from her eyes, but she dashed them away angrily. 'How could he walk out on the kids like that, without saying where he was going? He's being so fucking selfish!'

'What started it off?'

'Something stupid – I can't even remember. Only it wasn't a stupid row. Not really. We've bickered before but this was something different.' She sniffed unattractively. 'It been building for a while – well, you know that – and for the first time in ages, I really told him how I feel, but I don't think I did it very well. I wasn't – you know – assertive. I got a bit harpy-ish. But it's just so unfair. I look after everyone, and my needs always come last. All I really want is to be loved and looked after, you know, nurtured, and really *cherished*. Is that too much to ask?'

'No, I don't think it is. How do you feel about him now?'

'Bloody angry. But I'm just so confused.' Izzie paused and looked out of the window as Maddy drove. 'And the idea of never seeing him again is terrifying. Oh I'm sorry, Maddy. This must sound so trivial compared to what you've had to endure.

Anyway, I don't really want to talk about it. I can hardly bear even to think about it.'

Maddy put her hand on Izzie's leg. 'It's OK. I'm here when you do feel like talking. And don't worry about the Simon thing. I promise I don't compare. We have two different stories – that's all.'

When they got back to Maddy's, Izzie hugged her friend gratefully, then got in her own car to pick the children up from Janet's. Full of fish pie – why wouldn't they eat hers? – and worn out from playing with Tamasin and Oscar, they bickered in the back seat, but without conviction. As they approached home, Izzie's stomach contracted. What would she find?

A surge of relief mingled with panic. Marcus' car was in the drive. Letting the kids run on ahead, Izzie tried to pin down her feelings, as if they could guide her in her decision about what to do. Was she pleased he was back or not? Both really. At least she knew he wasn't dead in a ditch somewhere, but she didn't think she could face another row like last night's.

She needn't have feared. Marcus was drunk as a skunk, fully dressed and asleep on their bed. While the children tormented him, like Lilliputians pulling at Gulliver washed up on the beach, she quickly checked for empty bottles. There were plenty – at least he hadn't been driving drunk. That she could never have forgiven. She quietly extracted the children from their bedroom, ignored Marcus' slurred, 'Love ya, babe,' and got them ready for bed. She cleared up the mess he'd left, slamming things into the bin and enjoying the moral high ground as she gave in to her resentment, then watched crap on telly. By eleven, showered and in clean pyjamas, she lay down on the very edge of the bed as though on a precipice, and fell into a fitful sleep, punctuated by nightmares about missing trains.

But if Izzie had thought they were going to shuffle back to a flawed but tolerable version of normality, she was mistaken. Marcus was assiduous in his care of the children. If anything, he was far more patient than usual, but to Izzie he said only the barest minimum and never made eye contact. The frosty politeness was somehow worse than rowing. 'Tea?' 'Finished with the paper?' 'No thank you. I'll iron that shirt myself.' By the time they left for France, Izzie was at screaming point.

Ensconced on the plane, Maddy leant across the aisle while the kids grappled with their seat belts. 'Go on then, spill the beans.'

'Oh Maddy, he's being so immature.'

'You never really told me what was going on.' Maddy rummaged in her bag for Pasco's dummy. 'What sparked off that huge row?'

'It was coming here actually.' Izzie shook her head in exasperation. 'He hasn't been as bad as this for ages. The last time was when he was made redundant. That was hell but – well, I suppose I felt he had a right to be furious with the world. He says I neglect him, I always put him last. That's not true, is it?'

Maddy snorted in disgust. 'Honestly, Izzie, he's acting like a spoilt brat. He's a big boy – leave him to stew – he doesn't appreciate you anyway.'

'So you don't think it's me? I was beginning to wonder. Well, now he's giving me the polite stranger treatment.'

'God, that one! That sulking act drives me crazy. Maybe it's good that you're getting away for a while. It'll give you both time to think. You know, it's funny – in some ways he reminds me of Jean Luc's wife.'

Izzie had wondered about her but hadn't dared ask. 'Yeah? What went on there?'

'Oh she was a piece of work all right. A *really* spoilt brat. Gorgeous-looking – exquisite really – but cold as ice. We all hated her from the moment we met her, but he was besotted. Pascale, her name was. He did everything for her, spent a fortune on her and she always wanted more.'

'That doesn't sound much like me and Marcus.'

'No, that was more extreme. But it was another relationship out of balance, with one partner doing all the giving. It's not healthy.'

'No, I don't suppose it is . . .'

They broke off as the plane began to taxi, Jess and Charlie squealing with excitement as it picked up speed and lifted into the air. Will, blasé to the point of ennui, never took his eyes off his Gameboy.

'Tell me more,' urged Izzie, once they'd settled the children with drinks.

'Well, La Pascale never took to the country life – she was a Paris girl all the way. Started spending more and more time there until – well, you can guess. He called up one night and a bloke answered the phone. He's never told me what happened and he never talks about it – or her – now. And there are no pictures of her anywhere in the house. It's as though she'd never existed.'

'Gosh, that's quite romantic in a way. He's clearly got hidden depths. If I did that to Marcus now, I reckon he'd just spend his time in the pub slagging me off.'

'Well, Jean Luc's very Gallic and passionate, in his way. When he falls for someone, he falls big time, I reckon. Even though he's such a big flirt, I think he's still very idealistic about luuurve.' She winked extravagantly at Izzie. 'Maybe he's just waiting for the right woman!'

Izzie's outraged retort was cut off by Florence's wail as Will opened her little sachet of black pepper all over her cake, and the conversation had to stop for a while, but Izzie was pensive for the rest of the journey.

'Aren't small airports great?' enthused Maddy, as they quickly cleared customs at Montpellier and plunged through the arrivals gates. '*Ah, le voilà!*'

Jean Luc's face lit up as he saw them all, and he pretended to reel and stagger under the impact of the children's little bodies as they flung themselves at him. He greeted each one individually, teasing them and making them laugh. 'And where is my little Pasco? No – you've swapped him for a big boy! Izzie!' He whisked her off her feet and spun her round, before planting kisses on each cheek, and one just grazing the side of her mouth. 'I've been looking forward so much to your arrival,' he said softly against her cheek, then turned to Pasco. 'Come on, little man, I'll carry you. Your mother has enough to manage. At least you, Izzie, had the good sense to travel light. I hope we will all fit in the car – Pasco on the roof, maybe?'

Izzie had never been so pleased to see anybody. Straight away she felt better, and the contrast with the Marcus she'd left was overwhelming. In spite of herself, Izzie revelled in spiteful comparisons. 'Sod you, Marcus!' she muttered to herself as she followed the group. 'There are people who treat me well, even if you've forgotten how.'

Izzie threw herself into flirting back at Jean Luc as though her life depended on it. At first she wondered if it was wish fulfilment but, as the day wore on, she realised he too was taking every opportunity to touch her arm, make private jokes with her or talk very quietly so she had to stand closer to hear. At times she caught him watching her with narrowed, speculative eyes. Even Maddy commented on it. 'Blimey, you two are giving it plenty. Is this your bit towards the *entente cordiale*?'

Whatever the reason, Jean Luc's *mas* wove a magic spell on them all. For the children it was an irresistible playground, and they ran wild with little Pasco trying to toddle after them. There were plenty of bedrooms – Izzie counted at least eight as she wandered around, although several were being used to store paintings, books, sculptures and old furniture – but the children had all voted to sleep in the large attic room that stretched almost the length of one side of the building. Although Jean Luc had clearly not finished renovating the house, he'd prioritised the bathrooms. Huge rooms with enormous claw-footed baths, powerful showers, even armchairs with views over the field were irresistible to Izzie. She loved to soak in the bath until her fingers and toes wrinkled up, yet she so rarely got the opportunity at home. Here she would be able to indulge herself to her heart's content, without interruption, and she hugged herself in anticipation.

The buildings away from the main courtyard were all quite low. Stone built and with red-tiled roofs, the farm nestled into the landscape as though it had grown there, the lines of poplars stretching out like rays of light from a star. It crouched on the side of a gentle hill, like a contented, sleepy animal. Behind them the hill sloped gradually up to a distant horizon, sharp against the cornflower blue sky. Below them, a valley opened out like a beautifully drawn map in a children's book, revealing distant villages, pale gold, very straight roads, and oddly shaped fields. The whole view was softened by a shimmer of dust and heat, through which twinkled a far off, sinuous river – the Gard, Jean Luc had told her, a natural boundary to the farm – the course of which was plotted off into the distance in both directions by a fringe of dark green trees, occasionally pierced by a bridge or the odd house.

Within an hour of arriving, the children had all had a go on Coquelicot, a sweet, patient Appaloosa pony – even little Pasco, held safely in place by Jean Luc's big hands round his tummy. They had collected eggs from the biscuit-brown hens that scratched and huffed around the large pen in a far corner of the courtyard. They had chased each other up and down the external stone staircases, although Pasco was not allowed to join in that game, and they had tired themselves out thoroughly. By suppertime – roast chicken cooked on a spit in the functional but simple kitchen, with little potatoes roasted underneath in the fat – the children were already nodding off.

The three adults carried or guided the sleepy children

upstairs and encouraged those who were still conscious to clean their teeth. They all fell asleep within minutes of being tucked into the cool, slightly stiff white sheets, despite the novelty of all being together in a strange place. Maddy went to tuck Pasco into a travel cot in her room, while Jean Luc and Izzie puzzled over the baby listener borrowed from a friend for the attic dormitory, then plugged it in before they crept downstairs together. Izzie smiled secretly to herself, hearing the soft creak on the stairs behind her as he followed her quietly down.

They sat in the firelight, finishing their wine and, for the first time in what felt like weeks, Izzie started to relax. They chatted, laughed, fell silent. Everything felt easy and natural. Even Maddy was calm and sleepy-looking, and was the first to give in. Stretching and yawning very loudly, she mumbled, 'I always feel this way when we come here – I reckon I could sleep for ever. How do you ever get anything done?'

For a moment Izzie felt envy flicker in her at Maddy's casual familiarity with this magical place, and with Jean Luc. His low laugh rumbled. 'I get things done because I like to get things done. You know I've always been that way, Maddy. And you used to tease me about it when we were kids. But you were so lazy then, only living for pleasure. You've changed. Now you are like me. I know – in the morning you will be up at six, rushing around, hurrying everybody and making me crazy. No peace for anyone once you set your mind on something!'

They all laughed, and Maddy went up to bed, kissing Jean Luc on the top of his head as she walked past. Izzie made for the stairs a couple of minutes later, resolved she'd be up at six too. But Jean Luc didn't move, and held her eye as she bade him goodnight.

'You're leaving me all alone? I hoped you would stay with me a little.'

Her mouth went dry. 'I'm . . . a bit tired tonight. Perhaps I'll be a bit more rested tomorrow. Goodnight.'

He nodded and smiled, looking up at her from his chair by the fire. 'I hope so Izzie. *Fais de beaux rêves.*'

The next day they did, indeed, wake early. It took a couple of days to get everything sorted out in the barns Jean Luc had set aside for the boiling and filtering process, but the four women he had hired for the project were capable and hard-working, and soon caught on to the short-cuts and tips Izzie and Maddy had to pass on to them. They took it in turns to keep an eye on the children and Izzie had to operate mostly with sign language, but her few attempted words of French earned herself a particularly warm smile from Jean Luc. Once they had fully briefed the women and checked and rechecked the process, they were free to have fun.

Colette, who had joined them after spending a few days with her parents, was an extra pair of hands, so they passed the time taking the children out for walks, shopping trips to the market, and having impromptu picnics. The relaxing fresh air was having an effect, and there were no more early morning starts for anyone but Jean Luc. Izzie watched with pleasure as the shadows under Maddy's eyes gradually disappeared. But her feeling were not entirely altruistic. Once Maddy had crawled up to bed each night around eleven, she and Jean Luc fell into a pattern of sitting in front of the fire watching the embers tumble, drinking Armagnac, and talking about everything under the sun, his voice low and mesmerising.

It should all have been relaxing for Izzie too, but the combination of the warm early summer sun and Jean Luc's presence made her tingle with anticipation. Something had to happen, but she knew he was leaving it up to her. She let the children make the odd duty call to Marcus, but kept her own conversations with him as brief as possible. She resented the interruption. This wasn't the Izzie that had left, angry, resentful and confused, only a few days ago. She felt desirable and desired. In control.

On their last full day it wasn't until half past eight that Izzie sat back in the wooden kitchen chair, and pushed back her plate after a breakfast of fresh croissants. She looked across at Maddy, still in her pyjamas, hair uncombed, and stretched like a cat. 'I could take any amount of this. I'm just doing what I feel like, for the first time in years. I'm not thinking about anything or anyone else and I don't give a stuff about any consequences.' Her eyes glittered recklessly, and she leant forward con-spiratorially. 'It feels bloody fantastic.'

With plans for a huge farewell picnic under way, the children were all in a party mood and the preparation became steadily more elaborate. There was a barn that Jean no longer used about ten kilometres away, on a tributary of the Gard that widened into a tranquil pool – ideal for bathing. From the first visit, the children had claimed it as their own, and insisted on going there every day.

'OK, that's everything packed. It seems like a mountain of food, but if we're spending the whole day there, we'll certainly get through it.' Maddy squeezed another few ficelles into a space between the seats of an old Land Rover. 'Are you sure you can't come until later, Jean Luc? We've got *tarte aux cerises* – you've never been able to resist that.'

'Temptress – try to keep a little for me to have later. I have to go into town, but it won't take all day. I'll be there as soon as I can manage.'

'I don't promise anything. You'd better not be too long – that's all!' She glanced at Izzie. 'Are you all right, love? You look awful.'

Izzie felt it. 'I don't know. It's come on suddenly. I've got a ghastly headache, and I feel really queasy. Maybe I've just had too much coffee.'

Jean Luc turned to stare at Izzie for a moment. 'It's true,' he said. 'You're lips are pale. You should lie down.' He brought her a couple of paracetamol and a glass of water, which she swallowed gratefully. She sat hunched over on the step, feeling nauseous and shielding her eyes from the early morning sun, while the others continued their preparations. Jean Luc looked at her narrowly.

'Maddy, can you and Colette manage the children on your own for a bit? If Izzie rests now, I can bring her with me later.'

Maddy paused for a moment, and she caught Izzie's eye. A long look of complicity passed between them. 'Yes, of course we can manage. Izzie, take as long as you like. You need this. It will do you good. Just do exactly what you feel like, *you hear me?*'

Izzie smiled hesitantly. 'Yes, I understand. I think I'd better have a rest. I feel so odd!'

The children left her with barely a backward glance, and she watched as Maddy drove out through the arched gateway that led from the courtyard. Silence fell heavily between Izzie and Jean Luc, and they went back inside together. She sat down slowly on the window seat and Jean Luc leant back against the huge porcelain sink and folded his arms, looking at her. She felt as though she had never been so thoroughly studied in her life. His face was impassive but his eyes were roaming over her body, taking in every detail. She smiled a little. Normally, this intense scrutiny would unnerve her, have her twitching and fussing, chattering to try to dispel the tension. But she felt relaxed, powerful even, and revelled in the electricity that arced between them, filling the whole of the cool, stoneflagged kitchen. Her headache had receded – had already started to do so before the others left – but she had made a calculated decision. Dare she take the opportunity?

Still he watched her, looking almost amused at her cool returning stare. She was determined not to make the next move. After what seemed like hours, he stood up. 'I think I'm going to take you to bed.'

'Good idea. I'm sure I'll feel better.'

'You must treat these sudden headaches with respect. I'm glad I'm here to look after you.'

'So am I. I need to be taken care of. And you're the very person.'

'Can you walk by yourself?'

'I'm not sure.'

'Would you like me to help you?'

'Mmmm.'

He crossed the room almost before she had replied, and held out his hands to her. She could see he was breathing rapidly – so was she. She slowly raised one hand to take his, deferring as long as she could the moment when they touched. Then he simply took her in his arms, lifted her off her feet and carried her upstairs. After a moment's resistance, she let her head rest against his chest and closed her eyes. She felt his breath on her face as he took the stairs calmly, not hurrying, and his lips brushed her brow then settled on her head. She could feel him inhaling the scent of her hair and she shivered.

'Right,' said Pru, sweeping into the restaurant ten minutes late, looking glamorous in browns and beiges and wafting perfume after her. She ordered a glass of wine – 'Well, you're the only one who has to look pure and sweet' – and settled herself in her chair. 'Let's talk work first, then we can get back to being like it was in the old days. Much as I love Izzie, it's fun to have you to myself again.'

From her Mary Poppins-type bag, she produced a bulging file and handed it over. 'I've had Emma, my latest recruit, put together your press cuttings to date. I have to say it's staggering.' Maddy flicked through the pages. Some cuttings she'd seen and others were new: small pieces in the *Sunday Times*, *Independent* and *Telegraph*; larger features in the women's press; the big spreads from the *Daily Mail* and *Country Lifestyle*; Izzie and Maddy looking goofy in *OK!* mentions in the trade press.

'Pru, was all this from the initial press release?'

Pru blew out smoke from her cigarette, and Maddy leant forward to breathe it in. 'Some of it, but you'd be amazed. We are actually getting unsolicited calls and I've had to put one of my girls on to it virtually full-time. The word just seems to be spreading.'

'Like a rash.' Maddy skim-read the glowing praise, the confirmation that the product really was effective, but what struck her most was the theme all the copy kept coming back to: 'What this product proves,' one beauty writer had eloquently put it, 'is that we have invested too much in all that man and his endless capacity for invention has created. Too often we are blinded by the promises, often unfulfilled, that can be achieved from a test tube. We need to readjust our perspective, and look back to the earth from which we all emerged.'

'Bloody hell, this is heavy stuff.' Maddy's eyes were wide as she looked at Pru's rather self-satisfied expression. 'All we did was boil down a weed and put it in a jar.'

'Maybe, but you boiled down something else when you did it. You managed to pop the balloon – if I'm not mixing too many metaphors – that is man's relentless search for perfection.'

'Christ, Pru, you're talking to me, Maddy, not writing your next press release.'

'Darling,' Pru picked up the menu, 'most of the gumph in those features didn't come from me. I think I'll have a Thai Prawn Caesar salad.' She dismissed the waiter and put the menu down again. 'No, as I said to you right off, you have managed, whether you both meant to or not, to hit a nerve at a time when a nerve was ripe to be hit. We are on the verge of being able to reinvent ourselves by cloning, all in an attempt to achieve the only thing we haven't yet – immortality. Thank you.' She took a slug of wine the waiter poured for her. 'Suddenly we are scared by the speed of things, and along comes a product not just made using the basest ingredients the earth can provide, but invented by a woman who was a real earth mother—'

'Or so we think – she might have been the village bike.'

'Don't interrupt. I'm in full flow! A real earth mother, who knew what a woman's role should be, who raised her family in a natural environment, and you are the glowing, healthy proof that her genetic line was strong and true.'

Maddy looked at her in silence. 'But come on, this back-to-the-earth thing is nothing new. People have been ramming natural health and beauty products down our throats for years. You can't move for anchovy and horseradish skin toners and mango and chopped liver foot creams, you said so yourself.'

'Ah, but this is different. All that is within the framework of the modern age. It's all chrome and clean and clone-like. We are all buying into the same image, whether it's what we put on our bodies or how we decorate our homes. You've come up with something fresh.'

'Can we eat now?'

Pru laughed. 'I'm sorry. Got on my high horse a bit, didn't I?'

The waiter glided over and put down the salad for Pru and risotto with wild mushrooms for Maddy. A real treat. She loved the stuff but never had the time to make one for herself.

'So diatribe over,' said Pru through a mouthful. 'Tell me, how was sunny France?'

'Interesting. I think something went on between Izzie and Jean Luc.' Maddy fiddled with her napkin to distract her from the craving for a cigarette. 'She seems fairly enrapt by him. You know Jean Luc from the old days. He's criminally flirtatious and likes nothing more than a bit of encouragement, so much of the time I felt like a spare part. I'm not sure but I think they may have slept together.'

'Bloody hell,' Pru's eyes widened. 'She's going to have to be very careful the press don't get hold of that. I have to admit I'm quite surprised. She seems very innocent. What's her husband like?' She took another sip of her wine. 'Is he in the art world?'

'Well, he's not one of my faves actually. We just didn't hit it off right from the start. I suppose he had me down as some kind of airhead Sloane, with a big house and more money than sense. And now I've committed the ultimate sin of going into business with his wife and we're making a success of it. The better we do the less he seems to like it. Male pride I guess, especially as he was once in a big London advertising agency, but he was made redundant, and isn't really working at the moment.'

'Who did he work for?' Pru stuck her fork into the salad put in front of her.

Maddy took a mouthful of the delicious risotto, and let the flavours spread over her tongue. 'Oh don't ask me,' she mumbled, 'something something McCormack, I think.'

'Stock. What's his first name?'

'Marcus.'

Pru paused for a moment. 'Wait a minute. I know about Marcus Stock. Yes, I *certainly* know about him. And he wasn't made redundant.'

Maddy stopped, a forkful midway to her mouth. 'What?'

'No. It was quite a scandal at the time. Let me think. They were pitching for a big account – British Airways or someone like that – and Stock had been headhunted by a competing agency. Anyway as I recall he committed the cardinal sin, and tipped them off about what Mitchell Baines McCormack planned to pitch. He was rumbled and given the heave ho. It was all over *Campaign*.' She paused. 'Did Izzie tell you he was made redundant?'

Maddy put down her fork, suddenly feeling sick. 'No. Not as such. I think she said there was an agency takeover and that, as he'd had a pretty lean period creatively, he lost his job.'

'I'll say he's had a lean period. He used to be good, one of the best, but I don't think there's an agency in London that would have hired him at the time. No wonder they skedaddled to the provinces. Could explain why he's not keen on your high profile in the press at the moment. They'd have a field day with that one.'

Maddy leant back in her chair, disconcerted. Had Izzie known this all along? Was her story just to cover up and save Marcus' dignity? She couldn't quite believe that Izzie would have told her a lie – or at least been economical with the truth – but then she'd told her all about Marcus' job at their first lunch together. She was bound to be cautious with someone she hardly knew.

She worried about Pru's revelation all the way back on the train. If Izzie hadn't given her the full story then, why hadn't she been truthful since? God, Maddy had opened up enough about herself and her life and, gazing out of the window, she felt hurt. Didn't Izzie trust her enough?

But then there was always the chance that Izzie didn't know the real story. Marcus was such an arrogant man, and Izzie would have been unlikely to have read the trade press like *Campaign*, not when she worked in children's book publishing, which wasn't exactly cutting edge. No, she thought, I wouldn't put it past him to hush up the whole thing and just whisk Izzie out of London on the pretext that they couldn't afford to live there any more. Izzie was so wonderfully naïve, and so devoted to him, she'd have done whatever he wanted. But then hadn't she, Maddy, done exactly the same when Simon suggested – OK, arranged – for them to move out of London, and she had been just as guilty of not really questioning very deeply his work set-up. She'd just assumed. How dangerous assumptions can be. Armed with the information, and not quite sure what to do with it, she decided to think about it for a while, and simply observe.

'So how are you feeling?' She asked Izzie when she called her later that evening. 'Recovered from the trip?'

'Yes, yes fine. Piles of washing to do and the house in chaos, but it's nice to be home.' Either Marcus was listening or Izzie was being strangely off-hand with her. 'It's been crazy today though. Elements have been on the phone almost constantly wanting to chivvy up the next order. Lillian was at the dentist and Karen got the phone before I could get to it, so God knows what they thought, but I managed a schmooze which you would have been proud of.'

'Learnt at the knee of the expert schmoozer!'

'Naturally,' Izzie laughed, and sounded back to normal. 'How was Pru?'

'Quite philosophical. She wants to take us beyond hippy, and make us more of a statement against the mediocrity and image obsession of today.' She tried to précis, not quite so eloquently, Pru's spiel, but Izzie seemed to get the message.

'I can see what she means, but isn't that a bit of a tall order? We're only a couple of—'

'Housewives!' they said simultaneously. 'That's exactly what I said.' Maddy put her feet up on the table and lit her first cigarette of the day. 'But she seems to think we have hit a nerve, and that we must exploit it. I was thinking. Let's see if Peter can come up and we could have a meeting with him and Geoff about financing the new product launch. We could get on with sourcing the ingredients tomorrow, and then you can call Jean Luc and give him the *centpertuis* order.' She waited, expecting Izzie's coy giggle. There was a pause.

'No, you ring him, Maddy. Would you mind?'

Confused, Maddy didn't mention him again, or Marcus and the sacking, but the rest of the week was too mad anyway. The team worked flat out, with intermittent complaints from Crispin that at this rate he'd forget how to mix cement he hadn't done it for so long, and the next order was ready for despatch to Elements on time and in one piece.

Maddy's ear went pink she spent so long on the phone to

suppliers and to labs about accreditation for the samples of the moisturiser, and when she wasn't doing that, she was poring over Luce's book, and vats of more trial recipes with Izzie. There was barely time to mention anything, so preoccupied were they with proportions, temperatures and fragrances, and Lillian had to remind them not to miss a meeting with the website design team – an hour's meeting about flash plug-ins and html that might as well have been in Serbo-Croat.

'Is it just me,' sighed Maddy, flopping into a chair with mental exhaustion, 'or is the rest of the world talking bollocks?'

'Well, how about this for plain speaking?' said Lillian, smiling enigmatically as she replaced the phone. 'That was the alternative therapies buyer at Harrods. She wants to arrange a meeting.'

Lying on Will's bed a week later, curtains drawn against the evening sunshine, and listening to him read hesitantly about Biff, Chip and the Magic Key, Maddy felt as though she too had held a magic key and been transported by mistake into a new and strange world. Over the last incredible weeks she had been in negotiations with one of the biggest cosmetics outlets in the country, had been bamboozled by techno-whizzes, had been approached by the most famous department store in the world, all because of a weed recipe Izzie and she had cobbled together in her kitchen. Yes, the money was thrilling, and they had both gleefully signed a fat cheque to pay back Peter. The fees were secure, bills could be paid, and she had new car brochures – eco friendly, of course – sitting on the side in the kitchen just waiting for her to pick the colour for the trim.

But frankly it scared her. It wasn't so much the pots of healing balm per se, although they'd started to dominate her days and most of her dreams at night. It was what they had come to represent.

Here she was curled up with her little son, the same Mummy he had always known, and yet she was having to be someone else at the same time, acting out a role that was uncomfortable and farcical. What was she playing at, having Colette drive thirty miles to buy chicken nuggets and pizza for the children – there was only so much wholemeal pasta they could stomach – in case someone spotted her in the local supermarket? Only two days ago she had found herself with a copy of *Tatler* in her hand in WH Smith in Ringford, but had had to stuff it back on the shelf as if it was something smutty when Fiona Price had lolloped around the corner.

'Hey, Mum, you're hurting me,' complained Will and she realised she was holding him too tightly as if he, like the rest of her previous life, would suddenly evaporate. This time last year they had still been in London, and she'd never even heard of Ringford. Life had been simple, mapped out by an unchallenging routine of lunches and dinner parties, interspersed with copious bouts of shopping. Now here she was, a single mother, at the vanguard of a new sociological trend with implications she couldn't begin to grasp. What on earth would Simon have said about it all? Something funny and sensible and grounding, no doubt.

The sense of being on a bolting horse only worsened a couple of days later when Peter and Geoff arrived at the barn. 'It seems to me,' launched Geoff without preamble 'and I don't know anything about cosmetics, that you should exploit this success story right now and launch further products. Create a range and a stronger brand image.'

'We're on to it,' said Izzie, 'and we think we've got the recipe right for a moisturiser and a cleanser. We just need the accreditation, but I've a bit of a boyfriend at the labs and he'll make sure it's tested as soon as possible.' She picked up some notes from the desk. 'And now that we are ordering broadly similar ingredients but in substantially larger quantities, we're pretty sure we can get huge discounts on our orders.'

Geoff whipped out a pad and they all settled down to

number-crunch. 'You certainly have the capacity here,' he said, solemn and businesslike, 'to cope with the extra production, but you will need to get in more staff.' He lowered his voice. 'Your current . . . er . . . workforce is working well, but you are going to need to treble it.' He handed each of them a spreadsheet, and Maddy could just about work out from the sea of figures what their outlay would have to be. Next to it, he had calculated the potential income from extending the range, and had estimated the profit once costs were deducted. She had to look twice, convinced he had put the decimal point in the wrong place.

'Are you sure this is right?'

'Obviously it's a bit of a stab in the dark, but to the nearest grand I think I'm not far off.'

Izzie and Maddy looked at each other in silence.

'Time to buy back that piano I think,' smiled Izzie, delight in her eyes.

'I think you might be able to run to the whole orchestra!'

Chapter 14

As July settled in, it started to get cocky, chasing away the rain clouds to start off with, then all clouds, even the wispy, high-up ones that look like cherubs. There was day after day of uninterrupted azure, with barely a breath of wind. So where, thought Izzie, does all this dew come from? The bottoms of her drawstring hemp trousers were soaked on the short walk across the lawn to the car each morning. Of course, the grass was far too long, but Marcus had been assiduous in not doing anything beyond taking care of the children for the last few weeks. He took them to school and picked them up in his new car, a very efficient people mover with a name that sounded like a 1950s cinema chain, and wearing his fancy new duds – mostly linen, thank goodness, so the image remained intact.

He didn't seem to feel awkward with her providing the money for the new treats he was obviously enjoying. Or if he did, he hid it pretty well. It was so hard to imagine what he was feeling any more. He gave no clues. At first, Izzie had wondered if he would feel she was trying to buy her way back into his favour, by releasing some money for these and the other things they had needed for so long – like a new downstairs loo and new carpet in the children's rooms. But he seemed remarkably sanguine about the whole thing. In a way she'd been dreading him striking an attitude, going all proud on her, but when he didn't she felt peeved – and this troubled her. He didn't even comment when her piano turned up again – yet she'd probably have hated it if he had – just started to pile his discarded newspapers on it, as he had done before.

It hadn't been the first thing she bought after France. No, her guilt had been too overwhelming for that, and she'd started with the telephoto lenses he needed. Only once they were safely locked up in his darkroom could she think about what she really wanted. She'd been torn about going to the piano warehouse, in case it wasn't there any more. Finally, with a pocketful of readies and her heart in her mouth, she'd driven over there. At first, she didn't see it, and angry disappointment tightened her throat. She'd been about to leave, too upset to even ask about it, when the funny little man who'd come to value it suddenly popped up. He'd stared at her, blinking rapidly for a moment or so, then hurried to the office without saying a word. A moment later, he'd reappeared and bobbed up in front of her so suddenly, she'd yelped.

'Mrs Stock, isn't it? Were you, er, looking for something special?'

'I was just looking, you know . . . wondering if—'

'Your piano, the Bechstein. A fine instrument. The finest we've had here in a long time. It's not here . . .'

Her shoulders slumped. 'Oh . . . that's what I was afraid of. Well, I suppose—'

'No, Mrs Stock. I moved it out of here. Actually . . .' He stopped and fumbled for words. 'I moved it into the house. The temperature out here – it gets very warm in the afternoons. I've . . . I've been playing it myself actually.' He laughed sadly and shrugged his shoulders. 'I knew you'd be back for it, so I thought it had better be kept out of the way. I didn't want any children,' he shuddered, 'with sticky fingers trying it out. We can arrange for it to be brought back to you later this week.'

Izzie was overwhelmed and laughter bubbled in her throat. 'You were hiding it, weren't you? Trying to stop anyone else seeing it. I don't believe it! I was so afraid it would have gone. Thank you so much!'

He accepted her thanks with embarrassed pleasure, but had the grace to be shamefaced when she saw the price he had been hoping to sell it for – almost twice what he'd given her. Still – she was so pleased that she gladly split the difference, then added on some more. 'Consider it payment for board and lodging,' she called as she drove away, waving through the open window. And she hummed along tunelessly with Radio 3 all the way home.

But there wasn't much time to play it. An unsolicited plug from a flavour-of-the-month actress on *Parkinson* resulted in another surge of sales, and an invitation to appear on Breakfast TV. What an ordeal that had been! The *Paysage Enchanté* philosophy had been raked over on the comfy sofas, but considering their nerves, they both thought they'd handled it pretty well.

They can't have done too badly because the requests for the balm increased even further. Izzie's feet barely touched the ground, and it was only a phone call from her mother asking her what she wanted that reminded her that her birthday was looming. Marcus sure as hell hadn't mentioned it. If anything, he was on the defensive. 'But you never said!' he ranted a few days later. 'I'm not a mind reader! I just assumed you'd want to have a quiet time with us. I mean, you're hardly ever here are you?'

'I don't want a big fuss. I just thought you might have booked something. Dinner out, flowers and a babysitter, something like that. And I did hope I wouldn't have to buy my own cake this year. Come on, Marcus. It is a special birthday.'

She wearily began to clear the breakfast table. It looked like the piano would have to be her present to herself.

*

'What do you mean you're not doing anything?'

Izzie looked up from the desk. 'Well, I made the stupid mistake I suppose of leaving it up to him to organise something. Silly me!'

'It's your fortieth birthday, for heaven's sake, even reaching those heady heights is worth celebrating, though of course I wouldn't know.'

'No,' smiled Izzie wanly. 'You're just a mere babe.' She rubbed her hands wearily over her eyes, and went back to the spreadsheet in front of her. 'If we get Karen and Angie to do the early morning shift, then Donna to start at three, we should be able to keep the line running for about sixteen hours. Keep that up for a week and we'll have managed two weeks' production in—'

'No, I'm sorry I'm not going to let this drop, Izzie. It's your birthday, and you've worked bloody hard over the last seven months. I love a party and we're going to celebrate.' She thought for a moment. 'It's Friday, isn't it? Right, book a babysitter or persuade that Marcus of yours. You're coming over to my house.'

Driving home, late as usual, Maddy was incredulous that Marcus could have let the whole thing go without making some sort of effort. Birthdays for her had always been sacrosanct. When she was a child, Giselle had gone way over the top with them, no doubt to make up for her dad not being around, and Maddy would rush into her bedroom at some ungodly hour, confident that she would find a heap of deliciously wrapped presents on the bedroom chair. For her twenty-first, Giselle and Peter had told her to be at Heathrow with her passport, and they'd flown Concorde to spend the most fantastic weekend in New York, shopping as if their lives depended on it, and eating copious amounts to recover from the strain and exhaustion of spending so much money.

Simon had always made her birthday fun too, and she was

dreading that milestone in September. Their June wedding anniversary had been bad enough, though she had managed to cover up her distress from everyone else. Giselle had remembered of course, and surprisingly, she'd had a call from Cynthia. Contact had been pretty thin on the ground in that department, but this time Simon's mother sounded choked and weepy. That, Maddy supposed, had helped her be strong and she'd got through the day somehow.

For her thirtieth birthday, Simon had bought her a bath-bomb and, smiling at her barely concealed disappointment, had run a deep hot bath and got in with her – well, it had been pre-children. As the bomb fizzed and dissipated in the water, there at the bottom of the bath she'd discovered and fished out the beautiful square-cut diamond ring that she still couldn't bear to take off. She'd thanked him the best way she knew how, and the water that splashed as a result on the bathroom floor had ruined the cork tiles.

Sex in the bath. Would she ever have sex again? She was beginning to wonder. It had been nine months, and she wasn't sure she'd gone nine months without sex since she'd reached the age of consent. An old, single friend of theirs from London had always joked that if you didn't have sex for long enough, you ceased to want it. Maddy was beginning to see what he meant. The thought of getting into bed with someone else would seem like infidelity anyway. She was a widow – not a word she even let herself use – and she'd shelved that particular part of her life.

'It's Izzie's birthday on Friday,' she told Colette, as she came in the door and scooped Pasco up into her arms. 'She's going to come over here, in lieu of anything else to do, and I've got a little plan. Do you think you could help?' and grabbing a spare piece of paper, she started to write a shopping list for Colette.

Finding something suitable for Izzie's birthday was quite a challenge. In a normal world, Maddy would have had no hesitation in high-tailing it to London for the day, but she couldn't for two reasons. One: they were flat out at the barn and there would be hell to pay from everyone if she disappeared without explanation. Two: she was severely restricted as to what she could buy. She'd have loved nothing more than to spoil Izzie with a pair of sexy little Emma Hope kitten heel shoes, or that Anya Hindmarch bag she noticed her salivating over in a magazine. But thanks to Pru's restrictions, the only options available to her were from the farm shop. A bag of carrots for her fortieth? What the hell, it was a special occasion. She'd throw in a cauliflower too.

She strongly suspected that the present Izzie would appreciate most was a certain French farmer, delivered to her door with a ribbon around his neck. Izzie had actually been pretty quiet on the subject of Jean Luc since their return from France, and his phone calls had been less frequent to Huntingford House too. He was no doubt spending the time calling Izzie on the QT when Marcus was out of the way. What subterfuge! Maddy was thrilled for Izzie that Jean Luc was lavishing her with so much attention, even though she knew it was morally very wrong. She sent him a text message, alerting him to the impending birthday, though she was pretty confident that Izzie would have told him about it. She wondered later, as she turned out the downstairs lights and locked the front door, whether they had talked to each other about Marcus. I do hope not. Izzie needs Jean Luc's passion, not his sympathy.

Going up for her bath, she noticed a crisp copy of *Harpers & Queen* on the hall table, obviously discarded by Colette – or perhaps kindly left out for Maddy to help keep her sane. What a treat. Ten minutes later she was up to her ears in Floris Edwardian Bouquet bubble bath which she'd found discarded at the back of a bathroom cupboard (a Christmas present some years ago from Cynthia), was smoking her one surreptitious fag of the day (trying hard not to get it wet), and flicking through the magazine. God, it seemed like another world. Dinky little suits, delicious shoes, sumptuous fashion spreads. In the past she'd have turned down the corners of some of the pages and made a point of seeking out a bag or pair of trousers that took her fancy. Now it all seemed like forbidden territory. Look but don't touch. She did notice, however, that the beauty pages had a definite emphasis on oh-so-natural products, and were less about putting on the slap than going minimal. The beauty editor had made a strong story about the importance of clear skin, and the facing page had a luscious ad for Elements, 'now stocking the full *Paysage Enchanté* range'.

Throwing down the magazine beside the bath, she spotted the advertisement on the back cover: a beautiful, partially clad model, posing seductively in Armani. She pondered it for a moment. Now she might just get away with that. And, removing the soap and stubbing her cigarette out in the soap dish, she made a mental note to add another couple of items to Colette's shopping list.

Friday morning, and she made sure she got in early, giving herself enough time to string up some balloons on the balustrade around the office. It was a stunning day, with that chill of an early summer morning that will turn out to be scorcher. If they hadn't been so busy, it would have been fun to bunk off for a long pub lunch somewhere by a river and drink Pimms until late into the afternoon. Angie and Karen had been there since seven on the early shift, and dived on the bag of buns and doughnuts Maddy had brought with her.

'One each, children,' she laughed. 'They are supposed to be for Izzie's birthday breakfast.'

'We haven't forgotten,' said Angie, mouth full. 'I've bought her a little something. Nothing fancy.'

Lillian pulled up next in her lurid little green car. Getting out, Maddy saw she had in her arms an enormous bunch of garishly coloured flowers attached to which was a helium balloon with 'Happy 40th' spelt out in silver letters. She looked embarrassed but rather pleased with herself. By the time the birthday girl pulled up, the whole place looked really quite festive, and the anxious face Izzie had worn when she got out of the car dissolved into wide smiles of pleasure.

'What a treat!' she said admiring the pile of presents on her desk. Work had been suspended for an extra early coffee break and everyone was helping themselves to the buns Maddy had bought, supplemented by supplies of Lillian's famous doughnuts, and slurping fresh coffee courtesy of the redundant coffee machine Maddy had bought in from home specially for the celebration.

'Oh how sweet,' Izzie's enthusiasm could only be admired as she opened Angie's present, a dancing flower which played music as soon as anyone moved a muscle. Donna stepped forward with her offering, a wooden plaque in the shape of a big cosy mum, with the words 'I only have one nerve left and you are on it'. Karen had put together a selection of risqué bits and pieces: a pink thong with grey lace, one of those back massagers that resemble male genitalia (if you squint your eyes), and a jar of Lick it Off Me chocolate spread. Izzie showed suitable *éclat* here too and Maddy resolved that on her birthday, she'd ask for just cards.

Crispin pulled up in his van at the last minute – perhaps it was the smell of doughnuts. They hadn't seen much of him recently, because thankfully he was spending less and less time at the barn, and was finally putting in those windows at home he'd stored for so long. He dashed upstairs, breathless, whispered something to Lillian and handed Izzie a CD-shaped package. 'If you hate it I'll take it back,' he panted, making a lunge for the plate of food. But this time, when Izzie opened the paper and revealed a CD of Brahms concerti, her eyes filled up with genuine tears of appreciation. She gave him a big kiss on the cheek and he blushed suitably.

'Right,' said Maddy, getting into her car at the end of the day. 'Work's over now, Mrs Stock. It's POETS day, remember?'

'What's that then?' demanded Donna, stubbing out her fag on the barn step.

Izzie, Maddy and, surprisingly, Lillian too choroused, 'Piss Off Early Tomorrow's Saturday.'

'And anyway,' finished Maddy, 'old women like you should take it easy.' She ducked the ball of wrapping paper which came her way. 'See you at my house about eight-thirty. And do not fail me.'

Colette had fulfilled her shopping obligations brilliantly, and at nine on the dot, Maddy lit the candles, whipped out chicken tikka masala, sag aloo, pilau rice and piles of naan breads and poppadoms – the best the local take-away could provide – from the warming oven of the Aga, and laid them out on her poshest wedding-list dinner plates in front of Izzie, who had already made serious inroads into the cans of Carlsberg she had put out on the table.

'Oh what a complete and utter thrill!' Izzie's eyes widened with glee and disbelief at the sheer depravity of it. 'It's been aeons since I dared venture to the Indian. Is this really all for us?' Three-quarters of an hour and a tub of chocolate chip ice cream later, and they both sat with their belts undone and a look of stupefied satisfaction on their faces.

'Now, to raise the tone somewhat, the champagne!' and Maddy waddled to the fridge to bring out the chilled bottle, stopping to collect two delicate fluted glasses on the way.

'This reminds me. I had a lovely text message from Jean Luc,' said Izzie, trying not to slur her words. 'It was all in French, but I think he was wishing me well!'

'It could have been something sexy and suggestive.'

Izzie stuck her finger in the fluted glass to stop the bubbles overflowing from Maddy's rather misdirected pouring. 'I don't think so. Then Janet popped round with a bottle of elderflower wine' (they both wrinkled their noses) 'and a sweet bunch of cow parsley. She really is a darling.'

'Now for my present. Da daa!' And she whipped out the package from the kitchen drawer where she had stuffed it earlier. Colette's dash to London that day, despite nearly missing the train back, was worth the angst just to see the look of sheer pleasure on Izzie's face as she unwrapped the cool white linen top and wide-legged trousers from their delicious Armani tissue paper.

'Oh Maddy,' she breathed. And with no more ado, stripped down to her bra and knickers and put them on. 'I've never owned anything Armani in my life. I never thought I was grown up enough.'

'Well, if you aren't now, you never will be,' said Maddy, coming over to adjust the trousers as if she was dressing a window display mannequin. 'And anyway you deserve it. I just thought it was boho enough that you might get away with it, without looking like you have strayed too far from the sub-liminal message, man,' and she put on her best seventies hippy voice. Grabbing the wine and the glasses, she virtually herded Izzie into the sitting room. 'I'll do the washing-up later.'

They both sat in a heap of contentment, side by side on the sofa. Maddy lit a cigarette, and, without asking, Izzie helped herself to one too. 'Did Marcus give you anything then?'

'Oh some Jo Malone and the new Grisham he wanted to read, a stalwart at Christmas and birthdays, and he helped the children make me breakfast. I've always loved Coco Pops and apple juice.'

'Not together I hope?' and Izzie snorted so hard it took a good slap on her back to stop her coughing fit. There was a pause while she recovered and had another mouthful of champagne.

'D'ja know – this has been just the best birthday. I've loved it. Perhaps I'll be forty again very soon.'

Maddy looked at her in her new white linen. Something wasn't right. 'D'ja know. There's something missing. Follow me,' and grabbing both their glasses, led Izzie upstairs, only tripping once. 'Better shut the curtains,' she said, putting the glasses down on the bedside table. 'In case *Hello!* magazine has the paparazzi with their long lenses trained on the window.'

'Invite them in. Especially if they are good-looking.' Izzie slumped down on the bed. 'I hope your intentions are honourable. I love you, but not quite that much.'

'Oh, entirely dishonourable,' said Maddy giggling and opening her cupboard doors wide, started pulling things off the shelves and throwing them on the bed. Next she went into her bathroom, and pulled out make-up bags stuffed away through lack of recent use.

Maddy clapped her hands and, taking another swig of her drink, announced: 'Let's dress up.'

Over the next half-hour they behaved like children, trying on shoes and hats, discarding silk palazzo pants, skimpy tops and evening dresses and delving in the cupboards for more, wrapping two or three belts each round their waists. Izzie pranced about amidst the growing debris on the floor in one of Maddy's more beautiful Ghost dresses, champagne in hand and tottering on Jimmy Choos, swishing scarves like a catwalk model. 'Oooh,' she cooed. 'This is like an orgy.'

'It's been too bloody long since we wore decent clothes. Now the slap.' She picked up handfuls of cosmetics. 'Come and sit here. I'm your make-up artist for the night. Tonight, Matthew, you are going to be—'

'Dolly Parton?' suggested Izzie helpfully, wobbling precariously.

'Your wish is my command.' Maddy preceded to lay on, with as steady a hand as she could muster in the circumstances, thick layers of foundation, her best Chanel purple and green eye shadow and YSL eyeliner, swirling blusher in big circles on Izzie's cheeks, and her best Bobby Brown lipstick in a huge, exaggerated cupid's bow around Izzie's mouth. Izzie stood up precariously to look at the finished result in the dressing table mirror.

'Oh madam, you are so talented,' she giggled, her mirth rising. 'You have made me look so *beauutiful*. I hardly know myself. Watch out, Donatella Versace.'

'Well, dear, it's been a while, and I may have lost my touch a bit.'

'My turn,' said Izzie, swapping places, and after five minutes of artwork, punctuated by periods of painful laughter that made their stomachs ache, Maddy looked like a cross between Sophia Loren and Barbara Cartland.

'I think that look works for you. Perhaps not quite enough mascara.' She lunged towards Maddy, wand in hand. 'You need to end up with only about three big fat eyelashes, so I'll have to stick them together a bit more.' Maddy stayed as still as she could, for fear of losing an eye. Izzie took a step back to admire her handiwork, stumbling on a Lulu Guinness bag left on the floor. 'Perfect. D'ja know,' she propped herself up on the bed and refilled their glasses from a fresh bottle, 'now I'm forty I've made a decision. I can finally admit to all those things I've never had the courage to admit to.'

Maddy joined her on the bed and curled her feet up underneath her, nursing her glass in her lap. 'But am I allowed to play this game, being so young and all?'

'OK, you are honorary . . .' Izzie pronounced the 'h'. 'Honorary old lady for the night.'

'So examples then?'

'Like . . .' She waved her hands, casting around for an example. 'I know. I just hate thongs. Butt flossing. They feel like cheese wire.'

'Exactly,' Maddy nodded frantically. 'Make you walk funny.'

'And,' Izzie thought for a moment, 'I think Virginia Woolf was a dreadful writer.'

'Never read her, too intellectual, but Picasso's crap.' Maddy lit a cigarette.

'Aaah awful awful.' Izzie howled with laughter. 'Terrible! Pasco could do better. Picassssco!' She screeched again, 'What about films?'

'Four weddings and a bar mitzvah?' Maddy held up her cigarette like Kirsten Scott Thomas, and put on her clipped, brittle voice. ' "It's you, Charlie, it's always been you." Pathetic. Nothing more pitiful than unrequited love.'

'Oh! She was the best bit in it.' They both pondered a moment and Maddy filled their glasses again. 'This champagne's yummy. Oh Bellinis. Can't stand Bellinis. And I hate to say this,' she glanced at Izzie shamefaced, 'but I'm not good with olives either.'

Izzie gasped and put her hand over her mouth, her eyes crinkling with humour. 'But that first lunch. I practically cleaned out Ringford for them. You should have said.'

'Sorry,' she put her hand unsteadily on Izzie's leg. 'Didn't want to hurt your feelings, and pesto. I hate pesto and sun-dried tomatoes. So bourgeois!'

'But what would Sue Templeton say? She thinks they are the yardstick of class.'

'She thinks lacy loo roll covers are the yardstick of class!' They both screamed with laughter again.

'Polenta. Overrated nonsense,' said Izzie, getting more dogmatic. 'Whatever you do it still tastes like wallpaper paste.' She wrinkled her nose. 'And oysters – slimy and disgusting.'

'Taste like semen,' countered Maddy, and gasped at her own crudeness.

'Madeleine Hoare, you should be ashamed of yourself! And you a well-brought-up girl!' There was a pause.

'D'ja know, I've got a definite agenda for the next forty years.' Izzie took another sip.

'What's that then?' She'd never seen Izzie so drunk.

'I want,' Izzie looked up at the ceiling, deep in thought, 'I want a big fuck-off car. And I want to swan around in it with Dolce & Gabbana shades and look drop-dead gorgeous.' Maddy took in Izzie's make-up now smudged into one multi-coloured smear from the tears of laughter.

'Oh, I think you are halfway there already.'

'And . . .' Izzie slurred. 'And I want to snog Joseph Fiennes. And,' she was getting into her stride now, 'I want to bonk in a hammock.'

'I want to do it in a lift.'

Izzie fervently nodded her approval. 'Marcus and I did it in the bathroom at his parents' house!'

'At night?'

'No, half-ten in the morning. Very thrilling.' She paused and ran her finger around the rim of her glass. 'Why don't people snog once they're married?'

'I don't know. It's one of those things you sort of give up at the altar. I love snogging.' She struggled to remember what it was like. 'I love that moment when a man you fancy like hell bends his head towards you slowly and you just *know* he's going to kiss you. No one snogs any more, do they?'

Suddenly the mood changed and she glanced fleetingly at Maddy. 'Oh some people do.' She paused. 'Some people really do.' Maddy was alerted by the change in her voice and watched the tears of grief start to pour down her face.

'Did you snog Jean Luc?' She hadn't been going to ask that.

Izzie put her head in her hands, and rocked slowly, slipping into that twilight between happy drunk and maudlin wrist-slitting self-pity. 'Oh God,' she groaned. 'Can you stop the bloody room from spinning?' Maddy felt a moment of panic. Please don't throw up all over my precious bedspread.

Izzie raised her head, her eyes blurred and swivelling. 'D'ja know the worst thing of all about hitting forty? I've just realised all those things I know I'm never going to do. When I was

261

twenty I really thought I could do anything. It was all out there for the taking, and now here I am.' She took another swig of her drink. 'I really thought by now I'd have conducted the Berlin Phil . . . or been in *Vogue*.'

'But you have been in *Vogue*!'

'I meant on the cover, stupid.'

Izzie leant back against the pillows, and rubbing her eyes, spread her mascara even further down her stricken face. 'It's the things I haven't done that I regret. There were loads of things I wanted to do but I was too shy, but now I feel too old.' She looked across at Maddy, mournfully. 'And what if I don't have sex with someone else ever again? I mean, is this it?'

Maddy narrowed her eyes and looked back at her hard. Waiting.

Izzie held her gaze. 'Oh God, Maddy. What am I going to do?' She turned on the bed, eyes desperate and beseeching. 'Everything's going wrong. Is it all my fault? Why can't I make these things work? The minute one thing goes well – like the business – I go and fuck up my marriage. I love Marcus so much, and I just want it all to be back like the old days.' Maddy took her in her arms and let Izzie sob. The old days. This was not the time nor the place to bring up anything she had learnt about Marcus.

'It's OK. No harm done. Marcus doesn't even have to know.' She rubbed her back, as Izzie wailed harder, shaking her head. 'Come on, you old soak,' she said gently, and she eased Izzie off the bed, prising the glass out of her hand and they both weaved their way to the spare room. Izzie grumpily complied with having her new Armani removed, despite her slurred request that she be allowed to sleep in it, and Maddy, stumbling slightly, helped her into the bed. Izzie was barely under the sheets, when she heaved herself out again, struggled into the bathroom and wasted a good take-away and some very good champagne.

Bleary-eyed and shivering, she reappeared from the bathroom a few minutes later, and slipped into bed. Maddy wrapped the duvet around her, then, grabbing a tissue from the bathroom and squeezing on some baby lotion – the nearest thing to hand – she went back to wipe the worst of the make-up from Izzie's face. By the time she'd made a pathetic but slight improvement, Izzie was fast asleep.

Chapter 15

It was a very long time since Izzie had drunk enough to experience a top-class hangover. And now she remembered why. She felt ghastly. It wasn't just the ceaseless churning of her stomach, the gritty-eyed bleariness, the blotchy complexion and puffy face. It was that awful sensation that if she turned round without turning her whole body, her head would simply drop off. Maybe it would be better if it did, though. Then she might be able to get rid of the two little men with surprisingly heavy hammers who were taking it in turns to beat out the rhythm of Ravel's *Bolero* on the inside of her skull.

She gingerly made her way downstairs, gripping on to the banisters. She stopped, took a deep breath and tried to swallow. Nope – still no good. There seemed to be a large egg – maybe goose or emu – lodged in her throat. That would account for the bird's nest in her mouth. Ah, not far now. She'd reached the landing. Time for a little rest. Her body had evidently decided that it was just not up to the challenge. Perhaps that's what being forty did to you, or was it simply too much clean living? Oh yes – that was a warning all right, and one that Izzie would certainly heed from now on.

Because, despite how absolutely unspeakably hideous she felt right now, it had totally been worth it. It had been the very best fun ever. For the first time in – gosh – years, she had done exactly what she felt like . . . not counting that thing with Jean Luc . . . she swiftly put that out of her mind, and it had felt bloody marvellous. No worries about Marcus, the kids, the business, the image, the product, the market, the future. For that one glorious evening, she'd shelved it all. Even from the depths of her nausea, she could remember how good it had felt, and she wasn't going to give up on that now! She'd have to go into serious training – regular lager-champagne cocktails and korma chasers. Seize the day – or whatever. Now she'd rediscovered her inner adolescent, she wasn't going to let it go again! No siree.

Maddy had thoughtfully left a bottle of chilled Badoit water out for her when she left to do the weekend shop, and Izzie glugged it down, pulling a face as she did so. Disgusting stuff, but very cleansing for the liver, or so Jean Luc had insisted in France. Damn that man, what was he doing popping up like that again? She pushed him back down irritably, and continued with the liver cleanse as she poked idly through the contents of Maddy's fridge, hunting out the best hangover cure she could come up with – egg mayonnaise and anchovies in brine on wholemeal – then sat down heavily on a kitchen chair, her head in her hands. This was not good!

About forty minutes later, after a long hot shower and hair wash, trying out all Maddy's share of the Elements' haul, she felt almost human again. She sought out a pair of clean knickers – plenty to choose from – and put her Armani outfit back on. Provided she didn't look at her face, now thoroughly cleansed and generously daubed with balm, she looked pretty darned fine. Forty and proud of it! Turning this way and that in front of the mirror, she finally pulled a hideous face at herself, then blew a big kiss at her surprised-looking reflection and murmured huskily, 'You're gorgeous! Go get 'em, tiger!'

The bang of the front door downstairs and the sound of children running into the playroom alerted her to Maddy's return, and she trotted down, now starting to feel reasonably human. Maddy looked appraisingly at her and whispered her greetings. She was clearly no stranger to hangover etiquette. 'Ooh vertical! All right? Would you rather I didn't talk for now? We can do sign language if you prefer.'

'No 'sall right. The worst's over and I've had something to eat.'

'Good going! Wish you hadn't done it now? Any regrets?'

Izzie shook her head experimentally. Encouraged by the fact that it didn't fall off, she grinned and shook it emphatically. 'Not one! Not a single, solitary one! To tell you the truth, Maddy, it was the best time I've had in ages.'

Maddy dropped her carrier bags, rushed over and hugged her gleefully. 'I'm so glad you said that. It felt so nice just to be daft for a change. We've had to be so grown up and sensible lately. I was beginning to worry that we'd forgotten how.'

'I know what you mean. It's so weird when people ask us stuff as if we really know. And inside my head there is this mad urge to say, "I haven't the faintest idea, and what's more, I don't care. It's only face cream, for God's sake. The other stuff is all crap and we're just making it up as we go along." It's only my deep-seated fear of Pru that stops me sometimes.'

Izzie frowned, then swiftly pushed her eyebrows back up again with her fingers – too much, too soon. 'It's all bull, basically. Do you think they really imagine that we wear cambric undies and live like Bathsheba Everdene? Could they really be that daft?'

It was Maddy's turn to frown. 'Well, I think they sort of believe it and sort of don't. Maybe it's like fairy stories. You know that princess could never have really felt the pea through all the mattresses, but you go along with it because it's a good story and you want to feel good when she gets the prince in the end. Mind you, I always had doubts about that marriage. And the mother-in-law!'

Izzie shrugged and drained her second cup of coffee. 'I s'pose. Anyway, I'd better get home before I show my face and check out the state of play. I hope Marcus isn't going to do his martyr thing.'

'Give him a cordial kick up the arse from me if he is.'

'With pleasure!' Izzie stopped at the front door and turned back to Maddy. 'Thanks for everything, mate, and I luuurve my new outfit.'

'You're more than welcome to toss your cookies in my bathroom any time you like! Happy birthday boxing day!'

In the weeks leading up to the summer holidays, Maddy and Izzie focused on producing a new range of toners and cleansers for different skin types. With media appearances and interviews, as well as fitting in meetings with Pru, Elements and the other stores that stocked PE, they had very little time for anything else. But they weren't too busy to notice the changes that were going on around them. Everywhere they went, they found the same thing. Where a year ago, the look had been pared down, hard-edged minimalism, with a dash of po-faced cod-Eastern spirituality, now the press was raving about soft colours, floral patterns, loose and wavy hair, glowing pink cheeks. Far from feeling odd in their outfits, they both began to feel they were in the vanguard of fashion.

'Do you think men really notice fashion?' pondered Izzie one afternoon as they checked a delivery. 'I mean, Marcus is more than usually trend savvy, but even he doesn't pay any attention to what I wear.'

'Yeah, but maybe that's because you're his wife.' Maddy ticked off the list on her clipboard. 'Men are physically unable to focus on their wives after being married for five years or more.'

Izzie snorted. 'I reckon it's all our fault. It's misplaced maternal instinct. We turn our men into babies by pandering to their every whim, then get fed up with them when we get real babies that are much cuter. Suddenly we want men that are men again, but by then they've lost the knack.' She heaved another box on to a pallet. 'If only I'd had a pony to dote on during the early years of our marriage, I'd never have wasted all that time buffing Marcus' hooves or plaiting his mane, and I wouldn't have reduced him to this state of gibbering dependence.'

She stopped and stretched. 'Anyway, I'm subjecting him to a course in tough love now,' she said smugly. 'If he doesn't buy the coffee, we don't have coffee. If he puts a red sock in with his shirts, he wears pink shirts.'

'And how's he responding to treatment?'

'Hmmm. I'm getting a lot of huffing and puffing at the moment. And the spectre of the summer hols is looming.'

To celebrate the end of term – or perhaps to placate the kids for the impending weeks when their mothers would have to work full tilt – Izzie and Maddy had planned a party for the children. It was an e-mail from Jean Luc suggesting a visit, his first since their trip to his place in June, that had sowed the seeds of the idea. Izzie had downloaded the e-mail first, and glanced quickly over at Maddy, worried for a moment that he had e-mailed her at work by mistake. Then she realised how stupid she was being. He worked for them after all! Izzie was very aware that she'd been less than frank with Maddy over what had passed between them that day, but she really didn't know what to say.

'Oh look, Jean Luc's coming over! About time too.' Maddy, as usual, was full of ideas. 'Let's have a party right here, and invite all the staff, plus their partners, kids, whatever. Tamasin and Oscar will be starting back here too, so we'll have them, and Janet and Nick the Vic. Jean Luc won't know what's hit him!'

Izzie could feel anxiety rising. What would it be like when they met again? But Maddy chirped on oblivious, enthused by the prospect of balloons to buy, glasses to order, and sausages to prick. The party animal was in her element.

Marcus, however, was very cool about the whole idea when she broached it at home. 'Am I supposed to be honoured by this invitation? Do you really want me to come, or would I cramp your style – especially if that bloody Frenchman's going to be around?'

Izzie turned away quickly, and affected an air of nonchalance. 'What? I've no idea what you're talking about. Yes, I think Jean Luc might be coming. Dunno really. The whole crowd should be there. I just thought you'd like to meet some of these people I keep mentioning. Don't come if you'd rather not, though.'

He snorted. 'Well, don't overwhelm me, will you? I think I'd better come along. Perhaps I should regard it as protecting my investment, eh?' And he left the room.

The rest of the staff took to the plan with wild enthusiasm, with Karen and Angie coming up with more and more outlandish ideas, including fancy dress, a casino night, a sixties disco and a tarts and vicars theme – this last firmly overruled in view of the Grants – and had to be encouraged to think small. To keep them out of mischief, they were put in charge of food, and came up with the idea of having a hog roast. Izzie, mindful of her daughter's passion for piggies, quickly volunteered to provide a veggie alternative too.

'Orright,' conceded Donna. 'But none of that French cheese, y'hear. Makes me want to 'eave, that does!'

Izzie's anxieties intensified as the day drew nearer. It finally dawned clear and warm. Everything had been arranged with military precision. Since they planned to start proceedings straight after work, everyone rushed to get through the day's tasks and there was a pleasant buzz of industry in the air. The hog roast man turned up good and early, to get the fire going and the unfortunate pig cooked in time for the feast to start at around half past six. As the afternoon wore on the succulent smell wafted into the barn, spurring everyone on to greater efforts and they had finished an unprecedented batch of orders by the time the last apron was hung up. Donna, Angie and Co rushed for the loo with their party clothes, and a lot of ribald laughter could be heard as they effected the transformation from work to play.

Maddy, Izzie and Lillian stripped off in their office and took turns with the hand mirror Lillian had thoughtfully brought with her. Angie's boyfriend had arrived, and was soon rigging up armfuls of fairy lights in the trees next to the barn while his brother set up his mobile disco. Plastic dustbins full of ice were produced from the back of a van and tins of lager, many, many bottles of Bacardi Breezer, tins of Coke for the kids and a few bottles of Australian white were thrust into the icy depths. By this time, Colette had turned up with Will, Florence and little Pasco, and they were all hurtling round and round the barns with Angie and Donna's kids in a non-stop game of tag. There was still no sign of Marcus.

'Should I call him?' Izzie asked Maddy, looking anxiously at her watch. 'I said any time from six.'

'Absolutely not! It's not even half past yet,' replied Maddy as she cracked open her first Breezer of the night. 'Don't show him he's got to you. Just act cool. He'll be here – the kids won't let him cheat them out of precious party time, I promise you!' She looked up to a whistle. 'Oh look! Here's Jean Luc at last. *Salut, mon brave! Te voilà enfin. Viens boire un coup avec nous. J'ai du vin Australian, spéciale pour toi!*'

Izzie's heart lurched as she saw him. He pulled a face, and made his way towards them, past the bodies gyrating to 'Car Wash' blasting from the disco. He'd had his hair cut and was browner than ever, the sleeves of his washed-out blue shirt rolled up to show tanned forearms with the hairs bleached gold. He smiled broadly and within seconds he had wrapped her in his arms, kissing her softly on her head when she couldn't bring herself to raise her face to him.

'Hello, my two lovely girls. Now I've seen you, the sun has

come out. What a crazy idea to have a party outside in your terrible climate. Brrrr. I must stay by the fire all night.'

He turned to Maddy and gave her too an enormous hug, muttering endearments in her ear in French. Izzie could hear her teasing reply, and he laughed and seemed to tap her reproachfully on the arm.

'*Ça suffit!*'

Turning his nose up at a glass of Australian '*Merde*', he opted for a beer and, as Izzie resolutely tried to avoid eye contact with either him or Maddy, an awkward silence descended between the three of them. She began to make an excuse to move away, when Maddy gamely waded in with some shoptalk which eased matters for a while, until Maddy gave a shriek and dived away. 'Pasco! No! That's not a chocolate raisin. Put it down. Aah! Not in your mouth!'

Jean Luc laughed softly. 'I don't think rabbit droppings will do him much harm, do you?'

Izzie looked down into her drink, and was about to reply, when an increasingly raucous Karen shimmied up to Jean Luc and threw her arms around him. 'Bon jewer, gorgeous! Remember me?' Izzie grabbed the chance to step back into the shadows, and watched his perfectly pitched response to the girls. He looked relaxed and amused. How did he always manage to judge it right with people? How did he always seem to stay so controlled?

She melted into the crowd while he was occupied, and chatted with Janet and Nick the Vic, then tried to approach Crispin until she saw how engrossed he was in talking to Lillian. Still no Marcus. It was a little later, as she bent down to pick up a discarded hot dog from the grass, that she could sense Jean Luc standing behind her. She went to move away, but he put his hand out to stop her. Gently he drew her away from the rest, and taking her wrist, brought her hand up to his mouth for a soft kiss. 'Izzie, we must talk. Please.'

Reluctantly, she raised her eyes to his and sighed sheepishly. 'Must we?'

He smiled. 'Yes, we really must. You didn't reply to my e-mails. After what has passed between us, we should not hide anything.'

'I don't know what you mean. I'm not hiding anything!'

'Oh Izzie.' His voice was coaxing and she could feel her defence starting to drop. 'Maybe things didn't happen quite as we expected, but you can't deny that it was a beautiful moment. It has been so long since I was close with a woman like that.'

'Oh come off it, Jean Luc. I can't believe that.'

'No, Izzie, it's true. I don't take these things lightly, and the memory of what happened has been keeping me warm ever since.'

'But nothing did happen, did it?' she hissed. 'I mean, it could have. We both know that. And God knows I wanted it to, but I bottled out, didn't I? When it came down to it I couldn't go through with it. And ever since, I've been ashamed of myself for leading you on.'

He put his arms around her. 'Nooo! I thought that's what you felt but you mustn't. We were both guilty of flirting with each other. And I have no regrets about wanting you – but we both know that stopping when we did was the right thing.' She could smell his warm body through his shirt and when she looked up at him, she could see the paler, fine lines around his eyes where he had squinted in the sun. 'When we hesitated just for that moment, it gave us both time to think. Looking at everything, the way our lives are, it would have been a mistake to make love to each other. You're a passionate and exciting woman, Izzie. But you're also a married one. Very married, despite what you might think at the moment. You could not do it and neither could I.' He held her out at arm's length, gazing down into her face and she could feel the pressure of his fingers on her shoulders. 'But I feel very close to you. You will always be more than just a friend to me now. I hope you will feel the same about me?'

Izzie swallowed hard, and felt her body relax. Somehow, by making her talk and by being so honest, he'd made everything all right again, and a heavy shadow passed from her heart. Why couldn't she and Marcus talk like this? She smiled up at him, her eyes bright with grateful tears. 'I do feel the same about you. I really do. I would have just gone on pretending I didn't care, and I do care. I really do.'

'I know, Izzie. Now, let's have a drink together and you can teach me how to dance this . . . Macarena that your friends are all doing with so much *enthusiasme*. I think I will be rather good at it, no?'

She laughed. 'I'll see if I can find you some wine that doesn't taste of kiwi fruit and fresh tarmac, shall I?' Jean Luc moved towards the fire, rubbing his hands together as the evening cooled. She was almost knocked off her feet as Jess and Charlie threw themselves into her arms, chattering excitedly. So Marcus must have arrived. She looked over and saw him standing in the shadows – he hadn't noticed her yet – and followed his stare across the crowd. He was looking at Jean Luc with utter loathing. Izzie shuddered as she realised how obvious her attraction for Jean Luc must have been to him. Could she convince him that nothing had really happened? Would he ever understand? She grabbed a beer and walked towards him.

An hour or so later, and the party was in full swing. Izzie surveyed the scene from the safety of the barn door and smiled quietly to herself. She felt happier than she had in ages. The scent of broad bean flowers, an irresistible blend of Nivea and vanilla, filled the air and, in the darkening evening, the lights created a cocoon around all the assembled guests. Strange combination though they were, they all seemed to be rubbing along nicely. Pasco was still awake, wrapped safely in Jean Luc's big arms, and was watching the party with his huge brown eyes.

The older children were starting to get to that disinhibited stage that tiredness can bring and Izzie knew it would soon be time to leave. Marcus hadn't been as bad as she had feared; he had made an effort when she'd introduced him to Crispin and Lillian, and Angie and Donna had chatted him up shamelessly. He'd even got into quite a deep conversation with Janet but, she noticed, he'd studiously avoided both Maddy and Jean Luc.

Maddy came over, picking her way carefully past discarded glasses and plates, bearing three plates of carrot cake. 'Here you are, doll. Get stuck into that. The frosting is amaaaazing. A real Janet special.'

Izzie took the plate with enthusiasm. 'If Janet made it, sign me up. I'm so glad Oscar and Tamasin are coming back to work the summer. I've been dreaming about those burrito wraps she does. I can hardly wait.'

To Izzie's surprise Maddy waved at Marcus as he walked past. 'There you are, Marcus! Look, I've got you a piece of cake. You must try it.'

Marcus stopped and frowned. Izzie bridled. Couldn't he even make an effort when Maddy was going out of her way to be nice?

'Er, yes. All right. Thanks.' He put down his can of lager and looked at the cake suspiciously, then tasted just a little. 'Hmm. Not bad. Not really my type of thing though. I don't have much of a sweet tooth.'

'Oh go on, Marcus. I'm sure even you succumb to temptation sometimes.' Maddy seemed to be gushing. 'I'll tell you Janet's secret, shall I? What makes the frosting so very special? Can you keep a secret, Marcus? It's basically cream cheese, with icing sugar of course, then she adds Grand Marnier. That's the secret. Now don't go giving that away to any rivals, will you? You can get into awful trouble that way, you know. People have been sacked for less!'

Izzie was staring at Maddy in puzzlement. Was she pissed?

She seemed to be talking rubbish. But a snarl of rage from Marcus had her turning back to him in astonishment. He was gazing at Maddy as if he wanted to hit her. Instead, he threw the cake to the ground, turned on his heel and stalked away. She turned to Maddy, who was watching him narrowly. 'What the hell was that all about? Did I miss something? I've no idea what's got into him tonight. Should I go after him?'

Maddy shook herself. The expression on her face was almost one of pity, but she swiftly hugged Izzie. 'Maybe you should. I hope I didn't upset him too much. He really doesn't like cake, does he? See you tomorrow, mate.'

Izzie scanned the depleting crowd to find Jean Luc and say goodbye before gathering her troops. There he was over by the fire, on his own for the first time that evening. She made to go towards him. He, however, was looking beyond her, over her shoulder and with a fixed gaze she had never seen on his face before. She glanced round to see and stopped dead. Realisation dawned.

Glass of wine in one hand, Maddy idly pulled weeds from between the slabs in the terrace and chucked them into the hedge. She straightened up and stretched her back, stiff from crouching. Looking down the long stretch of garden, positively manicured now she could afford a gardener two days a week, she could see the boughs of the apple trees heavy with fruit. This time last year they'd picked them and eaten them right from the trees like real city folk, thrilled by the idea of fruit growing in their very own garden. What a year had passed since then. They'd arrived here, Simon chock full of enthusiasm and intentions for life as a country squire, she resentful that she'd had to pack up life in London and hike out to the provinces. Now here she was, Simon was gone, she'd met Izzie, the quality of whose friendship eclipsed anything she had known before, and they were famous. Famous for some fabricated image based on the countryside she still didn't feel completely comfortable with.

Her waistband didn't feel comfortable either. Without the fags – OK, she'd had the odd one – she'd been drawn to the biscuit tin for something to do with her hands and she'd definitely put on weight. Bugger. She'd never get into her size-eight capri pants, even if she was ever allowed to wear them again.

'Mum, when's lunch?' Will came padding out of the French windows in his football socks, swallowing quickly, the tell-tale smears of chocolate still around his mouth.

She ruffled his hair. 'I'm just about to come in and make the gravy. Come and sit on this bench with me for a minute.'

'What are we having?' he slid up next to her on the seat.

'Roast lamb.'

'Yum!'

'But you won't have room for any if you keep stuffing your face with biscuits.' He smiled sheepishly, revealing teeth coated in chocolate and crumbs.

'I was just looking at the orchard. Tell me,' she put her arm around him and pulled him close, 'do you like living here?'

'Oh yeah. It's cool. There's lots of places to play.'

'But what about your old school friends?'

'Well, I miss Harry and Dan. But I've got lots of new friends.' He swung his legs as they hung over the edge of the seat. 'But this house isn't Daddy.' Maddy felt a lump grow in her throat.

'Do you remember him here?' she asked gently.

'Not really. I think of him in the London garden and at the park. And I think of him on holiday on the beach.' She felt a massive wave of sadness that even these tenuous memories of Simon would eventually fade in Will's memory, and how Florence and Pasco would have nothing to hang on to at all.

'We had fun on the beach, didn't we? Do you remember him in his scuba diving gear in St Lucia? He looked like a frog, didn't he?' Will smiled wanly. 'And rock pooling on the Isle of Wight. Daddy always managed to find the crabs.'

'He cheated.' Will carried on swinging his feet. 'It was always the same one – he just kept pretending.'

Maddy laughed, uncomfortable with her son's melancholy. 'And I thought he'd fooled you, you clever chap. He'd be ever so proud of you, you know. How well you've settled into school and all the friends you've made.' Will shuffled and she realised she'd gone too far with the emotional stuff.

'I wish you were home more though.' This one took her by surprise. She knew she'd done some very long days at the barn, but had really hoped that, once she got home, she'd absorbed herself enough in the children that they wouldn't really have noticed. How stupid. Of course they would. The guilt made her feel sick.

'I know I've been busy, but what Izzie and I are doing is very exciting – and it means we might have enough money to take lots of holidays and have new toys.'

'I'd rather have you here.' She couldn't speak and simply held him closer.

'Can you make the gravy now? I'm hungry.'

'Come on then, old man.' She heaved herself up off the seat. 'Better feed you. Sometimes I think you have hollow legs.' And they walked back into the house.

The next morning, galvanised by guilt, she told Colette she would do the school run and packed Florence and Will into the new car. 'Just think, Florence darling,' she said, trying to work out how to turn off the fan and trying harder to sound as enthusiastic as possible, 'by this Thursday, you'll have done your first full week at school. Isn't that brilliant?'

'No, hate school. Don't want to go.' She kicked her feet sulkily against the back of Maddy's seat.

'Oh, you love it really. Lots of new friends to play with, and Will there to see every day at playtime.'

'Never going to school. Want to stay home and be with you.'

'But Mummy's never there anyway,' piped up Will. 'She's always at work.' Thanks, thought Maddy to herself. Shatter any illusions I may still have that I'm a half-decent parent.

'Haven't seen you for ages, Maddy,' chorused Sue Templeton and Linda Meades in unison, striding up to the car like Hinge and Bracket as she pulled into the school car park. 'Nice new car,' cooed Linda, peering to have a butcher's inside as Maddy hustled Will and Florence out, fishing his cap and Florence's folder from the floor, and kissing them both goodbye with a gentle push of encouragement. 'Very swish. You and Izzie must be doing well.'

'Didn't you see them on breakfast telly? They're frightfully famous,' Sue put in. How was it that she managed to sound so catty even when she'd pretending to be friendly? 'Very er . . . ethnic you both looked! Hardly recognised you.'

Linda, clearly more interested in Maddy's new set of wheels than her burgeoning TV career, was still peering in at the dashboard. 'It's ever so nice. Volvo, isn't it? Keith and I were looking at one the other day.'

'Oh well,' said Maddy, sliding past her into the driver's seat and looking down on the two women. 'It's the safety element that clinched it for me – you know how important it is to keep one's precious family safe. And it's so roomy – a real treat after the Fiesta.' She turned on the engine, shut the door and pressed down the electric window. 'That was so *pokey*. Know what I mean?' and, winking at Sue, she pulled away out of the car park.

Smiling broadly at her own joke, she belted over to the barn far faster than she should considering the car was still being run in, and pulled up in front of the doors just ahead of Geoff. Peter's Mercedes was already there. They'd tried to arrange the board meeting for after the end of the holiday, out of some pathetic delusion that they would be spending that time with their children. Fat chance. She suddenly felt irritable, and not just by Sue Templeton's cutting remarks, but at herself. Will's comments had cut deep, and she was struggling to work out the best thing to do.

It hadn't really been much of a summer holiday, though they'd grabbed the odd long weekend here and there, and Cynthia and Alan had very gamely entertained the children in Hertfordshire for a couple of days – though not entirely successfully by all accounts. Maddy should, she thought, have felt revitalised. All she felt was relieved that they were back at school, and she could shelve her guilt for six hours of the day at least.

She knew Izzie had found the holidays as hard to juggle, but at least she'd had Marcus at home some of the time – however resentfully. She talked little about him, except for the odd gripe, which Maddy found hard not to agree with. The thing she really couldn't forgive was how Marcus had duped Izzie. It was obvious from her puzzled reaction at the party that Izzie was completely in the dark about the circumstances of his leaving the agency. Marriages may have their little deceptions and, God knows, Simon hadn't shared his worries with her, but not telling your wife you had been fired and then playing a little game of lies for years? That was hard to justify.

Since the party and that stupid coded conversation about the carrot cake, she'd let things lie to see if Marcus would do the decent thing. He was clearly even more lily-livered than she gave him credit for. Arsehole, she thought to herself as she pulled in beside Geoff's Jag.

Geoff smiled toothily at her as he climbed out of the car. This was going to be an important meeting, with the figures for the first proper quarter of trading tucked away in his smart leather briefcase. 'You look lovely, Maddy,' he smiled at her appreciatively. 'It must be your celebrity.' What a creep, she thought, and shuddered. He walked over and handed her an inside page from the day's *FT*. 'Thought the headline might amuse you.' Maddy peered at the page, scanning the small column of short news stories.

'Sorry, Geoff, I can't see where you mean.'

He pointed a finger at the main headline at the top of the page. '*Luce Women go on Top*'.

'Very racy for the *FT*, don't you think?'

Maddy barely heard him, as she skim-read the news item. 'City analysts are predicting *Paysage Enchanté*, blah blah . . . brainchild of two women, will be looking to expand . . .' She let her eyes run ahead. 'Float on the AIM . . . logical move if they are to exploit their success and expand.'

'I wonder if Izzie has seen this.' If Izzie hadn't, she certainly knew all about it by the time they were all sat round the table, and had coffee in front of them. Geoff was full of it, and Maddy had strong suspicions who it was that had put the idea into the heads of the City analysts in the first place.

'It's a logical move, ladies,' he said, pulling his laptop out of his briefcase and rubbing his fingers rather salaciously over the mouse button. 'Now,' he said as he found the document he wanted, and swung the screen round to face them. 'Look at these figures.' Both Maddy and Izzie, once so clueless about spreadsheets, were getting quicker off the mark at working out the sea of numbers. They were both silent for a while, as they took in Geoff's calculations. Projected profits were one thing, but it was the current turnover figure which amazed them both.

'Pretty impressive, isn't it?' said Peter to break the silence. 'I'm sure it was skill and good judgement of course,' he added, with a smile, 'but you undoubtedly made the right move by centring production in this low-cost unit, keeping your employees to low enough numbers, and expanding your product range using very similar ingredients to the healing balm.'

'Well, I suppose it has kept the costs down.' Maddy kept her eye on the figures. 'And having Jean Luc doing the boiling process in France . . .' The four of them talked through several distribution points, suppliers who were keen to stock the brand and about other sources Izzie had unearthed for supplying the rose oil for the new moisturiser, but Geoff kept returning relentlessly to the question of expansion.

'But why would we want to float?' Izzie looked bewildered. 'We don't need to raise any capital, do we?'

'Not if you stay as you are,' Geoff tapped his pen irritatingly on his notepad, 'but businesses succeed because they don't stand still. You need to exploit your popularity now by building on your success, and outlets will be looking for products like yours to back up their poorly performing brands. Old Luce's notebook must be choc full of other recipes – can you exploit those? What about products for men? Shaving balms, that sort of thing. I know my barber is always waxing lyrical about such things and trying to get me to fork out for them.' Maddy glanced briefly at his immaculate hair, cropped close to his head, but leaving just enough to reveal the slight wave. All a bit contrived.

'Well,' started Izzie hesitantly, 'there are quite a lot more, I suppose, and I know Maddy has translated some.' She fiddled with her pencil absent-mindedly. Maddy wondered if she was thinking the same thing.

'Shouldn't we be consolidating?' She could see Izzie nodding her head in agreement. 'We haven't been going that long, and it could all be a blip, just a passing fashion.'

'Well if it is, it's certainly taken hold pretty firmly.' Geoff passed a sheet of paper across the table from the pile in front of him. 'These are the projected quarterly profits for the big cosmetics firms.'

In one column he had put figures for last year, next to the names of the biggest players in the industry and, in the next, those for this year. Most, if not all, showed a slight but noticeable dip.

'What does this mean?' asked Izzie, confused.

'It could mean nothing – the economy isn't brilliant and the FTSE is far from buoyant – but the message seems to be that women are turning away from conventional brands, and looking instead for a more wholesome image. Similar "earthy" brands to yours are showing good sales, but mainstream make-up brands are struggling. Look at this.' Geoff handed over another sheet showing sales figures for each product, again compared to last year.

'It can't be anything to do with us, can it?' Maddy found it hard to believe that their measly little pots could have made such an impact in precipitating mascara and eyeshadow wars, and for a moment she had a vision of lip gloss wands and eyeliner pencils doing battle in the aisles at Boots.

'Well, I'll be blowed,' Izzie was still staring at the figures. 'I never imagined when I left university that my contribution to the world would be putting a dent in national hand-cream sales.'

'So, ladies, what do you think?' Geoff as ever was keen to get back to business the minute he thought they were getting glib. 'If you are keen, I can put together a proposal for potential shareholders, and we could dip our toe in the waters, so to speak.' He was starting to pull out more papers, sorting them in an efficient sort of way that was beginning to get right up Maddy's nose. 'As a matter of fact I have started to jot down some ideas, not really worked up yet, but just the bare bones of an idea. Take a look.'

Geoff's bare bones looked pretty fleshed out to Maddy's inexpert eye. He had done a fairly thorough job of forecasts, sector trends, company profile, all laid out in a neat little document with bold headings and footnotes.

Suddenly she felt pushed around. Who the hell had asked

him to do this? Things were getting rapidly out of control. If they weren't careful, Geoff would have them PLCed before you could say Dow Jones Index.

'Just a minute, Geoff.' She smiled as sweetly as she could at him. 'This all sounds very interesting and has possibilities, but I think I speak for Izzie when I say we'd like to talk this through a bit more. You know, just see where we want to go from here.' A look of disappointment flitted across his face, and she saw for the first time a steely determination.

'Sure,' he said magnanimously. 'I just wouldn't advise you to take too long. There are lots of people out there who want to invest in an exciting new company with huge potential, and we need to strike while the iron's hot. My research shows—'

He was stopped mid-flow by Maddy's mobile phone ringing on her desk. Lillian picked it up, said, 'Yes, certainly I understand, I'll tell her it's urgent,' and came over to where the four of them were sitting. 'Sorry to interrupt, everyone.' Lillian leant down to mutter in Maddy's ear. 'It's school. Florence is in floods and inconsolable. They wondered if you would mind going over as soon as possible?'

Panicky, Maddy pushed back her chair. 'Sorry, folks, I'm going to have to leave you,' and she grabbed her bag and her phone off her desk, bolted down the stairs, and out to the car.

About a mile down the road towards school, her mobile began to ring again in her bag. By the time she'd pulled it out, she had missed it, and there was a voice message. Keeping her foot down, she pressed the buttons to listen, then slowed right down, a smile spreading on her face.

'Well, the sly old bird,' said Izzie, stirring her coffee in Costa's half an hour later. 'How did she get hold of my mobile?'

'We must have left them on our desks and, when she heard the way the conversation was going, Lillian picked yours up and dialled my number, had a conversation with, well no one really, then came over to pretend the school had phoned. I was halfway there when she sent me a rather frantic voice message – not sure mobiles are quite her thing – saying sorry, but she thought we might want rescuing. She was terribly apologetic, but God bless her. I thought we'd never shut Geoff up.'

Izzie scooped the foam from the top of her mug with her spoon and put it in her mouth. With her unruly hair, pink T-shirt and army green combats, she looked about twelve. 'What do you think about this flotation business? I mean,' she scooped up some more, 'I can see his point, I suppose. It would give us some cash to spend, and the figures do look good. And there are lots more recipes still we could do, and Elements are gagging for more stuff, but,' she paused and looked right at Maddy, 'it all sounds a bit scary, don't you think?'

'Bloody terrifying, and what's more I'm not even sure I want to go there, do you?'

Izzie leant back in her seat, and put down her spoon. 'God, I'm so glad you said that. I thought you might be all for it.'

Maddy laughed. 'Calm down! I'm not with Geoff on this. Actually Lillian's choice of excuse was shrewder than she thought. My first reaction when she said about Florence crying was, "I want to get to my daughter". Will has said a couple of things over the last few days about me not being at home and Pasco even called Colette "Mama". God, that hurt. I don't want to be some high-flying company director who has to shoot off to meetings and kowtow to shareholders.' She thought what Simon would think and laughed dryly. 'It's a joke really, me in that world. I think my sanity depends on being normal and at home.'

'I think my marriage depends on it,' Izzie muttered quietly, looking into her coffee.

'It's still bad, isn't it?'

Izzie sighed despondently and scanned vaguely around the room. 'Well, oddly enough he's been brilliant – ever since the party – but something isn't right. It seems forced, as if he's under some tremendous strain. And I'm missing out on family life. He's having all the fun with the kids – they did Warwick Castle on Saturday and ever since have had lots of in jokes about what a good time they'd had.' The tears welled up in her eyes. 'It's rubbing salt in the wound of my guilt. As if I didn't feel bad enough about all this already.'

Maddy felt uneasy. 'Have you had a chance to talk to him properly?'

'Not really. He keeps it all very shallow. And when the hell have I got time to talk anyway?'

Maddy picked up her bag. 'If this company gets much bigger, we can wave goodbye to parenting altogether. Come on, let's stall. I'll ring Peter and get him to tell Geoff to back off a bit.'

As it turned out Florence hadn't had a good day at all, and a very miserable little girl greeted Maddy at half past three. 'She's just taking a little longer to settle in,' said Mrs Rose, her teacher, over Florence's head. 'But it happens sometimes. She'll be fine,' and she ruffled her hair. 'See you tomorrow, dear.'

'I'm not going back,' whinged Florence in the car, and sobbed all the way home.

The following morning Maddy woke to heavy rain lashing against the windows, urged on by a strong autumnal wind. Feeling as lousy as the weather, she used every vestige of her persuasive powers to chivvy Florence along through breakfast and into her uniform, and eventually compromised on a Barbie hair band and pink socks.

'Her teacher wasn't too chuffed. Silly bag,' she said to Izzie when she got to the barns and shook the rain off her coat. 'She looked really disapproving – oh what the hell, I'm obviously a crap mother anyway.'

'Take a look at this,' Izzie slid the business section of the paper across the table towards her. 'Looks like Geoff was right.'

Maddy scanned the story, as she hung her coat over the chair.

Cosmetics giant Falcini Corp. announced today that chairman George Sayer, 52, would be stepping down. Sayer's resignation comes just as the company announced serious loses for the second quarter in succession. Commentators say the company's faltering performance comes as a result of being too slow to pick up on the end of the nation's love affair with mainstream cosmetics, and the soaring growth in natural brands. Companies like Elements and the American empire, Back to Basics, have shown healthy quarterly figures in comparison. 'Sayer has been pivotal to Falcini's success over the last ten years,' said a company spokesperson, 'but it is time to move on and grasp the challenges of the new mood on the high street.'

Izzie came and leant against the desk, her coffee cradled in her hands. 'Gripping stuff, hey?'

'Well,' said Maddy, 'if the mood really is a swing-back to some collagen-free existence somewhere between Queen Victoria and Fanny Craddock, then that can only be good news for us, can't it?'

Crouching down and lowering her voice, even though the radio was blaring downstairs and Lillian had yet to arrive, Izzie had a serious look on her face. 'But don't you think this means that what Geoff said yesterday makes more sense? I mean, if companies like Falcini are struggling because of some pendulum swing away from liposomes and provitamin B5, then isn't he right that we should be jumping on the bandwagon?'

Maddy looked at the article again. 'From a business point of view he is probably right – he does seem to know what he's talking about and frankly I trust Peter's guidance implicitly – but does that make it right for us?'

Izzie fiddled absent-mindedly with the pens on the desk. 'If we could raise the capital through floating – or whatever Geoff suggests – then maybe we would have enough money to get someone else to do the day-to-day stuff, and we could be more sort of development . . . you know, look at new lines and expand some of Luce's other recipes. Who knows, it could be diaries and tissue box covers next, in our very own design of tasteful sprigged floral print!'

'Have you talked to Jean Luc about all this yet?'

Izzie looked momentarily startled. 'Why would I talk to him about it? I don't speak to him.'

'Yeah yeah!' laughed Maddy, and before Izzie could reply, Lillian staggered up the stairs, wielding her brolly.

Much of the week was spent on the phone to Elements who, buoyed up by their cracking sales figures, were keen to secure promises out of *Paysage Enchanté* that new ideas were surging down the pipeline, and dealing with an on-going tiff between Linda and Karen over pallet loading. Crispin flitted in from time to time, which kept them all cheerful, but didn't seem to stop Angie discussing in minute detail the problems she was having with her coil and the riveting subject of her seriously heavy periods. Izzie sighed loudly at one point and muttered to Maddy under her breath, 'That idea about handing over the day-to day stuff is getting more attractive by the minute.'

Maddy was the last to leave on Friday evening – Izzie and Marcus were going out to dinner with friends – and she was just about to turn out the lights when the phone rang.

'Hi, Maddy, glad I caught you,' Geoff purred smoothly down the phone. 'Bit short notice I know, but I wondered if you would be able to have dinner with me tonight?'

For a moment she was flummoxed and she demurred, but it was what he said next that set the alarm bells ringing.

'I thought a nice bottle of wine, and we might have a chance to talk about the business away from the boardroom table?' So that's your motive, you slimy worm, she thought.

'I'm sorry, Geoff. Nice thought, but I want to see my kids. And Geoff, I never mix business with pleasure.'

'He what?' shrieked Izzie when she called her next morning.

'What a cheek! And why didn't he ask me? I could have done with being wined and dined!'

Maddy spent the rest of the weekend uncomfortable with the thought that Geoff Haynes was trying, however clumsily, to co-opt her. And his coolness when she turned him down was disconcerting. He was as quick to turn off the charm as to turn it on. She tried briefly to read a Sunday supplement analysis of the changing mood towards celebrity image, but chucking the magazine to one side, she turned, irritated, to the features section of the main paper, and began half-heartedly to read an article by Germaine Greer. The thrust of the piece was maternal role models, par for the course, but then Maddy began to read it more closely – the woman had clearly lost her mind. To Maddy's mounting horror, she seemed to be expounding the virtues of the mother role and the very beauty of the maternal lap, from where we should be learning the values of life.

'Oh Christ, the world has finally gone mad,' she squealed, threw down the paper, and went to join the kids in front of a video.

All day Monday there wasn't time to think, let alone talk. It was all hands on deck to get out a mass of orders, and even Lillian had to come down from her eyrie and the payroll to pot up. They didn't finish until well after eight, the girls having knocked off at five and, stiff with pain from standing up so long, Maddy almost crawled home, with just enough time to kiss a sullen and taciturn Will, stroke Florence and Pasco's sleeping heads, and crash out in front of the telly with a glass of wine and a plate of cheese biscuits.

She must have dozed off because she almost leapt out of her chair as the phone rang beside her.

It was Geoff. 'Have I woken you, Maddy? I'm so sorry.'

'What time is it?' She felt disorientated, her mouth dry and her head aching. God, he wasn't going to suggest dinner again, was he?

'About eleven-thirty, but I thought you ought to know. I've had an approach from Tessutini in the States.'

'Tess who?'

'Tessutini, you know the parent company for Face Facts and Agnès Broussard Cosmetics.' Maddy still wasn't sure who or what he meant, but she struggled to sit up and the plate of crackers slid from her lap on to the floor.

'And?'

'They have made an offer to buy *Paysage Enchanté*.' He named a figure. Suddenly Maddy was wide awake.

Chapter 16

Izzie had spent the evening thinking. Seeing the figures, accounts, projections printed out so neatly, had finally brought home to her just how far they had come in under a year. And boy, it had been a steep learning curve. But since July, thankfully, she felt she'd been on an up. And, incredibly, it was all thanks to Marcus.

Izzie marvelled at the way he was taking problems in his stride now. Just a few months ago, any frustrations would have sent him into a tantrum, followed by a prolonged sulk. Now he merely gritted his teeth and put it behind him. It was what Izzie had been hoping for all along. Now she realised – she hadn't really wanted Jean Luc, she wanted Marcus, only nicer, the way he had been in the early years of their marriage, the way he'd been before losing his job. And now she'd got him back.

The kids were much happier with the new, improved Daddy too. He was being the father to them she had always hoped and known he could be. But his transformation made her feel less needed and less wanted. What was wrong with her? Would she never be satisfied? If someone had asked her to write a wish list for the way she wanted Marcus to be, he would probably now score 80 per cent.

Izzie had a few theories about what had brought about this

change, but none of them entirely convinced her. Maybe it was the money. But this didn't explain why it only dated from the party.

Another possibility was that his obvious jealousy of Jean Luc had brought him to his senses. He was being very attentive now, always asking what she and Maddy had discussed during the day, when he'd never shown any interest before. He'd look at her almost anxiously when she came in at night, and wait up for her when she had to work late, instead of the 'I'm pretending to be asleep so I don't have to talk to you' approach he'd favoured before if she was in any later than ten o'clock. Hmmm – perhaps that was it, but was it really a healthy way to go on?

The third possibility was that there had been some trans-formation in *her*. Izzie knew that she bottled up her feelings too much, and had often not told Marcus how she felt about things, preferring to suffer in silence rather than have things out. But the whole Jean Luc experience had made her think differently. So she'd taken to being a bit more assertive in her requests instead of starting off in apologetic mode, and had started telling him how she felt about things. He'd responded well and there had been a couple of quite romantic occasions when he'd told her how much she meant to him, that he'd always wanted to look after her and protect her, and he'd always wanted her to think well of him. It was rather touching just how insecure he was – he'd never said things like that before.

Two things, though, were still bothering her. They hadn't managed to make love since well before the party, and Marcus had starting drinking more heavily. Could the two in some way be related? The sex thing was not for want of trying on her part. After the horrible row they'd had about her going to France, she hadn't wanted to go anywhere near him. But his considera-tion during the kids' summer holidays had made her feel so affectionate towards him – she wanted to show him just how much. But his interest had been flagging, to say the least.

She buried the thought, made herself a cup of tea and went to sort out the pile of clean washing in the sitting room. Marcus was nursing a large Scotch and sitting down, head back against the softly upholstered back of the new sofa, his eyes half closed.

'So what do *you* think, darling? Should we float or should we go on as we are at the moment?' she asked him, as she unravelled Jess's socks.

She suddenly realised she'd got her timing wrong. He raised his head and looked at her so bleakly, it shocked her. Then he shook his head helplessly. 'I don't know what to tell you. But I can't go on like this much longer. It's eating me up. I just don't know how much longer I can keep it going.'

With a deep, pained sigh, he let his head crash back against the cushions and shut his eyes again. Shocked, Izzie left the room, trying to work out what he had meant. Feeling unsettled and confused, Izzie put the washing in the airing cupboard, got ready for bed and was asleep by the time Marcus joined her.

Sweaty, troubling dreams of long corridors and public toilets with no doors plagued Izzie. In the distance, she could hear the bell for the end of lessons, but she couldn't remember which classroom she was supposed to be in, and didn't seem to have any books with her. The bell kept on and on ringing. Eventually she felt Marcus drag himself out of bed, swearing under his breath, then he was back, shaking her roughly awake and thrusting the cordless phone into her hands. She shook her head, trying to pull herself into wakefulness – was it her mother? Was somebody ill?

'Hello? Who is it?'

'Izzie, listen. Something extraordinary's happened.'

'Maddy? Wha . . . wha's up?' She squinted at the clock – only eleven-thirty, but she'd been so deeply asleep. She stumbled along the corridor to the bathroom so as not to disturb Marcus any further. Shaking her head to clear her thoughts and calm the panicked beating of her heart, she tried to focus on Maddy's excited jabber.

High on adrenaline, she switched off the phone. Could this be the answer to everything? She hurried back to the darkness of the bedroom, anxious to share the news. 'Darling, you'll never guess what. That was Maddy. She says that—'

'I don't give a flying fuck what that bitch says.' He heaved himself from his hunched sitting position at the side of the bed and stumbled towards her, his face ugly and contorted in the light from the landing. 'Who does she think she is, calling us at this time of night? She's got a fucking nerve. Rattling round in that bloody mansion of hers, she's got nothing better to do than try to push herself in between us any time it takes her fancy. That spoilt bitch – she's not going to ruin *my* life.'

'What the . . . ? What are you talking about? It's not that at all. She was only—'

'I know what she was doing,' he spat. 'I can see right through that slag even if you can't.' He stood there, hands on hips, in the shaft of light coming through the open door. 'She's got you just where she wants you, running round after her like some pathetic little lapdog. Can't you see how stupid you look? Poncing around in your silly little outfits, pretending to be oh so important. You might be fooling those tossers in London but you're not fooling me.'

Izzie reeled back from this outpouring of venom. Where had this come from? She knew he'd had too much to drink, but this was way beyond the whisky talking. 'For God's sake, keep your voice down, you'll wake the kids.'

'Oh the kids. Here we go! The loving mother.' His voice dripped sarcasm. 'Where the hell have you been for the last six months when they needed you?'

'You're drunk! Just stop it, now. Go to sleep. Just shut up, you don't know what you're saying.'

'I know exactly what I'm saying. I've had long enough to

think about it, all those evenings when you've left me alone. I've only got your word for it that you're even working—'

Suddenly she felt a wave of anger. 'Yeah, that's it, Marcus. Every night we knock off at five then go and pick up a couple of blokes down the Fox and Hounds in Ringford and shag them senseless. Is that what you want to hear? You're pathetic, Marcus!'

'I wouldn't put it past you. The only person you ever think about, apart from yourself, is that toffee-nosed bitch.'

'How dare you speak to me like that.' Izzie knew she was shouting, but she was past caring. 'You're happy enough to spend the money I earn when I'm working every hour God sends. You're so full of self-pity. You disgust me!'

He narrowed his eyes and glared at her, thrusting his hate-filled face towards hers.

'Do I now? Do I? I bet that French bastard can give it to you all night, can't he? Go on – tell me all about it.' Suddenly she was chillingly aware of how much bigger and stronger than her he was. Like a cold shower, the fear swept over her, completely eradicating all the good feelings that had been bubbling over just moments before. She felt vulnerable as never before. She was aware that a small rational part of her brain was calculating just how far it was to the door, and how quickly she could get to the children. 'And I bet you were just gagging for it, weren't you?'

He turned away, and staggered, then with uncontrolled violence he swept his arm across the top of her dressing table, sending everything flying. There was an unbearable crash, then stunned silence, and the smell of perfume from a shattered bottle slowly filled the air. She looked down at the debris in the half-light. A photograph of the children lay on the floor, their smiling faces distorted by the smashed glass. From along the corridor, she could hear Jess whimpering.

So the charade was over.

Very calmly now, she brushed past him as he stood there swaying and confused, and opened her wardrobe door. She took out a fleece and put it on over her pyjamas, then turned and left the room. 'I'm coming, darling. Mummy's here.'

Maddy rigged up beds out of blankets and duvets on the floor of Will's bedroom, whispering to Charlie and Jess to get under the covers, leant down to say how lovely it was to have them to stay at such short notice, and tucked them in to sleep. It would be quite a surprise for Will when he woke up in the morning, and she couldn't imagine how she'd calm him down enough to go to school.

She passed Colette coming up the stairs. 'I've made her a cup of tea,' Colette said quietly. 'She looks terribly sad.'

'Mmmm, I'm not sure tea will be strong enough. Can you just check for me that Charlie and Jess are settled?'

'Sad' wasn't really strong enough either. Izzie was still sitting huddled on the kitchen chair, dressed in pyjama bottoms, with a fleece pulled over the top. Her legs were pulled up on to the seat and her arms folded around them, cowering like an animal, her cup of tea steaming and untouched in front of her.

'Izzie, this is all my fault. I shouldn't have called so late – I was just excited and didn't think. It really could have waited until the morning.' She took a bottle of wine from the fridge and two glasses from the cupboard and sat down next to Izzie, who continued to gaze into space, her face betraying no emotion. Perhaps she was too mad with her to speak, but then why would she have turned up on the doorstep at half past midnight?

'I don't think I can go back,' she said finally in a monotone. 'I think he's really done it now. We both said things so terrible that there's no going back on them. It's like smashing a precious piece of porcelain or something.' She laughed mirthlessly. 'And he took care of that too.' Maddy pushed the glass of wine towards her, and watched Izzie pick it up without really noticing and take a sip.

'No, it's not, Izzie,' said Maddy after a while. 'Porcelain is brittle, but a marriage should be stronger than that. This has just brought to a head something that has been brewing for ages. OK, so the company has been a success, but he should be pleased about that, not making you suffer for it.' Izzie didn't respond. Dare she say anything about the agency or would it be so fundamentally destructive that there would be no mending the marriage? 'Look, Izzie, Marcus is pretty much out of work – even if it, er, wasn't his fault – and you were short of cash. What you have done has changed your whole lifestyle.'

Izzie was fiddling with the stem of her glass, running her thumb and forefinger up the length of it. 'Maybe, but it's been a hell of a price to pay, hasn't it?'

'Has it made you happy though?'

Izzie frowned. 'Yes and no. Meeting you, putting together the team, all this,' she waved her arm around the kitchen, 'has been fantastic, but in some ways it's made life a nightmare. I can't remember who it was I married any more. He's changed so much.'

'What about Jean Luc?'

'He's very special.'

She carried on playing with the glass and Maddy put her hand over hers and said gently, 'No, I meant, what about him? You have to ask yourself some pretty searching questions here. Do you feel happier with him now than you do with Marcus? Because I'm sure there is an option there if you decide that you have to leave.'

Izzie looked at Maddy for the first time since she'd sat down. 'No, there isn't,' she said firmly.

'But I thought—'

'I know what you thought, but we're not having an affair. But meeting him made me feel special and valued, and I suppose it's given me the strength to see what my marriage has become.'

'Oh yes, he's a past master at making you feel good, that's for sure. I ought to tell him about the Tessutini bid. He'll laugh like a drain.'

'He's been so easy to work with, hasn't he?' Izzie sounded vaguely regretful. 'Right from the start he was willing to help us out and be encouraging. If we accept the bid, it will affect him and the women who work with him. What shall we do about that? The bid I mean. It's unbelievable really.'

Maddy got up from her chair and dug a cigarette out of her bag. She'd had her ration for Monday, but it was tomorrow now after all. 'I was thinking about it after Geoff called tonight.' She inhaled deeply. 'It all seems a bit of a coincidence to me, when we'd been talking about floating and suddenly along comes an offer to buy us.'

'I suppose. But it could be fate.' Izzie sounded dismissive. 'It could just be the get-out that we're looking for. Face it, Maddy. Life's hell. We're having to live this completely false existence which is anathema to both of us – I mean,' she tried to smile, 'the way you've suppressed your primeval urge for Bond Street is nothing short of miraculous. But you know, it's destroying the most fundamental thing to both of us – our family life.'

Maddy fiddled with her lighter. 'Are you going to go back to him?'

Izzie sighed and took a cigarette from the open packet. Maddy suddenly felt a huge burden of responsibility. Whether she had meant to or not, by pursuing the idea of Luce's recipes, she'd created a situation which had changed Izzie's marriage perhaps for ever, she'd virtually forced her into the arms of Jean Luc – or at least she'd done nothing to stop the situation – and now she had even got her back on the fags.

'I don't know that I can,' said Izzie finally. 'I think we might all be better off apart for a while. And if this bid comes off, I could afford to be on my own with the kids.' Her face was distraught, her eyes big and frightened. 'Christ, Maddy, I don't know. It's so huge, isn't it? Here I am talking about leaving something that has been part of my life for fifteen years, but nothing I do makes the situation any better.'

'Do you still love him?' Maddy probed gently.

'At the moment, honestly no. In fact, I hate him, but I'm not sure I can bear to be without him. We used to have such fun. I wish you'd known him then, when the kids were first born, but since we moved up here some of that fun has gone. He's become prickly and well, chippy really. Always critical of other people. I used to think it was funny, but I don't any more. It's, well, it's bitchy really. Ugly.'

'Do you think he sees all this as a comedown? I mean, I don't know much about the advertising world, but it must be pretty glam compared to a wet Wednesday afternoon in Ringford.'

'Oh it was glam. In a shallow kind of way – you know, adverts for ketchup suddenly becoming an art form. But it was fun and exciting. I suppose I miss that sort of thrill and excitement too. But then I've loved all this. It knocks spots of copy-editing knitting patterns.'

Suddenly peckish, and remembering that she'd had nothing to speak off since lunch, Maddy went over and raided the biscuit cupboard and, from force of habit with Pasco, found herself unwrapping a KitKat for Izzie.

'You've changed, you know,' she said, sitting down again and mouth full of chocolate. 'Even in the twelve months I've known you. When I compare you to the woman holding the cake in Sue's kitchen, to the person who took on Finbar and the gargoyles at Elements. Things may have changed at home but you've found a self-confidence on the way.'

Izzie bit through the biscuit. 'Have I?'

'Yes, and it suits you. Perhaps, this might be overstepping the

Marc-us a bit, but perhaps you can now meet him on a level playing field. You've proved what you can do, and he's having to learn that you have changed too and he's going to have to treat you in a different, more respectful way.'

Izzie folded the foil from the KitKat wrapper into smaller and smaller squares. 'You make it sound easy, but I don't think it will be. He's bloody stubborn and he'll sulk. I don't think things can change for the better with the business getting bigger and bigger all the time.'

'Shall we go with the bid then?' Maddy asked.

Izzie shook her head, almost punch drunk. 'I'm too tired to think straight about anything, let alone something as big as that. Let's talk to Geoff and Peter about it, shall we? Can't we just go to bed now?'

Maddy couldn't really sleep, and at half past six she gave up trying, and went downstairs in her pyjamas and slippers while the house was still quiet. It was already light, though the sky was dull and grey with the threat of more heavy rain, and the kitchen felt warm and welcoming. She cleared up the glasses and ashtray from the table, laid out the bowls and plates for breakfast, and put on the kettle. As it began to heat, she dialled Jean Luc's number.

'Did I wake you?'

'Maddy darling. No, I've been up an hour. We've got a big day ahead to get supplies over to you. Celeste has been ill and we've got a bit behind. Are you calling to whip us into action?'

Maddy laughed. 'Oh yes, got to keep you on your toes! As a matter of fact, things might be about to change,' and she told him about Geoff's call.

'That's an amazing offer,' Jean Luc finally said after a long pause. 'Are you going to take it?'

'I don't know. Things have got pretty out of control here one way and another.' She told him about Izzie and heard him snort down the phone. 'I think the business is making him resentful and her unhappy. It could just be the best thing to bale out.'

'Well, she's a fool to give it all up for his small-mindedness.'

Tucking the phone under her chin, Maddy poured the boiling water on to a couple of tea bags in the pot. 'I don't think she knows what to do, but she's going to find it hard to go back. They must have said some pretty terrible things to each other.'

'People do.' That sounded heartfelt. What had gone on between him and Pascale at the end? she wondered. She had never rowed so painfully with Simon, not rowed about anything serious really, and in a way she was glad that she hadn't been faced with heartache like that to include now as part of his memory.

'Can I ask you something?'

'Maddy, you know, anything.'

She quietly closed the kitchen door, and lowered her voice – ridiculous when she was talking in French. 'I found out some time ago that Marcus was not actually made redundant from the advertising agency in London. He was fired.'

'*Merde*. Does Izzie know?'

'That's the point. I'm pretty certain that she doesn't. She ought to know. It's a monstrous secret to keep from your wife, but do I tell her? I could risk ruining everything.'

There was a long pause down the phone, and she thought for a minute he'd been cut off. 'Are you still there?'

'Yes, yes,' he said quickly. 'No, I don't think it is your place to say anything. He has to tell her, but you may have to make him do it. Can you speak to him alone?'

'I don't know how. I think the man's a jerk, and I think he knows I do. It would seem very odd if I suddenly phoned up.'

'*Peut-être*, but it's pretty important, isn't it? You really must speak to him somehow. Listen darling, I'm going to have to go. The girls are here. I'll speak to you soon. Take care, sweetie.'

She put down the phone. How the hell could she get to Marcus? Listening intently to check there was no one coming downstairs, she picked up Izzie's rucksack from the floor, and feeling horribly guilty, delved inside to find her mobile. God, it was a worse mess than her bag. She pulled out her purse, a sheet of paracetamol, half a packet of Softmints, and a bulging Filofax, before she found the phone buried deep with Lil-lets and a handful of Micro Machines at the bottom. It wasn't a mobile model she was familiar with, and it took her a couple of tries to locate the address book and to find 'Mmob'. She scribbled the number on a Post-It note by the phone, hoping to God it was his number, not Izzie's mother's. She even checked it wasn't her own. Cramming everything back into the rucksack, she hastily tucked the Post-It note into her own bag, poured Izzie a cup of tea from the pot and went upstairs to wake the household.

There wasn't much waking to be done. Will, on finding his bedroom had two new occupants, was frenzied with excitement, and his squeals had managed to rouse Florence, Pasco and Izzie, who emerged from her room looking like shit. Maddy pushed the mug into her hands, gave her a kiss on the cheek, and began to round up the kids for breakfast. Once she'd quietened them down long enough to work out who wanted which cereal, Colette appeared in the kitchen looking fresh and efficient, and Maddy skulked off for a shower.

'Come and pick something revolting from my wardrobe,' she called to Izzie as she passed the half-closed spare-room door.

'Can I borrow some more of that luscious underwear?' came the sleepy reply.

Once all the children had been dropped at their destinations, Izzie dug around in her bag for her phone, and quickly dropped it back when she saw there was no message.

'It's still early,' Maddy said encouragingly, turning onto the main road, still feeling guilty for having snooped.

'I don't know why I looked. I don't want to hear from him anyway,' and she turned her head to look out of the window. 'Can we get Geoff and Peter to a meeting today – bit short notice?'

'I get the impression Geoff would come and talk about it like a shot.' She passed Izzie her phone. 'Give him a call.'

As predicted, Geoff suggested a meeting late that afternoon at Maddy's house, and said he would speak to Peter. He stressed fervently to them how important it was that they talk to no one. 'It all sounds all very cloak and dagger,' said Izzie, hanging up. 'He had a sort of excitement about it as if it was Bulldog Drummond.'

'Meat and drink to these City boys – I could always tell when there was some takeover in the air with Simon. He used to come home elated and super efficient.'

'We could have done with his advice, couldn't we?' asked Izzie.

Maddy kept her eyes on the road ahead, thinking. 'I don't know. We never really talked about business things. I wasn't really interested, I suppose. Do you know,' she banged her hand on the steering wheel, 'I think this one is up to us. We've been advised by everyone from Pru to the ruddy man from the Trading Standards Office. We need to see what Tessutini are offering, and decide whether it suits *us*.'

'Can we all stay tonight?'

Maddy smiled. 'Have you got enough clothes?'

'No, but yours are nicer anyway.'

It seemed the City was as rife with juicy gossip as the Eagles' playground, and Lillian spent much of the day putting off calls from the press, which she did with aplomb. 'I don't know where they get their ideas from,' she said tartly, putting down the phone for about the eighth time.

'Geoff Haynes,' Maddy and Izzie mouthed simultaneously.

'Well, I didn't tip anyone off as such,' he explained later round the kitchen table. Peter was due any minute, hotfoot from the golf course, and Colette had taken all the children in Maddy's car to the play barn on the outskirts of Ringford, with thirty quid in her pocket and instructions to buy fish fingers and chips. 'It's practically impossible to keep these things quiet,' he went on, 'and there's nothing wrong with a little healthy competition. Someone might crawl out of the woodwork with a rival bid.'

'Do you think anyone would want us that badly?'

Peter appeared at the kitchen door and, relieved to see his familiar face and golfing clothes in the midst of this corporate madness, Maddy stood up to give him a warm hug, and put on her best Blofeld voice. 'So you managed to infiltrate our massive security system, hey, Mr Bond?'

'Well, I did nearly measure my length on Pasco's trike by the door. Very cunning!' He gave Izzie a warm embrace too, and shook Geoff's hand. 'So the big boys are wanting a piece of the action I hear.' She put a cup of tea in front of him.

'We haven't really started talking it through yet,' put in Izzie, 'but it seems like a pretty good offer.' Glad as ever to show off his aptitude for putting together impressive documents, Geoff distributed sheets of information, costings and estimates around the table, and they all pored over them.

'The way I see it, their offer is good, but could be better. I have factored in mail order, the Elements sales, and their interest in further products, plus other enquiries, so there is definitely an argument that within the next twelve months your profit margin could have increased greatly.'

'Mmm,' pondered Peter, 'who did you have in mind to negotiate the contracts?'

'Hewlitt Pritchard have always done the fine detail for me before. I can recommend them highly. In fact, I've already mentioned it to them.'

'Hang on a minute there, Geoff. Are we agreed on the sale?' asked Maddy indignantly.

Peter, sensing the need to put on the brakes, cut Geoff short before he could reply. 'That decision is yours. You two are the shareholders, and it is only for Geoff and I to advise and to help where we can. Tessutini's offer is good – it is a blue-chip company and you could do a lot worse – but three or four years down the line, if sales stay as good, you could make that much and more.'

'That's assuming that the mood doesn't change in the cosmetics market,' put in Geoff hastily.

'Granted,' replied Peter calmly, 'but I'm sure Maddy and Izzie are canny enough to move with and respond to the mood.'

There was silence as the men waited for a response. 'Can we meet up with them?' said Izzie after a while.

'Certainly.' Geoff was enthusiastic. 'I can arrange something for the end of the week or the beginning of next. They are based in the States as you know, so they'd need to get here, but Tom Drake, the CEO, is a great guy and I'm sure he'd want it all to be very amicable.'

'Do you know him then?' Maddy asked.

Geoff began to gather his papers. 'Er, not as such. But I've heard a lot about him on the grapevine. He's pretty well known.'

After Geoff left, Peter stayed on to see the children, who stormed back through the front door like the SAS, high on chips, excitement and E-numbers. Will talked non-stop to him, introducing Charlie, showing him new toys and telling him everything he needed and didn't need to know. It took all four adults to orchestrate bathtime, Charlie and Jess's homework, and stories, and Maddy persuaded an exhausted Peter to have a gin before he headed back home.

'Don't let Geoff push you, ladies,' said Peter, swirling the ice in his glass. 'He's an experienced operator, but he can be a bit – boorish at times. You are both at a huge advantage when they have come to you with an offer, but you will need nerves of steel and a vat load of craftiness – not easy when this whole situation is new for you.'

After he had left, Maddy and Izzie cobbled together an omelette from the contents of the fridge and, over a bottle of wine, talked and talked around the subject until they were hoarse. Slowly Izzie revealed more about the hideous scene with Marcus, and all Maddy could do was listen. Izzie cried, they laughed, they drank more, and eventually, dead on their feet and a little drunk, went up to bed.

Next morning, Izzie was more capable of taking Charlie and Jess to school and, after Maddy had dropped Will and Florence, she too started to head for the barn. Alone for the first time, she thought about all Izzie had said the night before. Perhaps Jean Luc was right, and it was time to take things in hand. She pulled into a lay-by, dug out the Post-It note with his number, and dialled, hoping he wouldn't recognise her number and not pick up.

'Marcus Stock.'

'It's Maddy.' There was a pause. A long one. 'Can you meet me somewhere? I would like to talk to you.'

'Have you got my wife?'

'She's staying with me, yes.'

'When's she coming back?'

'You will have to ask her that yourself. Will you meet me?'

'Er . . . why?'

'Because we have something to discuss.'

Next she called Lillian and made some feeble excuse about remembering she had to collect something in town, then drove out on the by-pass, towards Oxford and the roadside café Marcus had suggested. His car wasn't there yet – would he come? – so she went inside, almost knocked back in the doorway by the smell of chips, and ordered herself a cup of coffee, before sitting at a Formica-topped table as far from the window as she could and still be able to have a view of the car park. The other customers, an assortment of reps and elderly couples eating eggs and bacon, washed down with large cups of tea, looked at her curiously, making it quite obvious that she was an oddity in a place like this. It was clear that the ethos of *Paysage Enchanté* hadn't penetrated as far as here.

He finally pulled in to the car park fifteen minutes later, and pushed through the door dressed in jeans, T-shirt and a leather jacket, looking crumpled and unshaven. He ordered coffee from the counter and sat down heavily opposite her. These people must think we are lovers, thought Maddy, and had to stop herself laughing at the absurdity.

'This had better be important,' he said with no preamble.

'Yes, I think it is.'

He hunched over the table and ran his fingers through his hair. 'So, how is she?'

'She's fine, but pretty bruised.'

'Been persuading her all men are shits, have you?'

'No, cos they are not, and neither are you, though you are being one at the moment.'

He leant back in his seat as the waitress put down the coffee in front of him. 'Makes me laugh to see you in a place like this. Not exactly The Ivy, is it, darling?'

'Marcus, I couldn't give a monkey's what you think about me, though you've made it abundantly clear. This isn't about me, it's about your wife.'

'Why couldn't she have got in touch, then – did she have to send you as her go-between?' he scooped sugar into his cup and stirred his coffee round and round, far longer than was necessary. Was he being irritating on purpose?

'I think she is too hurt at the moment to speak to you. Besides, she doesn't know I'm here.' He clattered his spoon into his saucer. 'But I know that your marriage is never going to work if you aren't honest with each other.'

'Well, she certainly told me what she thought the other night.'

'Maybe, but there's something you haven't told her, isn't there?'

He looked up at her sharply, almost fearfully.

'Listen, I know all about why you left that agency—' He was about to say something but she ploughed on. 'Don't give me some flannel because I *know* – Christ, I made it pretty plain at the party – and this time you have to hear me out. I even know which ad campaign you were working on at the time.' She realised as she said it that she didn't, but was pretty sure he wouldn't challenge her. 'Izzie doesn't know, does she?' He looked away from her across the café and couldn't meet her eye. You bloody coward, she thought.

'How did you find out?'

'Never mind that. Don't you think that Izzie deserves to know the truth? And from you. God, Marcus, if she finds out from someone else – and with the press sniffing about us the way there are, it's only a matter of time – you can wave goodbye to any reconciliation. It's a bloody miracle someone hasn't blown the gaffe already.'

'It's none of your goddamn business, Maddy,' he muttered, looking down into his coffee.

'Yes, it is, because your wife turned up on my doorstep after midnight with Charlie and Jess and she was beside herself. I don't like seeing her unhappy. She's my friend.' God, she sounded like something from *The Godfather*.

'And she's my wife and the way we live has nothing to do with you.' He didn't sound convinced.

He was right though. It hadn't really. For a moment she couldn't answer. Only Izzie could make the decision to stay with him, but it had to be based on the facts. Maddy decided to take a risk. She gathered up her bag, to make a quick and suitably dramatic exit.

'The way Izzie is thinking right now, Marcus, she may not want to come back. She's a stronger person than you give her

credit for – or allow her to be. And nor is she short of admirers.'
She noticed with pleasure that his eyes narrowed at this. 'You've
made one major cock-up in your life, and you may be about to
make another.'

Marcus looked as if she'd slapped him. Perhaps no one had
ever spoken to him like this before, but what did it matter? He
thought little enough of her and some home truths from an
enemy might be the only way he'd hear them. 'I wouldn't be
surprised if she could not forgive you for hiding the sacking
from her – that's if you have the courage to own up at all – but
you might just be lucky. If you want to keep her, Marcus, then
you will have to be a man, instead of the coward you're being
now, and fight for her.' And feeling like someone in a B-movie,
she pushed back her chair, stood up and walked out, leaving
him hunched over the table.

Chapter 17

Maddy looked like an umpire at Wimbledon, sitting perched on the kitchen chair as she watched Izzie pace back and forth across the room. 'You're giving me a crick in my neck! Can't you stand still for a bit? I'll swear you're wearing a groove in the floor.'

Izzie stopped for a brief moment, and wrung her hands so hard that loud clicking noises resounded from her finger joints. Maddy shuddered. 'Ugh! Go back to the pacing. That's even worse.'

'Sorry,' Izzie called distractedly over her shoulder as she reached the French windows. 'I always get like this when I'm stressed. Something has to move. If it's not one bit of me it's another.'

Maddy stretched and yawned. 'I wish I'd known this about you earlier. We could have saved a fortune on our electricity bill at the barn by getting you a little wheel, like a hamster, and connecting you up to the mains.'

'I'm not always this stressed, thank goodness. In fact, I'm not sure I've ever been so nervous before in my life. I just don't know what I'm going to say. Or what he's going to say. Or what I'm going to say when he says what he's going to say.'

'You're clearly deeply bonkers.' Maddy shifted in her seat,

and reached for her coffee. 'But how do you feel? Surely you must know that.'

Izzie's frenetic pace slowed slightly. 'It's weird. I keep changing. It's like one of those optical illusions. You know – sometimes it looks like two faces looking at each other, sometimes it looks like a goblet. Well, it's like that. I keep seeing it two completely different ways, but there's no middle ground. I'm not sure I'll know what I want until I see him again. But I can't even begin to guess what he wants.'

'Well, he did contact you, so you have to assume he has something to say.'

'Yes, but what? What does he really want? Me and the kids or divorce and half my half of PE? Cos that's a possibility too, you know. You know, I'm not even sure I want to see him. I think I might call him and cancel.'

Maddy jumped to her feet. 'No! Don't do that. You have to see him sometime, and the longer you put it off the harder it'll be for both of you. It's time you were going.'

Izzie stopped and picked up her bag. She exhaled heavily, and let her hunched shoulders drop. 'And my Mrs Hardbastard act isn't really going to help, is it?'

'Nuh-uh! It's fair enough to be angry, but don't go in there all guns blazing. And Izzie . . . good luck.'

The hills outside Ringford were a favourite location for early morning dog walkers and after-school tree-climbing sessions, but in the early afternoon they were fairly quiet. Marcus' car was already there when Izzie pulled up in the lay-by. They looked at each other through the window for a moment, neither of them moving, then he got out and walked over to her slowly. He looked appalling. His eyes were bloodshot. He seemed so diminished from what Izzie remembered of that ghastly night that she couldn't, for a moment, imagine how she had ever felt afraid of him. He stood in between the two cars and tried a watery smile that flickered then vanished. After a moment, she opened the door and took a couple of steps towards him. 'Marcus.' She nodded curtly.

'Thanks for coming. I, er, wasn't sure, when you didn't return my message, that you'd turn up.'

'Neither was I. But there's no point putting it off, is there? We've got a lot to sort out.'

Marcus looked down. 'Yes. Shall we walk?'

They set off along the path. Marcus was on his best behaviour, holding the kissing gate open for her to go through first. As she waited for him on the other side, he fumbled in his pockets. 'Here – got you a bag of Minstrels.'

That nearly undid her. A pathetic enough gesture, but they were her very favourites. She managed a wan smile. 'Thanks, dar . . . thanks.'

They walked along slowly in silence at first. The afternoon sun still strong enough to warm them. Then Marcus started to speak. 'Please don't interrupt, Iz. There's some stuff I've got to tell you. I don't know what you're going to say about it all. It could be that you'll hate me for ever, but I have to come clean. It's been eating me up.'

Izzie glanced sideways at him as they walked along. What could it be? An affair? Fraud? The possibilities teemed in her mind like a cloud of buzzing insects. She had to force herself to listen – and slowly, hesitatingly, the whole story came out as they walked up the hill.

'. . . no one in the ad world would touch me after that,' he ended lamely. 'And I suppose I deserved it. But once I'd made the decision not to tell you, it all seemed so much easier. You've always been cleverer than me – oh I know I was quick with ideas and concepts, but that's all superficial. When it came down to it, I just didn't have what it took. I'd been successful, but I wasn't any more. I just couldn't stand it. And you didn't seem to notice anything was wrong – you were so wrapped up in the kids—'

'Now hold on, don't start this "You don't understand me" crap. This is about you and your decision to deliberately mislead me, and to keep me in the dark for ages, absolutely ages. We've been living a lie!'

Marcus threw his hands up to his face, digging his fingers into his scalp. 'I know, I know! But once I'd started it all, I didn't know how to change it. Everyone expected certain things of me, and I just couldn't bring myself to admit that I'd blown it. So I pretended. It was like I'd – I don't know – got on to a rollercoaster and couldn't get off.'

That was something Izzie could relate to all right. She stopped and turned to him. 'But, Marcus, you turned our whole life upside down, moved us out of London, made the children change school – just because of your *pride*. Ever since you were made . . . No, not made redundant. Let's start being honest – ever since you were sacked, you've made us all live a charade. And since the business took off, you've been behaving like a shit . . .'

She trailed off as she looked at her husband. Every line of his body was dispirited and defeated. Suddenly she realised the fundamental change in the balance of their relationship. He was no longer the glamorous golden boy she'd idolised. She was no longer the hesitant, unconfident one. Where did this leave them? Her throat closed painfully and tears pricked her eyes.

'I know how much this business means to you, Iz, but every time you tell me how well something's going, every time you go off to see Maddy and come back smiling and happy, every time I read something about you in the paper, I just feel like I've been kicked in the balls. I know I should be happy for you – but I just can't be. I'm . . . I'm so jealous of your success, and I'm still pissing about with my cameras, getting nowhere. I've achieved nothing! I'm crap at work, I'm a crap father, I'm a crap husband . . .'

His shoulders started to shake and his voice trailed off. The burning indignation she'd felt when he'd first told her his pathetic tale had gradually ebbed away and she felt empty and confused. She glanced at him, but moved no closer. Suddenly, she had to get away and let this revelation sink in.

'Look, Marcus, I've got to think about what you've told me. I don't know how I feel about anything any more. One thing I do know is that I can't trust you right now, and I really can't see how we can stay together after this. I think you'd better move out of the house for a while, till I decide what I want to do.'

Tears were running down his cheeks now, and Izzie had to turn away. His voice was hoarse and trembling. 'I didn't want to lose you! I thought you'd despise me for what I did. I couldn't think of anything else to do!'

The anger and indignation returned all at once, and she swung back towards him, eyes blazing. 'You could have trusted me! You could have shared this with me! But you chose to run away instead – and we've all suffered the consequences. I loved you so much, Marcus. I'd have done anything for you.' Suddenly she was crying too, hot tears that burnt her eyes and thickened her voice. 'We could have faced this together, like the team I thought we were. But you couldn't bring yourself to share your problem, and you can't bring yourself to share my success now, because you've been out on your own all this time. You don't even think of yourself as part of a couple any more. You've been moving further and further away with every lie you've told me. Face it, the last few years have all been based on pretence. I'd rather be alone than go on being lied to. I'm going home with the children, and I want you to move your stuff out by the end of the week.'

Izzie stumbled back down to the kissing gate, and fell heavily against it, bruising her hip. The sharp pain acted like a bucket of cold water, and she felt suddenly clearer. She needed to be alone and drove straight back to Hoxley.

Letting herself back into the quiet house, she braced herself for what she'd find – the carnage of a man left alone for a few days, but it seemed unnaturally tidy. He'd even remembered to put the bin out in an effort to please her. Perhaps he'd imagine they'd walk back in together – everything forgiven and forgotten.

She walked from room to room and shivered as she recalled all the moments they'd shared there, all the lies he must have told. How frightened he must have been, day after day, thinking he was going to be found out. Compared with that deep heartfelt dread, her worries about the company seemed trivial. But Izzie had Maddy to help her through, while Marcus had – no one. 'Poor Marcus,' she sighed, sorting through the post. 'You're like Humpty Dumpty – I wonder if we'll ever be able to put you together again.'

When she pulled up outside the school gate, half an hour later, she felt a surge of anger to see Marcus was already standing there. What the hell was he up to? There was no time to say anything as the children rushed over, delighted that both Mummy and Daddy had turned up in the playground to collect them. Their obvious pleasure at seeing him and the prospect of going home again to Hoxley all together threw her. Jess and Charlie debated hotly whose car to go in, until Marcus stepped in, speaking to them, his eyes fixed questioningly on Izzie. 'Go with Mummy. I've got to do some shopping. I might not be back until later.'

She looked at him stonily. This was a cheap trick, using the children to sway her, but as she watched them hanging from his sleeves and competing to tell him their news, her resolve faltered. She may not want to be with him, but what right had she to keep them from their father? She took a deep breath. 'OK, get something for the children's supper, and we'll talk later.'

His face lit up and he nodded fast in agreement. 'Yes, yes! I'll be back as soon as I can. Well, see you in a bit, back at home.'

And he ran to his car, turning to blow them all a kiss before he slid behind the wheel.

It was a long night after they'd finally got the children to bed. When she came down, Marcus laid an omelette on the table in front of her, and poured a glass of wine. A bottle later they were still talking in angry bursts, interspersed with tears from both of them. It must have been well after midnight when he finally persuaded her to give the relationship another chance, but Izzie knew she was less enthusiastic than he was. It was the children who had been her prime motivation. She was still so angry that, if it hadn't been for them, she'd have kicked him into touch.

The next day, she felt hollowed out and limp with exhaustion. Her car was due for a service, so Marcus, after a night on the sofa, followed her to the garage first thing, then dropped her at the barn before taking the children to school. She carefully avoided kissing him. It was too soon for that.

Throwing her jacket over the back of her chair, she put on the new coffee machine and sat at her desk trying to focus. Today was the meeting with the people from *La Boîte Bleue*, and she had to be on the ball. Sighing, she reached for the dossier Lillian had put together and began to read.

The *Boîte Bleue* chain had taken Europe by storm, its tremendous success based on the premise that women like to be able to pick products up off the shelf and try them out without being pounced on by sales assistants. The shops were exquisite; painted a wonderful Majorelle blue with mirrors everywhere, fantastic wash lighting and arrays of shelving with products laid out easily within reach. Perfumes lined the walls, while make-up and skin care were presented on racks running across the stores, the brands arranged in alphabetical order. They were like a sweetshop for grown-ups, and had been an instant success in Paris. Now there were branches in every major city in Europe, and Izzie and Maddy longed to be a part of it, tucked on the shelves between *Nuxe* and *Philosophy* – a fantastic position.

Izzie picked up and leafed through the sales pitch they had prepared so painstakingly at Maddy's kitchen table. She hoped it was convincing enough. *La Boîte Bleue* was the only store that they had actively gone after. And a hard nut to crack. If they could pull this off, what would it mean for the value of the company and for Tessutini's offer? But a sales pitch was a new experience for them. Were they ready for it? Izzie looked round. The barn was certainly looking good. Maddy had clearly been there until late the previous night, aided by Donna and Angie, and they had given the place a really good going over. The dodgy posters of Robbie Williams had disappeared and a giant vase of blood-red dahlias with deep purple foliage of cotinus stood in the middle of the 'conference' table. All the surfaces gleamed, and upstairs in the office the paperwork had all been filed away. Good going, girls.

But when Maddy arrived from the airport with Fabien and Joelle, the buyers, it was obvious that this wasn't going to be easy, and the expression on Maddy's face when she slipped in behind them told the whole story.

The New Ruralist look may have swept Britain, but it obviously hadn't reached across the Channel, or at least not as far as the Boulevard St Germain. These two were more than chic, they were über-chic. They were so *now*, they were actually more like the middle of next week – and boy, they knew it! Not a hair out of place, immaculately tailored, Japanese designer suits, briefcases that an astronaut would envy, they couldn't have looked more out of place if they'd tried. And trying was one thing they were clearly not doing. That, it rapidly became clear, was Izzie and Maddy's job.

Izzie tried the frontal approach, but her friendly greeting was met with coolly appraising looks and raised eyebrows. Offers of coffee were similarly brushed off. Joelle made a big deal of dusting off the chair Maddy had offered, before sitting down and opening her case, and said in such a soft voice that everyone had to crane across the table to hear her, 'Let's proceed, shall we? We have such a lot of ground to cover – the figures you e-mailed to us were not satisfactory at all.'

On and on it went with Joelle and Fabien making notes and occasionally exchanging significant glances. Izzie kept peeking surreptitiously at her watch, longing for the moment she could suggest lunch. But after another excruciating hour, during which Maddy dropped a whole pile of carefully stacked print-outs on the floor, and Izzie stapled her finger to a sheaf of documents, Fabien and Joelle (Izzie had secretly dubbed them Gomez and Morticia) simultaneously gathered their papers together, as though on a secret signal.

'I think we've seen quite enough. We'll go through our findings on the plane home and present them to the board tomorrow. You'll be hearing from us. Thank you for your time. If you could return us to the airport, please?' and off they swept in a voile of tantalising and costly smelling fragrance. Maddy complied without demur, all the stuffing knocked out of her, leaving Izzie behind feeling boneless and exhausted. She just hoped to God Maddy had remembered to scrape the children's biscuit crumbs and fluff-encrusted jelly tots from the seats in her car.

She was still sitting at the table when Maddy crashed in through the door, a couple of hours later. 'Oh thank God you're still here,' she called weakly. 'When I didn't see the car, I thought you'd gone. Have we got any gin? I need something to relieve the pain. It was only the vision of our product on those lovely sparkly shelves that kept me from opening the car door and shoving Fabien out on to the hard shoulder.'

'No gin, I'm afraid. How would some hot choc do?'

'Fine, just bring it on.' It was shoulders to the wheel then, until Maddy threw down her pen. 'I'm all in for the day. I'm going home for a nice hot bath and some heated-up spag bol. How are you getting home, by the way? Do you want a lift?'

'Erm, no. Marcus is coming to pick me up. My car's at the garage. We're going out to eat together – it's part of his charm offensive.'

'Eeeow. That sounds scary. I didn't want to ask but where are you two at the moment?'

Izzie put the steaming mug down in front of Maddy, sighed deeply and leant back in her chair. 'I don't mind you asking at all. I only wish I had an answer. He revealed something truly terrible yesterday about why he left the agency. It seems our whole relationship has been based on his lies for years. It's fundamentally rotten. So all the effort now just seems like putting a sticking plaster on gangrene. Don't you think?'

'Oh Izzie, I can't tell you that! Only you and Marcus can decide if there's anything worth saving. If he's come clean with you now about something in the past, you just have to start from where you are. I know it's hard not to look back – but it's getting you nowhere, apart from all bitter and twisted!'

'I know, I know. I'm just so confused. In a way, I want us to be a nuclear family, but I just wonder if that's—'

The phone rang, and they both jumped. Maddy answered, then her eyes grew round and she gesticulated frantically at Izzie. 'Hello, Fabien, how nice to hear from you again. How was your flight? . . . . Yes, Izzie is here with me now. Can you hold on for a moment while I put this call on conference?'

Izzie slid into her seat as Maddy put the call on speaker phone. She and Maddy stared at each other in anticipation. What could this be? Surely it was too early for a decision!

His intimidatingly flawless English accent echoed abruptly around the office. 'We have been going over the figures on the plane. We have concerns about your ability to supply all sixty branches. Your operation is too small at the moment. We don't see how you can do it.' They exchanged glances. Fabien was perfectly right. In their present form they couldn't hope to meet the demand that *Bleue* anticipated. The whole edifice was based on the 'maybe' that Tessutini would come through and take up the reins of production. Between the two of them, they fine-tuned their bullshit, throwing out rash promises about expansion, unit square metreage, staff recruitment and a new distribution deal which only had to be rubber-stamped.

At every turn, Fabien came back with another detailed query, and they lobbed them back as fast as they came. Was he convinced? Izzie wasn't so sure. Out of the corner of her eye, she saw Marcus come up the stairs and, seeing they were on the phone, he sat down quietly to wait.

'I can assure you, Fabien,' purred Maddy, 'our stock levels will be sufficient to cover any eventuality, and no, Italy shouldn't be the problem you envisage.'

There was a pause, and they could almost hear him breathing. 'I'm not happy with this,' he said, after what felt like an age. 'I don't think that I can recommend to my board that we go ahead.' They exchanged panicked glances. They could feel it slipping through their fingers. Izzie couldn't stand by and let this happen, so she jumped in.

'You don't need to worry, Fabien. We have a deal on the table that's going to make all the difference—'

Like a shot, Marcus was on his feet, gesticulating wildly, pulling his hand across his throat in a chopping motion, and mouthing 'no! no!'. Izzie faltered and looked bewildered.

Fabien's voice came smartly down the line. 'Really? Tell me more.'

'Er . . .' Izzie watched as Marcus scribbled frantically on the back of an envelope in front of her. 'Hold on, I have the figures here.'

Say nothing, she read. *Privileged information. Change tack.* The penny dropped and she exchanged horrified looks with Maddy.

'Er . . . the deal I mentioned is with a . . .' *warehouse in Rotterdam*, Marcus scrawled, 'warehouse in Rotterdam for . . .' she groped for inspiration.

Maddy waded in. 'Yes, we weren't sure we could tell you just yet, but we've secured a central distribution facility for our Europe sales. The confirmation has just come through this afternoon.' She grimaced, shrugging helplessly.

'Oh I see,' Fabien sounded sniffy. 'What a pity you couldn't mention it earlier. This might change things. That was my main concern. We like your products very much. I will talk to you in the morning.'

Izzie and Maddy mimed a silent high-five, pulling delighted faces at each other while trying to conclude the conversation in a sensible mature way. Thank God video-conferencing hadn't caught on!

'Fan-bloody-tastic!' gushed Izzie as the phone went dead. 'The way we finessed that thing with the distribution at the end. What a team! Wait till we launch this on Tessutini!'

Maddy was pale but triumphant. 'God, we so nearly put our foot in it big time. If it hadn't been for you, Marcus, we'd be screwed now. You've just officially saved our bacon.'

Marcus looked at Maddy for a moment, and Izzie watched him closely, semi-amused by his shyness. It wasn't like him at all! But she was glad that she was close enough to hear his reply. 'Well, it's an easy trap to fall into – saying too much, especially when you're trying to big yourself up a bit. You can't be too careful when you're talking to other companies. Everyone's got their own agenda.'

Yes, it had been a close one all right. And it had nearly happened without Izzie even realising. A moment's lapse. Saying what you know people want to hear. And your career is in tatters. Maybe that was how it had been for Marcus.

'This is surreal, isn't it?' said Maddy, as she pulled into the fast lane. 'I mean – less than twelve months ago we were cowering in Pru's vast office, and now we're off to meet the big boys at some swanky hotel.'

'I think I'm more excited about the swanky hotel – I always fantasised about staying at The Dorchester.' Izzie was rooting through the glove box, trying to find something to put in the CD machine. 'Oh God, please not Postman Pat. I'm just about ready to post his bloody letters up his unfeasibly large nose.'

'Do you think his nose was the same size as his . . . ?'

'Madeleine! Come on, we have got to work out our strategy here. Are we going to play good cop, bad cop, or are we going to be the hard-nosed businesswomen we are getting so good at? It worked for *Boîte Bleue*.'

'Frankly, I haven't got a clue,' said Maddy. 'I'm a bit scared really.'

'Have you spoken to Geoff about it?'

'He said that we should keep quiet and let him do the talking.'

Izzie was silent for a minute. 'He *is* on our side, isn't he?'

It troubled Maddy that this was just what she had been wondering for the last few days. 'What makes you say that?'

'Oh, I don't know. He's just a bit too keen sometimes. For all I know he'll whip some here's-one-I-prepared-earlier document out of his briefcase, and it'll all be settled before we can open our mouths.'

Maddy kept her eyes on the road, as they sped passed the exit to Princes Risborough and up the steep cutting in the hillside. 'I think that's when we have to remember who owns this company.'

The traffic down the Edgware Road was bumper to bumper, and they were running a bit late – Geoff had called twice already – by the time they found a space in the Hyde Park car park. They dashed down through the park towards the hotel, the early autumn leaves falling about them in the sunshine, before risking their lives crossing Park Lane.

'Right, Mrs Stock, uniform!' and they both pulled out their shades and put them on. 'I feel like the Blues Brothers.'

Izzie braced herself. 'It's one hundred and six yards to the meeting. We've got a full tank of gas, half a pack of cigarettes, it's light and we're wearing sunglasses.'

'Hit it!' cried Maddy and they stormed through the doors.

Giving their names at the reception desk, they were escorted like royalty, through the giant marble and gold hallway towards the Boardroom Suite. This was red-carpet treatment. Maddy had to remind Izzie to close her mouth as she gazed in awe around her. 'Pretend you come here all the time,' she said under her breath. 'You look like a five-year-old on a school outing. Think corporate, darling.'

By the time they had taken a detour to the ladies, titivated their lipstick, and found the private suite, they were seriously late. They knocked sheepishly, and the door was ripped open by Geoff, who was decidedly hot and bothered, and gave them a look of reproach, which made Maddy feel very small indeed.

'So sorry, gentlemen,' she said, in her coolest voice. 'You know how awful the traffic can be.' Stupid remark. At least two of those present lived in New York. She registered an imposing room, in Biedermeier style, awash with suits, all seated around a long rectangular table, with two places in the middle left presumably for her and Izzie. It was like being late to the wrong surprise birthday party, where no one seemed very pleased to see you. There was an uncomfortable silence, then Geoff bounded into action.

'Now, ladies, let me introduce you. This is David Seers and Steve Baines of Hewlitt Pritchard, our lawyers.' They shook hands politely. 'And Peter of course.'

'I think we've met,' said Maddy, and smiled broadly at Peter as his eyes twinkled and he winked supportively at her.

'And this is Greg Fienstein, Tessutini's vice-president business development.' Their hands were grasped firmly by a preppie-looking man, all tortoiseshell-rimmed glasses, who in turn introduced a man to his right, 'Brian Bridgeton, our lawyer.' More handshaking, then Geoff indicated someone seated over the far side of the table, 'and Tom Drake, Tessutini's CEO.'

The man stood up and came round the table. He was enormously tall and lean, and towered over Maddy and Izzie. Out of a sea of forgettable faces, this guy was impressive, and Maddy had to remind herself to look cool and nonchalant as she greeted him. Dark blue shirt and striped tie, suit trousers and, unlike the others, no jacket. He was not traditionally handsome – she supposed she'd imagined he'd be an Ivy Leaguer out of a John Grisham novel – but he was too rough cut for that, and he certainly had *presence*. She noticed neat cuffs as he took her hand in his cool, plate-sized one, and then she peered all the way up to his face. His hair was very short, obviously once dark judging by his dark eyebrows, but was now flecked with plenty of grey. His skin was slightly tanned – at Martha's Vineyard, no doubt – and she reckoned he must be in his mid-forties. But it was his eyes that engaged her. She couldn't really see the colour of them, but they were framed with laughter lines and they looked hard at her, with an assessing, rather presumptuous mirth. Well, she thought fleetingly, this would be eye candy if negotiations got dull.

Settled down in their places, opposite Tom Drake and his henchman, Maddy suddenly felt her palms go clammy, and she had an irresistible urge to hold Izzie's hand. This made the first Elements encounter seem like a picnic. She wanted a drink too, but she wasn't sure if it was the done thing to help yourself to the designer mineral water laid out down the middle of the table. What the hell. She leant across the table, and to her chagrin, couldn't quite reach, until Tom Drake slowly pushed the bottle and a glass towards her.

'Er, thank you.' Don't be pathetic, Madeleine.

With the *élan* of a man who had clearly done this many times before, Greg Fienstein got the ball rolling. 'Now that everyone's here, we can start. It is delightful to meet you, ladies. As Geoff said, I am one of the corporate finance advisers for the Tessutini Group, and I have to say how impressed we are with *Paysage Enchanté*.' He pronounced this in his Boston brahmin accent to rhyme with 'bay'. 'We have watched your progress with interest and, as we have indicated, are very interested in bringing your company into the Tessutini Group. We think it would complement our portfolio very well. We have always prided ourselves on having a stable of forward-thinking and innovative enterprises, and we feel we could fulfil the brand's potential.' He went on to repeat the offer made in their original communication, but hearing him say it aloud made it seem very real.

There was a pause, and Maddy slurped her drink inelegantly in the silence.

David Seers of Hewlitt's took up the reins. 'I understand my clients are interested in your offer to buy the *Paysage Enchanté* brand and associated goodwill, but have several points they would like to make.'

Geoff, in his element, swung into action at this point, and Maddy was relieved to let him run through the details they had talked about over the phone the day before. Clauses were discussed and counter-discussed across the table, product recipes and production processes detailed, wording tweaked and fine-tuned, staff pay-offs proposed and accepted, and after a while Maddy felt like a spare part. She tried not to let her eyes glaze over, nor to wander over to the other side of the table. The atmosphere seemed cordial enough, and Geoff was at his most dynamic. She could understand why Peter rated him so highly.

This is all going too well, she thought. They seem to be agreeing to everything, including maintaining the brand name and image, and we haven't even played our ace yet. Perhaps someone's going to jump through the door any minute and shout, 'Joke! Had you going though, didn't we?'

She kicked Izzie under the table, and scribbled on the pad in front of them, '*Boîte Bleue?*' Like passing notes in class, Izzie nudged Geoff and pointed to Maddy's note. He raised his eyebrows at it, quizzically. 'Just agreed big sales deal with them,' Izzie scribbled, and put the value of the order as discreetly as she could. Geoff's eyebrows shot up even further. 'Make us worth more?' she wrote underneath.

'Um, Mrs Stock has just reminded me' (boy, he was cool) 'that the company have just finalised a new order with *Boîte Bleue*, which would place the products in all sixty stores in six European countries.' He told them the estimated value of the order over the next twelve months. 'This, we feel, should be reflected in Tessutini's offer.'

'It is already a very generous one for a company that has not yet filed a year's trading figures,' said Fienstein, without flinching. 'On these terms we would expect exclusivity.'

Peter's voice came from the far end of the table. 'Perhaps, but your offer was made without this information, and this *Boîte Bleue* order is clearly quite a *coup*. You will know yourselves just what a demanding company they are to supply.'

Greg Feinstein looked at his boss, who wrote something in small writing on the top of the papers in front of him, then he looked back at Geoff. 'I think, yes, we can factor this increase in turnover into a new, slightly improved offer.' Maddy kicked Izzie again. Result!

'Our only issue,' said Feinstein, after a moment and glancing down at his notes, 'is with *Paysage Enchanté*'s desire not to relinquish the rights to the products should Tessutini decide not to produce them any longer.'

'Er . . . that doesn't seem reasonable,' Maddy blurted out without thinking. Judging by the looks of surprise coming at her from around the table, it was clear they really weren't supposed to speak at all during the proceedings and she felt like a juror who had suddenly said something inappropriate in court. She could feel the sweat prickling under her armpits, but ploughed on. 'Surely if you decide that *Paysage Enchanté* should not be continued, then it's fair game for anyone to buy the name back from you and start up production again, even if it wasn't us?' She'd directed her remarks to the tortoiseshell glasses, but she could feel Tom Drake's assessing eyes, full of humour, yet so damned arrogant, looking hard at her. She shifted her gaze to meet his.

He held her eyes. 'The company, at the moment, is yours and Mrs Stock's by rights too,' he said at last, 'until such time as you decide to sell. I'm afraid this is a clause of the contract on which we are immovable.'

Maddy looked down quickly at the draft contract in front of her. Suddenly she felt terribly protective about their little range of products. The fun Izzie and she had had putting together the story; the meetings with Pru and Elements; the cabbages stuffed into the veg patch; long evenings of agonising work that had gone into meeting orders; the girls back at the barn with their foul language and fouler jokes; Crispin and his visits to the weirdos in Wales; Lillian with her efficiency and surprising little hobbies. *Paysage Enchanté* was their baby, even if it had been somewhat unplanned, and she felt now as if they were having to put it up for adoption.

She turned to Izzie, her eyebrow raised in what she hoped would read as, what do you think?

Izzie turned back to the table and, in her best hard-nosed businesswoman voice, said, 'Am I not right in thinking there may be a requirement for us to stay on for a period of time as directors, to oversee the handover?'

There was a moment's silence, until Geoff and Greg spoke almost simultaneously. 'I think you'll agree, Izzie, that if production is to move to the States, it really wouldn't be practical.'

'Mrs Stock, set your mind at rest,' soothed Greg. 'Tessutini is one of the biggest cosmetics producers in the world. I can assure you there will be no hitch in the transfer.'

Izzie looked questioningly at Maddy. 'Er . . . can we have five minutes to talk about this please, gentlemen? Either we can leave the room . . . er, or you can.'

Once the Americans had closed the door behind them, both Maddy and Izzie slumped back in their chairs, not realising how tensed up their bodies had been.

'Is it too early for a drink?' Izzie asked Peter.

'With a bit of luck, darling, we can crack the champagne soon, but let's sort out this hurdle. Their terms are very reasonable so far – remarkably so really – but I think you may have to concede this one.'

Geoff gave a nervous little cough. 'Maddy, I think you will find that these sort of caveats are very normal in such negotiations. It is part of the purchaser's requirement to have complete control of a brand once it has been acquired. Don't forget the restrictive covenant – you will both be excluded from setting up a similar business for the next two years any-way.'

'I can see his point, Maddy,' said Izzie gently. 'Would we want to start it up again, even if they did stop production some time in the future? If a company like Tessutini decide after a while it's not really selling as much as it should . . . well, they'd take it off the market. They know the cosmetics market better than we do.'

'Everyone knows it better than we do, love. This whole thing has been by the seat of our not insubstantial pants.' Maddy smiled at her. 'Is there any chance of some coffee then?' Geoff picked up the phone to put in the order.

'It's all so very final though, isn't it?' Maddy continued quietly, so only Izzie could hear. 'Once they take it on, then it's goodbye to everything.'

'Maybe, but isn't that what we want? Haven't we decided

that we've had enough? All this spin's made me so dizzy, I don't know who or what I am any more.'

She looked at Izzie and could see the plea in her eyes. Selling the company was going to be the only way that she could salvage her marriage, wasn't it? Despite Marcus' eleventh-hour support during the shenanigans with Fabien, Maddy wasn't convinced his volte-face was genuine. How much longer would he tolerate Izzie giving every hour to the company? It had been one hell of a year for her and, if they didn't sell, the business would have to make a quantum leap to be able to supply *Boîte Bleue* at all. No way could they fulfil orders the way things were now, and how long would it take to realise an imaginary warehouse in Rotterdam? They'd be victims of their own sales bullshit. It was only fair to take the money Tessutini were offering.

But Maddy couldn't help feeling a strong flood of selfishness. Where would the sale leave her, except richer? She had no other life except for this. Their brief time at Huntingford House had been one of grief and *Paysage Enchanté*, but the day after the sale went though all she would have would be the grief. There was only so much shopping you could do in a lifetime, even for someone with her abilities in that department. And what about all the things Will had said? But what was left for her?

Izzie squeezed her hand. 'We've proved such a lot to ourselves over the last year. Think how far we've come since Ledfinch Manor and that awful Fayre, and the terrible smell in your kitchen. It was fun, but anyway it might not be the end. For both of us, it could just be the beginning.' She smiled at her terrible cliché.

They returned to the table for another hour of tedious semantics then, with a finality that felt like the end of a particularly arduous exam, Greg Fienstein wrapped up the meeting. 'This is all fairly straightforward and we will have it finalised within days, ladies, and then we will sign the agreement and have it ready for signatures.' He tidied his papers, slipped them back into his briefcase and put the lid back on his pen with a conclusive 'click'. 'I think for security reasons, we should leave the building separately, so if you could give us a few moments before you leave the room . . .' There was a general scraping of chairs as everyone stood up, shook hands, and made their farewells. Tom Drake took Maddy's hand again and, feeling bereft, she found herself saying, 'We've worked hard on this company, Mr Drake. You will look after it, won't you?'

His eyes crinkled into a smile. 'Oh, we know you have. That's why it's been so successful. We'll take good care of it,' and he picked up his briefcase, and walked out of the door, his minions following behind.

Maddy felt her body sag with relief. 'Is there light at the end of the tunnel, Iz?' she muttered.

'It's coming, babe! Just a few more days of being wholesome, and we can do what the hell we like.'

The traffic back was dire, bumper to bumper up the A40, stopping and starting until Maddy's clutch foot ached. The tedium was interspersed with calls from Geoff who gabbled his excitement into Izzie's ear. 'He says we should have the contracts by Friday,' she said as she cut him off after the second call. 'He's really fired up. Anyone would think it was his money.'

'We're going to have to give him a bonus of some kind I suppose.' Maddy looked into her wing mirror and tried to change lanes. 'I'll ask Peter what the procedure is. In the meantime, my girl, you're going to need a lesson in how to spend serious cash. Burn a hole in that plastic.'

For the next excruciatingly slow hour they planned what they were going to buy, Izzie's ideas getting more and more bizarre as time went on. By the time Maddy dropped her at her house, to be greeted by a cautious but friendly Marcus, Izzie had parted with most of her half on everything from an aquarium to a yacht painted lilac and manned by a crew of Adonis (or Adoni, they weren't quite sure of the plural).

As she finally pulled into her drive, Will and Florence flew out of the door, and it took her some time to answer their questions and listen to their news of the day. At last she dumped her bag in the kitchen and poured herself a glass of wine.

Will came trundling in after her. 'Mum, can I play on the GameBoy? Colette said I couldn't till I'd done my homework.'

'Well have you?'

'Yes.'

'Well then you can.'

'Mummy, can we have a disco?' Florence tottered into the room in her clippy cloppy pink shoes and one of Colette's pink sparkly T-shirts bearing the slogan, 'Like I give a FCUK'.

'Why not?' said Maddy, seizing the mood. 'Out on the terrace. I'll put the speakers in the doorway – Florence darling, you get the Abba CD.' She scooped up Pasco, went into the sitting room and flung open the doors. Yes, it was warm enough in the early autumn sunshine. Turning the speakers around, she slipped in the CD from Florence, and turned the volume loud. Will, too cool by far to join in, sat on the garden bench, engrossed in Pokémon on his GameBoy. Pasco began to push the soily tractor he'd found discarded on the ground through the flower bed, and Florence, grabbing Colette by the hand, began to gyrate to the music. Everyone happy, Maddy dashed upstairs, dug out and threw on her own FCUK T-shirt from the back of the wardrobe, some pink pedal pushers (bit tight now) she hadn't been able to wear under the Ruralist regime, and her beloved Jimmy Choos, retrieved her wine from the kitchen, lit a much-needed cigarette and went back to stand in the doorway.

'Come on, Mum,' shrieked Florence over the soundtrack. 'Come and dance.' Careful not to spill her wine, and giggling with the fun of it all, she joined the dancing line-up.

The music was so loud, and dance steps needing so much concentration, she couldn't possibly have heard the 'click, whirr, click, whirr' coming from the other side of the garden hedge.

Chapter 18

Izzie yawned and stretched, careful not to disturb Charlie who had clambered into bed in between them again sometime during the night. He'd given up coming into their bed a couple of years previously but, since the night she'd fled with the kids to Maddy's house, he'd woken every night and sleepily sought her out. She hadn't said anything. No point making an issue of it. Perhaps it would sort itself out in time. Perhaps her marriage too would sort itself out in time. Perhaps.

Charlie's long, dark glossy lashes lay on his cheeks and his mouth was softly open, his breath sweet and warm. Skinny as ever, he was getting tall now and she smiled to herself as she traced with her eyes the bump he made under the blue check quilt – not a little boy any more, but he was still easily thrown by changes in his life. What would be best for him and Jess? For their parents to stay together, despite their flawed relationship? Or for them to split up, live apart and carve up the children between them, a weekend here, a holiday there? The way Izzie felt now, the latter choice would be easier, or at least less painful. But she was not the only one involved. With Marcus around and the constant pressure to forgive, to analyse, to debate, she sometimes felt the top of her head was going to come flying off.

She felt tired – dog-tired. If someone had led her into a darkened room with a nice comfy bed and left her uninterrupted, she reckoned she could sleep for three weeks straight. And the prospect of actually being able to do just that was dangling in front of her. All they had to do was to get the signed contract back to the States, hand all responsibility over to Tessutini, bank the cheque, and take it easy – maybe not for life, but for a while.

Charlie stirred, saving her from any further thoughts, and slurred huskily, 'Kisses, please'. So imperious, so adorable. How could she love these children so passionately, yet feel so many doubts about their father? Jess came tippy-toeing in next and snuggled up on Izzie's other side, completing her bliss. Izzie nuzzled her hair, inhaling deeply and listened to an account of her latest dream.

Marcus, still on his best behaviour, had already set out to jog down to the village to get their newspaper. He was working hard at getting back into shape, perhaps remembering how irresistible Izzie had once found him. She shook her head sadly. It would be a long and difficult process if they were ever to build a relationship that worked for both of them. And without the business to act as legitimate distraction . . . He wanted the emotion. All Izzie wanted was some undemanding task to divert her. Could it be that Marcus was the one from Venus, while all she wanted was a nice cosy cave somewhere on Mars?

A gulp of tea and she was ready for action. She shooed the children into their rooms, pointed them at their school uniforms and retired to the shower. By the time she got out, Marcus had staggered through the door, wheezy but triumphant. He thrust the paper into her hands and made for the bathroom, stripping off his sweaty tracksuit as he went. She retreated to get dressed and have a quick shufti through the business pages. Aha! What was this little snippit?

Rumours are rife that upstart cosmetics company *Paysage Enchanté*, generally credited with having set the New Ruralist ball rolling, may be next on the menu for a Very Big Fish. A not-so orderly queue of bruised multi-nationals has been forming to snap up the tiny but perfectly formed PE, as profits from hi-tech cosmetics products have nose-dived. Who will be the lucky winner? No one wants to say for certain, but Madeleine Hoare and Isobel Stock, founder/directors, are unlikely to be losers if they sell out!

'Shit!' Izzie jumped up and pulled on her clothes at top speed. 'Shit, shit, shit!'

As she dashed downstairs, she registered Jess, now fully dressed, and Charlie, still strumming along to Queen in his underpants, emerging from their rooms into the hallway and exchanging horrified grins at her language. She reached for the phone. 'Maddy, have you seen it?'

'Yes. God knows how they got hold of that! Do you think someone saw us at the hotel and put two and two together?'

'Must have, I suppose. Drake's team were really cloak and dagger – just like *Secret Squirrel* – and it can't have been any of our lot.'

'Can't it?' Maddy sounded suddenly suspicious. 'I know Peter would never do a thing like that, but—'

'Geoff? Do you really think so? What a slimy toad!'

'Mmmm,' mused Maddy. 'Well, don't let's jump to conclusions and start accusing him. I don't even know what effect this might have. Do you think Tessutini would pull out because of it?'

'Nah! They're solid, I reckon. I'm sure they want us, and it confirms here what Geoff was saying about sales figures for the big cosmetic houses. At the moment, all publicity is good publicity.'

Less than an hour later, Izzie had reason to wish she hadn't tempted fate with that rash comment. They were at the office and feeling pretty smug. Having signed their part of the contract, they felt safe in coming clean with the girls about what was in store for them, although they hadn't yet said it was a cert. The initial shock at losing their jobs turned to elation as they explained the terms. 'So you see,' said Izzie, 'you'd each get the lump sum in addition to your three months' wages, but they'd probably be transferring production abroad fairly quickly, so you wouldn't have to work out the three months anyway.'

'What? Paid for sitting round on our arses? Sounds all right to me,' laughed Karen throatily.

'You can sit on your arse if you want,' chimed in Donna, 'I'm going to blew it all on a cruise.'

They were all laughing and talking at once, and Maddy had to put her finger in her ear to block out the noise as she answered the phone. Izzie noticed her problem, and ushered the girls back downstairs, with a promise to buy doughnuts at lunchtime by way of celebration. Still laughing, she sat back down and turned to Maddy. But her friend's white face and even whiter knuckles gripping the receiver wiped the smile right off her. She listened intently to the breathless, one-sided conversation.

'No, of course I'm not denying it. I'm just saying . . . But it's completely out of context and it's absolutely unfair to try to . . . No, you listen, please. It's outrageous to abuse someone's privacy like . . . This must be illegal. You can't do this. But why would you do this? I don't see . . . Is that all you have to say? Well then, no comment.' And she slammed down the receiver.

Izzie was befuddled. 'What the hell was that? Crank call?'

Maddy put her elbows on her desk, and dropped her head into her hands. 'If only. Oh God, Izzie, you're going to kill me!

That was the *Courier*. Miles Oakley, that sleaze-ball editor – he says they've got a photo of me, taken the other day at home. It was after that meeting with Drake and his lot. I was so knackered. God, why did I do it? I had a ciggie and a glass of wine, and . . . oh, it just gets worse. The kids were outside, and Will was playing on his GameBoy, and Florence was dressed up like a little tart and I was wearing an FCUK T-shirt. Oh, I don't believe it! The whole image gone in seconds. The bastard photographer must have been up a ladder somewhere.'

'They took a photo of you in the garden? But can they do that? Surely if it's your garden, it's private property, isn't it? What are they going to do with the photo? Surely they're not going to run it?'

'Yes, and on Monday. Front page, he said, the grubby little toerag. He said he thought their readers would "like to see what we get up to in private". He said they're going to compare all the things we've said in public with the reality.'

'Ooh shit! I hope they haven't been prowling round our place. They'd have a field day! Oh, but Maddy, I've just thought,' Izzie flushed and put her hand up to her mouth in alarm, 'Drake won't have signed by then. I mean, if we only signed yesterday, Hewlitt's won't have sent the contracts back to them yet. He'll have seen the paper – or someone in his organisation will before they sign. Do you think they'll go through with it?'

'No! I don't know,' Maddy wailed. 'I don't know anything. This could ruin the whole thing. We could end up with nothing. A complete laughing stock. No one will buy the stuff once this hits the news-stands. What have I done?'

Izzie took charge. 'Look, I'll make some coffee. You call Peter. He'll know what to do. Maybe we can make them delay or something. Get our lawyers on to them.'

Izzie could tell from Maddy's expression that Peter had not been able to reassure her. 'He says it goes to credibility,' she explained. 'The brand is based on a concept of integrity – well, we knew that. We worked hard enough to concoct the stupid image. He says without the image, the sales are almost bound to suffer. If Tessutini can't quantify the damage, they're just as likely to pull out. He said something about break fees if the transaction doesn't go ahead, and a thing called Section 151, but I'd kind of phased out by then. I could tell it was bad news though.'

Izzie blew her fringe out of her eyes. 'So does this mean we're going to have to find that warehouse in Rotterdam after all?'

'I don't think *Boîte Bleue* will touch us with a disinfected barge pole,' said Maddy bitterly.

'Oooh bum!' said Izzie quietly.

'My sentiments entirely!' Maddy sighed as she sat back down heavily in her chair. 'Bum indeed.'

After that, Izzie found it difficult to deal with the low-level elation that the girls were indulging in. Bumping hips together rhythmically as they went about their work and singing along to the radio, they looked so happy, as though someone had given them an unexpected present, or at least the promise of one. And so they had. The only trouble was they were going to have to take it right back again, and soon. Maddy was staring into space, and Izzie didn't like to disturb her. It could as easily have been her and she didn't blame Maddy at all. She hoped she knew that, but wasn't sure how to ask without raising the idea that she did blame her. Suddenly, Maddy jumped up.

'What was I thinking of? I completely forgot to tell you! I'm going away with the kids for the weekend. We're going to stay with some old friends, and I said we'd get there as early as possible, so I have to go and pack everything up now. Yup, right now or we'll be late. D'you mind?'

Izzie was slightly taken aback by this abrupt change. 'Course not. Do you good to get away. I really don't think there's anything more we can do about this now.'

'No, no. Of course not. Might as well forget about it and hope for the best.'

'Er, yeah. Well, have a nice time. I'll call you if anything comes up. Do you want me to call Geoff?'

'No. I think Peter's talking to him now. He'll call if there's anything new. I'd better head out. I'll call you later.'

And off she went. Izzie shook her head, and watched her leave. She hoped she'd be all right. This forced energy and brightness was a bit worrying. A weekend away would probably be the best thing. Izzie hoped the friends would take good care of her. But it wasn't like Maddy to dash off in the middle of a crisis – she hoped this hadn't pushed her too far. Her hand hovered over the phone. She wanted to tell someone, ask someone's opinion. All right – she wanted to speak to Marcus. Was that a sign of something? She couldn't be bothered to analyse it, though Marcus almost certainly would. All she knew was she needed to hear his voice. She dialled the number.

An hour later, she was back home in the kitchen. She'd given the girls and a rather surprised Lillian the rest of the day off, and explained that there might be some press interest. All had agreed stoutly to plead the fifth or at least defend the reputation of PE against the heathen journalists, like Crusaders taking the oath. Their loyalty was touching. So was Marcus'.

'What we can do, babe, is call round the agencies. See if anyone knows who's been sniffing round. I've got a few contacts at the *Courier* too, but they probably won't spill the beans. Give me and hour or so, and I'll see what I can dig up.'

With the bit between his teeth, he was like the Marcus of old, clicking his fingers between calls, scribbling notes, whistling tunelessly and jabbing out numbers with the end of his very chewed biro. 'Paddy? Hello, mate! It's Marcus Stock. Yeah, I know. Long time, no nothing . . . Listen, mate, I've got a bit of a favour to ask. A friend of Izzie's has got herself well and truly shafted by the *Courier*. Yeah, same old scumbags. Thing is, the photo was taken round here near where we live. Quite near Oxford, yeah. You gotta come up some time. Melissa and the kids too. Anyway, I was wondering, do you know anyone who's been out this way lately? Really? OK, thanks, I'll try him. Yeah keep in touch.'

So it went on. Marcus was making contact with people he hadn't spoken to in years for fear of being rejected, perhaps. Yet no one had brushed him off, as far as Izzie could tell from the one-sided conversation, and lots of them had asked when he'd be in London next. Maybe some good might come of this mess after all. On and on it went. Marcus followed up leads, ran in to dead ends, tried again. Izzie went to fetch the kids, leaving him to it. When she returned he was sitting back in the kitchen chair looking smug.

'I think I deserve a cup of tea this time,' he said triumphantly waving his notepad at her. 'I think I've got a result! Bloke called Pete the Greek. I don't know his real name – that's what everyone's called him for as long as I can remember. I've never met him, but I know people who have. He does a lot of this sort of thing, mostly for the tabloids. I've got a mobile, but he's not answering. What do you want to do?'

Izzie shrugged helplessly. 'Dunno. What can we do? Could I . . . offer him money, threaten to sue him, give him a knuckle sandwich? You tell me, Marcus – what should I do?'

'Wouldn't bother with threats.' Marcus got up and started pacing the room, hyped up by the thrill of the chase. 'That'll just piss him off. The newspaper's certainly paying a fair bit for this. If you can top their offer, he might sell it to you. Trouble is, the *Courier* won't take very kindly to him blowing them out at the last minute, so you'll have to make it worth his while.'

'What do you think? Twenty grand?' Izzie pulled a number out of the air.

'I should think that'd do nicely. All we have to do now is track him down. Hmmm. Hey, d'you fancy a trip to London?'

Izzie's eyes widened. 'Do you mean it? Should we go and find him?'

'Frontal approach is worth a try. And you haven't got much time, have you? One thing though, love. Drop the *Cider with Rosie* look, eh? Go for something nice and inconspicuous, like a trenchcoat and dark glasses. Could the kids stay at Maddy's?'

Izzie shook her head and frowned. 'No, she's run off to stay with friends. She was taking the kids straight from school I think, so she'll probably be there already. I might give her a call.'

'No don't. Let's call her when we have some good news. Don't want to get her hopes up too high. Shall I try Janet Grant, then?'

He busied himself phoning her. This was a new, improved Marcus, sorting out the kids' needs without being asked. She poured him another cup of tea – he did deserve it.

On Saturday afternoon they dropped the kids off at Janet's house and drove down to London. They'd arranged to stay with some old friends in Streatham. Shaun, another photographer, had given Marcus his best lead. 'His name's really Pete Kyriako-something or another. No one can ever remember what, so it's Pete the Greek. He lives over in Tufnell Park, dunno where exactly, but he's usually at the Flask in Highgate for Sunday lunchtime. They do a mean sausage and mash there and the beer's good. If he's not answering his mobile, that's your best bet. Have you left him a message?'

'Nooo. This is more of an undercover operation,' confided Marcus. 'I've never even met him but we need to speak to him, face to face. What's he look like?'

'This sounds exciting.' Maz (too graphic-artist-funky to call herself Mary) flicked her long plait over her shoulder and placed a huge bowl of pasta on the table in front of them, and slid on to the polished wooden refectory bench next to Shaun. 'He looks a bit like Kevin Kline in *A Fish Called Wanda*. Can we come along? I'd recognise him, and you might want moral support from what you say.'

'Oh yeah, do come along,' Izzie nodded. 'We'll stand you lunch. And if he's not there, maybe you'll recognise someone else there who might be able to help.'

Next morning, slightly the worse for wear, the two couples made their way up to leafy Highgate. Well, not quite so leafy in October, but still pretty gorgeous. They were sitting outside at one of the trestle tables in the large triangular forecourt when Maz leant across and hissed, 'Don't look round. That's him. With the blonde.'

They all looked round. He did, indeed, look strikingly like Kevin Kline. Not the seedy, furtive criminal-looking type Izzie had imagined. Instead, he was quite a tasty, interesting-looking bloke in jeans, with a Rolex he kept flashing, and a very expensive-looking leather jacket, but he was just a little too old for his designer stubble. Kleftika dressed as lamb?

'How are we going to do this?' Izzie asked suddenly.

Marcus was rubbing his chin thoughtfully. 'I can't see there's any way of doing it subtly,' he admitted. 'I hadn't really thought this through, I must admit.' Silence. 'Come on, Iz. We can't waste any more time, let's just improvise. Have you worked out how much you're prepared to offer him? Quick, he's going to the bar. Let's cut him off on the way.'

They sidled casually towards him as he approached. Marcus opened. 'Hi! Pete, isn't it?'

Pete smiled absently. Great teeth, thought Izzie. 'Yeah, that's right. How're you doing?'

'Fine thanks. Business good? Can I get you a pint, by the way?'

Pete had that vacant look of someone racking their brains to remember who on earth this was. 'Thanks, you're all right. I'm getting a round in for some people I'm with. Yep, business couldn't be better thanks, mate. What are you up to now?'

Izzie butted in. 'We're living in the country now. Near Ringford. Ever been out that way?'

He blinked rapidly, looking at Izzie properly for the first time and swallowed hard. 'Now hang on, what's all this about?'

'Oh, I think you know exactly what it's about and exactly what we want. Have you got the negative?' Marcus smoothly led him to a quiet table, speaking in a low voice. Izzie followed clutching her bag tightly.

'Why do you want to know?' He was looking distinctly uncomfortable now.

'Well, I think we could make you a better offer. Is it an exclusive with the *Courier*?'

'Er, kind of.'

Marcus sighed impatiently. 'Well is it or isn't it? How much are they paying you?'

Pete laughed shortly. 'You don't really expect me to tell you that?'

'Would ten thousand do it?' Izzie couldn't keep quiet any longer, and earned herself a glare from Marcus.

'Sorry, love. I can't do that.' He started to move away. Izzie grabbed his arm. 'Twenty, then.'

'You really want this, don't you? Look, I've told you, I can't make a deal.' He tried to peel her fingers off his sleeve, but she wasn't letting go.

'Fifty thousand. Please! You can't do this to us. It's just not fair.'

He stopped and sighed heavily, puffing his cheeks out, then looked her in the eye and spoke slowly. 'You're not listening. I *can't* do it. If it was just the paper, I might be up for it. You're offering enough. It's not that. Look, I've got nothing against you or your partner. I'm just doing what I've been hired to do.'

Izzie let go of his sleeve and her shoulders sagged. 'Isn't there anything . . . ?'

'Are you listening? I said no deal.' Looking back and forth

between their shocked faces he got up to leave. 'I've said too much, but it'll all be over tomorrow. There's nothing you or anyone can do about it now. For what it's worth, I'm sorry. Nothing personal.' And he went back to the bar.

Izzie and Marcus looked at each other in disbelief. 'What's going on, Marcus? Did you understand any of that?'

'No, I can't see . . . It sounded as if . . . No, I can't see what he's on about.'

'I'll just try and ring Maddy again. I guess I'll have to break the news and tell her what he said.'

A moment later, she was outside again, looking worried. The others were discussing what had just happened. Pete the Greek had left hurriedly, and was already disappearing towards High-gate Hill, with his blonde trailing disconsolately behind. 'I can't get through to Maddy. It goes straight to voicemail again, so I've just asked her to call me. Where the hell is she? Something's not right. I'll just leave a message on her voicemail at home too . . . Colette! What are you doing there? I thought you'd be in London or somewhere. What? So you've not idea at all? . . . Right. Well, if she calls you again, can you ask her to call me? Yeah, anytime, anytime at all.'

Izzie's heart was pounding in her ears and she knew she was sweating, despite the chill in the air. She flipped her phone closed and put in back in her bag, then looked round at the faces watching her expectantly. 'That was the nanny. She's at home with the kids. Maddy went off on Friday afternoon and said she wasn't sure when she'd be back. What on earth's going on?'

Maddy felt her mobile buzz in her pocket. Izzie again. This must have been the third call this morning. As she had done so many times since the calls had started yesterday, she pressed the 'cancel' button. She felt bad. The least Izzie deserved was an explanation for her disappearance, but just at the moment she couldn't face talking to her. Then after a moment she dialled home.

'Everything OK?' she asked Colette. 'Good. No, tell Will he can't have any chocolate until after lunch.' Suddenly a voice boomed out on the PA system, so grabbing her bag she made a dash for the ladies and an empty cubicle.

'Pasco feels a bit hot? Give him some Calpol, and keep an eye on him. It could be teeth, but if you're not sure, take him to the doctor in the morning.' Someone in the next-door cubicle pulled the chain. 'Sound of water? Er, I'm just about to have a bath actually. Yes, very echoey . . . these friends have a big house. Fabulous bathroom. Big enough to have a party in.' She could hear two women come into the loos, talking loudly. 'Better go, Colette. Someone else wants the bathroom before me. Speak to you later.' She clicked off the call, then slowly and deliberately turned off the phone.

Back in the main concourse, she looked up at the board. Slipping her phone into her bag, she pulled out her ticket and boarding pass and headed for passport control. It seemed ages since she'd been on a plane. How she'd missed all the rigmarole of check-ins, taxiing, and that sensational thrill of taking off.

She'd never been on a trip like this before though.

Finding her seat in Club Class, she stashed her overnight bag in the overhead locker and settled down. The man beside her looked up and smiled briefly before returning to his paper. She couldn't have expected anything more. She'd left in such a rush this morning and, wiser after recent experience, she had made damned sure she was wearing her Ruralist 'uniform' to the nth degree: dung-brown boiled wool suit, buttoned to the round-collared neck, box pleat skirt and her flattest, frumpiest pumps, all covered up with her woollen shawl. It had pained her to buy it, but, boy, it had done her some mileage. She'd stuck in a couple of Florence's cotton flower clips she'd found on the side in the kitchen to keep her hair back off her face, innocent of make-up. All she was missing was the guitar and she'd be good and ready to arrive at the Von Trapp mansion.

Pulling out the newspaper, she braced herself, hoping that the picture hadn't been brought forward a day and, relieved to see it hadn't – or at least not in this paper – she tried to concentrate on the news. Instead her voice shouted at her in her head: what the hell are you doing? Is this really what Peter meant by a 'vat load of craftiness'? Somewhere in her thoughts Simon's face kept appearing too, shaking his head with disappointment at her. But everything hangs on this, her rational brain kept butting in. Even if her momentary lapse on the terrace last week stymied the sale, they could wave goodbye to the company's future. Who on earth would be fooled by the *Paysage Enchanté* message when it was being peddled by a fagsmoking, wine-drinking slut who let her son play GameBoys and her daughter prance about in dainty pink high heels and an obscene T-shirt?

She dropped the paper and groaned, watching the tarmac fly past out of the window. She couldn't be sure whether the lurch in her stomach was the take-off or the nausea she'd felt every moment of the day and night since the paper called on Friday.

She didn't move until her brunch had been served (and ignored), and the movie began. It was some thriller nonsense with George Clooney, but even his come-to-bed eyes couldn't engage her interest. All she could see were someone else's eyes staring back at her. He'd sounded surprised when she'd called on Friday afternoon, but with the ease of someone getting so used to the art of deceit, she managed to convince him that she'd had the trip planned for ages, how this was the only flight she could get (well, that part was true at least), how her brother was so looking forward to seeing her on Monday, and that it made *such* good sense to deliver the contracts by hand. Yes, he'd said, he'd come back from the weekend early and would be at JFK to meet her at lunchtime.

'Bye, Maddy,' he'd said deeply down the phone. 'See you then.'

Now as she looked out of the window at the candy floss of cloud beneath them, so clear you could almost stick your hand out and touch it, she wondered what she planned to do now the arrangement was made. Would he be free for the rest of the day? What about family? God! Perhaps he had a wife? The thought hadn't even occurred to her. He might simply drive her back to her hotel, take the contracts and drive back to his apartment, somewhere deeply fashionable no doubt, and be greeted by a pretty wife with her station wagon and three blonde beautiful children. She'd have stayed on a bit longer at the beach house, Maddy imagined, to make the most of the day, and would unpack the weekend bags efficiently in their gorgeously stylish kitchen, and ask him if it had been a complete *bore* to have to break up the weekend and drive to the airport on a Sunday. She'd be beautiful too, no doubt about that, perhaps an ex-model he'd met through the business, with long glossy dark hair and a fabulous figure. No, Maddy shook her head, she's an overweight battleaxe, with varicose veins and a penchant for double cheese bacon burgers. Unlikely.

She must have slept for a couple of hours, because she awoke to hear the cabin crew announcing the time it would be when they landed in New York. Adjusting her watch, she glanced up to see if the loo was vacant, then took down her bag from the hold, and wended her way down the aisle. She locked the door, dumped the bag on the lid of the loo and faced herself in the glaringly bright mirror. She breathed in and then out slowly through her mouth, dropping her shoulders, delved in her bag and laid out make-up, razor, tweezers neatly in a row as if about to perform an operation. All ready, she set to work.

When she sat back down in her seat half an hour later, the man beside her glanced up at her return, but this time there was no vague assessment and dismissal. He looked fixated, then with slow deliberate ease, he took in the smoothed bobbed hair and the flawless make-up (she'd had to spit on her mascara it had dried out so thoroughly through lack of use). His gaze wandered down over her breasts, outlined clearly under her soft pink shirt, and over her waist and then to her thighs, where the short wrap-around silky skirt stopped, and down, down her long tanned legs to her spiky brown Jimmy Choo shoes, with their delicate little tie straps wrapped around her neat little ankles. His eyes wandered back up to her face, and she smiled at his obvious appreciation. She clearly hadn't lost her touch.

'Special meeting in New York?' he said with a Stateside drawl.

'Oh yes,' she purred. 'Very special.'

She was, however, out of practice with the heels, and had to manoeuvre her way off the plane, down through the boarding tunnel and out on to the JFK concourse with studied care. She'd forgotten how high shoes made you wiggle your bum suggestively, and she felt like an updated version of Marilyn Monroe in the railway station scene from *Some Like it Hot*. It was all very hard work and, by the time she got through to Arrivals, she had to rearrange her face from intense concentration to the sexy, devil-may-care impression she wanted to make. I hope he's here, she thought, because I don't think I can keep this up much longer.

She wasn't disappointed and she saw him, head and shoulders above the crowd of people awaiting arrivals, before he spotted her. He was looking away somewhere over to the left, which gave her time for a serious panic attack. She felt her arms turn ice cold. There he was, dressed casually in long-sleeved T-shirt and jeans, his hands jammed firmly in his pockets, and the grim reality of her journey was made real.

His head turned back towards the stream of travellers and she saw him scan the group. She stopped and stood still, her Louis Vuitton overnight bag in her hand and her Prada 'good-luck' handbag over her arm. His gaze flicked over her and on to the people coming through behind and around her. Zap, then they were back and focused right on her. Slowly, like a cat, he smiled and she knew that he had got whatever ill-advised message she had wanted to convey. No going back now.

Skirting those around him, he met her as she passed through the barrier, and without saying a word, she held out her overnight bag to him. I may feel like a tart, she thought, but he can treat me like a lady.

'Well hi,' he said slowly, and putting down the bag, put his hands on her shoulders and gave her a kiss on the cheek. Her nose filled with the smell of soap and beach.

'Have you had to drive a long way?' she asked with mock innocence.

'Not too bad on a Sunday morning. At least some New Yorkers sleep in. Let's find the car.' He strode off and it was all she could do to keep up. Those ghastly flat pumps had their advantages after all.

She imagined some large car the make of which would elude her completely, but was surprised when he unlocked the door of a silver Porsche Boxster. Not exactly a practical family car, she caught herself thinking. She slipped as demurely as she could into the passenger seat, letting her skirt open a little over her thighs, and surreptitiously slipped her feet slightly from her shoes. Not too much that they would swell and she'd be unable to get them on again, silently thanking Giselle for teaching her the finer points of social survival. He slipped in beside her.

'Where are you staying?'

'60 Thompson in—'

'Soho. Yes, I know it well. Excellent choice.' She heaved a sigh of relief. Her Friday call to a New York girlfriend had paid off, though she was pretty 'pissed' that she wasn't to be included in Maddy's flying visit.

He drove fast, as she suspected he might, and made little attempt at conversation. How could she ensure he wasn't going to drop her, pick up the contracts and shoot off to domestic bliss, leaving her high and dry before her flight home tomorrow? The whole idea was to keep him as occupied as she could, but if the worst came to the worst there were more painful ways to bemoan your ruined career than a night in New York. She gazed out of the window, to avoid looking at his big brown hands on the steering wheel as they headed down the Van Wyck Expressway towards Manhattan. God, how she loved this city. It always thrilled her – not quite as much as Paris, granted, but infinitely more than London. New York was sex. Fast, dirty and exhilarating. Except, of course, that it was full of Americans.

He broke the silence. 'So what time are you meeting your brother?' Brother?

'Oh Crispin' – well he was kind of brotherly – 'er, he doesn't come back until tomorrow, so I'll meet him for lunch.'

'Where does he live?' Oh Christ. She scrambled through her memory bank. What the hell was Ruthie's address?

'Um, out near Queen's. Not very salubrious, but he lives with his girlfriend who's a designer. They're visiting friends for the weekend.' Keep it vague, Madeleine, before the hole gets too damned deep to dig your way out.

'Right.'

'But I thought,' she ploughed on, 'I could give you the contracts today, then it's done. I'm very grateful you could pick me up. I hope I haven't pulled you away from an exciting weekend.'

He kept his eyes on the road, but smiled. 'Oh, nothing I couldn't leave. It's a long time since I spent a Sunday in town anyway. Bit of a novelty.'

They talked vaguely about the New York Maddy knew, and she asked him about the office and where he lived – even more fashionable than she had imagined – until they pulled up in front of the hotel. Suddenly she wasn't sure how to handle it from here.

'Shall I check in and then bring down the contract?'

He turned off the engine and rested his hands on his thighs, turning towards her. 'Well, you've dragged me away from the beach. Let's at least have some tea, or whatever you Brits do in the afternoon.'

She smiled, unable, she suspected, to keep the triumph out of her eyes. 'OK.'

'I can leave the car not far from here. You get yourself settled in, and I'll be back in half an hour in reception. And Maddy,' he added, 'lose the heels.'

Her room was everything the *Paysage Enchanté* ethos wasn't – cool, chic, understated thirties minimalism – and she revelled in it. Big wide bed, with suede headboard, and crisp linen sheets; white, brown and grey tones everywhere, even on the tiles in the bathroom. She wandered about in excitement, opening cabinets to reveal DVD and CD players hidden away oh-so discreetly, looking out of the window down Fifth and Broadway towards the Empire State, until she almost lost track of the time. Emptying out the contents of her bag, she shook out her clothes, and stripped down to her underwear, throwing everything over the chair. After a shower which would have merited an award for speed, and careful not to wet her hair, she dressed as fast as she could, reapplied her lipstick and looked in the long mirror. Not bad. The go-natural regime they'd had to stick to all summer had left her with a good tan on her legs, which had survived their first shave for months, and now they glistened with the moisturiser she'd slavered on after the shower. You may be riddled with deception, but you've got a fine pair of pins, Madeleine Hoare, she told her reflection. Simon always thought they were her best feature. Don't think about Simon.

Tom Drake was waiting in the funky, rectangular reception

area, flicking through the paper. What if her picture was in there, she thought suddenly. Don't be ridiculous. The Americans had never heard of her. He folded up the broadsheet and as appreciatively, if a little more subtly than the man on the plane, took in her low-cut white top, short wrap-around skirt (this one in pastel beiges and pink – she'd loved them so much in Harvey Nicks last year she'd bought three in different colours) and down her legs to her low-heeled pumps.

Nonchalantly, she put her pink cashmere cardigan around her shoulders. 'Shall we go?'

She hadn't known what to expect. She'd hoped to God it wouldn't be too uncomfortable and contrived. What she hadn't imagined was that it would be fun. They walked together down Thompson Street in the warm afternoon sunshine, and just carried on walking. He took her for coffee and a muffin in Soho, then they strolled down to Ground Zero. He talked about the fact that he'd been out of the country on September 11, and what it had been like to return to the carnage. They went on to Central Park, and found themselves stopping and watching a juggler entertaining children under the trees. They drank more coffee by an impromptu softball game, and all the time no mention was made of contracts, buy-outs, cosmetics. He talked little about himself, just the odd fact here and there – he'd gone to Yale, his parents lived up near the Catskills, he had a sister who worked in Paris. Instead he turned the questions on her, and she found herself telling him about the children, the house, living in London. She almost let down her guard when he mentioned that he knew about Simon's death, but skilfully turned the conversation round to neutral ground, like how much she loved Paris, holidays in Cap Ferrat, the weather. Anything rather than think about home, the business, the reason she was here.

At one point she almost came a cropper, when he asked her about her family. She told him briefly about her father's death and Peter's arrival on the scene. 'He was a saviour to my mother and me.'

'And your brother?'

'Oh no, he's much younger. He's only my half-brother, Peter's son. Much, much, *much* younger than me.'

By seven the light was beginning to fade, and cars with dipped headlights sped past them as they made their way back to the hotel. What now? The shit would hit the fan in about seven hours, UK time, when everyone opened their newspapers at breakfast. That would be 2 a.m. New York time, and she was pretty sure someone from London would be hot on the phone to Tom Drake with the happy news that his new little acquisition was not all it appeared. If she didn't get him to sign tonight, the deal would all be blown. Non-disclosure would be the least of their worries. Goodbye everything.

Time to launch Operation Drake. She stopped at the doorway, and turned around to him, addressing somewhere between his chest and his chin. 'Thank you, Tom, that was fun. Er, would you like to come in for a drink? I believe there's a new rooftop bar. We could watch nightfall.'

He was standing very close to her, hands back in jeans pockets, and looked down at her. 'Let's go one better, Maddy. Will you have dinner with me?'

She'd bought herself another few hours. It was all going to plan. They agreed to meet in Thom's bar at eight-thirty – she tried to give him as little time as possible to reduce his chances of receiving any phone calls – and went into war paint application overdrive. After a second shower – well the room cost enough, she might as well empty the hot water tanks too – she lifted out her palest pink La Perla underwear (the only set she hadn't let Izzie get her hands on – Oh God Izzie, what would you think of all this?) and slipped in on. She smoothed stockings over her legs, and pulled on her short, black Lycra dress, standing in front of the mirror to check it didn't show too much stomach now she was almost off the fags. Phase two: on went the foundation, the soft pink eyeshadow, the straightest line of eyeliner she could manage with shaking hands, then she dried her hair until it was smooth and sleek.

She knew she looked great, but if anything he looked better. If this situation hadn't been so bizarre, so contrived and unforgivably planned out, then she could think of nothing more appealing than dinner overlooking Manhattan with this very good-looking man in his open-necked sea blue shirt and clean, pressed chinos, sitting at the bar. He had a cocktail waiting for her, and she found herself almost downing it in one. Steady on, old girl. You've only had a muffin since this morning, which was five hours longer ago than it should have been.

Another cocktail later, they were taken to a discreet little booth in the restaurant and, in her increasingly hazy mind, she wondered whether he had asked for this in case anyone he knew spotted him with someone other than his wife. Or perhaps they had an 'arrangement'. Or perhaps she was too ugly and he never took her out anyway. He ordered wine, and she piled into the bread as elegantly as she could to try and absorb some of the alcohol now coursing through her. I hope to God I don't need a pee, because I'm not sure I can stand up.

'So what will you do once the company is sold?' he asked her through the candlelight once they had given their order.

Curl up and die? Maddy thought. 'I don't know really. The last year has all happened so fast that I haven't had a chance to think about anything at all really. I expect Izzie might go back to her books, but I'm not sure I'm fit for anything.'

She watched his hands as he fiddled with the fork in front of him. 'Oh, I disagree,' he said laconically. 'I expect you could do any number of things you set your mind to.'

'I'd like to spend more time in France.' She hadn't thought of it before, but now he had asked her, she really thought she would. Perhaps she might buy a house with the proceeds of the sale, somewhere in Provence, or near to Jean Luc. Jean Luc. God what would he think? She could imagine him strolling over to their table now. 'What are you doing, Maddy darling? Are things really so desperate?'

The food, exquisitely laid out on large plates in front of them, looked too good to eat, and Maddy wasn't sure she could anyway. She felt confused. She knew what might be in store, but what concerned her was how much she wanted it to be. That part of her that had laid dormant since Simon died had suddenly and unexpectedly burst back into life. Whether it was the dress, the candlelight, the booze, or just those bloody arrogant, amused eyes looking back at her, she wasn't sure. All she did know was that she felt as horny as hell.

She toyed with a rocket leaf and the scallops. What should she do now? She was well out of practice at this game, but it didn't take a master's degree to know that he wasn't here to pass the time. If she wanted him, she was fairly sure he was there for the taking. But did she need to? Was it really a critical part of the plan? If she handed over the contracts now, he would go off home now and go to bed – alone? with his wife? – then he'd wake up tomorrow, go off to work, find out about the photograph and . . . well, that would be it, no doubt. What she needed was for him to sign the contracts, tonight, and then she could be off out of New York tomorrow like a ferret up a trouser leg. She kept the conversation going, while the remaining part of her brain tried to sort everything through.

He seemed willing to join in her little game, and answered her questions about movies and books with the same dry, slow humour. Yes, he liked movies, but nothing violent. No, he thought British movies were crap on the whole, and that Hugh Grant should be shot. Yes, he read books, but none she would ever have encountered. She bristled at this. Did he think she only touched chick-lit or something? No, he replied, but he doubted Norman Mailer or Gore Vidal was quite her thing. Yes, he loved music, and reeled off a list of obscure British bands.

'Big CD collection?'

He smiled wryly. 'Too big.' He paused. 'And there's something else British I admire too, Maddy.'

'Such as?' She took another sip of her wine, then rested her chin in her hand, head to one side, a seductive look she knew worked a treat, and awaited his reply.

He leant closer towards her and fixed his eyes on hers. 'Your incredible double-decker buses!'

She laughed so loud the Japanese couple at the next table turned in reproach. 'Well, I'm glad something about us floats your boat. They must be worth coming all that way to see.'

He knocked back the rest of the wine. 'Oh yes – the style, the eccentricity, the colour!' He put down his glass. 'A true masterpiece of design. But of course there are other things too.'

She was more cautious this time. 'And what might they be?'

He leant close again. 'Your gorgeous lips.' He was looking at them. 'I've wanted to kiss them since I first met you.' Maddy didn't know what to say. She could feel the colour rising up her face. This was supposed to be her show. She was supposed to be making the moves, and he had taken the wind right out of her sails.

'Er,' she faltered, desperately trying to cope with it. 'Well, right.' Don't lose sight, woman, of what this is all about. The contract. Perhaps she could persuade him to sign it now. She leant down to her bag. Damn, she'd left the papers upstairs when she changed bags. Oh fickle fortune or Freudian slip.

'The contract. We really ought to sign it while I'm here. But I've, er . . . I've left the contract up in my room. Do you . . . ?'

It was the wrong way to phrase the question. Very quietly he said, 'Yes, Maddy, I do.' He stood up and waited for her to join him, which she did blindly, then he led her to the lifts. As the doors shut behind them, she felt trapped by the intimacy of it and turned towards him. He turned at the same time and, stepping towards her, put his hands either side of her against the wall, and gently, oh so gently and slowly, not touching any other part of her, lowered his head and kissed her on the side of the lips, on her cheek, down to her neck, before returning again to her mouth. He tasted so good, she opened her mouth to him, and let him slip his tongue inside.

The lift stopped smoothly, and as the doors opened she pulled away panicked, delving into her bag for the key card. She put her hand on the light switch, but he stopped her, the room already lit by the lights of the Manhattan skyline, and turned her round to face him.

She dreamt there was a fire alarm at the barn, and everything – all the girls, Izzie, Lillian and the children were stuck inside. She couldn't open the door so she smashed her hand against the fire bell again and again to stop it, but still everyone inside banged against the door screaming to be let out.

She sat bolt upright. The early morning light was coming through the still-open curtains. Where the hell was she? She took in the room, the sheet pulled over her, her clothes strewn all over the floor, a sea blue shirt and chinos, and then looked at the figure lying asleep beside her. He was lying on his front, his face turned towards her, and both arms hugging the pillow under his head. She could hear his slow steady breathing, and lay back down again carefully so as not to disturb him.

She turned on her side, making herself look at his face, yet ashamed by the intimacy of watching him sleeping. He looked so relaxed, that face that only hours earlier had been twisted in the ecstasy of passion. She had been wrong about him. He was a passionate man. She ached from his lovemaking. She could still feel him inside her, his kisses all over her and the way he had called out 'Jesus, Maddy' as he came. Yes, it was passionate, but it was far from right. And what made it even worse was how much she had enjoyed it, revelled in it.

The digital clock said six-thirty. Her flight was at midday. Would he waken in time to get to work? And what about the contract? She slipped out of bed for a pee, trying to avoid her flushed and ravished face in the mirror and, on the way back to bed, slipped the contract out of her bag. She squinted at it in the half-light. What a price to pay for one signature. She threw it down on to the chair and slid back into bed next to him. He stirred and moved his body closer to hers.

She must have slipped back into that deep, deep early morning sleep again because, when she woke, he was gone. And so was the contract. It was half nine, so she showered as briskly as she could, put on the pink shirt and skirt she'd worn on her arrival, made as good a fist of repairing her face as she could, and thrust everything else into her bag. She checked her handbag for her tickets and there at the top was a note on hotel notepaper. She read it, screwed it up and went down to reception to settle the bill.

'No breakfast, madam?' said the receptionist.

'No time I'm afraid. Could I just have the bill? And could you call a cab for me please?'

He punched in some keys on to the computer screen. 'Your account has already been settled for you by Mr Drake, madam. I'll call you a cab right away.'

Stunned, she picked up her bag and went down in the lift to street level. Without her even registering, a cab pulled up, the door was opened and she climbed inside.

'Where to, Miss?' the cabbie asked in a strong Bronx accent.

'Kennedy, please.'

He pulled away from the kerb, and she fixed her gaze out of the window as Monday morning New York City shot by beside her. People were bustling to work, road sweepers were moving like snails beside the sidewalk, shops were opening up their iron grilles for business. As she watched, registering none of this and feeling like a whore, the tears rolled down her face. Oh God, Simon, I'm so sorry.

Chapter 19

Only two trains of thought occupied Izzie's mind from the moment Pete the Greek walked away: what had become of Maddy, and what the fall-out of the exposé would be. That the deal was off was no longer in question. And the chances of PE surviving such a publicity disaster were slim, to say the least. It was over. The whole mad roller coaster ride was finished, and it was time for them all to return to earth with a bump. They'd come so close to solving all their money problems, but they were back where they had started.

Now there was nothing left to fight for, Izzie sat back limply in the pub and let the other three speculate on why Pete had turned down such an enticing offer. Marcus reckoned he was on a retainer from the paper and didn't dare to cross them. Shaun's more cynical view was that Izzie had shown her hand too quickly, and that he was expecting her to track him down again and offer more. Maz had come up with a theory that brought in the Mafia and MI6, but, there again, she had been downing Pimms with serious intent.

Izzie was past caring. Once the other three had finished their lunch – she no longer had any appetite – Marcus scooped her up, they picked up the car from Maz and Shaun's place, and he drove her back home. Before going to pick up the kids from

Janet's, he poured Izzie a hot bath, slopped in as much product as he could lay his hands on, and left her to it. By the time he returned, Izzie was in bed and fast asleep. Not even Jess and Charlie's resounding kisses on her cheeks could wake her and eventually they gave up trying.

The next day was a different matter. The disadvantage of going to bed at six o'clock, Izzie told herself crossly, is that no matter how tired you are, you'll be lying wide awake and bored out of your skull by four in the morning. And so she was. By half past four, she'd given up even trying to doze and went downstairs to make herself some tea. Nothing on her e-mail, nothing on her voicemail. This was getting beyond a joke. Was it time to report Maddy as a missing person? No one else seemed as worried about her whereabouts, when Izzie had done a frenzied ring-round the previous day. Not Colette. 'She took a little bag with her, and some beautiful shoes. Wherever she is, she is fine – you will see, Izzie.' Not Janet. 'Perhaps it all just got a bit too much for her. The two of you have been working so hard and, you know, it's not been all that long that poor Simon was taken . . .' Not even Peter, whom Izzie had rung after much soul-searching, and had made promise he wouldn't tell Giselle anything. 'She's a good girl, Izzie, my dear. This had been a hard blow to her. Give her time to come to terms with it, and just be there for her when she returns.'

This had all sounded quite reasonable the day before. But now, sitting at the kitchen table in the dark, with a mug of Assam going cold in front of her, all Izzie could imagine was that her friend must be dead in a ditch somewhere by now.

Izzie had never been much for ironing, but by six o'clock, she'd done a great big pile of it. As displacement activity, it left something to be desired – she now had Maddy abducted by crazed terrorists with terribly chapped skin and was feeling more anxious than ever, but ooh the lovely neat tea towels. She took Marcus a cup of tea and dressed deliberately in her florals –

you couldn't be too careful. 'Right, Marcus, I've got to go and get it. Can't put it off any longer.'

'Would you rather I went?' came a sleepy voice from underneath the quilt, obviously hoping she'd say no – that was more like the old Marcus.

'No thanks. I've got to face the music sooner or later. Might as well be now. Can you get the kids ready for school, and I'll take 'em in today.'

The atmosphere in the newsagent's was electric. All the staff were standing round in a knot, talking and nodding. When Izzie walked in, they jumped apart and none of them looked at her. She pretended to browse at the magazines for a bit, then plucked up her courage to go to the counter. 'Morning, George. *Courier* please.'

George, a tweedy figure with a startlingly red moustache, pantomimed searching behind the counter. 'Sorry, Mrs Stock. We haven't had any in today. Delivery problems, probably.'

She smiled and nodded. 'Thanks, George. I do appreciate it, but there's no need to hide it on my account. I really do have to see it.'

Reluctantly, he brought out a copy and laid it face down on the counter, refusing to take her money. 'No, really. I can't expect you to pay for that . . . that rubbish. Just take it, m'dear. And remember, we're all behind you and Mrs Hoare.'

She nodded her thanks, touched at his consideration, and folded the paper in two, not daring to look at it until she reached the safety of her car. It was far worse than she'd feared. The photo was grainy in quality and had obviously been blown up, but they'd caught Maddy smoking hands-free, and taking a particularly deep drag that sucked her cheeks in and wrinkled up her brow, while holding a very large glass of red wine. She looked like trailer trash. Haggard and in deep concentration, she seemed to be standing in an odd dancing posture. Will was head down, looking anxious and bewildered, Florence was sticking her little bottom out and pouting furiously. It couldn't have been worse. And the headline! 'What a Hoare!!'

The editorial, as usual for the *Courier*, was snide and insidious but without actually committing to any facts that you could contest. There was that usual sickening cocktail of prurience and prudery – endless innuendo combined with supposed moral outrage, and although there were no photos of Izzie, she hadn't been spared. They'd found out she and Marcus were having problems. Damn them, they'd even found out about his sacking, and they'd implied that he'd been a shadowy figure in the background, masterminding the whole image of the brand and manipulating her and Maddy like puppets. God! Could they have sunk any lower?

She returned home, sick to her stomach and dreading having to show Marcus. His reaction, over the Bran Flakes, was a surprise. After a quick glance, he tossed it aside. 'Tomorrow's chip paper, love. I was expecting something of the kind. They've made me sound very clever, though. Maddy's PR mate will be annoyed that they've given me the credit for all her hard work.'

'Pru! I hadn't thought about her. I'll have to call her from work. Come on, kids, time to go.'

Marcus looked thoughtful for a moment. 'I'd better pick them up today. Once this story breaks, you won't be off the phone all day. Good luck – I think you're going to need it. Just remember, this may change what some people think about us, but they're not the people that really matter. And it can't change who we are inside.' He gave her a slightly awkward hug – the first for ages. 'Stay strong. I'm here if you need me.'

At the barn, the girls were there early, clustered round the door like hens waiting to roost. When she turned up, they broke into a ragged cheer. 'Don't let the bastards grind yer down!' 'I'm never buying that paper again!' 'What would I want with a bonus anyway? Only burn an 'ole in me pocket!'

Even before she unlocked the doors, they could hear the phones ringing inside. 'Let the voicemail pick it up. Maddy would call on my mobile anyway, and I can't be bothered speaking to anyone else just now.' They shut the door firmly behind them, and sat down to discuss the outstanding orders, uncertain whether to make more product or not. Lillian, flicked through the print-outs and gave her opinion. 'Well, we've got plenty of everything, so it seems a bit daft not to carry on. Perhaps PE will become a collector's item. We've certainly got enough for two weeks' production of balm, and one week of the toners and cleansers.'

Izzie shrugged. It was hard to summon up the enthusiasm she'd felt only a week earlier, before they'd even met the Tessutini team, and had a carrot in the form of a big juicy payoff dangled in front of them. 'I don't suppose it really matters what we do now, so let's stick to the schedule as planned. So it's . . . balm today. Let's go for it! But first, coffee all round. I know I could use one.'

When Izzie dared to switch on her computer, she downloaded a barrage of e-mails – some supportive, some not, some requesting interviews. But nothing from Maddy and nothing from Tessutini – yet. Voicemails were roughly the same. Lots of reporters requesting interviews and comments on the story. Izzie ignored it all, and focused on getting through the day as normally as she could. Until about eleven, when Pru swept through the door, arms outstretched. 'Those fuckers,' she spat. 'The timing couldn't be worse. Obviously the deal will be off. I should imagine someone's waking Tom Drake with the unwelcome news at this very moment. I wonder what he'll make of it. There's one slight possibility that I'm a bit concerned about . . . But, no, no.'

Izzie was on the alert at once. 'What slight possibility? Is this another problem?'

'Weeeell, it could be.' She dumped her bag on the desk. 'I

shouldn't have mentioned it really. Not until I speak to your lawyers. It's just that if you can be shown to have misrepresented the facts, Tessutini could claim some damages – you know, legal fees and all that.'

'What? You mean that in addition to them not buying us, and us losing all our credibility, we might have to pay them compensation as well? Oh, my God. How much is that going to be? We'll be worse off than when we started. Oh where the hell are you, Maddy?'

Pru looked uncomfortable. 'You see? I know I shouldn't have mentioned it. It's only a possibility. Tom Drake knows you're tiny. He almost certainly wouldn't do it, unless—'

'Unless what?' Izzie shrieked.

'Well, unless he wanted to be vindictive – but there's no reason why he should be. Look, can we stop talking about this. It's only speculation, after all. What we really should be focusing on is damage limitation. It'll be tricky, but I think we could get a big sympathy vote for Maddy here. You know, the single working mother thing. We have to make it look like a blip. In a way it might help to make the two of you look a bit more human – you know, warts and all.'

'What kind of warts did you have in mind?' Izzie asked cautiously.

'You know . . . something we could turn to our advantage. I mean, look at George Michael! And Liz Hurley didn't go global until she got banged up by that disgusting man. Sometimes bad news is good news these days. It just depends on how you handle it.'

'If it's a choice between coming out or getting pregnant again, I think we'd both opt for the comfortable shoes every time. But come on, Pru. Let's face it. The whole PE story was based on a pretence. Without the myth, there is no PE. It's over, and I think we're just going to have to accept it.'

'Izzie, it's not over till the PR lady sings. Let me have a crack at this. I've got a tame psychologist. He'll deconstruct the picture and give it the right spin. Anyway, *Courier* readers are emphatically not your customer base. I don't see this making a huge difference, to be perfectly frank. Let's get pro-active. I'll handle the press—'

'Izzie!' called Lillian, who was manfully fielding the constant stream of phone calls. 'It's Jean Luc. He's calling about your latest order. What should I tell him?'

At last! Someone who could talk sense. 'I'll take it. Hello, Jean Luc? Yeah, it's me. Now listen carefully. We've got a problem . . .' Ten minutes later, Izzie replaced the phone with a sigh of relief. He was on his way over the England, and had come up with the brilliantly simple idea that Izzie should get hold of Maddy's home address book, and contact all her friends to find out where she had gone. She phoned Colette to make sure she was there, but the number was engaged. Maybe Maddy was back, or had contacted Colette. Izzie checked that the spare set of keys Maddy had given her was in her bag, then headed for the door, leaving Pru to help Lillian fend off the demands for comments and interviews. The soft popping of a flash bulb and the click of a shutter, teamed with the sudden burst of light, sent her reeling back inside. 'Izzie – just a quick quote—'

'Pruuuuu! Get down here quick. There's a couple of photographers outside. I need you.'

Pru came clattering down the wooden stairs, smoothing her hair and checking her lipstick. 'Let me at 'em!'

At the same moment, Izzie's mobile rang. It was the secretary of St Boniface's, and she didn't sound pleased. 'Mrs Stock, I think you'd better come and collect Jess and Charlie straight away. We've had a reporter trying to talk to them through the railings outside the playground, asking them what they had for supper last night, and offering them money for a look inside their lunchboxes.'

She hung up, having made profuse apologies – although,

come to think of it, it wasn't actually her fault – when Marcus called. 'I won't be coming over to the barn for lunch after all. There's a couple of blokes lurking in the bushes across the road – journalists, I reckon, and I don't trust myself not to thump them if they ask me anything. I did manage to get the washing in off the line, though. Didn't want them getting snaps of your undies.'

She explained the problem at school, and Marcus let out a curse. 'Bastards! How dare they go after our children. I'll thump them anyway. Right! Change of plan. I'll go and get the kids now and bring them back here. You'd better see what's happening at Eagles. It won't be any better.'

'No, don't you go and fetch them. They'll follow you. I'll call Crispin. He's out on a job today. If he can pick them up, I'll phone the school and let them know.'

Right, so that was the children sorted. Colette's mobile and the landline were still engaged, so Izzie sneaked out of the barn by the back door while Pru was holding court at the front, jumped in the car and zoomed away before anyone noticed. Glancing in her mirror to check she wasn't being followed, she felt a bit like James Bond. Too bad she didn't have any gadgets to help in her mission. An automatic in-car mascara applicator would be a start, and how about a perfume dispenser built into the headrest – instead of choosing between diesel and petrol, you could choose between Clarins and Diptyque. She was musing on what else would come in handy as she drove through Ringford, but snapped to attention when she saw Pokey-Sue (their new nickname for her) talking animatedly to a tall, rather interesting man who was emphatically not her husband, and who gave the impression of hanging on her every word. 'Way to go, Sue-eey. Once a Pokey, always a Pokey!' Izzie whooped to herself as she drove past, giving Sue a cheery wave.

Remembering Marcus' warning, she slowed before the turning to Huntingford House and, sure enough, there were several cars parked on the verge, each containing two men. She turned in without indicating – well, there was no one else around, and was amused to see them all jump to attention as she sailed past. She tucked the car by the barns and made for the back door, opening it with the spare key.

'Colette!' she called. 'It's Izzie. Are you all right?'

A cupboard door creaked open, and Colette and Pasco emerged, Colette looking terrified, Pasco delighted. 'Encore! Encore!' he chirped, keen to carry on with the game.

'Oh Izzie, I though it was one of them! They have been calling here all morning. I took the phone from the hook in the end. I don't know what to say to them.'

Izzie hugged the frightened girl and tooted Pasco's nose. 'So you still haven't heard anything from Maddy? Listen, can I take her address book and see if I can track her down? Do you know where it is? Oh thanks.'

'Izzie, I don't know what to do about collecting the children. I know there are people in the garden. I don't feel safe.'

'I think we all need to stick together for now, and I've already asked Crispin to pick the kids up from school. He'll drop them back here with you – unless of course you want to come and stay with us?' Colette opted to wait at home for Maddy, but promised to lock all the doors and ignore the phone.

Whatever Marcus had said to the journalists had worked. There was no one to be seen lurking outside when Izzie returned home. Crispin had dropped the kids off, but hadn't stayed. 'He said he wanted to check that everyone at the barn was all right. He looked quite worried, actually,' said Marcus. 'If this wasn't so awful, it would be quite fun. Like that first time we stayed at your parents' and I had to hide in the cupboard when your mother walked into your room.'

Izzie laughed, but turned quickly away. She didn't want to get into nostalgia trips with Marcus, especially not about the days when they couldn't keep their hands off each other. He was being brilliant, she couldn't deny it, but this enforced proximity was not what she'd had planned. 'I'm going to go through this address book now. Jean Luc suggested I should try all her friends to see if they know where she is.'

Marcus looked down and started laying the table for supper. Why had she mentioned him? It was deliberately spiteful, and now she'd hurt him she wished she hadn't. Was this going to turn into one of those awful 'can't live with him, can't live without him' scenarios? She picked up her mobile and started at A.

By P she'd still had no success at all. Most of Maddy's friends hadn't even heard from her in the last six months, and the pretext she'd used on them all – that Maddy had taken her contact lenses by mistake – sounded lame even to her. Marcus had organised the kids into a game of Twister – strictly indoors, they were still unsure if there were any lurking paparazzi – and supper was all cleared away.

Later, Marcus read to Charlie and Izzie gave up the hunt and went to tuck Jess in. She'd requested a 'Mousey Brown' story, an invented saga that had been going on for years, and Izzie complied as far as she could. But her thoughts kept turning back to Maddy. She would have to call the police tonight. Once she'd phoned Ayesha Zafari, one of Maddy's old friends from school, she'd have run out of road. 'Mummyyyy! You've already done one where Mousey Brown gets stuck in a tuba. Make up a new one.'

Her pathetic efforts at invention were interrupted by Pru's phone call. Not having kids herself, she was unaware of the problems that a seven-thirty phone call causes, and went on at some length.

'Well, at least I've found a halfway decent hotel in this godforsaken place. Yes, I know you invited me to stay, but no one, repeat no one, sees me without eye make-up, and since you don't offer en-suite facilities, I can't run the risk. Now brace yourself. I think this is going to get worse before it gets better. I was accosted by some hunky reporter in Ringford this afternoon. He was asking anyone and everyone if they knew anything about you, and I fear he may have had a few takers. Don't get the paper tomorrow. I'll get it, and come round to your place. Are you keeping the children off school again tomorrow?'

'No, I think we'll risk it and hope it's all blown over. I can't bear to give in to some state of siege. Can't think of anything worse, frankly.'

'I think you should stay out of the frame though.'

'But we need provisions. The cupboard is bare, Jean Luc's on his way here tonight and if Maddy still hasn't turned up, Colette's bringing the kids back after school tomorrow.'

Pru got efficient. 'I'll bring supplies with me, since you've got a houseful. What do children eat? Same as humans?'

'Probably not the same as you, Pru. Erm, pasta, ketchup, sausages – not fancy ones, mind, cheese – not Stilton, mild cheddar – apples, milk, Coco Pops, bananas. I think we can manage otherwise – oh, and loo paper, there's an exponential relationship between the number of kids and how much you get through.'

Pru made a gagging noise. 'Please, too much information. I'll be round first thing, then I'd better go and hold the fort at the barn with Lillian.'

Izzie finished settling Jess and looked in on Charlie. Marcus had fallen asleep next to him mid-story, and was snoring softly. She poured a large glass of cold white wine, then sat in the kitchen on her own. She still hadn't quite grasped the fact that they were going to be broke again. In her mind, she'd already spent the money Tessutini would have paid them. This was like waking up from a wonderful dream – and she didn't like it! She heard a soft tap on the window, and jerked her head up to see Jean Luc's face.

She let him in, and he enfolded her in a warm hug. He smelt

a bit travel worn, and looked exhausted but as gorgeous as ever. 'What a mess!' he commiserated. 'Your English newspapers are the worst in the world. Has she made contact yet?'

'No, nothing at all. I just don't know what to do.'

Jean Luc stretched and rubbed his eyes. 'Well, the most important thing is to pour me a drink.' He produced a bottle of wine from his holdall. 'After that, I'll have some ideas, but until then I'm no good.'

They were soon sitting comfortably across the kitchen table from each other, both nursing their wine and eating Bombay mix she'd bought specially when she knew he was coming over, a weakness he'd divulged shamefacedly on a previous visit.

'Thanks for coming over so quickly. She will need people she loves around her when she gets back.' She glanced at him, wondering if he'd pick up the hint, but he was still staring into the ruby depths of his glass. She pushed a bit harder. 'I think she blames herself for what's happened, but it could just have easily been me. She's so hard on herself. Without Simon around, she thinks she has to take care of everything, but it's too much for her. She won't admit she needs anyone though.'

Jean Luc shrugged in resignation. 'She wasn't always like that. First there was Peter to look after her, then Simon with his stupid braces and his big City salary.' Izzie was shocked by his hostility. He'd never even mentioned Simon's name before. He went on, 'I think she's different now. She never had to provide for herself before, but she's proved she can. But she's so proud. And she's been hurt. She won't let anyone get close again, I don't think.'

Izzie hesitated, then took the plunge. 'Jean Luc, how long have you been in love with her?'

He looked up suddenly in surprise, then smiled in rueful admiration. '*Mon Dieu*. I thought I'd done a good job of hiding it.'

'Not good enough, I'm afraid. I knew there was something

that day in France. It wasn't just you doing the decent thing, was it? Then at the party, I saw you watching her. The look on your face gave it away.'

He stood up and went over to the window, staring out into the darkness. 'Izzie, I'll say it again. In France I could so easily have made love with you. I wanted you so much. But her bloody face is always in my mind, fucking up all my relationships.' He laughed mirthlessly. 'My wife couldn't stand it and she was right. It's always been Maddy. Always.'

His intensity took her breath away. How ironic. She remembered that far off drunken night, Maddy posturing with a cigarette and laughing cruelly, 'It's you, Charlie, it's always been you.' Poor, poor Jean Luc. Had Maddy any idea at all? She hoped not for his sake.

Suddenly he turned back and leant over the table imploringly. 'Izzie, there will never be anyone else in my life who comes close to her. I will love her always, but please don't tell her. I couldn't bear her rejection. This way I can still see her. Please, promise me?'

They heard floorboards creaking as Marcus levered himself out of Charlie's bed and headed downstairs. His eyes screwed up against the light, he stood in the doorway, staring in puzzlement from one to the other. Izzie got up from her chair, squeezed Jean Luc's arm reassuringly and nodded. Then she took a glass of wine over to her husband, and smoothed his sleep-rumpled hair tenderly. 'Darling, try this Cahors Jean Luc has brought over. It's delicious. Come and sit down and join us. I'll make up the bed in the spare room.'

Suddenly, her mobile beeped a message, then a moment later, Jean Luc's joined in. They exchanged startled glances and pressed the read buttons.

When Maddy woke at last the house was silent. They'd clearly left for school. She tried hard to open one eye and focus on the clock. Ten-fifteen. She rolled over on to her back and groaned. She could have slept for another week. Perhaps she was getting old, but jet lag had never got to her like this before. Gingerly sitting up and swinging her legs of the bed, she began to focus her mind on the past twenty-four hours.

The children had been thrilled at her return the previous night, and at being allowed to stay up late enough to greet her. They seemed happy enough with the paltry offerings she'd managed to cobble together at the airport shops. Judging by the look on her face, Colette wasn't as convinced that a baseball hat quite made up for putting up with the kids and a horde of paparazzi for a couple of days, but she'd have to make it up to her later. She hadn't bargained on Crispin and Lillian being there too, but she thanked them profusely for their moral support, kept her explanations to the minimum and waved them off into the night in Lillian's little car.

Once she'd packed the children off to bed, she'd turned her mobile back on. As expected there were several messages from Izzie demanding to know her whereabouts, each more desperate than the last. One too from Jean Luc, not so panicky of course, but no less concerned. She'd replied to them both by text saying she was OK, and she'd be in touch. But the best news, the most joyous news of all, a voicemail from Geoff, which must have come sometime late yesterday afternoon. He'd had confirmation from Tessutini that the contract had been signed and finalised, but could she call him regarding the photo in the paper? She didn't know whether to laugh or cry at this. Had Tom seen the pictures? She didn't imagine for one minute that he hadn't. But who could say whether he'd signed before they'd landed on his desk?

She pulled back the curtains and looked out at the wet, windswept garden. Twenty-four hours ago she'd been zipping though a warm, sunny Manhattan, disgusted at herself and frantic with worry that the whole deal had been blown. A few hours before that? Well, perhaps that's why she was so tired. She was very out of practice after all. Now here she was, a rich woman. Richer than she could have imagined – though by the skin of her teeth. And with nothing to do with herself.

First she had to put Izzie's mind at rest, and she wanted to do it face to face. She turned towards the bathroom. Time for a shower. The best fun would be putting on her favourite old clothes that hadn't seen the light of day for months, and she was going to pile on the slap too.

Feeling rather odd and unused to tight trousers and kitten heels, she jumped in the car and headed off towards Hoxley. It felt like a million years since she'd been down this way, or at least now she felt like a different person. Despite herself, she felt a wave of lust as she remembered Sunday night, and quickly buried it. That kind of thought wouldn't do at all.

She pulled into Izzie's driveway, and almost careered into the back of a Range Rover. Oh my God, it was Jean Luc. She thought the call had come from France. What was he doing here? Leaving her car jammed in the gateway, she squeezed past the bushes, soaking her back on the wet leaves in the process, and headed for the door. She had barely put her hand on the door knob when it was ripped open by Izzie, who threw herself into Maddy's arms.

'Where the fuck have you been?'

'And hello to you too!'

'I've been worried sick.' She looked it, her hair stringy and greasy, her eyes red and tired. 'I nearly rang ruddy Interpol. I've been calling and calling.'

'Didn't you get my message?'

'Yeah, but not until late last night. Where have you been? Things have been frantic here.' She led Maddy into the kitchen, and there were Marcus and Jean Luc sitting over half-drunk cold coffee cups with newspapers strewn all over the table. Now that made an interesting tableau.

'Maddy!' They both stood up. 'Where the hell have you been?'

'What a happy greeting from everyone! Any chance of a cup of coffee? And where's this infamous photo then?'

Marcus handed her the *Courier*.

She shuddered. 'Does it make my bum look big?' she asked looking up at the three faces gazing at her.

'Christ, Maddy, it's been frantic here. How can you be so trite?' One look at Izzie's face and she knew she had to get serious.

'I'm sorry, I should have been in touch earlier, but I couldn't.'

'The papers today are even worse, darling,' said Jean Luc in a sombre voice, and pushed over more pages from the table. They had clearly been poring over them all morning. She scanned the copy, with Izzie pointing out particularly choice bits to her.

'Well, good old Pokey-Sue,' Maddy laughed. 'She's really stuck the knife in, hasn't she? The old bat. She's right off my Christmas card list. Will always eating McDonald's indeed! And I don't think I'll be buying Minstrels in the village shop either by the look of it. Oh lovely Linda Meades. She didn't hold back either, did she? And who's Mrs Evelyn Williams? Never heard of her.'

Izzie lost it completely. 'Maddy, don't you realise what this all means?' she stormed, hands on hips. 'There is no way that Tessutini are going to sign now. I tried Geoff this morning but he's not answering the phone.'

'Perhaps he's topped himself with grief.'

'Maaaaaddy!'

Maddy realised she'd been teasing too long. 'Oh sweetheart, fear not. They signed yesterday. It's all settled.' There was a stunned silence.

Izzie opened and closed her mouth. 'How?'

'Because, my darling, I took the bloody contract to New York and . . .' she paused, 'and delivered it to Tessutini by hand.'

'You did what?'

'Broadway sends its love.'

Izzie sat down hard on a chair. 'I don't understand. Why didn't you tell us? This has been about the worst weekend of my life.'

Maddy sat down beside her, pushing the coffee cups out of the way, and put her hand on Izzie's. 'I'm sorry. I know I should have, but I couldn't just in case it all went wrong. Those pictures were all my fault. I could have blown it for you, the girls, you, Jean Luc, everyone, and I had to sort it out myself. It just sort of came to me on Friday, so I went to London, to Hewlitt's, and collected the contracts – they were a bit surprised and said it was highly irregular – then I booked a ticket – which wasn't that easy either – and I rang To . . . Tessutini and said I was coming to New York anyway. They seemed a little surprised, but, well if I learnt anything over the last twelve months, it's how to bullshit, and they seemed happy with my explanation. Thanks.' She picked up the coffee Marcus placed in front of her, and cupped the mug in her hands. 'I didn't see them actually put their names on the bottom, Geoff told me they had yesterday.'

'Did you speak to him?'

'No actually, he left a message, but then . . . I didn't have my phone turned on.'

'I know,' said Izzie, her eyes on fire with anger. 'I must have called you twenty times. Don't ever, ever do that to me again! It was like the time when Simon died. I was worried sick.' Her eyes filled with tears and Marcus squeezed her hand. Maddy leant over and gave her a kiss on the cheek.

'Izzie, I know it was wrong, but I had to do it. Anyway, it's done now. We're in the clear.' She pulled something out of her bag. 'I got this for you – best thing Kennedy could offer I'm afraid.' And she handed the package to Izzie.

As she pulled open the bag and fished out a bottle of Clarins 'Relax' bath foam and the flimsiest, pinkest laciest knickers from the bag, Izzie looked momentarily bewildered then, sniffing, a broad smile came over her face and she threw her arms around Maddy.

'You bloody cow!'

'Now listen. Here's orders. You go and get in the shower. Gallons of hot water, big squirt of that, then new knickers on and your very best combats and naughtiest T-shirt.' She helped her up, and directed her towards the kitchen door, patting her on the bum as she went. 'And Izzie, don't forget the make-up. We can celebrate!'

As Izzie made her way upstairs, wiping her runny nose childishly on her sleeve, Maddy turned back to the men sitting silently at the table. There was a pause.

'She was very worried, Maddy. You shouldn't have done that to her,' said Marcus after a moment. She looked hard at him.

'I know, and I realise now that sometimes we all keep things from people when we should tell them, don't we? But this time I think I was really doing what was best.' He clearly registered what she was saying, then nodded his head slowly in agreement.

'I didn't just do it for myself, Marcus. I went there because it was the only way. I still don't know whether Tessutini saw the pictures before they signed, but that's academic now. I was just trying damage limitation.'

'You must be tired after so much travelling,' Jean Luc interrupted, perhaps sensing the uncomfortable atmosphere. 'Have you had a breakfast? I bet you haven't.' He walked over to the toaster. 'One slice of this revolting cardboard stuff or two?'

'Two please.' Marcus was still looking at her. 'Truce?' she said quietly.

For the first time he smiled a genuine smile at her. 'OK, truce. And thanks, Maddy.'

'I did it for my mate.'

'I know.'

She was halfway through her second piece of toast, and reading more thoroughly the hatchet-job news items in the tabloids on the table when her mobile rang.

'Hello?' she said, mouth full of crumbs.

'Maddy, it's Peter.'

She swallowed rapidly. 'Hi.'

'You've certainly got yourself all over the papers, my love.'

'Yes, I know. Reputation in tatters. I don't think we'll have our own TV show now, do you?'

He laughed deeply. 'Unlikely, but you never know. Look what disgrace did for the Hamiltons.'

Maddy giggled. It was good to hear him knock the whole situation back into some sort of perspective. 'Listen, Maddy, I don't suppose you've seen the *FT*, have you?'

'No, frankly, but we pretty much have every other paper here. Do they do a gossip column?'

'Not of any interest. But, Maddy, there's a feature about the sale, and it's got some information in it you may not want to hear. Can you get hold of a copy?'

She fished out her purse and her keys, mouthed to Marcus and Jean Luc that she was just nipping out to get some fags, and ran out down the drive to her car ignoring Jean Luc's frown. The nearest place she knew might have a copy was the garage on the by-pass. No joy. Two shops later, and still no *FT* – well, it was hardly popular Ringford reading matter – so she headed for the centre of town and, pulling up on a double yellow line and sticking on her hazard lights and sunglasses, she ran into WH Smith.

She didn't open the paper until she was in a lay-by on the by-pass again. There on page three was the story: 'Tessutini Buy And Bury *Paysage Enchanté*'. Bury? What was this?

As predicted, American cosmetics giant yesterday announced the acquisition of the small UK natural cosmetics brand *Paysage Enchanté*. The amount the company paid for this young, but highly successful enterprise has not been disclosed, but commentators suggest the figure was well beyond the company's value. 'We thought it would be an excellent addition to our portfolio,' said Tessutini CEO, Tom Drake, in New York last night – the empire also includes US brands like Agnes Broussard – 'but we have subsequently decided that it is uneconomical to transfer the manufacturing operation.' 'This move is extraordinary,' said Graham Fields, of bankers HBFR. 'One can only imagine that in view of falling profits in this sector, Tessutini decided to buy the brand in order to take it out of the competition.' Tessutini's share price fell a further ten points after news of the takeover.

Maddy dropped the paper on to her knee. The bastard! The complete and utter bastard. They'd been shafted. All that bunkum about 'valuable asset' and how impressed they were with the company. They just wanted them out of the picture. What galled her most now was how much more they should have asked for the sale. If they were that desperate to get rid of them, they might have stumped up even more.

She looked out over the wet fields and the hills beyond, shrouded in a blue haze with the threat of more rain. What had she done? She'd behaved like a bitch on heat, and had slept with Tom Drake for nothing. Well, to no significant end anyway. He'd have signed the contract even if she'd appeared topless on page three of the *Sun*.

Cars shot past her, sending spray up behind their wheels. People rushing about in their busy lives, and hers felt as though it was in ruins. The money in the bank was one thing, but shame was the price she had had to pay. She could feel her heart pumping hard. What would Geoff's reaction be?

She picked up her phone and tried to call him. Where could he be? It struck her as odd that he hadn't called or made contact in some way. He must be as surprised as she was by the news.

She started up the engine again, and headed back to Hoxley.

Izzie, fresh from her bath, hair fluffy and uncontrollable as before – but clean at least – was clearing up the breakfast debris.

'Got the knickers on?'

'Yes thanks. They're scrummy.'

'Now you're rich you can keep your thieving hands off mine, OK! Where're Marcus and Jean Luc?'

Izzie closed the dishwasher and turned it on. 'Jean Luc took one look at what Pru had provided for lunch – she's at the barn and coming back later – and announced he was off to the deli to buy a celebration lunch. He took Marcus with him, which was quite tactful I thought.'

'He's being great, isn't he? Marcus, I mean.'

Izzie leant against the humming machine, drying her hands on a tea towel. 'I suppose so, but it's all a bit forced. Remember having a row with your best mate at school and then making up, and lending her all your favourite crayons to make sure she was still your friend?'

'And probably your Sindy too.'

'Quite. All a bit false really, but things feel more equal now. We've both learnt something, but we'll have time to think about it when all this shit is over.'

Maddy pulled out the paper from her bag. 'It's not the end of it, I'm afraid. We've been well and truly screwed.' Oh the irony of that statement.

Izzie scanned the story fast, her eyes racing over the copy. When she raised them again to Maddy, they were wide with emotions that ranged from disbelief to abject fury. 'Why?' she asked weakly.

'It seems we made more of an impact than we thought.' She went over to Izzie's fridge, hoping to find a bottle of wine. It was still early, but what the hell. Pulling out the cork from the half-full bottle and smelling the contents – well, you couldn't always be sure with Izzie's fridge – she poured them both a glass.

'It wasn't just us. I think as Pru said some time ago, we just hit some back-to-nature nerve when it was ripe for the hitting. Don't worry, the pendulum will swing back and people will all be doing something equally silly before long.'

'But it all seems such a waste.' Izzie had the look of someone who had been boxed around the ears and was reeling.

'No, Izzie, it wasn't a waste at all. It was amazing. Unreal actually.' Her zeal increased. 'We had a ball. We were brilliant, we were inspired! And now,' she grasped Izzie's hands, nearly spilling her drink, 'we are rich!'

They hugged each other as hard as they could and danced an awkward little jig around the room.

'We all ought to party. Have you spoken to Geoff?' asked Izzie between gasps. 'Where is he by the way? You'd have thought he'd have been a bit nearer the coal face of things.'

'I was wondering that too. Shall we try to call him again?' Maddy dug out her phone, just as it started to ring. The screen showed 'Private number'. 'Perhaps this is him. Hello?'

'Hi, Maddy.' Her face blushed deeply as she recognised that deep accent and she turned away from Izzie as quickly as she could and left the room.

'Hello. How did you get my number?'

'There isn't much I can't find out if I need to.' She fumed at the arrogance of the man, and hated that in spite of herself the timbre of his voice managed to make her shiver. 'It had to be done, Maddy.' She knew he wasn't referring to the acquisition of her mobile number.

'Were we that much of a threat?'

'Potentially yes. It wasn't just you though. It was the way you were leading people, whether you meant to or not. You are both cleverer than you thought.'

She wandered into the sitting room and sat down on Izzie's piano stool, silently running her fingers up and down the keyboard. 'But what about the photo, Tom? I suppose that wouldn't have changed anything?'

'Oh no,' he said gently. 'It wouldn't have mattered a jot. In fact, it was more of an insurance policy.'

A germ of suspicion began to grow in her mind. 'A what?'

'In case you refused to sell. We had to bury the brand somehow.'

'You bastard! You arranged the whole thing!'

There was a pause down the line. 'We'd had you both covered for ages, just waiting until you made a slip-up. Unfortunately, it was you who did it first.' He waited for her to say something.

'Do you really imagine that just by burying our brand women are going to come flocking back to liposomes and anti-oxidants? This wasn't just about cosmetics, it was about the way women feel about themselves today. They are so over-committed and neurotic about juggling childcare and working, and you are even playing on their insecurities about their looks. We gave them a chance to reassess it all.'

'Maddy, I have shareholders to answer to. I'm not interested in some half-assed sociological theory. We know our market. It was my job to turn around the company's faltering fortunes. We had to get rid of you somehow, and it was buy you or discredit you.'

'How thoughtful.' Buy you? From somewhere in the back of her mind another realisation dawned. Where had the buy-out idea come from? Her mind ran over the events of the last few weeks since Geoff's late-night call about the offer, and Geoff's enthusiasm to push it through, and Geoff's very tiny, tiny error when he had revealed that he knew Tom Drake was a 'great guy'.

'You were in with Geoff, weren't you?'

Tom laughed deeply. 'He's a very useful guy your Geoff.

I'd had dealings with him and Hewlitt Pritchard before and, oh serendipity, found out he was working for you. I simply contacted him and told him it would be worth his while to persuade you to sell to us.'

'And was it?'

'Oh I think so.' No wonder they hadn't heard from Geoff in days. He was probably sunning his carefully honed body right at this moment on a yacht moored off Antigua, slimy little git.

'God, you had the whole thing covered, didn't you?' Incredulous at the deceit of it all, she could feel her anger rising. 'You didn't miss a shot. You knew about Simon, Marcus Stock, even the state of Izzie's marriage, *Bôite Bleue* too probably—'

'No, you actually surprised me with that one. It was good going to land them, I'll give you that.'

She wouldn't be stopped. 'What else did you know about us?'

'Well, I sure as hell know you don't have a brother.'

'OK, so I lied, but it was nothing compared to the depths of your deception. And what else is there? Do you know what my kids eat for breakfast? My mother's national insurance number? The colour of my underwear?' What on earth had made her say that?

'Yes, Maddy. I know the colour of your underwear.'

She saw red. 'And that too. Was that part of the plan? God, how you must have enjoyed watching me make such a fool of myself. And you just held out your hands and let me fall into them. Was that all in the great scheme, Tom? Well, was it?'

There was a pause. 'No Maddy, that bit wasn't in my plan. That was something else. That was the real thing.'

She thought about his note he'd left in her bag at the hotel. 'And that's your idea of "something else", is it? A curt little message saying, "That was an unforgettable way to close the deal"?'

'That wasn't all I put though, was it?' Maddy didn't answer. 'So *would* you want to resume negotiations?'

'Frankly, I'm too damned angry to want to do anything with you. And how do you think I felt when I discovered you'd paid my hotel bill? Christ, Tom, that's what men do when they spend the night with a hooker.'

'OK, Maddy. I'm sorry. That was insensitive, and perhaps I didn't handle it too well.'

'Too right. And then you sneak off without signing the contract—'

'I was always intending to sign it – photo or no photo – but I had to have it witnessed. Would it help if I told you you look beautiful when you are sleeping and that Sunday night blew me away?' She felt her stomach turn. Damn him.

'Why didn't you tell me you would have signed anyway?'

There was a pause. 'That would have taken away the fun.'

'You bastard.'

'Would you have slept with me anyway?' For a moment he didn't sound so confident.

She heard Jean Luc's Range Rover pull up in the drive outside her window, and the men's voices as they got out. Then a second car behind it. Maddy craned to look out of the window and saw it was Pru's. 'Tom, I have to go now. There are people here.'

'Before you go, Maddy, I'm sorry it had to be like this. It was strictly business. But what happened between us, that was all about you and me. And it's not over.' That arrogance was back again.

'Oh, I think it is, Tom. Find someone else to screw over.' And she cut the line dead.

She turned round slowly at a movement behind her and saw Izzie leaning up against the door jamb, arms crossed, eyes narrowed. 'I'm sorry I couldn't help catching the end of that. Is everything all right?'

'Er, yes, I guess.'

Izzie thrust her hands into her pockets and scuffed her foot on the carpet. 'Maddy, I've no right to ask this, but you didn't do anything stupid in New York, did you?'

The front door opened and Jean Luc, Marcus and Pru barged into the hallway, arms laden with carrier bags, talking animatedly. Maddy and Izzie looked at each other before the moment was lost and celebrations took over.

'Stupid?' said Maddy quietly. 'Maybe. But sometimes we all do things we regret. Izzie, Marcus needs your forgiveness. You both need to put it behind you.'

'Yes, mate. I think we're getting there.' They linked arms and went into the noisy kitchen to join the others.

Epilogue

'Hi there. It's me.'

'Hi! I was going to call you, but our flight was delayed and we didn't get home till really late.'

'Did you have fun?'

'Just brilliant. Will and Pasco are brown as berries, but poor Florence. She spent the whole time with her Legionnaire's hat on and factor zillion slathered on an inch thick.'

'Poor love. Did you relax?'

'Oh, you bet. Colette just let me sleep and drink rum punches until I was comatose. Moving house took more out of me than I thought.'

'How's the apartment looking?'

'The work's nearly finished. These bloody Parisian builders tried to muck me about though, but I don't think they realised they'd taken on Attila the Soft-furnisher. They finished the children's rooms while we were away, though they painted Will's the wrong bloody colour, and now they're working on the kitchen. But exciting news – the other place is coming on brilliantly! Jean Luc's promised that by the time we get down there next week the pool will be finished. Can't wait for you to come and see it.'

'Flights booked already. We're arriving Good Friday. Anything you want me to bring?'

'British cigs of course, and don't forget the Tunnock's caramel wafers!'

'Already packed in bulk, my dear. That's taken care of our excess luggage. Can't believe you've got a place in the country. I thought you'd vowed never to set foot on a blade of grass ever again.'

'Will insisted on a garden – it was a major factor in the moving-to-France negotiations. I'll just try not to look at the view, and go into Montpellier and breathe in some diesel fumes every now and then. But how's things your end? How does the bathroom look?'

'Since I cadged all your ideas from the one in Huntingford, it's really beautiful, thank you.'

'Stoke Newington builders come up trumps, did they?'

'Do you mind, Maddy, we're definitely Islington now!'

'If it's north of the park, it's bandit country to me, old girl! Never mind that, I'm itching to hear about the wedding.'

'Oh, you really missed something. It was lovely. The sun shone, Charlie and Jess looked angelic, even though he managed to spill Coke down his pageboy outfit. The groom scrubs up pretty well too.'

'And come on, tell, did she wear orange and green?'

'No, strictly virgin white, but the flowers were as garish as you'd expect and clashed beautifully with her hair.'

'Good old Lillian! Did she salsa?'

'Like a good 'un! The best thing though was the wedding cake – the most enormous pile of doughnuts you can imagine – about a foot high in every flavour under the sun!'

'And did Crispin eat them all?'

'Almost. It was sweet – they shared one, biting from both sides until they met in the middle – like *Lady and the Tramp*. It was all so romantic – though Donna and Angie got absolutely slaughtered and Karen ended up paddling naked in the pond. I meant to tell you, that idea they had for the mobile sandwich van has come off. They've called it – wait for it – Buns 'n' Butties!'

'Oh please!'

'They're doing a roaring trade, so Crispin tells me, and they're the toast of every building site in the county. I thinks it's as much the abundance of cleavage as the quality of the bacon sarnies that's clinched it.'

'Nice to know they put their pay-off to good use. Well, that's one happy ending. Did Marcus enjoy the nuptials?'

'He was pretty busy doing the photos – which are terrific – but I think he genuinely did.'

'How're things going in that department?'

'Much better. We're spending time together and it feels like a more grown-up relationship. I can't say it's violins and roses all the time, but we have our moments. He's had a few job interviews and he's back in the loop. Thank God for the minuscule attention span of the advertising industry.'

'Has Jess forgiven you yet?'

'She won't admit it, but I think she's settled at last. She's got herself a little girl gang in her class, and I hate to tell you, but we've plugged right into the after-school activities circuit. Violin, ballet, intermediate particle physics. You know the kind of thing. I'm becoming a regular *Guardian*-reading hyper-mummy.'

'Nothing new there then. Boy, I don't miss that Eagles' car park. The most we do after school is trot round to the Jardin du Luxembourg, all us mummies in our Miu Miu kitten heels clutching our teeny weeny handbags, and watch our stylish offspring on the climbing frame. Not a Pokey-Sue or a pair of gold loafers in sight.'

'Sounds dead elegant.'

'Well, it has to be an improvement, especially after the dirty looks I got when our gaffe was blown. Bloody Geoff and that photo. If I ever see that man again, I'll shove his laptop where the sun don't shine. And Peter was so upset about all that. It haunts me. Do you think we convinced him it wasn't his fault?'

'Good God, Maddy, you couldn't have done more. He's a smashing bloke, and he's too honest for the way the City is now. There are few gentlemen left like him. Speaking of gentlemen, how's that dishy French fancy? Is your new house far from his?'

'About half an hour's drive. He'll be thrilled when he doesn't have to come up to Paris to see us any more. Of course I haven't seen him since we went away, but we've been in daily contact from my sun-lounger.'

'Were you demanding regular updates on the building work?'

'Erm, yes and no actually. It was just a good excuse to get him to call. I sort of miss it when I don't talk to him.'

'Oh yeah?'

'Oh come on, I've known him all my life! I feel so comfortable with him after everything that's happened – I don't have to explain anything, he knows me so well. And he's so good to me. The children miss him too – of course, it's for them really. Look, Iz, can I ask you something?'

'Course you can. I've worn your knicks, haven't I? There's nowhere we can't go. Shoot.'

'Well, I know you and Marcus are solid now, but . . . what did happen between you and Jean Luc that day at the *mas*?'

'Why ask about that suddenly? That's ancient history.'

'I know. But all you said is that you weren't having an affair. Did you even . . . are you . . . do you still have feelings for him?'

'I think he's a very special man. But OK, cards on the table. We came close that day, but it wasn't right for either of us. Anyway, he had someone else on his mind. Still has in fact . . .'

'Oh. Oh, I see. Is it serious?'

'Would it bother you if it was?'

'No! Well yeah, I think it would. He's been acting a bit odd around me lately, and I wondered if there was something going on. I'd hate him to be hurt like he was with Pascale. He's like a second skin to me and I feel . . . well, his happiness is important to me. But tell me about this other woman. Is he still in touch with her, do you think? Is he in love with her?'

'Well, yes I think he might be.'

'Are you sure? How do you know?'

'He's mentioned her to me in confidence. I reckon she could just be the woman for him – he's pretty smitten, and do you know? I'm beginning to think she might feel the same way.'

'Oh . . . oh right. Should I ask him about her?'

'Yes, Maddy, I think you should, and as soon as possible. You just might be surprised what he has to say . . .'

'Did he tell you what she was like?'

'He didn't have to. I've already met her.'

'No way! Oh God, Iz. Is she gorgeous? What if I hate her?'

'Don't worry. You won't. She is gorgeous, and she's the best mate I ever had . . .'

Acknowledgements

Thanks are due to our brilliant friends who've answered many hypothetical and occasionally off-the-wall questions with patience and imagination. These include: Rupert Symons, Mark Kalderon, Philip Lelliott, Marie Laure Legroux, Dolores Smith, Julie Weiner, Elaine Townshend, Lord Tombs of Brailes, Peter Byrom, Janine Watson, Marie Gerrard and Wynford Dore. And thanks to those experts too numerous to mention who fielded our weird phone calls and even weirder enquiries: the nice man at the Trading Standards Office, the beekeeper, the desk sergeant at Stratford Police Station, the person at the accreditation office, and many others. Most of all, love and gratitude to our long-suffering husbands for putting up with our distraction and for providing endless cups of tea.